THE TEMPEST

BLACK CARBON #3

A.J. SCUDIERE

GRIFFYN INK

This one is for all my pandemic friends. The Tempest is just one of several books I've written while on lockdown. Thank you for keeping me sane and for just being there. I hope we come out the other side okay. Because, honestly, we were all pretty nuts before we got shut inside our houses for a year.
Thank you.

It's also for anyone who has survived a catastrophic weather event. Parts of Alabama are prone to twisters. The entire northeast was under water or snow a handful of years ago. Texas just had a deep freeze. Things are getting weird. If you've survived, then this one is for you. I admire your fortitude so much, I wrote a whole series about it.

ACKNOWLEDGMENTS

Books like this require research. There was too much involved to name each person who helped. But thank you to everyone who's traveled with me to help make this series more realistic. Thank you to everyone who shared stories of the twisters they've been through. You helped make this book better.

1

The rumble sounded like a freight train bearing down on her as Joule drove along the virtually empty highway. Her head turned from side to side, looking for the threat. She'd been told that tornadoes were supposed to sound like trains, and that Alabama had tornadoes.

Her breathing shortened and her chest tightened, even as she tried to talk herself down. She scanned the skies and saw nothing. She should be safe.

Joule hated being ever-alert, but it had to be some level of post-traumatic stress. Lord knew, she'd had enough trauma in her life.

The flashing red light signaled a four-way stop, and as the large, dirty white pickup loomed to her right, she saw that the driver seemed wholly unconcerned with whatever disaster was bearing down on them.

Why had she gone to pick up supplies by herself?

Unable to linger at the intersection and assume she was safe if she sat still, she took the ninety-degree right-hand turn with her breath held.

"Are you kidding me?" she yelled into the empty space in the

car, to the groceries sitting in too many plastic bags, to the flashing red lights and long, wooden signal arms crossing the road.

It had sounded like a freight train because it *was* one.

With her foot on the brake, Joule breathed at least a little easier as the red and white-striped bars came to a rest and the small motion toward her right grew into the oncoming engine and the probably thousand cars that it was towing at high speed.

The train was going to take a while and the grocery store had already been far enough away to make her worry about the ice cream melting. The prolonged stop turned her worry to certainty. If she had a spoon, she'd dig the ice cream out of the bag and eat it now, so that at least someone got to enjoy it.

Instead, she watched the cars whizz by and turned the radio on, hopping through the stations.

Country.

Country.

Christian.

Country.

Metal.

Sighing, she went back to one of the country stations. There were a few country songs she liked, and the back beyond of Alabama was not going to be the place to find an alt-rock station.

For a moment, she contemplated the nerves and jitters that came with starting a new job. She figured her anxiety was likely compounded by the fact that it was her *first* job.

Though she'd scooped ice cream very part time at Snyder's for two summers before the night hunters had come, and she'd waited tables and had a few internships, this was her first career-move *job*. And moving to new places and confronting new things was not her forte.

A life-threatening crisis—a real emergency—she could handle. A simple relocation was harder on her nerves.

The job was between Arab and New Hope, two small towns in northwest-ish Alabama. But being between towns meant there was no apartment-style housing for the crew, so HR had decided to house them in small groups in rentals.

She and Cage—thank God she was with her brother!—and Sarah and Deveron were all in a little two-bedroom house that the owners rented out under the catchy title of "Desperado's Hideaway."

The owners had traded the queen bed in the largest bedroom for two twins—when they signed the one-year lease, but there was still some kind of cow skull on the dresser as "decor." It didn't fit in the drawer where Sarah had tried to hide it, so it was now stashed under the dresser like some kind of bovine boogie man.

Joule sighed into air that was full of kicked up dust from the passing train. She would be living in "western rental-chic" hell for the duration of the assignment.

Looking to the right, she saw the end of the train approaching.

Was there a caboose? She found herself getting excited to see it. She'd lived near railroad tracks in several different places but couldn't remember ever seeing them *used*.

Her phone dinged from its prop on the dash.

—Where are you?

—waiting on a train. Back soon.

The last car whizzed by right then, looking sadly not red and without any fancy railings where a passenger could stand and wave at the passing countryside.

Though the train itself was a disappointment, the silence as it left was a welcome relief. The grinding, gushing noise had grabbed her gut—there were tornadoes here. But not *here*. That was the reassuring part. Though much of central Alabama was its own "tornado alley," her new employers had chosen this particular area specifically because it had a low annual tornado count.

Building a solar farm was only a worthwhile enterprise if it stayed put and sent power to the nearby towns. Theirs was a prototype landscape system that would rotate with the sunlight and conserve its own energy on cloudy days. Eventually, it would hopefully replace fossil fuels for this quarter of the state. But only if tornadoes didn't rip it out of the ground.

Putting the car into drive, Joule reminded herself, *When you hear a train out here, it's actually a train.*

But as she drove through a slightly more populated area, she saw what had once been a cafe or a library or a shop ... she couldn't tell. The roof was caved in on half of it, the windows all blown out. Although the damage looked old, the parking spaces in front were still covered in glass shards.

The place had been abandoned after some large hand had seemingly ripped it in half.

She turned toward home, the road rougher here, and headed toward Desperado's Hideaway and the only people she knew.

2

C age sat uncomfortably in the metal folding chair, his legs stuffed under the folding table. His chair was crammed in next to his sister's and he tried not to bump elbows in the tiny, folding room.

It was actually a trailer that had been set up at the edge of "the lot"—although there wasn't much to distinguish what was "the lot" and what wasn't.

He cradled the coffee in his hands, the heat suffusing into him and providing comfort where there was little to be found. He was grateful the four of them had managed not to spill any in the car that he and Joule shared. The gravel road out here had given them a serious test of their balancing abilities.

Now they were all crammed into the tiny space, even though he didn't know who they "all" were yet. They had been given three days to arrive and settle in, but this still felt far too soon to be getting to work.

He didn't know the area. And he was pretty sure their small, elderly sedan was not going to survive long on these roads, and he hoped this wasn't the best coffee in town.

He and Joule had opened their identical laptops, as had

everyone else. They looked like a classroom as Radnor walked down the aisle, his broad shoulders and pink polo shirt taking up all of the available space. When he hit the front of the room, he rotated and moved his hand as he clicked a button lighting up the screen behind him.

Though his dark skin might have blended into the background, his voice boomed through the tiny space. He lifted a hand to shade his eyes, as if the projector were sunlight. "All right, I want the old guard. Raise your hands. Show who you are."

He scanned the room as though checking that all the right people had their hands up. Cage did not. Day One on a job definitely did not make him "old guard" of anything.

Cage had noticed that the others in the room were a variety of ages and dressed in different ways. Though no one wore business suit, he saw everything from khakis to jeans, to even one pair of overalls. That was his roommate, Sarah, who somehow still managed to not stand out.

Radnor once again raised his hand and peered through the darkened room. "Kelsey. Hand up. I want all the people who've been here since the beginning of the project."

Kelsey, it seemed, caught on and she now confidently held her hand aloft.

"All right. We've all seen them. Now it's the newbies. Hands up," he demanded.

This time, Cage and Joule shrugged to each other, but their hands went into the air, along with Sarah's and Deveron's. Glancing around the room, Cage found that almost half of the group were newbies.

"All right," Radnor called out again, waving his hands dramatically. Everybody had been seen and all positions addressed. "Put them down."

Cage wondered if he was supposed to memorize who was new and who was Radnor's "old guard" in that short period of time. But he would just have to wait and find out. His new boss was plowing forward.

"Before I get started, I want to be sure everyone understands. We're on a time crunch for a number of reasons. We started this project about six months ago. Some of you newbies were hired to come in and help with Phase Two. We were on track, and we did this."

Jabbing his hand toward the screen, as though that helped the clicker, he popped up a picture of a cleared field with spanking new pylons being sunk into the ground. In the next picture, people were taking measurements and Cage recognized some of the people who were in the room.

"We got the environmental impact report done. We got everything measured, and we started the install." He pointed to the picture and then to the wall. "This setup is less than one mile that way ... and then we got *this*."

When he clicked the images again, Cage again saw the same field, only this time, some of the pylons were bent. Debris was strewn all over the field, wood and metal and plastic everywhere. Smashed dark glass fragments revealed that some of the solar panels had not survived the onslaught.

"So now we've been kicked back for two reasons. One, we lost the work that we already did." Radnor was striding up and down the stubby aisle now, hands on his hips. Those who were sitting closest to the center of the room were leaning back to avoid his elbows as he rotated, his anger at the situation radiating through the small space.

Radnor appeared not to notice. "And two—we have to redesign. Clearly, what we had was not as strong as we thought. So, here's where we're aiming next."

He jabbed at the wall again, his hand dwarfing the tiny remote that he held. This time, the picture showed on his back and his shadow was cast directly into the middle of the image. His heavy sigh and a few choice swears were clear as he tried to get himself to the front corner of the room and out of the way.

This time the image was not a photo, but a drawing. Cage tilted his head to examine it.

"This is the new plan. We've expanded. So we've moved to a new location. Also, the hope is that the new location won't take quite the hit that this last one did." Radnor looked around the room again as though searching for a team of superheroes that he just knew wasn't there. "We need a redesign. Old guard, hands up again. Newbies, I want you to look at them. When they tell you something won't work, ask them why. And listen."

He paused for only a moment. "Now newbies, hands up again. Old guard, I want you to listen when they give you new ideas. We can't dismiss stuff just because we don't think it will work. *We need ideas.*" He emphasized each word in the last sentence.

There was nothing like coming into a project in crisis, Cage thought. He could have gotten a job where he wore a suit and showed up at an office building every day. But he wouldn't have been with his sister, and honestly, what good biology jobs existed in office buildings? At best, he would have been wearing a lab coat.

He and Joule had opted for this. No office buildings, just temp trailers like this, field work that was plausibly backbreaking. He didn't really know what to expect.

Radnor was still waving his hands around. "We need to think outside of the box!"

Cage watched as Joule's glance flicked toward him. She managed not to roll her eyes, but he could still see the thoughts in her head. *Did he really just say "outside of the box"?*

Cage nodded that yes, Radnor had. But the man was speaking—or booming—again, and they needed to pay attention.

"The goal is to take today to examine the old site." Radnor

gestured for emphasis, and Cage once again sipped the coffee in front of him. His had cream and sugar. Next to him, he could smell that Joule's version was black. *Seemed fitting.*

"I want us to get as much as we can out of today, though you will be able to come back and re-examine this site later if you need to. This building—" He pointed up over his head, "—will remain here and we'll be erecting another like it, but larger—" He smirked as though he understood that he'd been whacking his new employees with his elbows as he paced around. "For today, I want all hands on deck and everyone talking. Out we go!"

As Radnor marched down the short aisle, he blocked the light again. Setting his clicker on the last table and carrying nothing in his hands, he hollered to them all. "Leave your laptops but bring your phones. Take pictures and make copious notes."

He threw the door open, letting in the sunlight as he led the way outside. As Cage pushed past him with the growing crowd, he heard the man mutter, "We're going to need them."

3

J oule stood in the field simply surveying both the work and the damage in front of her. She was a newbie—as it had been clearly declared—and she didn't have anything of value to add yet.

She'd have sweat dripping down her spine in another hour or two. It wasn't just hot in Alabama, the air was heavy and thick. She'd had three days to learn to dress better, but she'd opted for "first day at the new job" clothes: new khaki pants and a white button-down shirt, and her boots.

Sarah, in her overalls, clearly had no such compunction. Though Sarah was a recent grad from another school where Helio Systems recruited heavily, she'd grown up nearby. Joule should have listened when her roomie had looked at the nicely pressed shirt and said, "That might melt before noon."

Radnor had sent them all emails requesting they be here at eight a.m.. And while, right now, the sun was not fully overhead yet, the day was already far more humid than Joule was used to. Each time she inhaled, she felt the extra weight of the air and resented the extra energy just to breathe. *Tonight she would shower in cold water,* she told herself. Tomorrow, she would dress smarter.

The group trekked out into the middle of the open field, a not-short distance from the tiny, temporary building with its window-unit air conditioning chugging along in the background. As she high stepped forward, she missed the AC already.

Looking around, she noticed Radnor's newbies were sticking together, many of them wearing boots as clearly un-broken-in as hers were. She and Sarah and Cage and Deveron were still clustered tightly together and Joule wondered if some of the other little gatherings that had formed might also be roommates.

As they approached the edge of the lot, Joule's eyes flicked back and forth. The pale blue footers jutted from the ground as if escaping their graves. Though some of them were still straight, most had been grotesquely bent and twisted.

What did this? Was it the same thing that had collapsed just half the store she'd seen the on the way back from getting groceries? The site had been cleared since the tornado, and the permanent damage was the only thing that still showed.

She raised her hand, though she hated being the center of attention. Radnor instantly hit her with, "You don't have to raise your hand, Mazur."

She nodded, wondering how he was going to distinguish her from her brother if he was using last names, but now wasn't the time to ask.

"What was the rating on the tornado that went through here? The one just outside Montgomery was F6."

"There's no such thing as F6," one of the newbies corrected from the other side of the gathering, as if she were ill-informed.

Joule raised one eyebrow at him, but didn't get any further as Sarah jumped in. "The Montgomery tornado was the first one the experts are dubbing F6 officially, though they aren't sure the new rating will take. They've discussed extending the scale for going on ten years."

"Thank you, Carter," Radnor bellowed. His voice didn't seem to have a setting other than "booming." "The one here was an F3."

"And it still did *this*?" Cage asked from right beside her. *Thank God for a good twin brother,* she thought as he pulled the focus to himself.

"It was a new design," Radnor reminded them. He had told them that before they moved out here, even before they graduated. She assumed all the other newbies had heard much the same thing.

"New designs are always amazing until they're tested," he sighed and went on to add that he was grateful the design had been tested before they fully built the site. "But if it was going to fail, we want it to fail early and hard. Before too much could be lost. "

"Then it was a success," Deveron whispered wryly next to her, and Joule fought the grin that pressed at her face.

That was an interesting way of looking at it. She pushed her expression back to neutral and saw that only Sarah remained stone-faced, giving nothing away.

"All right, we need another division!" Radnor announced, his pink Helio Systems Technologies polo shirt now shining even brighter in the sunlight. His jeans had splotches of white, as though he had painted his home in them at some point previously and his stained boots had shoelaces that showed their age.

"Environmental team over here!" He pointed, and Joule watched as both Cage and Sarah slowly stepped away.

"Engineering over here!"

She high-stepped through the grass to join the second cluster and noticed that, within each group, the old guard and new guard were fairly well mixed.

"Project managers to the back," he boomed. "Y'all are going to fan out. I want you walking back and forth between the Enviro and Enge teams. Listen in on everything! Record whatever you need to. Each manager needs to talk to each team member at some point today. Everybody's job is to solve what went wrong. We meet again tomorrow morning at the new site to discuss what new ideas we have."

And with that, he dropped his hands to his side and looked at them as if to say "Get to it!"

Joule and Deveron headed toward one end of the field and, as they got closer to the last of the pale blue metal pieces, she noticed several of the old guard were moving in.

"Brad Barker." One of the guys held out his hand, and Joule took that moment to look at his feet. *Yes, old boots.* Radnor's old guard.

"Joule Mazur." She held out her hand in return and she let Deveron introduce himself as two more of the old guard came up behind Brad.

"Saskia Kaczmarek," the woman said, her fine features looking as old-school European as her name.

The other woman was clearly Indian. "Chithra Murasawa."

Radnor hadn't subjected them to the dreaded ice-breaker games and, while Joule had appreciated not having to "stand up and tell us a little bit about yourself," she now thought it would have been nice to recognize faces. She filed the ones she had.

It was Chithra who led the way. "I want to stand at the end and look down the line. Let's see what we all see."

Joule followed along. Helio had promised her on-the-job training, but Radnor had basically just thrown them all out into the field as though he were rolling a big bag of dice.

"You can see the path the tornado took. Look," Saskia added. Joule nodded along, tipping her head first one way then the other.

Before Chithra asked, *What are you looking at?* she filled in,

"The beams are not all bent the same way, which makes sense, because a tornado has varying wind speeds and directions. But it's interesting to me that there doesn't seem to be a real pattern. Some of the structure is still standing, even in the middle of the path."

She held one hand up along her sight line. The damage provided an odd picture. "What was different about those beams?"

"Let's go find out," Chithra suggested, and she began marching through the field, seeming to know the others in their new little group would fall in behind her.

Joule followed along, aware that she was the newest of the new kids. Sarah had the advantage of having grown up around here and being smart enough not to wear clothing that would stick to her. Joule plucked at her shirt, letting air under the fabric. Her only consolation was that a handful of others were also marked by their shiny new boots and too-warm clothing.

They trekked the tornado's path, passing other small clusters of their teammates. Joule saw Cage in the distance, not looking at pylons but taking pictures of the space between. His "Enviro Team" was likely getting pictures of endangered flowers or lizards or something.

When her little group arrived at the one beam that was most upright in the middle of the path, they instantly quieted and took a moment to examine it. But there were no obvious answers.

Damn, if it didn't feel like *Day One*. She looked behind her at the horizon and the wispy white clouds that danced in the sky. *Good*. Nothing was bearing down on her.

Yet.

4

—————

"Did you get yours?" Joule held her phone up, tipping it back and forth to catch her brother's attention.

Her first paycheck from Helio Systems Tech had been deposited into her account. She'd had paychecks before, but nothing like this—nothing that wasn't accompanied by pulling wadded bills out of her apron pockets at the end of a shift waiting tables.

"I want Italian," she said. "*Good* Italian."

Cage wasn't paying attention as he tapped hurriedly at his phone, pulling up his own bank account. "Got it."

It had taken three weeks to see their first paycheck. Between doing the first rounds of work and then waiting for the paycheck cycle to finish, she didn't feel quite so new anymore. Some of the shine had rubbed off, surely.

They'd spent a week in small teams, designing new pylons. The second assignment was testing what they'd designed. When their work made it through initial testing, the other teams were brought in to try to squash their victory.

Cage and the environmental teams had completed new surveys of both the old site and the new one. He'd complained that some of the work was a direct repeat, but Sarah had pointed out that it had to be redone. Getting it wrong again would mean starting all over. Mostly, it seemed the Enviro teams trashed the new designs for violating all kinds of environmental norms. There was nothing quite like her own brother questioning all her work.

He'd asked her in jest, at one point, "How much paint does a woodland creature have to ingest before we have feral mutant hamsters on our hands?"

She'd stared at him then, not caring that both teams were watching them. "That's not funny."

It was Sarah who chimed in, "I heard there a was a place outside Chicago that had mutant dogs a while back... that actually killed some people—"

Joule and Cage stared only at each other. They stayed silent in the eye of the conversation that swirled around them.

"They got rid of them. Didn't someone make a video about how to kill them?" Mitch had asked. He was old guard and definitely not the person Joule would have guessed would be up to speed on that story. He was also smarter that the next four of them put together. She waited for him to make a comment she couldn't quite wriggle out of.

"Yeah," Sarah said, magically hauling the conversation back around without realizing it. "Your sister's right. We could get dangerous feral hamsters, and it's not funny." But then she'd turned her gaze to Mitch. "So how much paint would it take?"

Now Cage pocketed his phone, looking at his sister with a warning in his eyes. "Around here, Italian only means pizza. And even that is only so-so."

He was right, the others agreed. The pizza was barely passable.

"But I really want pasta," Joule moaned. "I want Chicken Piccata. And green beans sauteed in garlic."

She felt the need for green veggies in her whole body, and if she had Mexican or barbecue one more time, she was going to lose her mind. Though both seemed to be specialties of the area, Joule was already burning out on them.

"What we need is to start cooking for ourselves more," her brother said, as though they needed to hone kitchen skills.

But the twins knew enough. Their parents had made sure that they each knew how to make a variety of basic meals. They'd shared an apartment over the summers, and they'd stayed with their grandfather for a while during a long break and cooked for him. But now Joule was realizing it had never become an everyday skill for them.

"Yes, we do," she agreed as she stepped beside their nearly-empty fridge and opened it as if to present evidence. "But today is not that day."

"We're taking Sarah and Deveron with us?" her brother asked as she pushed the fridge door shut to an unsatisfying thwack.

"Well, first we have to find an Italian place. And then, yes. We should also invite Mitch and Chithra and Brad." She rattled off the others that she knew who hadn't moved their families down to Alabama, like Saskia had.

"Now you're talking about reservations," her brother warned as he retrieved his phone again to find a restaurant.

"Any place that has the chicken piccata I want will take a reservation." Joule pulled her own phone out to join the hunt. "And it will also be far enough away that we'll have time to make it happen."

An hour and forty-five minutes later, they were two towns away, having finally found the Italian restaurant that agreed to their nine-person reservation at the last minute.

"I don't know." As Sarah looked skeptically at the storefront, she shoved her fists down into the pockets of her sweater. Tonight, her leggings neatly matched her boots, meaning Sarah was at her dressed-up finest.

Not that any of them needed to look nice. Greco's occupied a brick storefront in a strip mall. The Papyrus font in red, white, and green lettering wasn't out of place between the pet supplies store and the nail salon.

"Well, we're here now," Joule said, and heard her own mother as the words tumbled out. "I don't know what it will be, but it will be an adventure."

She strode inside to the small hostess stand that looked like a lectern stolen from a community college. The hostess herself appeared to be about twelve. But by the time she held the menu, Joule was sniffing the air and saying, "It doesn't look like much, but it sure smells good."

Even Sarah was agreeing.

An hour and a half later, they all had bags of bread and left-overs folded in tin foil swans—because the waiter thought he was special. The jury was still out on that, but the food had been wonderful.

"Okay," Sarah conceded. "We can go there again."

"But first," Cage replied, "we need to start cooking for ourselves."

"Do you mean me?" Deveron pointed to his own chest. "That's a skill I do not possess."

The others were waving goodbye and climbing into their own cars. Though they were all headed the same direction and would follow each other down the road for a bit, the four room-mates had all come in Sarah's car. It had taken a deep breath for Joule to finally relinquish her burning desire to be in charge of the car, but Sarah knew her way around much better than Joule did. Maybe she could let it go, only for tonight. It was difficult to sit in the backseat and not have a method of escape. It was simply one of the leftover pieces of her past, but it was one that was worth leaving behind.

So she sat in the backseat with Deveron and looked out the window.

"You okay?" He seemed to have guessed something was off.

"Yeah." But the word gave away that she was tired now, loaded up on carbs, and definitely ready to tap out for the evening. She changed the subject and hoped no one noticed. "Last night was the first night that I remember not waking up for the train."

"I told you you'd get used to it," Sarah's announced, her cheer at being right emerging in the sing-song tone.

"And I believed you," Joule said. "How could I not? I woke up every night and saw you on the other side of the room, eyes closed, snoring like a baby. So I knew it could be done. But last night was the first night *I* did it. And now I can't wait to get home and try for a repeat performance tonight."

She was even hoping to sleep in. Though Radnor had summoned them on one of the Saturdays, there were no call times for this weekend. She caught Sarah's attention in the rearview mirror now. "What's on tap for tomorrow?"

Sarah had served as their local chaperone for the past several weeks, making sure they got enough "Alabama" to know their way around. "I don't know. It's been three weeks, and I'll be honest, there isn't that much more to do or see around here."

She waited a beat, thinking. "There are a few wineries, but these are definitely Alabama wines. Not as well-known as France or California, for good reason. We could hit Noccalula Falls, if you want."

"What is it?" Deveron asked, joining in on the weekend planning for once. He always tagged along, but hadn't expressed real interest until now.

"Just a nice little park and the falls. And there's a statue of the woman it's named after. You know, there's a plaque and it's pretty. You'll get some local landscape."

Joule and Deveron looked at each other. That was pretty much their usual work: study the bedrock, avoid hurting the plants and critters. But without Radnor peering over their shoulders, it would be better.

"It's worth the drive," Sarah added, as though she'd decided to sell them on the idea only now.

From the front passenger seat, Cage uttered a single choice word: "Shit."

Before she could even ask, he turned around and held his phone up. "The radar is showing a bad storm coming in."

"Tomorrow?" she asked. There went the falls ...

"No. Right now." He turned around to face her, pointing to the tiny screen. "It's ugly. And it's coming up right behind us."

5

C age stood at the window next to Sarah, each of them holding back one of the curtains. He let his knuckles touch the cold glass to keep Sarah from seeing that his hand shook just a little.

Joule was hiding in her room, deep in a book, earbuds in so she could pretend there wasn't a storm. But Cage stood watch, as if keeping an eye on it would hold the storm away—as if his tension would keep him safe. He knew better, but he still stood at the window, watching.

"Was that a shingle!" He jerked as something black swooped by. *Was the house falling apart?* He was grateful he wasn't the owner.

"Maybe," Sarah answered, in a far-too-calm voice. Then again, one of the things he'd learned in the past several weeks was that Sarah didn't show her hand often.

"Losing shingles doesn't concern you?"

"It does." Then she echoed his own thoughts. "But it's not my house. And nothing's leaking ..." She looked up as if to check that she was correct.

Cage let his gaze follow hers, but she kept talking.

"Helio Systems will get us a new house if this one's broken."
She was still gazing out at the yard, in flux with high winds.

All of that was true, but ... "I'd rather not be in this one
when it breaks."

Sarah looked him then, laughing. "It won't break. Not for
this." Then her face went back to its normal passive expression.
"It might, however, flood."

Ice chilled his veins at the word, and he forced himself to
watch over the backyard and *breathe*. He counted the familiar
things in the grass: the smoker that had stood empty, as none of
them knew how to use it. The green-painted picnic table. The
log the squirrels kept hopping along that Joule had taken to
leaving her toast crusts on. It had taken them a whole week to
find out the gently sloping area beyond Squirrel Log did, in
fact, lead down to a creek.

Floods were not his thing. It was difficult to keep his voice
level. "Does that happen often?"

Sarah's expression grew wary. "More often lately than
before."

Though her words didn't say it, he felt the implication that
she was mostly referring to one incident. So he next asked the
question he dreaded, but that's why he was out here watching
the world blow by. "Was there anything *in* the water?"

"No. The water itself is bad enough when it happens."
Sarah shrugged, a too-small gesture for the next words out of
her mouth. "It took out a handful of houses and swept away
some cars, though. We lost some neighbors."

She said it as though the neighbors were of the same conse-
quence as the cars or the porches. "I heard that out west, some
bull sharks came inland with the waters."

Cade didn't respond. He couldn't. He wasn't ready to tell the
story.

Sarah seemed to catch on that he wouldn't say more, and
she turned to him as if to comfort. "This isn't a rainstorm. The

radar looked really bad, but it picks up mass, you know—
density—not water. So sometimes it looks like rain when it's
really something else. Pressure. Clouds. Who knows?"

He did know that. He'd been prepared for a rain that would
raise both the creek and his heart rate. "I'm not used to seeing
things blow by horizontally."

A piece of white paper whipped through the yard, followed
quickly by a plastic bottle tracing the same path.

"It's just high winds." Though she was watching alongside
him, she sounded mostly unconcerned. Cage was terrified.

He still didn't quite trust the nonchalance she projected.
He'd believe it when she returned to the brown leather couch
and the quilt with the skull design and watched one of their
three channels of TV. But Sarah stayed at the window, eyes on
the gathering damage. "At least we're not in Tornado Alley."

That was the whole point, he thought. A solar display that
was toppled by tornadoes multiple times each year wasn't cost-
efficient. Building damaged the environment, so rebuilding
each year wasn't economically *or* environmentally feasible. It's
why Radnor was breathing down their necks now.

He knew this storm probably wouldn't tear up any of the
newly-installed test posts, because they had to build them to
withstand more than this force. As harsh as the weather looked
from here, Sarah was right. It wasn't much.

Central Alabama had experienced one of the new F6
classes earlier in the year. An F3 had come through here. The
good news was that, according to frequency, if they could
build the solar array now, they should have an average of a
ten-year span before it would need to be repaired again. But
averages weren't storms and they worked only if it didn't get
worse.

Unlike Joule, who was hiding in her room and not watching
the storm, Cage preferred to keep his eye on the problem. He
and Sarah stayed at the window, silent for a few more

moments, each of them holding back their side of the curtains. He was trying to hide the tension that suffused every cell, but...

"Is that *snow*?" *In Alabama?*

The big, fluffy, white pieces blew across the yard. First, just a few came through, confusing him. But when they gathered steam and he saw the flurry of fluffy white ...

"Hold on!" Sarah laughed at him as she dropped her side of the curtain. She headed out the door into the back sunroom.

"Wait!" *Was she going outside?*

"It's just wind." She tossed the words too casually over her shoulder as she headed onto the back porch.

His jaw clenched and he told himself she'd be fine, even though the screens that enclosed the porch billowed and shook furiously around her. Several of the small, painted wood pieces had blown from their perches and Cage spotted the decorative piece with the red, white, and blue star crammed into the corner, now upside down. He waited for the wind to pick it up again and aim for Sarah.

But it didn't.

Unlatching the back door, Sarah fought the wind for a moment. She put one foot onto the step, then followed with her head and one hand, the other holding tightly to the frame. Cage grimaced, waiting for a stray shingle—or worse—to smack her, but it didn't happen.

Instead, she snatched one of the little masses of "snow" from the ground and brought it back in. She handed it to him as she leaned against the door and bolted it shut with a misplaced grin.

"It's cotton!" he said, squishing the soft mass between his fingers. It felt just like a store-bought cotton ball.

"Yeah. It looks like the wind stripped somebody's field."

Cage was still examining the piece she'd brought back in. Sarah was unfazed by it, but he turned it over with wonder. "It comes off the plant this way?"

"In the wind, all the time." She'd already turned to look out the window again, as more debris blew through their yard. This time, the smoker tilted a little in a big gust, but Cage was now more impressed with the white fluff blowing by.

What he held in his hand looked like a slightly dirty, unraveled cotton ball. He examined it for another moment, thinking about the fields he'd passed all the time since moving here. "Is this somebody's crop? Did their livelihood blow away?"

"If it's a big company, then this loss—" she waved her hand at the yard where the white was already thinning out, "—isn't enough to wipe them out. If it's a family farm, then the cotton probably isn't their only income."

Cage turned the cotton ball over in his hand, as if he were still inspecting it, but his thoughts had pulled elsewhere. He knew the disasters he'd encountered might have been odd or unique. But it didn't matter if the disaster was big or small. It mattered how hard the disaster hit you.

He jerked and dropped the cotton ball as something smacked against the window.

6

"What misfuckery is that?" Joule asked, leaning forward from the back of the car, her hand clutching the fabric of Cage's seat as she pulled herself forward to look.

She'd survived last night's nasty windstorm and she was letting Sarah drive again. *She was growing as a person.* But it sucked monkey balls, because now she wished she were at the wheel and could see more clearly.

A line of people in work clothes and boots held signs and shook angry fists in the distance. "Is that for us?"

It couldn't be, she thought. She watched the side of her brother's face as he, too, frowned.

"It can't be." Deveron spoke as though he'd plucked it from her brain. "We're building a solar farm. I mean, who even cares?"

But Joule noticed that Sarah was slowing the car.

"Oh, it's for us," her roommate confirmed as she scanned the crowd. Her hands tightened on the steering wheel as she muttered, "You have got to be shitting me."

Joule wanted to push and ask how Sarah knew, but decided

Sarah would reveal it in her own good time.

The car slowed more as they got closer. The protesters were now pushing in and crossing the road. The car in front of them came to a stop and Joule felt her own forward momentum abruptly end. The people surrounded the lead car, but Joule turned around to look out the back. Several more angry pedestrians had come in behind them. With the protesters blocking the road in front, Sarah's car was fenced in.

Joule wasn't really one for panic. It was true, she'd survived a lot of things the others around her had not. Still, these were just people, not killer animals—and she didn't even know yet what they were angry about. But as the protesters crowded the cars, she was able to read a few of the signs.

"Solar = noise pollution, heat pollution, water pollution."

She frowned. *That wasn't right.* The whole point of the solar farm was to reduce pollution. Her head turned the other way and she saw a sign that said, "Take your solar farm and stick it where the sun don't shine."

That didn't even make sense. She read the third one she saw out loud to the car. "Solar equals cancer? But *how*?"

Sarah sighed and leaned back, banging her head against the headrest a few times in irritation. One hand gripped the steering wheel, the other reached up to her hair, and she explained. "The oil and coal companies give them information that's only partly true. So these people have heard about the gases that are inside the solar panels."

"Right," Joule agreed, though she dragged the word out. "But those are literally trapped inside the panels. Unless they're cracking them open and sucking it down, there's no cancer to be had. In fact, I don't think we're even sure if the gas inside the panels *would* cause cancer if you *did* suck it down. It's just not really on the 'approved foods' list."

"You and I both know that," Sarah said as she waved her

hand in front of her, palm up, to gesture to the people who stood in the road in front of the car. "But they don't."

Joule tried to lean back and let the tension leach away. There was a little truth in all of it. The accusation of heat pollution existed because putting in a solar panel did raise the temperature near the panels. An array as big as theirs could raise the field temp a few degrees.

But that was why *half* of their team members were environmentalists. She couldn't help herself, and she opened her mouth again. "Do none of them understand that I spent the last three weeks being shot down by you two, because I can't use a paint that a hamster might ultimately ingest about a gram of?"

"Again," Sarah sighed harshly into the car, "You know, and I know—"

But she didn't finish the sentence. The passenger side door of the car in front of them flew open and Melinda Gonzalez hopped out. Apparently, the lead environmental tester had had enough and wasn't ready to be late to her job. Protesters be damned.

"You need to let us through." Her voice was firm and borderline angry. Joule heard her say she was one of the management team. Apparently, Melinda Gonzalez also had a *bitch switch*, because the kind teacher Joule had seen before was gone. "You have two choices. You can get out of my way or I can call the police."

Joule was pretty sure she heard the large man who was getting in Melinda's face grumble, "It's public property. We have a right to be here."

As Joule watched, her hand clenching the door latch, ready to hop out and defend the woman, Melinda didn't flinch.

Gonzales was taking none of this shit. "One, public property or not, you're obstructing a roadway. That's illegal. And two, it's *not* public property. The Helio Systems property line is about five hundred yards back that way, asshole."

Ooh, Joule thought, *that was a nice punctuation.*

But the man leaned forward almost into Melinda's face, definitely aiming to use his size to intimidate. Even Joule towered over Melinda, but Gonzalez was already leaning forward, using his move against him. Though the conversation seemed to be happening between two people, Melinda was letting her voice carry, maybe so she'd have lots of witnesses. Joule made a mental note but was listening raptly again as Melinda leveled another accusation.

"This is *my* property, not yours. Anything you do is assault. And anything I do is self-defense. So bring it." She jolted forward at him and Joule felt the smile creep across her own face when the man jerked back at the sudden, if small, threat.

When he only stared for a moment, making no further gestures, Melinda turned away from him as though he were no longer worth her time. This time, she addressed the crowd at large. "I'm calling 9-1-1 now. And I saw an officer on the road, right back there, less than a mile," she threatened, pointing. "He'll be here quickly. You won't have time to get off of my property before you get arrested for trespassing. And you *will* be arrested. Helio Systems will prosecute to the full extent of the law."

Joule watched as the peripheral people started to shift away at the threat. They probably didn't have the money nor the time to fight a corporate giant. Who did? But it was odd, sitting in the car and feeling like she was part of the machine. Even if she knew most of what they were protesting was untrue.

Melinda was already dialing her phone and Joule watched as the crowd now dispersed in earnest.

Go Melinda, she thought and at that moment, she realized if she ever wanted to move into management, she wanted to be Melinda Gonzalez.

The crowd might be leaving, but they did so belligerently, moving close to the cars, holding up their signs to be sure the workers inside could read them. The man who'd harassed Melinda came close to her again, but Melinda just offered an expression that said he wasn't worth her time, and climbed in, slamming her door.

Joule breathed easier with the manager out of harm's way. Even as Melinda pulled forward, the man leaned in as if to look into the car for contraband or such. Sarah started the motions to follow along.

But as she shoved the gear shift into drive, her head snapped to the left. The lead man had leaned down to her car window and was looking directly at Sarah ... as if he knew her. And he was making a motion to let her know he was watching.

7

"That's a nice T-shirt, Cage." Izzy laughed at him as she passed by, carrying specimens up to the main tent.

They'd not seen him in just a T-shirt before, but today he'd tied his hoodie around his waist. He was known for being perpetually cold, but the Alabama humidity had broken him yesterday. He was hot and he didn't like it. He wanted his jacket on, but needed to do the work, and the work made him hot.

He, Sarah, and Mitch were back at the same job today—doing the sweaty task of catching field mice and anything else they could get their hands on. Even Sarah—finally in a better mood after the encounter this morning—was singing "Little Bunny Foo Foo" as she emptied the traps.

Cage already had three containers stacked under his arm as Sarah held out another. "Take this one."

He double-checked her field sticker with the trap number and exact GPS coordinates of where she'd found the little guy. Inside each clear plastic box, a single creature scrambled about. Cage now held two field mice, a lizard, and a huge centipede.

He headed away from their little cluster of workers before she could hand him another box, or before Mitch could get any ideas. Walking slowly at first, Cage waited for his critters to settle down. Normally, they were a little anxious at first, then got used to the container and eventually handled the field checks like recalcitrant teenagers. But not today.

Was it yesterday's wind storm that had them all stirred up?

The field solar array was huge and it took him quite some time to trek his way to the main data tent Helio Systems had set up on the edge of the field. He passed people that he knew along the way, saying hello to each of them as he went.

The job was finally settling in, though the work itself was more backbreaking than he'd expected. While he had racked up plenty of experience in school doing fieldwork internships, the hands-on part of his education had been spotty at best. He'd had fun and, at the end of the two weeks, he went home, ate all the pasta, and slept it off for a few days.

Now he was on his fourth straight week and he'd been working a minimum of forty hours each week. Radnor was hard-pressed to get his project back on the original schedule, and that pressure was falling to the team. Cage didn't mind. He knew what he'd signed up for.

Though they spent Thursdays in the lab, they were still on their feet all day. And the meetings on Fridays, when they got to sit down, were actually the most effort. The meetings got crazy as Radnor pushed them all for "more ideas!"

Though Cage had come here believing he was prepared, he hadn't quite been. Still, he was finally settling in, and his muscle memory was catching up. So was his stamina. He didn't fall into bed quite as hard anymore. And his career choice was feeling more like a choice, and less like a trial period.

He'd been worried for the last semester of school, wondering if this was going to be the time that he and Joule finally went their separate ways. She was his only remaining family—aside from their grandfather, who insisted the twins live their own lives rather than move in with him. They'd lost both parents—dramatically, and in short order—about five years earlier.

Their first year at school hadn't been any easier. While normal twins might have happily gone their separate ways for college, and certainly for work afterwards, he and Joule had made the effort to stay together.

At first, he'd thought himself happy with the arrangement with Helio Systems Technologies but now he wondered if he actually liked the work, or if he just liked that it kept him close to Joule. Now, marching across the too-hot and too-humid field, with four plastic containers barely tucked under his arm, he felt that he'd made the right decision for him, too.

The field mice scrambled for purchase in the plastic boxes. His own crappy writing labeled three of the stickers on the containers. Though Alabama wasn't home, the job was becoming where he belonged.

"Hey Cage," Leah called out as he almost stepped on her. She'd been down in a particularly tall patch of grass, nearly hidden. "Want to take two more?"

Checking his location, he shifted the boxes. Balancing six wasn't easy, but they weren't heavy, just awkward, and the animals tended to shift their weight suddenly. His job was to not drop them. He'd done that once before and felt like such a shit. So he double-checked this time. "Two more mice?"

"Yup. Tiny little guys," she replied, holding her containers aloft so he could see inside.

It wasn't far to the tent now. "I can make it." He shifted his own containers, letting her stack another two on top. Steadying them with his chin, he continued carefully picking his way to the main lab tent.

"That's quite a haul you've got there," Melinda greeted him, back to her usual cheerful self after going full badass bitch at the protesters this morning.

"Not all mine."

"Everything's initialed?" Melinda asked, as though that wasn't the standard protocol, and as though she wouldn't murder them all if everything wasn't filled out properly and double-checked.

"Of course." He'd checked each of his own stickers before stacking the boxes. And while he hadn't made a big show of it, he'd checked Sarah's and Leah's work, too, before agreeing to bring their samples in. He'd seen Melinda go off on one of the newbies with improperly labeled catches, and while these weren't his boxes, he was the one delivering them. That made him equally responsible—and he wouldn't want Melinda to turn on him the way they'd witnessed that morning.

"We're getting behind," Izzy called out from the other side of the tent, her gloved hands wrapped around a lizard as she removed him from his box for initial weights and measures. Then she looked up at Cage with a gleam in her eye. "Want to stay in the main tent? Help with data? You know you want to."

"Sure!" he laughed. He held up one finger, grabbed his walkie, and asked Sarah and Mitch if they needed him more in the field than the tent needed him.

He breathed a sigh of relief when they said they could spare him. As much fun as trapping was, it was in the broad sun. The tent was in the shade. Staying here through the midday inferno would be a blessing.

Within a few minutes, he was elbows-deep in tiny animals, measuring them, weighing them, tagging them. Though Cage found the work interesting, the animals were not fans. He felt for them, and it diminished his joy in the data. He next transferred every number from his notebook into the one of the two laptops set up for statistical analysis.

"Be sure to do a body check for ticks," Melinda called out.

Shit!

There wasn't a column for that, and he'd forgotten. But luckily, none of his boxes had been sent back out into the field yet. So three minutes later, he was giving a particularly irritated field mouse a full parasite check when Izzy yelped from the other side of the tent.

8

C age laughed as Izzy scrambled to catch the mouse that had made a break for it. Her words rang clear through the heavy air. "Little suckers are jumpy today!"

She called out, "Gotcha!" and Cage watched as she covered the little mouse with both cupped hands. Then he laughed again when she jumped as he got away.

"No, no, no!" she yelled, chasing her tiny escapee around the table and down one of the legs.

"Did you get him? Do you need help?" Melinda called out. She and Cage would have both rushed to help, but each had their own tiny animal in their hands.

"Got him!" Izzy hollered out and held the mouse aloft in her victory. But the comedy only lasted a moment before they all turned back to their own work.

Still, the interruption seemed to provide the break Cage had been looking for. Trying to sound casual, he asked Melinda, "So why did the protesters think that the solar array is going to cause water pollution?"

Too much of the protest didn't make sense to him, but this

was maybe the easiest, most straight-forward question to ask. He not only wanted the answer but wanted to see if he got shut down just for asking...

He and Joule had researched Helio Systems before they joined. Staying together was a priority, and Helio offered that, but they hadn't been willing to join any company that was adding to environmental changes in the wrong direction. He'd seen the damage some corporations were doing, and there was no salary he could fathom that would make it worth his while to be part of that.

Melinda took a moment to answer, and it made him wonder if she knew. She seemed to be hunting for the right thing to say, but even so it came out a little half-assed. "Everything causes pollution. Everything that changes the environment, that is. And this is no exception."

Though she still held a lizard in her hand, she seemed to have forgotten as she gestured with it toward the open field. The tiny, blue-striped reptile didn't appreciate being waved around, so he wrapped his little claws tighter around her glove. She didn't notice.

"Is that really it?" Cage asked before thinking. "I was assuming it's the paint from the pylons leaching into the fields. Or something like that."

From the other side of the tent, Izzy joined the conversation, seeming to have gotten her mouse in line now. "There's also a lot of concern about what's inside the panels. Specifically, most solar panel designs contain cadmium, lead, and antimony. Those are the ones that get protested."

Izzy was probably only a few years older than him and his sister, but this wasn't her first project with Helio. Her answer was solid and informed, and he found he was willing to learn the ropes from her.

"But the panels don't break open," Cage said. "I mean, they

aren't supposed to. We don't break them open each day to make them work."

"True, but the breakage problem is twofold," Izzy replied, placing the mouse she'd just tagged back into his container and making her notes on the corresponding sticker as she talked.

It was all second nature to her. And Cage, who'd almost let a small batch back into the field without recorded tick-checks, hoped he would grow as confident as she was, and soon. He turned back to his lab notebook, double-checking everything and making sure that his conversation wasn't degrading his work quality. Melinda wouldn't stand for that.

As he opened another lid and placed the proper marks on that sticker, he listened to Izzy. "And the F6 tornado that just came through Alabama would have likely cracked open some panels on a field like ours."

"But that didn't happen here," Cage replied.

"Right, and that's part of why we're building here. But F6 tornadoes do now exist." She turned to Melinda. "Do you know if that one hit any solar arrays?"

"There aren't many solar arrays in Alabama to begin with," Melinda lamented as she tapped on the computer, entering her own latest round of data.

"Anyway," Izzy went on, "tornado or not, what's inside *is* dangerous. The second issue is what happens once a panel's life is over. The older solar panels—dating back to the '70s—aren't in use anymore. And they're so toxic, it's horrifying! In general, the panels do last a long time, but we still don't know what to do with them when they're spent. And the protesters don't seem to understand that the pollution from what we're doing is far, far less than the environmental damage caused by things like coal and fracking."

She paused just long enough to take a breath and Cage found himself smiling at her happily delivered lesson.

"Right now I, personally, think water is the cleanest energy source. But it's not going to be enough, so here we are with solar."

"So what about our panels? Are they dangerous when broken?" Cage asked.

"That's exactly the point of all this research," Melinda chimed in. "Specifically, that's on *us* as the environmental team." Melinda smiled at him. "Once we're finished cataloging the wildlife, we get to crack open a few of these bad boys and see what damage the inside causes."

Cage raised an eyebrow. He hadn't known that.

"The trick is to make the most solar energy with the least amount of environmental damage," Izzy said. She went on about cadmium and landfills and drainage problems.

It made sense and, while it was more than what he'd asked, he loved a good, nerdy conversation. Putting the lizard he held back into his container, he double-checked the sticker against his notes ... again. Though he'd finished the six that he'd brought into the tent with him, field workers had arrived with fifteen more animals while they'd been talking.

Melinda didn't tell him to leave, so he picked up another specimen as Melinda countered Izzy. "But none of that is happening here. So yes, the solar array is going to cover part of the field and it is going to change the environment a bit. And it is an eyesore. But barring a massive accident, the protests don't make sense."

She offered a heavy sigh. Maybe because she'd had to face down one of the most intimidating of the protesters this morning. "All this work we are doing is to keep the array going—producing power for *them*—even in the event of harsh weather or other heavy damage. So all the things you're talking about, that's still not happening *here*."

Izzy seemed increasingly frustrated. Cage grasped his field mouse tightly so that he wouldn't have to watch it as he looked up to see her expression. Her tight, dark curls were scraped back into a ponytail and her T-shirt proclaimed that "Penguins don't smoke weed." It made Cage question the snarky shirt he'd thought about wearing today. He'd rejected it for being even more unprofessional than his national park T. Maybe he could have gotten away with it.

Izzy waved her hands—luckily without a creature in her grasp—and seemed not to notice that Cage was watching her more closely now. But her tone matched her face in aggravation.

"Those protesters weren't protesting general pollution in the future! It wasn't a 'save the environment from the evil corporation' thing. They were acting like our very presence here is tainting *their* water, *their* Earth, and *their* sky."

"Well," Melinda sighed, "there's enough truth in it and enough questions that, when they look stuff up, it seems reasonable. A good Google search will support that. There *is* antimony and cadmium in most solar panel glass, so I get that. However, the real problem with the protest here isn't any of that. It's that it's *personal*."

The knock at the door was hard and heavy, so Joule took extra caution as she pushed herself out of the deep leather couch and headed toward the front of the house.

The night had grown so dark, she wasn't able to see who was on the porch, other than that it was someone relatively large. The only way to find out was to open the door.

She threw the bolt as the pounding continued. She was speaking even as she pulled the thick, wooden door back. "Hello?"

"Where is she?" the man demanded, his head craning one way and then the next, trying to see past Joule. He looked vaguely familiar, but the threat in his voice was more concerning than her recognizing him.

Joule frowned hard, trying to get his attention. When that didn't work, she moved into his path, blocking him from coming fully inside. He had to mean Sarah, but she wasn't going to volunteer her roommate's name. And maybe he had the wrong house? "I'm sorry. I don't know who you're talking about."

He looked at her as though she must be stupid or deliberately holding back on him. Well, he had the second part right.

Still, he wasn't the first person Joule had faced down. For a moment, her mind raced to the fact that she had her bow and arrows stashed in her closet. If she could just make it to her room, she could defend herself, if need be. The thought solidified as the asshole on her porch growled and shoved her aside and stormed into the house.

"Hey!" Joule shoved back at him but he was already past her. Also, he was so physically dense that her move had little effect. He yelled out, *"Sarah! Sarah, get out here!"*

Luckily, his harsh tone brought not only Sarah, but Cage and Deveron, too.

The man seemed a bit surprised by the small army that had formed in response to his entrance. Sarah had been in their room. Deveron had been in his as well, and Cage had been out of sight, around the corner at the dining room table working on some collection of data he'd gathered during the day. None of them were taking shit from the intruder.

But then Sarah surprised her, stepping up and getting in his face. "What is it that you want, Jerry?"

She knew him well enough to do that?

"I saw you in that car," he accused.

"Of course, you did." Sarah crossed her arms over yet another pair of her ever-present overalls. "I *work* there. You'll see me going there five days a week."

He stared hard for a moment as though to make her back down; Joule was glad that her roommate wasn't taking any of it. Sarah was hard to read sometimes, but tonight that was probably a good thing.

When Jerry didn't say anything else, Sarah added, "I saw you on *private property*, staging a protest."

"Of course, I'm protesting." He was moving ever closer, his finger pointed and jabbing at her chest.

Joule walked forward. She'd faced worse creatures in her life and knew when an animal was about to pounce. With a lightning-quick move, she smacked his hand away like he was a toddler, but harder.

Clearly, she'd surprised the shit out of him. It seemed he'd not expected the now-quiet blonde observer to actually strike out.

But Joule wasn't done. Responding in kind tended to make things escalate. Animals on the hunt had to be forced to concede Fueled by her anger at having her home invaded and hearing a threat issued in her own living room, she issued one of her own in return. "Get the fuck back!"

She stepped into his personal space now, next to Sarah, and hoped that the fire in her eyes looked like she was willing to rip his face off with her teeth if she had to. As long as she kept moving forward, as long as she kept up the threat, she would have an advantage.

He stared at her hard for a moment, finally ignoring Sarah. But though his voice was harsh and aimed at her, his words were those of an offhand dismissal. "This is between me and her."

Not willing to be dismissed, Joule crossed her own arms and planted her feet, now standing shoulder-to-shoulder with Sarah. Or close, as Sarah was a little shorter.

"No, it's not," she countered him with confidence. "And don't treat me like I'm stupid. I'm not. None of us are. *You* barged into *our* home and threatened someone I live with. Don't act like it's not between you and me. I've already had enough of your shit. You can be decent, or you can take your monkey ballsack of a face and get the hell out of my house."

Beside her, though Sarah's lips stayed pressed in a straight line, Joule could feel her shoulder moving. Sarah was trying desperately not to laugh. Joule had a feeling Cage and Deveron were doing the same behind her, but she was keeping her own face straight, as though "monkey ballsack of a face" was merely so apt a description that it wasn't even humorous.

Jerry's mouth dropped open with the insult, but Joule was still riding her forward momentum. Ignoring the man for a moment, hoping he caught the insult that he wasn't even worth her attention now, she asked, "Do you want to talk to him, Sarah?"

Sarah tipped her head one way as if shrugging, as if saying maybe she had time for this, maybe not. But she addressed the man in front of her. "Only if you're decent about it, Jerry."

"You shouldn't be doing this!" he accused again, his eyes once more focused on Sarah, who apparently wasn't going to call him out—at least not quite as harshly as Joule did. But Sarah wasn't taking any of his shit either.

"Nope. You'll have to do better than that. Last chance. You can sit at the dining room table and have a reasonable conversation with me, or you can leave. Those are your only two options. Because as Joule said, this is our house, not yours."

"This isn't over!" He once again jabbed his finger toward Sarah's chest and, once again, Joule smacked it downward, this time harder and with her fingers curled so he felt the sting of fingernails. She did not take threats in her own home. She'd seen harsher shit than him.

"Don't you fucking touch her, you flaming piece of shit!" she now shouted in Jerry's face.

Jerry's eyes betrayed him, flaring at the harsh string of swears. She didn't care, and her "don't screw with me" stance earned her a glare before he turned and headed out the door. He slammed the front screen door behind him as he left. It was a sound Joule had previously heard about through country music. Over the past few weeks, she'd come to think of it as a friendly, neighborly noise. Now, it was unsettling.

Even as she heard his car start up, she had the vague feeling that he'd memorized her face. Sarah had told him her name, and he would be able to easily find her.

As his taillights faded down the long drive, the threat still hung in the air.

10

Cage was thrown toward the dash when Sarah hit the brakes, the car skidding to a stop on the gravel just before it crashed into the pile of branches in the road. He hadn't quite smacked into the windshield, although he got a good little jolt from the seatbelt, which he ignored and watched Sarah look from side to side.

It had been five days since Jerry had come to the house. The protesters had shown up each morning after that, waving their signs, and each time Jerry had been there, front and center. He'd spent some money or time or both on the big signs that he could only hold one corner of.

The night he'd been to their place, Sarah had plopped onto the couch afterward and explained. "He's my cousin. We played together as kids. I was always the smart one in high school, and he was the jock."

Cage had looked to Joule. They didn't have that. They saw their cousins at holidays, and even not then sometimes. Their parents had moved around with their work and then, once they were gone, and after grandma had passed, they hadn't seen their cousins at all. The twins had lived in a town of high-IQ scientists, they'd lived near the think tanks, and they'd lived at college. What Sarah was describing was as foreign to him as Alabama itself.

Sarah had leaned back onto the couch, her head tilted onto the cushions as she stared at the ceiling. "He graduated two years before me and went from high school football hero to factory worker. He wasn't happy about it. He didn't get any college offers like he thought. Then I graduated as valedictorian—"

"That's cool," Deveron had interrupted. "I wasn't valedictorian."

"Well, there were only sixty of us, and some of my competition was a lot like Jerry." Sarah had stuffed her hands into her pockets. "He watched me move away and get jobs and come back for holidays. We haven't really spoken in years. Now, I don't know if this protest is just something to do, if it's personal against me, or if he really loves the grass and the trees and thinks we are poisoning his home."

"Could be all three," Joule had mused, and the conversation ended there.

In the meantime, they'd seen the protest crew here each morning as they drove in. They were gone by midday, seeming only to want to harass the workers as they arrived. But Cage had noticed that Jerry was staring Sarah down as she pulled the car through the crowd. She'd seemingly become their designated driver, with all of them piling into the same seat each morning. So Jerry was easily positioned to lean near her window as the crowd slowed the car down. Sarah had ignored him, looking straight ahead.

Cage was beginning to wonder if maybe Jerry was the leader of the protesters.

Sarah put the car into park, as she had no other options. The branches had been dragged across the road for clearly that exact purpose. He could see she was clenching both the steering wheel and her jaw.

Cage squeezed her arm to steady her. "I've got this."

From the back seat, Deveron leaned forward, too, clapping his own hand on Cage's shoulder. "I'm with you."

The two climbed out from opposite sides of the car, intending to simply clear the branches and drive through. Cage hoped the protesters were done interfering, but he kept his attention on them in the periphery.

As he leaned over to grab a gnarled branch, Deveron whispered in a low voice, "We're not the first ones here."

"Right, *they* were here first." Cage picked one of the smaller branches and chucked it to the side.

"No, we aren't the first *Helio Systems people* on site today. That means they're throwing the branches back into the road every time there's a break in the cars entering."

Cage picked up another of the pieces from where it blocked the road. *Not the lightest*, he thought as he tugged it off the roadway. Behind him, the protesters started in with a chant that they hadn't been doing when Sarah stopped the car. At least, not that he could remember. The fact that they'd started up again, and that Sarah's was the only car here right now, meant this roadblock was specifically for them.

He sighed, having already had enough of this bullshit. Like Sarah and Joule, Cage was more than willing to sit at the table and have a conversation. He was more than willing to look into any accusations. He didn't want to work for Helio Systems if the company was actually poisoning land. With the remainder of their parents' life insurance money still in the bank after they finished college, they could afford to walk off the job, if the situation warranted.

So if the protesters were right, he wanted to know. If they weren't, then this was bullshit. And the method was bullshit, either way. So, using his momentum, he swung the branch around and hurled it away from the road, nearly whacking some of the close-by protesters.

Turning to them, he gave a neatly insincere shrug. "Oh, sorry."

Beside him, Deveron laughed softly and did the same with another branch, chucking it near to the protesters on the other side of the road. As the branch sailed and they hopped angrily out of the way, he called, "Look out! Guess I don't know my own strength."

Cage knew he was being childish, but he didn't care until he spotted Chithra Murasawa—one of the managers—walking toward them. She'd followed the gravel drive from the field out to where they were now stuck. She had to have seen what they were doing, but she didn't call out, thus letting them get a few more good throws in before she stepped over the last of the large branches and softly told them, "Hey, you should be careful where you toss those."

Then she called out louder to the protesters, "Hey! You should be careful where you're standing!"

"They are throwing branches at us!" one of the women called out.

He was doing no such thing. He was throwing branches *near* them. And not over the property line—assuming he remembered correctly where it was.

Cage watched as Chithra navigated past the car and walked a little farther back on the drive. She seemed to be examining the situation—and maybe eyeballing the property line?— before turning around and coming back. He'd worked with her often enough to like her quite a bit. She had a calm, easygoing style.

"They're heavy," Cage told her. "Really hard to control—"

He motioned to the protesters to move back before letting another branch fly into a more open space, "—as these good people here can attest to, since they mistakenly managed to keep getting them all back in the road. Which I'm sure is an *arrestable offense*."

He let the last several words hang in the air for a moment. It was Chithra, who was now much closer, who said loudly, "Oh, it definitely is an arrestable offense."

She casually pulled her phone from her back pocket and began taking pictures of all those nearby, who suddenly began hiding their faces behind their signs. As they turned back toward the cars, she continued to snap photos. Then she spoke to Cage and Deveron in an overly loud voice. "I can't see their faces in the photos... but it doesn't matter. I took much clearer photos as I drove in this morning. This is just to prove that they're still here an hour later."

"It's public property!" a different protester yelled out, as though that made it all okay.

Chithra seemed to have realized that Jerry had it in his head to lead the little group. She quickly understood that the smarter move was not to go after him, but the followers. So ignoring Jerry, she faced the group on the other side of the road. "It doesn't matter if it's public property, you still need a permit to gather. I'd like to see yours."

The others began looking at each other frantically, maybe having trusted Jerry to have this organized. But even as they scrambled, Chithra kept pushing.

"It's also illegal to block the roads. And I don't know what you all think we're doing here, but most of what's on your signs is incorrect." She motioned to the posterboard and paint many of them still held aloft. "We are a large corporation. We've put too much effort into this solar array to let you ruin it over things that aren't true. So you need to know, I took pictures on the way in this morning. And yes, after your first little stunt, we installed video cameras at the front of the road. So we have pictures of every face that has gathered here unlawfully for the last five days."

Cage watched as the crowd grew silent. One by one, the signs lowered and the people looked at each other, wondering if she was going to have them arrested. This strategy was far more effective than his flinging branches had been.

Chithra wasn't done with them yet. "We understand you're upset. You should know, you've all been invited to the table. We'd love to have a talk with you so we can all figure out what we need to do to make this safe for everyone—for our workers and for those of you who live here."

Again, the protesters looked to each other, their expressions indicating they'd heard of no such thing. Chithra realized this was news to them and she spoke softly this time, only to Cage and Deveron. "Can I hit you guys up for a ride back to the tent? I was going to stay on guard, but I think they're leaving now."

Without waiting for Cage or Deveron to answer, she called out to the protesters again. "Perhaps your leader here, Jerry Whitman, hasn't told you, but he's known for five days that we've offered to have an open meeting to answer any questions. Everyone is welcome."

As she nudged Cage on one side and Deveron on the other, the crowd began to turn on Jerry. That was some brilliant tactical work. She'd walked in, spoken clearly, and made them all mad at the person doing the most damage.

She spoke softly to the two of them again, her tone a little more urgent than Cage expected, given that the crowd was already beginning to disperse. "Get back in the car *now*."

Cage quickly surveyed the road. It was clear enough. A few twigs had snapped off the branches, but nothing that was any threat to the car's undercarriage. Climbing into the back seat, Cage wedged himself with Joule and Deveron, so Chithra could take the front.

Sarah shoved the gearshift into drive, though her jaw was still clenched tightly and she didn't say anything. She plowed the old sedan over the branches, keeping her speed even and her angry gaze straight ahead. All five of them stayed quiet until they were pulling up to the grassy area where they parked near the main tent.

Cage had expected another day of fieldwork. They'd moved on from smaller mammals and lizards to collecting the last week's data from the field cams for the larger creatures. He was ready for that kind of work. Instead, everyone was gathering in the tent, the crowd growing larger as several cars pulled in behind theirs.

As Sarah parked and Chithra opened her door, the manager turned to the four of them before she stepped out. "We have bigger problems than the protesters."

11

C age laced his fingers together to keep from fidgeting. Instead, he found he was clenching his hands. At the front of the tent, Radnor was talking, waving his own hands in front of a projection screen showing a map of the entire US. It seemed most of the audience—the Helio Systems team—was sitting rapt in their white folding chairs, trying to catch up.

"We ran the data before we started the project," Radnor said, waving his hands across the whole of the map. "And we picked this site. However, we've been running the data again. With the latest addition, we've noticed a big change. Dr. Murawasa?" He motioned to where she stood at the side and the manager stepped readily into place in front of the screen.

Not just a manager, Cage thought as Ragnar introduced her. That was quickly followed by, *So she'd known.* Not just that there was a meeting but specifically what the meeting was going to be about.

The team had been told not to take notes, but having something to do would have kept him from fidgeting. He tapped his toe in a steady rhythm to release part of his energy and clenched his fingers tighter together.

Next to him, he felt more than saw Joule's eyes flick his direction, as if to ask, *What is this?*

The project had already had a major setback before they and the other newbies had arrived on the scene. Was this going to be another catastrophe?

Stepping forward, Chithra—apparently *Doctor* Murasawa— pointed at the map. It seemed she was a meteorological data analyst. Once again, he wondered why he and his sister had been hired, fresh out of school.

Up until they'd arrived on site the first day, he'd foolishly believed there would be workers here as well—people hired to move things around and install everything. And, when he was honest, he'd believed he would have at least some status in the hierarchy. But apparently, no, they were the lowest rung of this ladder.

He pushed his attention back to where Dr. Murasawa was pointing at several specific points on the map and expecting her captive audience to follow. "We were looking at tornadoes first, because that is what this section of Alabama—" she ran her hand up the middle of the state, "—is known for."

Waving her hand along another section running up through Tennessee and Kentucky, she added, "I think most of you know, but just in case, this area north of us is well-known for strip mining. When we head toward the Virginia and West Virginia area, we see more energy from more standard coal mining scenarios. Either way, we're looking at fossil fuels. Our main goal is to come in, create an alternate system, and maybe make some systemic nudges that change the culture toward becoming more fossil-free."

Cage involuntarily tipped his head toward his sister and saw that she'd done the same. The protesters out front indicated the last part was not going as smoothly as intended.

But Murasawa wasn't dwelling on that. "This section of the country does have a tornado issue, and we've been building to suit that. However, we're now looking at other data. Because the area isn't known for flooding—despite having heavy rainstorms —we'd run the calculations and when they came out as minimal risk, we didn't worry. Much of the Alabama area has a wonderful watershed system..." The screen changed to a brightly colored topographical map, but Cage's mind was flashing other thoughts.

Oh shit, he thought, remembering what Sarah had said about the creeks rising. As he watched, the map expanded again, shifting the focus from Alabama to the entire continent of North America.

"The rest of the world aside, we've seen massive flooding situations here—" She pointed to New Orleans. "Here." She pointed to Houston. "And here."

All heavily localized to the south, Cage thought.

"Miami, New Orleans, mostly coastal towns," she said, even as he thought it. "And those places were prepared for flooding. It's not new, though recent floods have been reaching new heights. Now, we add in more recent years. We've seen too many 'hundred-year' floods. Nashville had one in the late aughts." She pointed to the middle of Tennessee. "The entire Southeast US suffered extensive flooding in ninety-eight. And the Palo Alto area had one just under four years ago." She moved her hand across the entire map to the other side of the country as Cage felt his stomach clench. Joule's fingers slipped in between his, grasping his hand. *They had been there.*

"In recent years, the spring flood outlooks don't hit the Alabama area." The map changed again, showing water flow and bright purple flood warning areas far to the north. "But we have seen 'hundred-year floods' hitting in record numbers, and flood levels of thirty-plus feet. These tend to happen because of mountain runoff. It wasn't so much the quantity of rainfall in one area—though that is problematic—but that pooling and watershed runoff created fast-moving water and rising flood lines. If we go back and look at Texas, we can see that their scenario had that as well."

The entire team was now turning heads and looking at each other. They weren't supposed to be in a flood zone. Wasn't that the whole point? They were in Nowhere, Alabama for a number of reasons. Cheap land and open space was important, but lack of catastrophic natural disasters was crucial. And after the number of disasters they'd seen, that had been a huge pull for Cage and his sister.

"But what does all this mean?" Dr. Murasawa was smart enough to openly ask the question they were all thinking. "Two things. One—as we look at the topography of this area, we should be relatively okay."

She moved her hand around showing the map that had switched back to a topo map of the state. The colors indicated high ground and low points, and this time, Cage was trying to follow the key and make sure he was interpreting it correctly. Joule moved her hand away from his to point. Though their area was higher ground for Alabama, it was lower than the surrounding areas.

"The mountains feed down to us," she whispered.

"It's inevitable. The water path is why we have valleys here." He quoted his Environmental Systems class from sophomore year. When he'd been sitting in class taking copious notes, he'd never imagined the information might impact his survival.

Dr. Murasawa stood silent at the front of the room . Then she turned to Radnor and shrugged, her demeanor changing instantly from teacher-mode to more conversational. *She must be going off script.* For a moment, she looked out over the crowd and Cage thought she might have caught his eye. Then she started into a story. "But point number two is something I overheard. A week ago, I was having dinner at Los Jalapenos."

The crowd laughed. It was one of two wonderfully authentic Mexican restaurants, and the solar site sat directly between them. Everyone had eaten there. Cage could imagine the scene as she continued.

"I overheard the local news station meteorologist at the table behind me." They'd all seen the over-tanned and over-coifed Jason Wilcox on the news. "He said he was concerned about the upcoming rainy season and whoever was with him—his wife, I don't know—said 'but we have one every year.' He said he was concerned about flash flooding this year and listed several key times during the fall season that he thought these things might occur. He told her that she should mark his predictions down..."

Dr. Murasawa looked around the room. "I don't know if *she* marked it down, but you can bet I did."

This time the tent erupted in small laughter, and Cage realized he wasn't the only one who felt he knew Dr. Chithra Murasawa. They all did.

"It was no big deal, I thought, but it did make me go home and pull the data and re-crunch the numbers. As Radnor said, we crunched everything before we chose this location to build, but that was two years ago."

This time, the entire tent fell silent, and Cage felt something ominous bloom in his chest. If there was anything he didn't like talking about, it was floods.

"This last year's data does change things, and not in a good way."

12

"Not high enough," Joule called out to her team members, her tape measure in hand.

She raised the end well overhead until it bumped the bottom side of the top lip of the pylon they'd just installed. It had been exactly eight days since Radnor and Murasawa had made the big announcement that everything was changing yet again.

Joule had told Cage the night before, "We were hired for a year, but I'm beginning to think we'll be here longer."

The year had been estimated as enough time to install the array, get it working, and for the Helio Systems team to monitor it before handing it over to a more permanent crew. Now, it seemed they might never make it to the part where they monitored a working solar array.

She simply didn't know if all the setbacks were normal or not. She looked up at the top of the pylon and shook her head at Mitch, as the wind whipped her hair around and the back of her neck prickled.

Turning, she scanned the open space behind her. The trees

seemed to creep closer at the edge of the field as the sky slowly grew darker. It should have been bright and sunny, but Joule knew the storm was rolling in—not just because she could see the light fading, but because she felt it in her bones.

Though she couldn't pinpoint anything specifically suspicious, the wind offered the sensation of fingers walking along her spine, as well as the feeling of being watched. Joule narrowed her eyes and swept her gaze through the forest with a glare, as if to say, *I see you.*

Honestly, she suspected it was Jerry out there, searching for something to turn the protesters against them again. Though Sarah had had many kind things to say about "old Jerry," "new Jerry" wasn't proving to be the kind of person Joule would want to hang with.

Luckily, the protesters had left after Dr. Murasawa had, in one fell swoop, both threatened them with arrest and informed them that Jerry was holding out on them. They hadn't returned.

Tomorrow was Saturday, and though technically they were all supposed to have the day off, the town hall was scheduled for two p.m. Everyone was invited to come and ask their questions. Most of the tiny town and some people from the surrounding, bigger townships were expected to show as well.

Though neither Joule nor Cage—nor anyone that she knew closely, really—was scheduled to be on the panel that would answer questions, the project workers were all intending to go. She wanted to hear the answers for herself.

"But how much height does the solar array add?" Mitch was asking, bringing her thoughts firmly back to the matter at hand. She lowered her tape measure and noted the height.

"And what about the hydraulics?" Dev asked.

Radnor had cycled them back around to being in the same group this week. It was an odd arrangement, but what did Joule know? For a moment, she wondered if that's why she and her brother had been hired—because they would go along easily with anything asked of them, not knowing any better.

"If we have hydraulics at the top," Dev said, "we actually have to go higher. We don't want to risk water getting into the system."

"*Dirty* water," Joule added without thinking. They all looked at her. *Shit.*

She shouldn't have opened her mouth. This was not her favorite topic, but five pairs of eyes were on her. "Floodwater. It's dirty. Look around."

She waved her hand toward the ground. "All the leaves will be in the water. Twigs and more—"

"Which will be far worse in the fall," Mitch interrupted, and she nodded along, glad to turn the conversation over to him. She didn't want anyone asking how she knew so much about devastating floods.

"How exactly does the water get here?" She was trying to push the topic of flooding onto the others. So she looked around but couldn't tell whether she was standing in the bottom of the bowl or at the top of the mesa. None of that was visibly available information.

"Probably directly." Mitch looked up then to each side as they all tried to ascertain what might direct water to this particular spot. It was Leslie who pulled out her tablet and began tapping until she had a topo map of the area where they stood.

Holding it out toward the rest of them, she pointed. "Here, here, and here."

She was noting the higher peaks near them. "They might drain this way."

"Drainage is bad," Joule said as she realized she was too dumb to keep her mouth shut. "Drainage picks up everything it runs over—mud, dirt, sometimes gravel. Anyway, it's not clean water. It's usually too dirty to even see through if you put your foot in it."

"So, anything we do, we need to calculate well above the floodwaters." Mitch nodded along as he spoke.

"How far above?" Leslie asked the group at large.

"It's a good question." Mitch took the lead. "How long is the array supposed to stay in place and function?"

Joule didn't know the answer to that. In fact, she would have thought Mitch did.

"We have to calculate for the growing likelihood of problem," Mitch continued. "Flooding now is worse than it was a decade ago, which was worse than it was twenty years ago. If our array is to stay on for ten years, then we have to calculate for how bad a decade from now *could* be. If the array is supposed to continue working for twenty or thirty years, the floodlines could be much higher."

"But the flooding could also be something we get under control," Leslie countered. "In which case, we would have over-calculated."

"True. So what's the error if we over-calculate?"

They all looked to each other, and Joule would have felt put on the spot, but she was growing used to it. Mitch, she'd learned, enjoyed spitball answers—even the stupid ones—so she blurted out, "Extra supplies."

"More money invested than needed," Deveron said at the same time.

"Whatever environmental damage the extra height causes," Lindsey added, and Dev ran with that.

"We would have to sink the pylons lower to counterbalance the height. And it might require different materials to make them stronger, taller."

"So it's not negligible." Mitch nodded, once again looking up toward the top of their test system. "But if we under-calculate...." He left it hanging.

"We lose the whole array," Lindsay filled in, saying what they were all thinking.

Once again, the winds picked up.

"I don't know how much longer we can stay out today." Mitch looked away from the pylon and off toward the edge of the sky. "Storm's coming in."

13

"Oh, that was painful." Cage watched as Sarah moved to shove her hands into pockets that weren't there. Maybe she thought she was wearing overalls again.

"That hurt me in my cold little heart," Joule replied, tossing and catching her keys almost casually as the wind whipped her curls to Medusa-like life.

The four of them were some of the last to leave the squat, tan building that housed the local Lions Club and today, the big meeting. The parking lot was almost empty, the day as gray as dusk. Not a good feeling for four in the afternoon.

A storm had been threatening for almost twenty-four hours now, the winds and gray skies lingering since early yesterday. Radnor said it was a good test of the equipment. Though on the drive home last night, Dev had commented, "The only real test is an F6 tornado—"

"Bite your tongue!" Sarah interrupted with the quick reprimand, though Cage was already countering that they only needed an F3 or F4.

"That's right," Sarah pointed out. "That's about the worst

that comes through this section of Alabama. And again, that's why we built the array here."

But though he'd been ready to quip about running a tornado test yesterday, now—with the weather growing stranger by the second—Cage was wishing they hadn't even mentioned it.

The parking lot was almost empty. The only other cars left were those owned by the Helio Systems Tech employees who still lingered inside to clean up after the verbal carnage. A few other clusters of his coworkers were trailing out behind them or already pulling out of the lot.

"Hey," he commented with concern. "We should check the car. That didn't go well in there, and I'm wondering if someone might have keyed it."

"How would they know which one we were in?"

"All they need to do is recognize the cars we drive in every day. They came often enough to know..." Sarah approached Cage and Joule's car and, instead of reaching for the door handle, she wandered around the back. She motioned the others to circle around.

"What?" Sarah asked when Deveron leaned down as if to look under the car.

"Check everything. Key marks, dented bumper, slashed tires." But he quickly backpedaled. "I don't see them! I'm just checking everything."

"Will we even know if they dented the bumper?" Sarah asked.

"Rude!" came almost immediately from Joule.

But Sarah's question wasn't out of line. Their car was older and a bit dinged up, but it had been with them through college. They'd bought it after the last one had been damaged by the flood. The longer it stayed with them, the more Cage felt a kinship for it—as if the machine itself were a living creature, ferrying them back and forth to work. As though he'd failed by letting the last one get flooded and totaled.

When the car checked out, they climbed in, closing the doors against the wind as Cage breathed a little easier. Nothing in the town hall had gone smoothly. He'd expected a meeting of the minds, that the Helio people would see how they'd misframed their message or failed to get the necessary information to the public. He'd believed the public would hear that the crew wasn't poisoning the well water or ruining their deer-hunting season. He'd expected to feel better now.

He didn't.

Joule started the engine as Sarah turned to face the middle of the car and said, "I was considering getting a cat." The words hung for just a moment before she added, "Is anyone opposed?"

The other three looked to each other, Joule shrugging while keeping her eyes in front of her as she pulled the car out of the spot and headed toward the lot exit.

Sarah spoke again, maybe trying to clear up a very lackluster response. Had she expected them to be excited? "I guess maybe more importantly: is anyone allergic?"

Both of the twins shook their heads. Cage, in the backseat with Dev, waited for his roommate, who also shook his head but still managed a protest. "I'm not cleaning the litter box, though. And I don't want to smell it."

"Agreed," came from Joule as she wheeled out over the curb and onto the main road. Behind them, the last three cars were starting up and pulling out, leaving the lot and his hopes empty.

At least a conversation about a cat would help him shake off some of the irritation from the meeting. Though there had been people who asked questions about things like water pollution, Radnor had clearly told them *no*.

"There's no water pollution from the array. No more than

when you paint your house and less than when you wash your car in the driveway." He'd answered the question of whether they would have to look at "the eyesore of that ugly solar field," with "You're more than welcome to grow bushes or trees at the edge of your property, so you don't have to see it."

That hadn't been very tactful, but he'd followed that right up with, "You will also, regardless of that, get a much lower power bill." Radnor hadn't been the best person to put in charge, Cage realized. He'd answered many of the questions, but not with the soft touch that might have gone over better.

Though a good number of the locals seemed to understand and take the information for what it was, in the end, Jerry—no surprise there—had led a charge accusing Helio systems tech of stealing jobs.

It was Dr. Chithra Murasawa who'd stood up and looked around the room, the frown on her face asking if all of those attending were stupid. But the words that followed made Cage understand. "You are aware that there's an application system?"

Some had nodded their heads, but others hadn't. Murasawa filled everyone in, even Cage and Joule. "If anyone loses a job because of us, we will hire you, and we will provide all the training for that job."

"But how will it pay?" One of the angry workers had shot off the words as an accusation.

Murasawa handled it as though he'd asked in a kind and inquisitive tone. "We've done salary comparisons. We pay for training and at each level, and we pay better than the local power plant is paying."

She'd been ready to sit down, her information dispensed, everyone educated.

But Jerry protested. "I work at the power plant. It's what I do. This is my job, and it's what I'm trained for. I shouldn't have to get trained for anything else."

All the Helio Systems workers could see Dr. Murasawa's

tight smile as she fought to keep from barking out a laugh. "No one is guaranteed a job forever. Not me. Not any of us at this table. But we're offering you a job with less physical impact to your body and a better outcome for your neighbors."

It was a good, if subtle hit, but Jerry missed it or didn't care. He barked out a laugh, as though his power plant job was perfectly safe.

"And at a higher salary," Dr. Murasawa had repeated, pushing the words through her teeth. Radnor had tugged on her sleeve, suddenly the voice of tact.

"Well, I don't want to work for you," Jerry shot back as though it was an insult.

Cage thought working with Jerry would be a punishment in itself, and he wanted to stand up and say, "Good!" But Dr. Murasawa managed to keep her calm. "Okay. However, the offer still stands."

She'd looked out at the rest of the crowd, made up of some of their own workers and many locals who were apparently afraid of disrupting a life built on less than steady systems. They weren't anxious to change anything that wasn't actively hurting them. "We are offering jobs for anyone who loses a power systems job because of our arrival. We will need ongoing support for the array, and we want to put local people into those jobs. We'll train."

Cage thought it was a more than equitable solution, but the meeting had devolved into yelling and complaints. No one was happy. The mayor had to stand up and tell everyone to be quiet and orderly. And even after she did that, the questions still sounded more like accusations. He wanted to believe it could have gone better, but he hadn't been prepared for the entrenched anger that the company faced.

Now he looked out the window as Joule came up to the turn that would take them home. As they pulled up to the blinking red light, he saw the intersection looked the same as so many others—a Dollar General store sat on one side of the road. Opposite that, a Marathon gas station and a Jack's fast food straddled the pavement.

Joule didn't move when it was her turn, but as the last ones at the intersection, she wasn't holding anyone up. She turned her head toward the back seat. "Drive thru for milkshakes?"

"Oh God, yes!" Next to him, Dev looked as though the day's first decent offer had finally come through.

Putting the car in motion again, Joule went straight instead of taking the right- hand turn that would have taken them home. The wind buffeted the small car as she pulled into the long line, which was probably populated by others leaving the meeting.

While they waited, the wind kicked up higher. This time, when she returned to the intersection, she was facing the other direction. Taking a left, she headed for home.

But when Joule jerked her hand on the steering wheel, the whole car jolted with her.

And all four of them felt and heard something smack the side.

14

"Drive!"

Sarah's harsh command from the backseat shot through Joule like a jolt of electricity. Even though she didn't quite know what was happening, her hands clenched the steering wheel and she pushed back into the bucket seat.

Her jaw clenched and her vision narrowed.

She was approaching a stop sign.

"Drive!" Sarah yelled again from the back seat. "Run the sign."

Joule's eyes frantically scoured the roads, but from the left, the pavement turned sharply, the trees obscuring her view of oncoming traffic. She slowed so as not to get slammed by a surprise truck barreling around the corner.

"There's a tornado behind us!"

There was no other reaction but to hit the gas, and Joule passed the sign without any more hesitation. She was tense in her seat as though she controlled the gears and axles herself. Though she should have trusted her roommate, Joule turned her head and looked behind them.

Sure enough, following the path of the road was a gigantic, gray whirlwind.

Unlike the ones she'd seen as a child, this storm wasn't a whimsical twist of floating leaves twirling its way down the street. Her memory floated back to her mother showing her how to feed different colored leaves into the swirl to mark their paths. She'd been a tiny tornado scientist watching in wonder that day.

This wasn't that.

This was a funnel with distinct edges. No one needed to throw a car into it to see where it went. This one was a massive, dark gray column, ominous and loud.

Joule pushed the gas pedal as far down as it would go, but even the sudden burst of speed wasn't enough as Sarah yelled at her. "Faster!"

There was no "faster." Still, she jammed the pedal harder.

"Shouldn't there be a siren?" Deveron was asking in her rearview mirror.

Joule didn't know. There had been no warning, only Sarah being smart enough to read the weird weather and check behind the car. Joule could see both her rear passengers had turned and were staring out the rear window now. Their hands gripped the back of the seats like small children on a road trip, but this was anything but.

Breathe, she reminded herself. But it only resulted in one deep gulp that she then held tightly, using the pressure to fuel her brain.

"There aren't sirens out here," Sarah answered. "People are too far apart. It's too expensive."

More expensive than replacing all the homes? Joule thought, even as she realized that Sarah's voice was now calmer... now that her own reaction was blowing up.

She took a curve in the road and then, once again, pressed the gas pedal down as far as it would go. These roads were not made for speed. They'd not been kept up—old country roads with the paving only in random spots, if they were paved at all.

The car bumped and swerved as she tried to maintain speed and yet miss the potholes. The open space behind them let her know the tornado still chased them. It lagged for a moment but then sped up. Suddenly, it loomed close behind her, taking up most of the rearview mirror. She would have been shaking were she not locked so tightly into position.

Her brain raced, watching the road in front of her. Her eyes darted back and forth, tracking the beast that tracked them as if it were hunting.

Joule thought back through everything she'd been taught. It didn't sound like a train. Though it was noisy, it roared like wind. Like a white noise machine with the switch changed from "gentle" to "horrific."

Maybe it was too far behind them.

She was putting space between it and the car again, though whether that was from her skills in outrunning it or because the gray beast itself had backed off, she didn't know.

Joule hated not knowing. If she didn't know what she'd done, she couldn't repeat it.

She flinched as another noise came, her whole body jerking —along with everyone else in the car—as something else screeched across the side of the car.

Though she managed to stay on the road, she felt the car take the hit. Forced to lift up on the gas, she tried to take the harsh turn without running up on two tires. That was a win in itself.

The road itself challenged her with hidden turns and uneven pavement. The last road had been straight and easy by comparison. Her heart pounded in time with her hands jerking the steering wheel side to side, as if it knew she would function better fully in sync.

She gulped another lungful of air and held it again.

And the Twister disappeared from the rearview mirror.

"Where is it?" she demanded. *"Where is it?"*

Her heart pounded in her ears. And maybe that was why she could no longer hear the sound of the tornado.

"It's small," Sarah said as she put her hand on Joule's shoulder. As if that might make her calm her shit down. It wouldn't. "It might die out."

That was small?

But Joule realized that, while Cage and Deveron were still shouting about where it might be, Sarah's voice sounded almost relaxed. Honestly, once Joule had started driving away, her roommate had sounded as if everything would be okay. Joule tried to take that in. If Sarah could keep her shit in her basket, so could she.

"Where am I going?"

They were the only car on the road. As if everyone else was local, and far too smart to be caught out when there was a tornado about.

"Where is it?" Deveron pressed, still twisted around in his seat.

Cage, too, was turning all directions, acting as tornado spotter but failing to find anything. "I don't know. I'm looking for it!"

"Head home." Once again, Sarah was a calming voice of reason.

Joule knew where "home" was. Desperado's Hideaway was where she would drive on autopilot now, and she knew all the roads around her. She swerved again, knowing that the pothole was just over the small rise, and automatically missing it.

"Is home safe?"

She was thinking it as Cage asked. Just like a twin. She was once again grateful they were still together.

"And where do we go at home? There's no basement," Deveron pointed out, though neither of them was looking at

Sarah. They were still trying to figure out where the tornado had gone.

The lack of it was more nerve-wracking than seeing it had been. Now Joule felt as though it would pop back up at any moment, ambushing her rather than giving a solid chase.

"No basement," Sarah said, "but there is an interior closet." Again, her voice was measured while the other three were flipping out.

Joule scrambled far too fast for the road. Gravel kicked as her nerves made her speed climb higher and higher, until even Deveron was telling her slow down.

"If we go in a ditch, we're completely screwed."

That much was true.

The roads sloped off steeply to either side. Whether there was water in the runoff ditches, she didn't know, but she didn't want to find out. And she sure as hell didn't want to discover it by being nose down off the side of the road.

"It's over there," Sarah said, and Joule tried not to jerk the car as she looked.

Even before she said it, the others in the car were feeding her information.

"It's a waterspout now," Cage told her. "It must have gone out over the lake."

They couldn't see the lake from their home. But it wasn't far away as the crow flies, hidden from their back window behind the large, beautiful, and mostly serene hillside that flanked the small house. Joule had liked the landscape—both the hills and the lake. Maybe only until today.

Knowing she shouldn't, she turned her head, watching over the trees as the water climbed into the sky.

Now the spout was no longer gray. It was white. As if the water had cleaned out the debris the twister had picked up.

And it still didn't sound like a train.

She raced down the short road leading toward the house.

The car fishtailed as she hit their turn, but she didn't care. She offered a glance as they passed the only other house on their drive.

There wasn't any movement inside—nothing obvious through the large windows—and she wondered if the couple who lived there had already hunkered down in their bathtub, or their closets, as Sarah had suggested.

Gravel kicked and sprayed behind her, as her wheels dug ruts in the road. Right now, she didn't care. The underside of the carriage pinged from the rocks she kicked up, but it barely registered in her brain.

As she took the last turn into the driveway, she could see the waterspout still hovering over the creek.

"Don't they die out over water?" she asked, pulling the car into the carport and slamming it into park.

"Sometimes," Sarah said, though just "sometimes" wasn't reassuring.

Whatever else her roommate told them was lost in the wind as the four of them opened the car doors and let in the full extent of the whipping white noise.

Joule felt her hair leap up, as though the wind was trying to tear it out of her scalp. Her clothing pressed against her, flapping in the gale. And for the first time, she realized it was raining, too. With the wind throwing the raindrops around, they hit with a zing.

"Inside!" Sarah pointed and demanded as though she'd given them this instruction before and they simply hadn't paid attention. Her own hair was blowing wildly around her head as she grabbed at the edges of her jacket to keep the wind from stealing it.

Cage ducked suddenly to avoid something flying past. It moved too quickly to properly identify it, but seeing it sail by made Joule's heart kick, when she would have thought it was already beating far too fast and hard for that to be possible.

He grabbed her arm, tugging her behind the other two. Only then did she realized she'd stopped. She'd been standing in one place, peering out at the backyard and over the hill, her instinctive human need to watch the devastation.

But intelligence won out over curiosity and she followed Sarah up the tiny stairs that led to the side door. It had bothered Joule before that the screen door opened out and there wasn't even a porch to stand on. Now it seemed a ridiculous arrangement when they were struggling to get four people inside.

Once all of them were in, Deveron turned and threw his weight against the door, pushing it until it fully shut. He struggled to get the bolt closed and tested it, since it never seemed to want to stay clicked on its own.

"Bathroom closet!" Sarah said, leading them toward the hallway and keeping the foursome centered in the bulk of the house.

The main room that Joule and Sarah shared had an attached bath, but it also had a window. The hallway bath had a separate room for the toilet and the tub and a door that closed it off from the sinks.

Slamming the doors and giving away the impression that maybe she wasn't as calm as she seemed, Sarah shut them into the small space that was far too tight for four.

"We can shove in by the washer and dryer," she offered.

Though Joule was tempted, shoving herself into a closet to escape danger was a place she'd been before—and one she didn't want to return to.

The four of them now stood shoulder-to-shoulder. Supposedly safe, they looked at each other as if to ask *what next?* Sarah was the only one with any experience at this.

But Joule found no answers on her roommate's face either, so she put voice to what they were all thinking. "What do we do now?"

15

"No, I don't know where the radio is," Joule snapped back to Sarah, as the two men looked at her roommate with the same crazy expression. "I also don't know where the crank is to start the car engine."

Sarah gave her a deadpan look before sweeping her gaze around the small group. Apparently, they were all found equally lacking. "Stay here."

Before they could protest, Sarah had dashed into the hall—the space she'd just declared unsafe. Shaving the door closed behind her, she left Joule, Deveron, and Cage looking to each other as if to ask, *What just happened?*

Though she couldn't see anything from their windowless space, Joule couldn't avoid hearing the rage of the wind outside. It slapped at the house with whatever debris it had picked up and whipped around. She wondered if there was a whiteout of cotton in the air, and she fought down the prickling of anxiety. All they could do was sit in the safest place in the house. And wait.

But Sarah—who'd been adamant that they hunker down and wait—wasn't doing it herself.

It was Deveron who first put words to Joule's thoughts. "Look, she's the only one of us who seems to know what she's doing."

Even as he finished saying it, the door flipped open and Sarah, keeping her body limited to the lower half of the open space, duck-walked through and quickly shoved it shut behind her.

Why not just stand up and run through? Joule thought that would be quicker, but Cage managed to voice the question.

"Keeping myself low in case a window goes out," Sarah explained. "Don't want to get hit by any flying debris."

Though the explanation made sense, Joule had been avoiding thinking about the tornado getting *into* the house. Sarah was still offering up her impromptu tornado safety lessons. "If you're exposed, you get down and you crawl around. It protects your torso, too."

Jesus, Joule thought. For all the wind and the noise that sounded like someone had left a massive grinder on high, this storm *still* didn't sound like a train. In fact, every time she'd heard a train, it had been a train. And now that she'd actually seen a tornado, it didn't sound like a train at all.

She was super salty that her limited information had turned out to be incorrect.

But Sarah was already fidgeting with the dials on a small radio she had grabbed, and Joule didn't have time to remain angry at whomever had sold her that useless bit of goods. The radio wasn't old-timey, as Joule had anticipated. It was sleek, black, and high end.

"This is our lifeline." Sarah held it up for a moment. "We don't have tornado warning sirens out here, but we do have access to updates even in a power outage. In fact, we should probably keep it in this room, since this is where we'll come if we see another one."

If we see another one, Joule thought. That was something she didn't want to contemplate. Being chased down the street had been heart-stopping enough. She didn't want to become jaded to them the way Sarah had.

Or maybe Sarah was just handling the pressure well and she'd freak out later. For the moment, her roommate played with the knobs and found the emergency broadcast station. The voice came through loud and clear, updating them on what was happening and where.

At first, they listened with rapt attention, but after a while, Joule started to tune it out. The information repeated and only a few useful bits drizzled in over the next hour or so. None of it changed anything for them. They simply sat on the floor, waiting it out. Joule was grateful that she was too uptight to have to use the bathroom or get hungry, but she decided she was going to lay in supplies for "the next one."

Mentally, she made a list of good things to have—snack bars, crackers, some bottles of water. She'd want a coloring book and some crayons maybe. Puzzles, something to damn well *do*.

If we see another one. The words ran through her head in a sarcastic loop.

"This was supposed to be a low-tornado area!" she complained aloud, as if the weather should understand where it was and wasn't supposed to go. But it certainly hadn't understood that this last decade.

Sarah shook her head at Joule. "This *is* low tornado."

Joule and Cage blinked at each other as the words processed.

It was Cage who spoke up this time. "I've seen exactly zero tornadoes in any of the other places I've been—until today. I might not have lived here very long, but I've now been chased down the street by a tornado. It doesn't feel *low* to me—"

"Listen!" Sarah interrupted, jostling the radio a little bit as if to draw their attention.

The voice over the system let them know that this twister was currently being classified as an F1.

"*F-1?*" Joule cried out. "That was *huge!*"

"You won't think so once you've seen a bigger one," Sarah told her, still remaining outwardly calm. Too calm.

"I hope I never do. This is supposed to be a low tornado area!" She reiterated the clearly incorrect idea.

"But there's no part of Alabama that's a *no-tornado* area." Sarah sounded like she was trying to be comforting, as if anything she said would calm the other three down. "In fact, there's no part of the US that's a *no-tornado* area. They can happen anywhere. It's just a matter of how frequent they are."

"Well, I'm with Cage. I've seen exactly zero of these fuckers before now." Even as she said it, Joule noticed that some of the noise outside had died down. But the voice on the radio crackled back to life, and this time they listened as it told them where a funnel had been spotted. In fact, there were *two*.

Christ. Joule sighed, but didn't say it. *Why should there just be one?*

They had apparently seen the larger of the two. The other was also classified as an F1, but wasn't quite as big.

Another hour of staticky updates passed before the voice declared the danger gone.

"That's it," Sarah said, standing. "We are now free to roam about the house."

They all stood up, stretching their legs, and following her lead. But Joule still asked. "I can use the bathroom now?"

"Good idea," Deveron replied, clearly having been needing the facilities himself.

But they still waited for Sarah to nod before Joule headed out to the bathroom attached to her bedroom.

"Be careful out there," Sarah cautioned. "Our first job is to assess the damage."

16

C age looked over his shoulder, but nothing was chasing him. He told himself to calm down, but his alert system wasn't getting the message. He knew about adrenaline, about parasympathetic responses and all the hormones and messenger systems involved... and he still couldn't turn it off.

He was walking through the field again, the sunshine feeling deceptive on his shoulders now. As if it were just waiting to pounce, to toss a tornado at him. He should be comfortable with traipsing his collections across the open grass to the tent, but for the past several days, he'd fought the urge to flee.

Today, for the first time, the specimens he was carrying weren't fauna, but flora. Beside him, Leah carried her own stack of small boxes with clippings. Seeming to read his mood, she told him, "It's not tornado weather."

But from the other side of him, Micah added, "But we don't always get them with weird weather. Sometimes they come out of nothing."

Cage glanced over his shoulder again. That was not comforting information and it didn't help with his ongoing effort to relax. As each day passed without another tornado, he'd grown a little calmer. He'd *believed* a little bit more that it would be okay. But he wasn't there yet, and he was now figuring that it would only be time that really made the nerves disappear.

"They *usually* come preceded by weird weather, and you can't spend every sunny day petrified that a tornado is going to appear out of nowhere!" Leah shot back. The two were having the argument into the air around him. Cage felt as if he was absorbing their words, but Leah continued. "Honestly, it's just as likely that a hellhound would show up to drag you to fire and brimstone."

That made his eyes flick directly to her, wondering if she had any idea what the odds of that were. *He did.* And he sure as shit didn't want to add the night hunters to this mix.

Though he and Joule had remained jumpy for days after the storm, Sarah had been her usual, calm self. But she was a local and Cage wasn't using her as a barometer. It was these other transplants—others who hadn't been in 'Bama before— that he thought were getting over it far too quickly. Had they somehow easily survived the disasters that seemed to hit everyone sooner or later? Or was he standing between two incredibly lucky people?

In college, one of his friends had been through an avalanche and a blizzard. Another had lost a good portion of his family to a mudslide. Most of his group had developed a keen awareness of nature and its ability to take away human life in the snap of a finger. They'd been through a lot together. But the weather had been going haywire for quite a few years now. Floods, storms, landslides, and more.

And now, a tornado. It seemed the next thing on his checklist.

"I'll just count myself lucky that the county repaired the gravel," Cage muttered. He and his roommates had been able to drive up to the house last night as the work crew had finally made it out to their house and machined the gravel back into the driveway. They'd finagled Sarah's car out of the driveway instead of Joule's, simply because the undercarriage was slightly higher. Neither of them had the kind of vehicle made for four-wheeling.

Even though it had only hit the end of their long driveway, the "tiny F-1" tornado had come too close to the house, plowing a ten-foot-wide ditch through the gravel. It had even left a trail where it had danced along the edge of the property.

The first trip over the damaged section had been slow, rough going. Sarah had carefully picked her way around through the damage, the car bouncing as it dipped into unseen holes. They'd been worried it would get stuck, and Sarah had quickly declared she and her car wouldn't do that again.

So the four of them had been walking the length of the driveway and leaving Sarah's car parked at the end of it for most of the week. There hadn't been much choice, unless they found someone willing to pick up all four of them and drive them into work every day.

"Why did they fix the gravel?" Leah broke into his thoughts.

"Because the tornado ate it. The edges were creepy, super clean cuts—as if made by a machine," Cage told them.

"Holy shit!" Micah responded. "I didn't know it hit so close to you. It didn't get your house, did it?"

This time, Cage shook his head. The storm had hit his driveway, and that was close enough.

"You, Leah? Did it get close to you?" Micah leaned forward to see her face across Cage, who still walked in the middle as they approached the tent.

"No. I mean, we went to our safe room and listened to the radio, like everyone else, but I didn't even see it." She shifted her attention to Cage. "Did you see it?"

"Hell, yes. It chased us down the road. We were on the street when it first hit."

"Why were you out?" She sounded as if he'd been asking for trouble.

"Because we needed dinner?" he replied, as though it might be obvious. Had everyone else around the area figured out that a tornado was coming? Well, everyone except Sarah, who seemed to otherwise know everything about Alabama life and dangers.

As he thought about it, he realized that maybe he'd been unaware because of the late evening. Or maybe Sarah hadn't thought anything of the weird weather—maybe Alabama got enough of it that she wasn't worried. But it sure worried him now.

The three of them reached the tent, handing off the samples to Izzy and Melinda. They all knew by now to help sort the specimens and wait while everything was properly checked in. Though Cage often liked to be quiet and focus on his work, Melinda seemed more than capable of multitasking. "Everybody good today?"

"Sure," he replied, as did the others, though he felt his shoulder shrug as if to ask, *Why today?*

"Did you see the protesters on the way in? They're back." So Melinda had caught that he didn't understand why she was asking.

"I saw them, but they didn't block the road or anything. They sure seemed extra angry," he added.

They'd come back with a vengeance, three days after the tornado. Maybe they needed to get their houses repaired or their insurance claims filed, he didn't know. But they had returned in record numbers. Though they stayed on their side of the property line, this time the signs suggested that the tornado was the wrath of God rather than just a weather system. The protesters also seemed to think that God was emphatically anti-solar energy and emphatically pro-strip mining.

Cage wasn't sure if he was right with God or not, but he had a hard time finding a belief in his heart that could match the signs.

Itching to turn around and leave because Chithra had given them a full load today, he looked to Melinda. "Are we good to go?"

"Yeah," she said, not looking at them as she pulled the first samples from their containers. But even as he stepped from the shade of the tent into the full sun, he heard her behind him saying, "Well, this is weird."

17

"We're off for the next three days. I'm not unhappy about it," Joule said as she passed the bowl of broccoli to Deveron.

"That's what I heard, too."

"It's official. Radnor emailed everyone." Cage let some of the bowls pass him by as he dug into what was already on his plate.

Three days off work meant five days in a row completely off, Joule thought.

"Yeah, but it's not vacation," Sarah interrupted her happy thoughts.

Joule looked around the table to see if any of the others were having the same response. "I'm *off* off. I don't have any assignments."

This wasn't a work-from-home job. Radnor had simply said, *stay in and stay safe.*

"But we likely won't have power for part of it," Sarah said, only this time Joule understood, and she was prepared.

The days off were because a storm system was coming through. Between the field and the local infrastructure, it wasn't going to be safe to be driving into work most days—*if* it was as bad as predicted.

This time, they all knew where the candles were. They knew where the radio was and where the hand crank flashlights were. There were now energy bars waiting in the bathroom closet.

One of the baskets in the closet held toilet paper while a second held laundry detergent and supplies. But the third now contained all their emergency backups, including the radio.

"Are there fresh batteries in the radio?" Sarah asked around a bite of broccoli. The radio had a hand crank backup, just like the lights, but batteries were the preferred option.

"Already done," Joule said. Her lesson had been learned. Despite the coming storm and the predicted high levels of rain, she found she was feeling better. She always felt better once she had a plan in place.

This wouldn't be like Stanford. She repeated that to herself enough times to calm down, and she reminded herself that the jitters were from the high of the tornado. She was still coming down from it.

Last night had been the first night this week that the train hadn't awakened her or driven her to tornado-like nightmares. So she could handle the power going out and the incessant sound of rain. It had been a number of years, and she'd weathered a number of storms since the Stanford disaster.

The next morning, she woke late to the pattering on the roof and a growling stomach. Grateful the stove was gas, which would still work even if the power went out, Joule made breakfast.

They'd checked and double-checked the gas lines and outlets. They'd walked the property and looked for failure points. She and Dev were engineers, after all. Everything tested fine and she had a plan.

She had hot food, a good book, and a full fridge. So she told herself not to worry that the rain was picking up steam. Though it took a little bit of conscious effort, she managed to get lost in a mystery novel. When her eggs were gone, she transferred herself to the couch and watched an action flick on one of the cable channels.

By the time the movie ended, Sarah and then Deveron had rolled out. Her brother had the ability to sleep all day when given the opportunity. It would be at least noon before he was up.

Sure enough, Sarah had made them all grilled cheese sandwiches and tomato soup from a can by the time Cage appeared in the main area, his hair sticking up on one side.

"Oh, thanks!" He grabbed his plate from the breakfast bar as he headed to the table. While the rest of them were lazing about, he was alert and chattering. "So, Melinda found this bizarre plant yesterday."

Across the table, Joule felt her eyes narrow. "What was it?"

"We're still trying to figure it out. She's pretty impressive. She can identify most of the animals, down to specific species, just with a glance." He dipped the sandwich into the soup and took a bite.

"But she couldn't identify this one?" Sarah asked. Sarah was also part of the environmental team, and Joule wondered if maybe this strange plant wasn't a big enough deal for the news to travel yet.

"No, she couldn't identify it *at all*." He paused a moment. "It might be invasive, or lone, or endangered. We don't know."

"Damn. Invasive or endangered may very well change the configuration of the array," Joule hopped into the conversation. They'd done numerous calculations accounting for the possibility of the treeline getting higher nearby and casting longer shadows. They'd calculated for winter days and lower sun.

But the clipping her brother had brought to the lead environmentalist might just change all of it.

18

J oule clinked her glass to Sarah's. Almost eighteen of her Helio Systems teammates sat around the long table. Plates of fragrant Indian food sat decimated in the middle.

Their three days off had been met with a storm that managed to only knock out the power for a few hours Thursday afternoon. Friday had bloomed bright and humid, but it was too late to call the employees back.

They'd set to work with a renewed vengeance the following Monday, and now the corner pylons that formed the base of the array were finally set. Though this wasn't an official work dinner, that was the reason for the celebration tonight.

Joule was glad to be having a night out with friends. More work graced the horizon, but the team had achieved a major breakthrough. The pylons should be able to withstand high winds, hail, and twisting forces—like tornadoes. They would hold up even under the high pressure of flood water, should the creeks rise. They'd even tested for blizzards and mudslides, though neither was expected to occur here.

While everyone was laughing and having a good time, Joule

felt something tugging at the back of her brain. She was still thinking about the protesters showing up every morning. Sometimes they harassed Helio Systems team members at dinner or if they ran into the workers on the street.

That might be one of the reasons that this had been the suggested celebration place. The owners were pleasant and welcoming of the solar team. The town itself was becoming more divided. Some of the bigger landowners—with larger power bills—were grateful for them. But still, there was always Jerry leading his band of protesters. They seemed to no longer be mad about pollution, but now were angry about God, despite the fact that there had not been another tornado.

"More?" Chithra held the plate up for her.

The tall and thin-to-the-point-of-willowy woman had managed to put away three plates of food tonight. Joule had made her best attempt to do the same, but now she held her hand up to stop. "I'm stuffed."

Still, she looked at the remaining plates and wondered who was going to get the joy of the leftovers. And who was going to get to do the math for the check. *Probably the engineering team.* But as she looked around the table, she realized that she was glad that the two teams had intermingled quite a bit. For the first time, it occurred to her that that might be why she and Cage had gotten these jobs.

One of the things that had attracted her to the position was that the company was big on innovation. While Joule had found that most places like to *say* that, very few actually wanted to *hear* from their lowest-level employees. But the description of the intermingled teams had grabbed her.

Now she wondered if the company was utilizing her twin-relationship to build the community between the enviro and engineering teams on site. Given the interlocking designs of the teams, Joule wouldn't have been surprised to find out it was a manipulation they'd done on purpose. But she realized these people were now her friends.

She liked Mitch. He was fun and an excellent boss, always making sure everyone was getting what they needed. She liked Chithra; the woman's management style was not flowery in the slightest. She got shit done. And was more than willing to answer any question, no matter how big or small, or how stupid. And Radnor, for all of his bluster, seemed to understand that his employees needed to care about the project and each other.

She wondered what would happen when the job was over. Would she and Cage be offered permanent positions with Helio Tech? What were the odds they'd wind up on the same project in the future? If they were permanent Helio employees, they might not get to decide where they were placed.

She took another swallow of the pale ale in her glass. Not her favorite, but it went well with the spiciness of the food. It also quelled some of the concerns in her heart as the conversation rolled happily around her. Why couldn't she just soak that in?

"Okay," Sarah called out so the whole table could hear her. "What's the over/under that the new buckeye plant—the *one lone* bottlebrush buckeye—causes the array to be moved or delayed?"

Others were shouting out options and timeframes and placing bets. Joule joined in.

"How much do you want on that?" Sarah asked, pen poised over the napkin where she was copying bets down.

"Oh please!" Joule chimed in, laughing. "I'm not betting money by way of a napkin with curry stains. Half of you are too drunk to even remember this—"

"Y'all ain't drunk, are you?" Sarah called down the table, her own southern accent creeping in. Her tone let Joule know that, yes, Sarah was at least tipsy enough to lose the napkin.

"No!" came from all along the table.

"Sorry, I want a real bookie and a receipt!" Joule smiled at them as though she'd ever done any of those things.

They finished their drinks and Sarah pocketed the napkin. Joule wanted to bet on the likelihood that it went through the wash and the ink ran. But the unease sat just at the back of her brain through the remainder of the evening.

Sure enough, the engineers had fought over who got to divide up the check. The managers volunteered to cover the appetizers. Joule wondered what would happen when they headed into work tomorrow. Would the protesters be there again, signs held aloft? Would it be more or fewer of them?

But as they headed out to the car, the wind kicked up her hair again. The night had been still when they arrived, but now a roll of dark clouds was coming in from the south. And something in the air tasted *off*.

19

"Ready?"

Cage wasn't. "Almost."

He pulled the long, slim cylinder from the soil, leaving a three-inch-diameter hole and a few wriggling bodies in its wake.

Cutting earthworms in half shouldn't make him feel bad, but it did. He felt bad when he cut roaches in half, too. And the roaches down here grew to an unusually large size. Cutting them in half seemed a cruel and unusual punishment.

As he pulled the last bit of the long metal device loose—heavy with dirt and half-earthworms—he held it out toward Leah. "Here."

She stood with a tablet in one hand, waiting. It had taken the two of them almost twenty minutes to push through all the layers of dirt and embedded rock, and even small invertebrates. But it took less than twenty seconds to activate the plunger on the top and release the soil—along with anything that was trapped inside—into the clear, long container Leah had waiting on the ground.

"Hold on," Cage told her, grabbing his phone and getting ready, as she stepped back and let him take his pictures.

"Got it?" she asked before slowly sliding the metal cylinder out from under the sample. As she did, the dirt fell apart, separating itself as Cage took a few more pictures and noted the measurements.

Together, he and Leah started to poke at the dirt, using thin, pointed metal rods to see what layers would crumble with a little prodding and which simply held their shape.

"We need light," he commented, looking over toward Micah, who was working in the small tent their team had set up on the far side of the field.

He and Leah each picked up one end of the now heavy container, leaving the tools in the grass. Preserving their sample was far more important than cleaning up.

The red canvas top of the pop-up tent stood out against the landscape, looking as if they'd stolen it from somebody's back patio. But right now, the legs were tied and weighted with heavy-duty sandbags, and the top, though vented, still managed to flap noisily as the winds picked up.

The two of them stood by, holding the sample between them. Just as they arrived at Izzy's table and placed it under the light, Chithra blazed into the small tent and made a sharp motion that they were to take everything down.

"Now," she told them, the tension in her voice surprising him. But he didn't get to ask as she snapped into the general air around them. "Everything!"

"It's barely noon," Cage muttered it to himself, but Chithra gave him a harsh look, then pointed skyward as though he hadn't been paying attention. The fact was, he hadn't.

The clouds had been dark since last night, but nothing had happened, so he'd gone about his work. But his manager was right. The reason they needed the tent with the light in it to see their work was because the sky was so overcast—even at barely-noon.

Radnor had been reluctant to send them home again after the last time he'd miscalculated, setting them behind. Honestly, they could have worked through the rain. It wouldn't have slowed them down. According to Radnor, a little water wouldn't hurt anyone. So now, Cage wondered why Chithra had suddenly ordered them to shut it down.

"What do we do with the samples?" he asked.

"Mark them and box them." But Chithra was already headed to the next team before Leah had said, "But our half earthworms will die."

Chithra turned back, her harsh words slicing the conversation with Sarah and Kevin. "Put them in the box!"

With a shrug, Cage sent Leah back to the site to pick up their tools while he struggled to label the half-finished work. His eye kept dashing to the sky. *Where was his sister?*

Despite the strange request, it hadn't taken him very long to box and mark everything. He was immediately pressed into service helping to take down the tent. It required four of them to get it down with the wind fighting them and attempting to lift the top right off the poles.

Today, he'd worn his jacket over the T-shirt, and it flapped around him the same as the tent. Cage was relatively certain that his clothing would have made a noise if he could have heard it over the harsh thumping of the canvas.

They collapsed the tent accordion style, and as each of the four of them walked their leg toward a center point, he looked over his shoulder and back toward the other side of the field. But he didn't see Joule.

She was here on site, he knew, but he forced his attention back to the task at hand and let Micah hold the heavy, collapsed tent. He and Izzy used Velcro straps to tie it.

"Where's the bag?" Kevin asked as he looked at then pointed to the ground at his feet. "It was right here."

It took a few moments before Leah returned and figured it out. She pointed and commented, "It's stuck in the tree."

As Cage turned to see where she was looking, he spotted the red bag plastered halfway up the trunk, the wind holding it in place.

"I've got it!" Leah was running off before anyone could stop her.

Cage's heart beat a little easier as Leah returned with the matching canvas bag, and the three of them slipped the folded tent down inside, pulling the drawstring.

"What else do we need to get?" he asked, even as he stubbed his toe on one of the sandbags still sitting where the post had been.

"I left the main field bag," Leah commented, "but we can grab it on the way back."

Between the tools and tent and sandbags, the six of them could barely manage to carry their gear back to the car as the wind whipped their hair around and plastered their clothing to their bodies.

It might have been fun, had he been younger and more naive.

As the team trekked across the open space, Cage found himself sneaking a glance toward the edge of the trees and wondering if he could see night hunters roaming in between the trunks.

Even as he reminded himself it was just his imagination, he startled at the harsh of the siren stopping all five of them in their tracks.

20

"We don't *have* sirens here," Deveron commented to Joule as both their heads snapped at the harsh sound.

She was frowning without meaning to. It took a second to recognize it wasn't a siren, but a bullhorn. Even as Joule figured it out, Radnor's voice came over the line. "F 2 in Horton."

That was all he needed to say.

"*Holy shit.*" But her words were swallowed as her boss must have pressed the button again and the sickly electronic siren noise filled the air once more.

Radnor was making a running loop around the field—which she'd never seen him do before—and aiming the siren first one way then another. Periodically, he would stop and plant his feet, pressing the device to his mouth to say once again, "F 2 on the ground in Horton."

She hadn't wanted to look up the information before, but now she regretted not knowing how much bigger an F2 was than an F1. At the time, she'd mentally told herself she didn't need that information because she'd had her tornado scare and she was done with it.

She and Deveron quickly packed their tools. Her hands moving with almost no input from her brain, and she had the handles Velcro'd together and the whole thing scooped up and ready to go.

She was starting across the field as she felt the first drops of rain hit. Large and soft, they were almost whimsical amidst the panic that was trying to force its way through the field and through her system. Joule fought down her fear. She could see the other teams around her moving quickly, trying to clear out in an efficient manner while holding their own worry at bay.

The siren stopped for a moment and Radnor's voice came over the bullhorn again. Only this time all he said was, "Shit."

Unable to help herself, Joule laughed. She turned to find Deveron doing much the same. *Probably hysteria and panic response*, she thought but she'd giggled a little harder.

But when Radnor's voice came back, she quit.

"F 2 in Arab."

Once again, Joule turned to Deveron. They'd covered some distance, but the field was huge. They were nowhere near the main tent yet. "Did he get it wrong the first time?"

Arab was a different city from Horton, almost thirty minutes away. But even as Deveron shrugged in reply, Radnor's voice came over the system again. "Two twisters on the ground."

Joule froze.

Horton and Arab were on almost opposite sides of the array field. They were standing somewhere in between what was now *two* tornadoes—but the real question was, where would the storms be in relation to them in five minutes?

That all depended on which way the twisters tangled and turned. And that was unpredictable. They could move slowly. Turn on a dime. Plow a ten-foot-wide precision cut through a gravel driveway or eat one half of a store—like she'd seen in town.

"Everyone, head immediately to your cars, and go home." Radnor blasted the siren once, almost like a car horn, rather than a wail now.

After three short blasts, which Joule didn't think they'd been trained to interpret as anything other than an attempt to get everyone's attention, her boss began reciting safety information.

"Find shelter. Don't hide under bridges, they're not safe. The engineers know the physics will actually increase wind speeds. Don't try to outrun it. Get out of the car, get into a low ditch."

It took her a few moments to realize he must have pulled something up on his phone and was reading the instructions out to everyone. Periodically he would stop and add his own commentary or blast the siren like a horn again. Still, he moved around the field, aiming it in every direction and looking for all of his employees.

She could tell when he ran out of instructions, because his voice became more forceful. "Everyone to the tent! Check in with Chithra before you leave. We need to be sure we've claimed everyone."

Radnor wasn't one to give in to panic, not that Joule imagined, but she could hear a hint of terror seeping into his voice as she and Deveron raced across the field, tool bags still in hand.

"Leave your equipment behind," Radnor called out. "We don't care, keep yourself safe."

"The tornado's really not close," Deveron told her. His breath and his clunky movements as he tried to run with the heavy toolbag at his side cut into the words.

Joule still understood and she agreed. But Radnor wanted them to run. In fact, in just another second, he yelled out over the bullhorn again. "Faster! Please drop your bags."

And it took the two of them another few moments and Radnor repeating himself to realize their boss was aiming the bullhorn at them. Both of them were still clutching their tools as though they were saving graces—as though they could simply remove a lug nut from a tornado if it came their way and stop it in its tracks.

Dropping her own bag, Joule elbowed Dev, who seemed to have not caught on that he was still clutching his like a lifeline. As she heard his bag hit the grass not far from where she'd left hers, she grabbed his free hand and waved to Radnor, letting him know that they'd finally understood and were following instructions better now. She was breathing heavily, her heart pounding.

She couldn't take another disaster.

Hand in hand, they bolted through the rain and toward the tent as Chithra and Leah stood there, calling out first names as people went by.

"Jeff!"

"Sarah!"

Each person waved, knowing they'd been accounted for, before diving through the now heavy rain toward their cars. Several were revving and pulling out as Joule told herself that Sarah wouldn't leave without them.

"Kevin!"

"Peter!"

"Wendy!" she heard as she headed into the flimsy shelter of the tent.

"Joule! Deveron!"

It surprised Joule to realize that she had an emotional reaction to each name. Though she was no fan of Peter's, she was glad he'd been checked off.

As she moved around to sneak a peek at Chithra's clipboard, the woman turned the other direction inadvertently cutting her off. So Joule tried again, but Chithra's constant effort to scan a moving crowd meant Joule couldn't get a read on the list.

When she turned again and caught Joule's questioning gaze, Joule simply asked, "Cage?"

But Chithra just narrowed her eyes and didn't even have to glance at the list. She knew everyone going by. And she shook her head at Joule. "Not yet."

21

The thundering noise made Cage look up.

He saw it looming above the trees, even as he heard the siren sound on the bull horn click off, replaced only by Radnor's quiet, "Oh crap."

In the distance hovered the wide, dark gray funnel. The sound was something between a grind and constant thunder as it plowed toward them. Cage imagined it scrubbing the earth as it went, just like the clean line through the gravel drive, but this time maybe even miles wide.

Radnor, having found his senses, this time merely yelled, *"RUN!"*

His breathing stopped, but Cage didn't need to be told twice. He quickly found himself in the middle of a chain, all four of them having locked hands without thinking about it. It was probably a horrible idea, but none of them were letting go. He, Leah, Micah, and Izzy were all running together as a single unit. When Leah stumbled, Cage and Izzy—on either side of her—yanked at her hands, pulling her back up.

As she mumbled, "Thank you," Cage thought that maybe

they'd dislocated her shoulder. But a dislocated shoulder would be the least of their worries if the tornado caught them.

The funnel seemed to have stopped moving and hovered in the distance. Or plausibly, it was like watching another airplane from your airplane window. If it didn't appear to move in space, it meant the two were on a collision course.

Maybe no matter where he ran, he was on an inevitable course with this funnel. If the one he'd seen before was an F1, then this was nothing of the sort. This was not the F2 of Horton or the one from Arab. This was their own whirling, screaming monster.

Though his mind told him in the end he'd find out the beast was only an F2 or F3, right now he was confident it was a seven or an eight and that the Fujita scale would rework their numbers because of this one.

As they approached the middle of the field, he finally spotted movement on the other side. He couldn't hear it, but he saw as cars revved and turned, pulling out of their spots and peeling away from the lot. He watched ahead, still running, still hoping his foot placement was solid, because he wasn't looking at his feet. As far as he could tell, neither were the rest of them. His feet pounded the earth and he thought *just keep going just keep going.*

He spotted Sarah's blue car as she backed up then slammed it into gear. As she pulled away from him, Cage could see Joule's face in the rear seat, her hands flat against the glass as Sarah drove away.

Thoughts moved rapid-fire through his brain. *Were they leaving without him?*

It didn't matter. It was best that they were safe. And he could ride with Leah or Micah or with any of them. No one would refuse him a seat in their car.

It was best that Sarah and Joule were getting away, because this time when he looked up the monster was closer.

Wider.

Darker.

Angrier.

The four of them were flat out bolting now, free-range *running* for their lives. Behind him, Radnor brought up the rear of the small fleeing crowd, and Cage had no doubt the man was identifying every employee. His harried voice was still calling out instructions. "Get in your cars and drive away! Don't drive into it. Go north! Go north!"

There was a pause, a new set of directions. "If you can't get in a car, get in a ditch. Hold on to something buried deep—a tree or a pipe. Strap yourself to it if you can."

The words were broken up by his heavy breaths as Radnor worked furiously to save everyone. He left the bullhorn turned on and maybe mistakenly broadcasted his encouragement and directions each time he found someone. "Get up. Get up, Jason ... Come on."

Cage breathed only a little easier knowing that Radnor was gathering the fallen.

As they approached the edge of the parking lot, Cage again spotted Joule through the back window of Sarah's car. *Why weren't they gone?*

His sister's hands were waving frantically, pointing at him, and he realized they weren't going to leave without him. He would have waved them on, but he was so close. They'd lined the car up, and now Sarah slammed it into reverse, aiming directly toward him. Gravel spewed as the bright blue bumper came directly at him and the others.

His heart thumped as he dropped their hands, moving the last few feet and closing the distance. In no time at all, he was peeling open the back door and climbing in, pulling Izzy on top of him. Micah and Leah both refused, yelling into the high winds that they had other rides, that the others were waiting for them.

"Go!" Sarah yelled at them, her own window down, her hand motioning them as she watched to be sure they made it to the other cars. The wind whipped through her hair and all around her, stealing her words. In fact, Cage wasn't sure if he'd actually heard her voice, or just seen her mouth move.

But Leah and Micah were off in two different directions. In a moment, they had both climbed into other, already populated cars. Cage was asking the one thing he could, "Deveron?"

But again, the wind and noise stole his voice. And even as he asked, the front door flew open and Deveron slid into his usual seat.

"Go!" his friend yelled, and Sarah was off before Dev even had the door closed.

As Cage looked out the back window, Izzy tried to situate herself, partially climbing over him and smushing herself into the middle space. He tried to put on a seat belt but couldn't make it click and instead reached out and braced his arm against the back of Deveron's seat. With his head cranked around to look out the back window, much like his sister on the other side, the twins watched as the wide beast hit the edge of the field, pulling up enormous trees by their roots and sucking them into the sky.

22

"**N**orth," Cage yelled as they hit the main road. "Go north!"

He said it the second time, in case Sarah hadn't heard. How could she hear with the windows down?

She'd opened them to let the wind flow through the car rather than shattering the glass. But as she made the sharp turn onto the small highway, he felt a precarious dip in the back of the car. The tire missed the pavement and his stomach pitched as he worried about going nose down into the ditch.

Across the back, he and Izzy and Joule clutched the seats in front of them, as though that would save them if the car suddenly dropped seven feet. The ditches on either side of the roads here were deep. The advantage to that was that they would already be low to the ground, in case the tornado went directly over them. Unfortunately, he would bet there were no pipes, nor anything solid, to hold on to if it rolled right over them.

He'd never seen anything like the wide, curling monster. Though Sarah had pulled away before he could see more, he found he was grateful for that. He'd watched three tall trees get ripped out of the ground—roots and all—the dirt that pulled up with them disintegrating quickly into the air that disappeared into the gray. As the trees were quickly whirled away, he wondered how long it took them to reach the other side of the funnel or to come back around to the front. Would the tornado eventually just drop them somewhere?

Underneath him, the tires squealed as Sarah raced down the road. They all knew they weren't supposed to try to outrun it, but there was now no other option.

The pylons they'd sunk in the field, though they should hold up to the force of at least an F5, had not been tested, and they were too big for human arms to wrap around them and hold on. Although the best hope for anyone stranded in the field would have been to belt themselves to the pylon anyone still out there probably would have been ripped away in a heartbeat.

Cage found himself wondering if all the Helio Systems people had made it off the field because it looked like the tornado was barreling across their construction even as Sarah squealed away from the site. He hoped everyone including Radnor had abandoned the area ...

Behind them, he watched as one of the other cars turned and headed south.

Wrong direction! The thought screamed through his head, but he didn't say it out loud. What good would that do?

It was Miranda's car. He recognized it and his heart stuttered at the serious gamble his boss had just made. There wasn't time to dwell on it. Sarah was yelling frantically into the open space of the car.

"What do I do? What do I do? Where should I go?" She had one hand gripping the steering wheel as the other smacked against it.

Joule, ever calm in a crisis, leaned forward to make herself more easily heard.

"Unless we get too close to it, stick to the freeways. If we get on one of the smaller roads, we won't be able to go as fast."

"Oh, I can go as fast," Sarah said, the threat finally sounding less than frantic. But she said it as though it were merely a matter of hitting the gas pedal.

Joule, still outwardly breathing easily, replied, "Not on gravel roads, not with those potholes, not with those turns. If possible, stick to the highways."

Cage could barely hear the words. Maybe it was only because he knew Joule as well as he did that he deciphered what she said. But he was tapping her on the shoulder and pointing out the back window once again.

Behind them, the monster had reappeared. Now it seemed to have moved toward the north end of the Helio Systems work site.

He was offering up a silent wish that his colleagues were safe as he saw a pale blue metal pylon launch into the funnel and disappear.

He gasped, but as he tried to process it, the image was gone. It was so fast that he had to wonder if he'd only imagined it. But next to him, Izzy breathed out, "Holy shit," in a nearly reverent tone.

At the same time, Joule muttered, "Holy flying monkey balls."

He would have laughed at the contrast had they not been stuck in the small car, fleeing for their lives.

"It's tracking us," Izzy breathed the words, her awe apparent between the wispy tone and her wide eyes.

Though Cage knew that kind of anthropomorphic attribution to a weather system wasn't smart, it definitely did feel as if they were being actively searched out.

"Sarah!" he yelled, "Keep going forward. But take the next highway *to the left* that you can find."

It was coming closer, the distance between the car and the

storm shrinking with every passing moment. It was possible they couldn't outrun it at all. But his brain was absorbing everything, the way the edges were somehow both rough and clear. The feeling of a limited space but the absolute destruction that dwelled inside it. The clear need to stay beyond the borders of the storm.

He'd told Sarah to turn left, but then he doubted the call.

Everything was a gamble. The funnel could turn on a dime. It could stop and hover, it could speed up. It could easily outrun cars. Tornadoes were known for that.

He wasn't as well-educated about them as he should be, but he'd looked up a little after the first one. He'd decided to stop learning, as the information had become more and more disturbing.

Funnels could cause an almost infinite amount of damage. They could appear and disappear at any time. They could form, touch the ground, and snatch a whole house into the sky, then be gone—all on a blue, clear day.

The first one they'd encountered had made his heart pound. And that had been even when they were sitting in the small room with the four of them feeling relatively safe. Though the windows had shook a little at the time, the walls hadn't.

But now, the car was rattling as the twister closed the distance.

The gray funnel took up a wider and wider section of his vision.

Sarah was aimed toward an intersection, the red light blinking as it swung wildly from a far-too-thin wire that threatened to snap at any moment.

"You have to turn!" Even as he finished yelling it, the tires squealed, and it felt as if the car rocked up on the outer two.

Joule and Izzy slammed into his side, as Sarah cranked the

wheel around the sharp turn, completely ignoring the flashing red light.

Though he knew he was in the car, Cage cringed and ducked in the fear that the large traffic light would come through the air like a projectile aimed right at them.

But maybe the light wouldn't kill them. Maybe the car would roll and they'd never make the turn... his stomach pitched again as the car tilted higher and higher toward his side.

He tried to calculate the kinematics of having Joule and Izzy's extra weight slamming him against his door. The momentum of it was horrible. But the weight of the car compared to their own weight shouldn't be enough.

The thought cut off as the car bounced back to its original horizontal orientation and the breath he was holding whooshed out suddenly. Maybe from relief. Maybe from the added weight of Joule and Izzy scrambling back to the other side.

"Seat belts!" his sister snapped, though she was the only one who seemed to be able to buckle hers.

He and Izzy were completely unable to get the ancient silver tabs into the slots.

"Here," Joule yelled, snapping Izzy into place and reaching across to try to help her brother. But as he felt her hands grab the webbing of the strap, Cage turned around, making her job nearly impossible.

The wind whipped through the car and stole his voice the first time he yelled it. So no one heard.

He cranked himself back down into his seat, his heart pounding from what he'd seen. There was likely nothing they could do, but he would try. And Sarah would try. And they would all hold their breath and see if it worked.

Leaning forward, he ripped the seatbelt from Joule's hand.

He was not going to be buckled in. It simply wasn't going to happen.

He tapped at Sarah's shoulder far too harshly for it to actually be the *tap* that he had intended.

"Sarah! You have to go faster!"

"*What*?" she yelled back to him, barely turning her head.

How had she not heard?

He tried again. "You have to go faster. *It's right behind us.*"

23

J oule's fingers dug into whatever she could hold onto. It wasn't much. The door handle offered her left hand some stability and the edge of the seat gave her something to smush.

Those were the only two things that had any effect.

There was nothing she could do about the car rocking as it sped along, trying to outrace the monster. Nothing she could do about her hair getting pulled and twisted one way or the other. Nothing she could do about the roar in her head and on the ground behind them.

Her grip was tight and her muscles tense in hopes of not slamming into Izzy or Cage as Sarah took the sharp turns. But there was every possibility she was just hanging on to hang on. They were all petrified of the noise and gray bearing down upon them.

At least Sarah had something to do—operating the steering wheel, taking her aggression out by mashing her foot into the gas or the brakes. Joule could only hang on and deal.

The car bounced with a pothole, or maybe Sarah had run over a piece of someone's house that had already been ripped away... Joule's eyes bounced closed with the movement and, for a moment, she just listened. It did sound somewhat like a train. The roar was akin to white noise, a coffee grinder, and a train all spun together as the beast crept up behind her. The heavy sound took over until she couldn't hear anything else—even the pounding of her own heart or the words her brother, a mere two feet away, was yelling at her.

As she turned her head, feeling as though she moved in slow motion, Joule could only see Cage's mouth moving. But somehow she still made out the words.

"It's too close!"

She watched as Izzy turned and looked out the back window once again. Joule could see her friend's eyes widen at the sight.

It was stupid, she didn't need to see it, but Joule automatically turned to look too.

Unlike her brother, she didn't yell. Instead, she reached forward and smacked the back of Sarah's seat, getting her attention the only way she could guarantee. Leaning forward, she hollered out. "It's too close, Sarah!"

"I can't go any faster," her friend yelled back, her voice breaking with stress or fear.

The conversation was difficult. Their faces had to be close to even hear each other as their voices were ripped away by the high winds whipping through the car. Joule ducked suddenly as a piece of trash flew in her window, slapped across her face and Izzy's and then hit Cage in the chest before it flew out the other side.

She ducked again as the second piece came through—surely that was a telltale sign that they were far too close to the tornado itself. Letting go of her death grip on the door handle for just a moment, Joule pushed the button raising her window. It was Izzy who reached out slapping at her hand. "You can't close it."

"No." Joule shook her head, "Not all the way. I'm trying to narrow the gap."

As she watched, Cage's window started to rise too. She'd left about five inches of space, hoping that was enough to keep the windows from shattering outward—or inward. Hopefully it was also enough to keep the larger pieces of trash from coming in and hitting them again.

"I can't go any faster!" Sarah cried again as she whipped her head to the side. Another piece of something had come barreling into the car. Sarah jerked and the car reacted as she tried not to get hit.

This one didn't go right out the other window but fluttered in its own whirlwind. Deveron jerked back before recognizing that it was safe, even if it shouldn't be here. And they all paid too much attention to the plastic bag as it settled in the footwell.

"Can we turn?" Cage yelled, leaning forward, his head whipping back and forth as he looked behind them and then out the front window.

Deveron had tried to pull out his phone, presumably to pull up a map, but the car jerking back and forth had made him drop the device several times. Joule didn't even try.

"I don't know!" Sarah yelled. "Anyone?"

But if they'd driven this far before, Joule didn't remember. They'd certainly come out on some meandering afternoons, just checking out the roads and the scenery, but she didn't remember this one specifically. Joule had no idea even which direction they were heading. The sky was dark purple now, and they'd taken several too-fast turns.

There had to be a crossroad, though. If they kept going, they should come to an intersection with a flashing red light. It was an Alabama law or something.

What she wouldn't give for the familiarity of a Dollar General store perched on a corner. But she didn't see any.

The twister got closer and closer behind them until the wind was strong enough to make the car rock. Joule wasn't sure if the answer was to keep driving, or run the car nose down into the ditch and hope the tornado skipped over them.

She glanced out the back window again and felt her heart kick higher than she'd known was possible. She was going to explode in a few moments if she kept breathing at this rate.

The funnel behind them was huge. It had to be an F4, she thought—but her brain was racing at too high a speed to make any reasonable decisions right now.

"Here!" Deveron yelled, his finger pointing outward and almost bumping into the windshield because he was leaning so far forward. *"Turn here!"*

In the darkness, none of them had noticed the intersection before it was upon them. There was no flashing red light, and Joule was horrified to realize that the cables that had once held the traffic signal box were snapping in the wind. The light itself was nowhere to be seen, probably picked up and flung far away already.

On her right, she caught a movement. She couldn't have heard it—she couldn't hear anything. A large truck raced through the intersection in front of them as Sarah slammed her brakes. The truck's mudflaps slapped in the high wind and it made no effort to stop.

Joule couldn't fault the driver, though, as Sarah once again jammed the gas and cranked the wheel in a hard left. There was no light anymore, and the only evidence she could see that there had once been orderly traffic was a green road sign, twisted and bent at the base, now lying flat against the ground.

Whoever was in the truck had likely spotted the tornado and missed seeing Sarah's little blue car. But Sarah took advantage and tucked in behind the larger vehicle now, maybe stealing the drag wind and using it to their advantage. Joule wondered if it would make them faster or just save on gas... a truly absurd thought for a life-and-death moment.

But as she pondered the physics of it, she breathed easier for a moment.

Cage had turned around, watching behind them again as they veered. "Is the Twister still headed on its track?"

Joule turned and looked, her relief flooding her system and maybe the whole car. It was no longer chasing them, but running along the perpendicular road they'd just been on. She watched for a few more seconds, grateful that they'd managed to get out of the chase.

"Oh, thank God." She breathed out the words, unable to swear or come up with anything snarky to throw into it.

But then, as she watched rapt out the back window, the raging gray funnel stalled.

Was it dying? she wondered. That would be wonderful. *Just let it stop, hover for a moment, and then quit.*

It could do that. But it didn't. Instead, the stall was only momentary. The noise softened for just a few seconds before it began to rage again, the volume picking up as it widened before her terrified eyes.

Joule saw it turn, now moving off the road and coming directly for them. A small farmhouse sat in its path and, as Joule watched, the home exploded. Ripped shingles, cracked lumber, and broken appliances were sucked upward and scattered to the sky like an angry offering.

She didn't even have a chance to scream as the two-by-four came flying toward the back window.

24

C age felt the car shudder as he grabbed for Izzy trying to shove her out of the way of the flying debris. Joule tried to duck toward the footwell, but she was thwarted by the seat belt. He watched as it locked her into place with the sudden movement.

Thankfully, Izzy was just held by a lap belt. As the two-by-four split the window directly behind her head, she at least managed to slam her torso forward. Cage and Joule, instantly realizing their predicament, threw themselves toward the sides of the car. He slammed up against the side with no belt to hold him back. For a split second, he thought the car door would fly open from the hit and he would roll across the street as Sarah and everyone else drove on.

But it didn't happen.

Reality was bad enough. The end of the two-by-four— splintered and jagged—swept through the space their heads had just occupied. The pristine shade of the wood let them know that it had been ripped very recently from the center of a house, untouched for who knew how long until now.

The piece swept through the space in the back seat before

clunking against the trunk and disappearing. He would have believed he'd imagined it if not for the spray of window glass that coated his jacket. He'd thought the window was designed to crack but not shatter... the wood must have hit with an incredibly high speed to have peppered the entire back seat in pebbles of safety glass.

Sarah was still screaming at the noise, and even as Joule and Cage fought to sit upright and assess the damage, the car weaved back and forth. Sarah was fighting to keep the small SUV on the road.

"We're okay!" he yelled, hoping to calm her down even though he didn't quite know that they were.

He and Joule looked at each other and both shrugged frantically. His sister was okay, and if he was injured, he hadn't figured out where yet. But as he looked back, squinting against the high wind and grainy feel of the air, he realized they were in more trouble than just two-by-fours shattering the window.

"You can't outrun it!" he yelled again as Sarah twisted the wheel first one way then the other, trying to steady the car on the road. The whole thing bumped as one of the wheels bounced off the shoulder and grabbed at the gravel on the edge for a moment. When Sarah turned the other way, they bumped again, hitting the curb.

Cage suffered a brief bout of fear that the bump would be enough to make them airborne and let the tornado lift them. But the small car slammed back to the road, rocking on old shocks, as Sarah once again screamed, unable to control the vehicle.

Having overcorrected for the last mistake, she had them aimed across the road to the ditch on the other side. There was nothing she could do now, except hold the wheel steady and pray.

Out the front window, Cage watched the truck in front of

them manage to stay between the lines, but it disappeared into the distance as Sarah braced against the steering wheel.

He watched everyone in the car tense as the car pitched over the side of the road and nose down into the ditch.

It felt as if they fell forever. Time stretched out as the wheels bumped over ruts and rocks and roots. The only one not buckled in, Cage slammed into the back of Dev's seat. As the car twisted, he scrambled, grabbing for whatever he could. He held the door handle for a moment, until a bump jerked the handle out of his grip. He flailed, reaching out again, bracing against the side or the ceiling and trying desperately to minimize his impact.

He waited with breath held for the vehicle to flip, but it stayed upright as it slammed nose-down into the ditch. Cage pitched forward, bouncing against the back of the seat in front of him and sliding into the footwell as he watched everyone else get yanked back by their belts. In his peripheral vision, he saw Izzy bend fully forward and then slam backwards, only to fly forward again.

Cage reached out to grab her but realized his own folly as soon as he tried. There was no holding on to anyone or anything in the middle of a car accident. Behind him, the noise grew even louder. And he wasn't sure how, but he managed to distinguish the engine from the surrounding noise of the storm. The car buried its nose in the dirt in a grinding halt and a puff of smoke. It was dead.

But they weren't. *Not yet.*

Though Cage couldn't see anything behind him with the back window aimed directly upward, he saw the five of them stuck in the car, the others all hanging from their seat belts.

They were nose down and needed a moment to gather their thoughts and get oriented, but they could hear the storm getting closer. The sky was growing darker as he took two breaths, but it was two breaths too many.

Why wasn't it already on them?

Was it further back than he'd thought?

"Get out! Get out!" Joule yelled, and he could hear his sister reiterating Radnor's instructions from earlier... was it only twenty minutes ago?

"Find a pipe. Find a tree root. Find something you can hold on to. Strap yourself to it, if you can!"

She was already scrambling to get out.

25

C age felt the car move as he watched Izzy and Joule pushing the buttons on their seatbelts and dropping forward. They were all trying to get out before the car became a casualty of the tornado bearing down on them.

There was no time for pleasantries as he pushed on his door, hoping it would open. It didn't give, and he wondered if it was dented in from the ride down into the deep ditch.

Joule managed to get hers open, the sickly groan of angry hinges signaling her quick success. With it open, it was now parallel to the ground, and she was testing it to see if it would hold her weight as she climbed out onto it. Her hair whipped in the high wind and Cage still couldn't open his eyes fully against the stinging grains of Alabama dirt or cotton or anything else the storm had picked up.

"This way!" She motioned back to them. She must have been six to eight feet off of the ground, but the car was wedged tightly against the side of the ditch pitching up behind them. Joule began maneuvering to reach back for Izzy who in turn reached back for Cage, once again forming a human chain.

That was probably a bad idea. But he wasn't willing to let go of the only people he could hold on to.

Deveron was out the front door on his side, already climbing down and around the front, possibly a precarious position. If the tornado slammed the car around, or if gravity changed its mind and it tipped forward, Deveron might get caught underneath it. But he didn't seem to notice as he also motioned for them all to get away from the vehicle as fast as they could.

It was probably the smartest decision and it was worth the risk as Cage saw no other options. He was climbing out onto Joule's still open door as he heard Sarah below him banging on the window.

She was stuck.

Cage motioned Izzy and Joule away and turned back to help. Beside him, Deveron pressed his face to Sarah's window and tried to yell. "Do you have a tool?"

It took a moment for her to understand, but when she did her face lit up. Scrambling within the confines of the seatbelt, she reached around in the space, but came up with a silver "car accident tool" as Cage had always called them.

She quickly lined up the point and smashed out the window. Next, she tried and failed to climb out, discovering she was stuck. But she figured it out and twisted around again, slicing at her seat belt with the back of the tool.

"The seat belts!" he called to her. "Get the seat belts!"

Sarah frowned at him for a moment and didn't understand. So as she climbed out the jagged window, bumping glass pebbles into the wind, he snagged the tool from her and rolled back into the interior.

Five passengers. Five seat belts, though Izzy's center back belt just went across the lap, coming out very short. He scrambled through the car, slashing and trying to pull out the longest strips of webbing he could. But the car didn't want to yield the belts. They'd locked into place with the accident and he was left with only short chunks.

He didn't know how long it took before he crawled back out, but when he did, he was slapped by the ends of the straps he now clenched tightly in his fist. The wind had no respect for any of them and they moved along, buffeted by trash and parts of things the storm had already destroyed.

"Duck!" he yelled as he saw a piece of a roof fly overhead.

They all complied, though it had been too far above them to do anything.

But this was no longer arm- or leg-sized pieces flying by. That had been a recognizable chunk of someone's home. He wanted to look back up, but kept his head ducked low. The only reason they weren't getting thrown about like straw was because they were down in the deep ditch.

While that was clearly saving their lives right now, they were stuck without trees. No pipes. Even the exposed roots were small and flimsy. But when the storm rolled over them— and it would be a miracle if it didn't—the pressure changes would suck them right out of their hiding spot.

What Radnor had said was right: People always thought it was safer to climb under a bridge or into a large pipe, but it was actually worse.

Deveron grabbed onto Cage's free hand, taking the tool and reaching out to Sarah, who was now linking up with Izzy and Joule. The five of them picked their way along as quickly as it could. In his mind, the time stretched for ages. The storm would catch them faster than he could think about it.

But they moved forward, not ripped from where they stood. Not yet.

The ditch already had some standing water, though as he looked down, he saw that it rippled in the high winds. Nothing was still, not even down here.

They moved as quickly as possible, but it was slow going.

They couldn't outrun the storm, and it sounded as if the winds had targeted them again. He couldn't see beyond the edge of the ditch to be sure. He only knew that the day was getting darker and the air getting louder. It didn't bode well at all.

"We have to find something to hold on to!" he called as loud as he could, but he wasn't sure he was heard at the front of the line.

It might not matter. There wasn't much of anything down here to hold onto except each other.

It was a balancing act full of bad choices, and what they decided would determine if they lived or died. Small trees, which they could wrap themselves around and hold on to, would likely be easily pulled out by the storm. Bigger trees that might withstand the wind, they wouldn't be able to hold on to.

"Are there roots? Anything strong?" He began trying to tie the ends of the seatbelts together, knowing they were running out of time.

Was there a house nearby?

It would have pipes and at least a more solid structure than anything in the ditch. Then again, he'd seen what happened the last time a house went up against this monster.

What they needed was a house with a basement, but they would have to leave the ditch to find one. And they couldn't leave the ditch.

"There!" Izzy yelled as she bolted forward. Cage could feel her tugging even though he was at the end of the line. "A pipe! There's a pipe!"

They all jostled toward it and he felt his ankle roll beneath him. Still he pushed on. A rolled ankle wasn't going to stop him. The group clustered up as Deveron and Cage moved faster, climbing up the sides of the ditch so they didn't run into the women in front of them.

He aimed forward, running until the pipe came into view. Though cutting the seatbelts was his best move so far, they still needed to tie themselves to something. They needed time to tie the straps together, then more time to strap everyone to the pipe.

Time they didn't have.

The noise was so loud, there was no way to even explain what he was doing or what the plan was. He managed to hand one or two of the strips to Joule, who seemed to understand what he intended.

She crouched down next to the pipe and wrapped the belt around it, then she looped it around her waist and tied it in a square knot.

Now, with her hands free, she moved to do the same for Sarah, who was already catching on. Cage tied himself onto the pipe as well, thinking that it was like an airplane in jeopardy: he couldn't help anyone else if he didn't get himself situated first.

In order to get all of them tied to a small section of galvanized pipe sticking out of the ground, they would have to sit back to back. They were doing well, getting everyone tied in with shaky, terrified movements and fumbling fingers. But then, the last belt proved to be too short, and Joule began to untie hers.

It was a tricky proposition, and Cage wondered what she was doing. *Was she going to simply give Izzy her strap and risk the winds herself?*

But she motioned for Izzy to sit next to her and he watched as his sister tied her belt to Izzy's shorter—otherwise useless—piece in a firm square knot. Joule yanked on the knot, testing the now longer, joined one. Then she wrapped it around the both of them, her fingers working rapidly to make the last square knot and get them both anchored inside the loop.

The wind would wrack the two of them against each other, there might be broken bones—but his sister had just risked her life to save Izzy's. Despite his own near-certain death as the storm grew to painful noise levels overhead, he was proud of her.

Leaning back, he felt Deveron behind him. He couldn't see his friend—couldn't see much of anything in the painfully gritty air—but he could feel that the other man and Sarah were behind him. On his left, Joule finished doubling down on the knot that held her and Izzy both to the pipe and Cage grabbed her hand, holding on tight. Probably too tight.

As the wind hit, he shut his eyes completely against the debris. He heard only the clamor above and the voice in his head repeating that they'd survived worse... though he didn't quite believe it.

As the wind began to tug at him—at all of them—he felt the ground slip away.

He hated having his back to the pipe and wished could have turned and wrapped himself around it. But, had he done that, there would only have been room for him. Trusting the pilfered seatbelt webbing to hold onto them was an exercise in faith.

It seemed forever that the heavy-handed gusts whipped and buffeted them. Beside him, Joule squirmed. He was getting pulled hard, the seatbelt digging into his stomach as it held him back.

The storm tried to yank him away—to yank all of them away. The wind tried to take his shirt, then his arm, then his head. But they all miraculously stayed attached. The pipe itself swayed in the ground, as if the storm knew it would have to take them as a unit.

Small stings told him he was getting cut by flying debris, and the whiplash changes in wind pressure made him think the tornado was right on top of them. He couldn't tell. Were they almost done? Or just beginning?

His blood was getting pulled with the forces and he felt the dizziness creeping in. He fought back the fear that—for all that they had done—the pipe would give way. If it did, all of them would be lost.

He couldn't see anything. Though he tried to open his eyes a crack, the barrage of tiny particles in the air battered his face and he squeezed them tightly back together for protection. He couldn't hear anything but the deafening roar that yanked at him and then slammed him back against the pipe or against Deveron. At least that meant his friend was still there. Still, he must have groaned at the hard hit.

Beside him, once again, Joule clutched his hand. But she was tugged and tugged until he realized their arms were outstretched.

How could that be?

She was tied in next to him on the pipe, they couldn't reach *out* unless...

A faint sound that poked at his brain and his heart tuned in —it was Joule, yelling, though he couldn't understand what she said. Once again, he fought to crack his eyes open. Though it hurt like hell, he realized that her seatbelt had come loose.

He was the only thing holding on to her.

Letting go of the pipe with his other hand, he risked reaching up and gripped her wrist with both hands, holding on for everything he was worth. The wind was tugging her upward, her feet flying over her head, hair whipping one way then another, her clothing flying like flags around her. Her open mouth yelled at him to *HOLD ON*. He thought he heard her, though he was confident he couldn't actually hear anything.

And Izzy?

Cage couldn't see Izzy at all. For a moment, he flashed back to another time when rushing water had also tried to steal his sister away. In that moment, when he had held onto her hand, he had thought he would lose her. But he hadn't.

And he wouldn't lose her now.

Their grip held.

So he clenched his fingers tighter around his twin's. She was his only remaining family member, and he was going to hold on with everything he had.

But everything wasn't enough.

In a moment of dark roaring noise, whipping wind, and shuddering ground, he found his hand was empty.

26

"Wake up, man."

Cage moaned as he was jostled about. He heard Deveron's voice through the ringing in his ears, but everything else was strangely, disturbingly silent.

"Whah?"

He didn't finish the word, couldn't—his mouth didn't work. As he lifted his hand to the side of his head he felt the groan and ache of sore limbs.

"Is it over?" he asked, but as he heard the sound reverberate through his thick skull, he knew he hadn't formed them correctly. Cage tried again, "Is the tornado gone?"

"That one is," Deveron told him, the words clear and crisp in the empty air.

"Come on, Cage." Sarah's words came at him from the other side, and he turned his head, still not seeing her. "You've been out for a little bit."

He felt her hand on the side of his face, tapping gently. He jerked back to get away, but the movement made so many things hurt. Then Cage realized he'd seen nothing because he hadn't yet opened his eyes. As he blinked himself slowly into the bright, clear light of day, he remembered getting jostled back and forth by the winds and debris bashing at them.

He'd felt as if he was drowning, unable to even breathe in the high winds. They'd grabbed and tugged and thrown them all every direction, as if by an unseen hand or a riptide. The last thing he remembered was his head smashing backward against Deveron's. This time when he reached up to his skull, Cage felt the lump.

"I got one, too," Deveron said. "Sarah thinks her arm is broken."

That made Cage twist his head quickly and look. Though the light burned his retinas, he saw his friend was holding her right arm across her body as though it was in a sling, but there was nothing holding it there.

"Here," Cage told her, reaching for the knot at his waist, trying to undo the seatbelt. Every time he'd been thrashed, it had ratcheted the knot down tighter—exactly as he'd hoped. That was what had kept him safe. But now it kept him stuck.

He felt Sarah and Deveron's hands join him, and the trio spent several minutes working on it, finally managing to get him free. Apparently, they'd both worked themselves loose before he'd come to.

Standing slowly, Cage felt aching muscles protest as if they'd gone unused for a hundred years. Bruises made themselves known as he rolled his shoulders and put weight on each foot, but none of that was surprising. He thought about stretching his arms above his head, as if he could simply yawn and welcome a new day.

But even as he thought about it, he realized— "Joule? Izzy?"

The names jumped from his lips, harsh and accusing, as Sarah and Deveron shook their heads at him.

"It got them," was all Sarah said.

"But I had Joule!" he protested, remembering holding onto

his sister's hand. He clearly remembered reaching up and locking her wrist in his firm grip.

But Sarah simply shrugged her one good shoulder. "And I had Izzy... but they're not here now."

She'd said it almost casually, as though they were missing samples on the job site. Cage was curious if maybe she was still in shock.

He'd seen enough trauma in his life to know that that was more a probability than a possibility, and he didn't fault her lack of emotion. In fact, it was probably the better course. Emotional people did crazy things.

As he quickly shut down the worry and fear blooming in his chest, he thought once again of his father. It had been bad enough when his mother died, but his father... Hell, Cage still wondered if Nate might show up one day and say, "Here I am. I did it!" But the fact was, the twins had presumed their father dead a long time ago. And that was harder than knowing their mother had died and how.

Looking around at the ditch that now held broken tree branches, debris, another car, and even an intact section of brick from someone's house, he braced for the horrifying thought that he might have to deal with his sister going missing, too. Never finding her might be harder than knowing she was gone.

Was he the only one left?

No, he told himself, putting a vise around the feeling and twisting it hard until it cut off. Emotion wiped clean and determination now pushed to the forefront of his thoughts, he told the others, "Let's go find them."

"How?" Deveron asked.

"I don't know," he admitted, but he wouldn't let it stop his forward momentum. He couldn't afford to think about it; he had to act. "So, let's figure out how to find them."

"We need to find everyone we can," Sarah pointed out. "We

have no idea who else is missing. And then we'll get all the Helio Systems people together—"

All the remaining *Helio Systems people*, he added mentally, but kept his mouth shut.

"—and we'll get a big search party."

He wanted to say no, to tell her she was wrong, that he could close his eyes and psychically find his twin. But none of that was true. He didn't have that feeling in the pit of his stomach that he did with his father, the one that said she was gone. That, at least, was a benefit, but he didn't know if that was a true connection or just pure logic. Because for all that Nate had wandered off in an emotional tizzy, Joule, just like Cage, had learned to shut it down.

If there was any chance she was alive, Joule would make logical decisions and get herself found. Their dad had *wanted* to get lost. Cage ignored the sharp stab that stole his breath every time he had to think about that.

But the others were already working, and he needed to join in.

"First, we have to get out of this ditch." Deveron looked up at the side. Even as tall as he was, the top of the ditch was still over his head.

"I don't know if I can climb." Sarah used her good hand to point to her bad one.

"We'll pull you up," Deveron was already volunteering, and Sarah was nodding.

Even as Cage reached out to hold onto her good hand, they heard large wheels stopping on the road overhead. Doors slammed and two faces peered over the edge of the ditch.

"We've been stopping every so often and looking in the ditch!" The man said it as though they were searching for treasure. He grinned at the three stuck below and Cage realized he and his friends were the treasure: People, found alive.

"We saw the tracks where a few cars went off the road a while back."

So they weren't the only ones, he thought. Not surprising.

The round face with the short red beard grinned happily and called, "Need a hand?"

27

"Just use your feet," the man called down.

Cage was trying to do that, but clearly failing. The harness wrapped around him did everything to help lift, but Cage also had to reach forward and grab onto the climbing ropes pulling him upward to help steady himself. The ground was soft and loamy, and the whole endeavor was awkward at best.

He'd just watched Deveron go up like a goat, and then he'd helped with Sarah—who was nothing approaching agile-footed. They'd all bit back their yelps a few times as her feet had slipped and they waited for her to land on her bad arm. She'd managed to prevent it each time, but Cage hadn't managed to not wince.

He was now the last one to get out of the ditch. Boomer and Bob, who must be twins, had their huge, red, tricked-out truck well outfitted for this kind of rescue.

"Slow and steady," Boomer called down to him.

Or at least, Cage thought it was Boomer. He didn't have them straight.

"Gotcha," he called up with a smile, though he thought he'd

been going steady. He tried to move even slower.

When he got close enough to the top, the other brother leaned over, reached down, and clasped Cage's wrist like a bear trap. Cage grabbed on tight, appreciating the lift, but his mind flashed to the times that he and Joule had done the same.

This time didn't matter. *Joule wasn't here.*

Forcing his thoughts back to the task at hand, Cage reminded himself that he had to get out of here first if he was going to find her.

"Three..." Boomer counted out to him as Cage put his last steps into place. "Two...One!"

He cleared the top of the ditch and stood on his own, the harness finally relaxing against him, no longer grinding his skin and muscles into bones and revealing more new bruises with each step.

Cage wondered if he, too, had broken bones. But since he couldn't pinpoint anything specifically, he didn't mention it. Probably, it was just paranoia.

While Sarah and Deveron had been hauled upward and he waited at the bottom of the ditch for his turn with the one harness, he'd pulled his phone from his pocket. It came out almost in pieces, making him wonder how it had stayed in his pocket at all. It was cracked and bent and completely useless.

He wanted to show the rescuers a picture of his sister and ask if anyone had seen her. But that couldn't happen now. Cage had been wondering if Sarah or Deveron had pictures of Joule on their phone—and if their phones were in any better shape than his?—when Bob had seen him and called down, "Don't worry about it. There's no service yet."

But there would be, Cage thought. And he'd need to find a place to get pictures of his sister downloaded. As he stood at the top now, with Bob unclipping the harness and taking their webbing and supplies back, he realized the back of their truck was already full of tornado refugees.

A woman sat with two young children. The smaller one had her arm in a makeshift sling and the other held a once-white towel to his forehead. It was now soaking up a nice patch of red blood from a cut he must have gotten. The mother sat with her arms around the little ones, her face streaked with dirt and tears. Beside her, three men sat across the back of the cab. One had his knees up, elbows bent, and head down in between. Cage couldn't see his face.

Some of the people looked vaguely familiar. Then again, he'd been working in this town for several months now. He'd been in the restaurants and the stores, and he'd surely seen their faces somewhere. This slice of Alabama wasn't that big, although somehow he hadn't met Boomer and Bob before.

"Don't think you're gonna get your car back any time soon," Boomer was telling Sarah. "It's lost until someone comes by with a working winch to tow it out." He paused, scratched his head, and delivered more bad news. "You're probably not high on the priority list."

Cage had already figured that out after the five-day lag in getting the driveway fixed so they could get up to the house. His and Joule's car had been hostage at the house because it couldn't navigate the road to leave. He could only hope this went faster.

Sarah had her own wishes, it seemed. She shrugged her one good arm and told Boomer, "Hopefully it'll run without too much work."

Their conversation continued about who to call and what she should do next, but Cage didn't pay much attention. Finally free of the harness constraints, he pushed all his thoughts aside for a moment and did a full rotation to look at the road.

It was littered with toppled trees, wood pieces, shingles, pieces of pipe, chunks of insulation, and anything you might find in a home. A kid's cup nestled in the grass nearby and a hardback copy of Pride and Prejudice lay at his feet. As he leaned over, he felt his body protest the movement, but he picked up the book and discovered that only the two pages that had been face down on the road had dirt and gravel on them. He wiped it off out of habit and the book was as good as if he'd pulled it off the shelf.

Folding it shut, he wondered what to do with it, but he was distracted by something pink. On his left, smack in the middle of the road, was a single, pristine slice of bologna. Beyond that, a twisted water heater and a window frame blocked the lane.

Boomer and Bob had navigated the damaged roads to get to them. And as Cage peered as far as he could in each direction, he had to wonder how they'd managed to get their truck around some of the obstacles. Then he wondered how they would get everyone back to wherever they were going.

His next thought was how to find his sister.

But around him, no one else was thinking, and everyone was moving.

"Get up in the truck," Boomer told him, as the man helped Sarah into the bed with the other foundlings. Deveron tugged on her, using her good arm. Cage was the last one, and they were all now waiting on him.

But he didn't move.

Boomer seemed to sense his hesitation and provided some information. "We're gonna get you folks to the community center where they've got everything organized."

And it occurred to Cage, as he surveyed the motley crew waiting on him in the bed of the truck, that they were waving him in. They understood the protocol to get to the community center. Though this might be *his* first devastating tornado, it wasn't theirs.

He wanted to run down the street and scream for his sister, but he wasn't going to find her that way. He had no choice but to climb into the truck.

28

Her alarm was going off. The odd noise was incessant, but repeating in an odd pattern. She reached out to slap it, but missed, her hand landing in grass.

"Ugh." She heard her own voice, and it was less complaint and more groan. Slapping her alarm hurt, so she tried something else. She lifted one leg, placing her foot flat on the bed, but that hurt, too.

Again, the alarm made its odd, organic beep.

"Shut up," she yelled at it, but though she managed to form words this time, her voice seemed to be set to whisper-volume.

It beeped again, only this time the sound was lower and more drawn out. *The beep was afraid.*

Now Joule frowned. Beeps shouldn't convey emotion.

She rolled her head slowly toward the sound, but the crackling noise that motion made concerned her more than her scared alarm clock. Still, she smacked her hand down in several different places, but didn't manage to hit the alarm. It rewarded her with another long, low buzz.

Prying one eye open, she immediately shut it again, hoping to stop the bright glare. Next she tried slowly opening both eyes. Joule didn't know how long it took to get her eyes open and focused, but when she looked around, her head still made that strange crackling sound.

The field was a mess—trees down, broken limbs everywhere. The place she lay was littered with trash, and as she rolled her head to the right again, she caught a glimpse of white next to her eye. Reaching up, she pulled a dirty plastic bag from behind her head. At least the crackling noise wasn't coming from her.

"Ew." She heard the sound of her own voice, creaky as if from disuse. And in that moment, everything came flooding back: lashing herself to the pipe, her and Izzy getting thrashed around, bashing into each other until the knot on the belt had come loose.

She'd grabbed onto Izzy. Sarah had also grabbed on to Izzy. Joule had grabbed onto Cage. And it still hadn't been enough.

Where was Izzy?

Joule sat right. *Where was Cage? Deveron? Sarah?*

Her head throbbed from the sudden movement, but she ignored it. There was no one here. She was in a field, alone.

The odd alarm went off again. This time, her head snapped toward the sound, though her muscles protested and her brain pulsed. She was leaning back on her hands, propping herself up in spite of the dull pain in her right arm, but she was more concerned with finding the odd sound.

"Mrrrrrrwow."

A little black head popped up.

A tiny kitten. It was out walking in the grass. It felt better, somehow, to know that maybe she wasn't completely alone. Holding her hand out, Joule waited until the small thing came directly to her.

Another little growl-meowl let her match the sound to her concerning alarm clock. *Well, thank God she hadn't managed to smack it off.*

Not generally a fan of babies, Joule still held her hand out as the tiny feline sniffed at her fingers. This one was hard to ignore. It only took a moment for the creature to deem her friendly and leap into her lap where it pawed at her shirt.

"Where are you from?" she asked as though it would answer. Of course, it didn't, so she looked around.

Kittens—ones this tiny—didn't run around solo. "Where are your brothers and sisters? Where's your mama?"

Again, it had no reply.

The lack of response left the day eerily silent but otherwise gorgeous. The sky was too-bright blue, the wash of color a background for fluffy white clouds that chased each other across the cerulean expanse.

Joule could only look up. If she did that, then the day was perfect.

When she looked down, the damage was the only thing left to see.

On the far side of the field, she could see a dirt rut, or at least the edge of it. She couldn't see the other side.

But she sat there, despite the need to stand up and inspect it. When she finally decided to stand, the kitten clung to her shirt. With gentle hands, Joule put it on the ground. *Best to leave it here for its mother to find.*

Aiming toward the ditch, Joule eyeballed the distance, curious now how wide it was. Wondering if she could compare it to the ten-foot furrow that had been carved in their gravel driveway, the last time this had happened.

She laughed to herself, as if there had been a "last time this had happened." The "last time" was nothing like this time. This time, she woke up in a strange field, alone. But seeing the ditch was an achievable goal, and she pushed forward.

Though she didn't want it to, the kitten followed along. Despite her headache, Joule was a quick mover, her steps high in the low grass. The kitten wasn't able to keep up. In fact, the grass was nearly to its eyeballs. As it fought to stay up to speed, it mewed for her.

Joule looked back at it. "You can't come with me, kitten. You need to find your mama. Or let your mama find you."

If only her own mama was still alive to come find her...

As she looked around, she realized she wasn't in the field where she worked. There were no pylons—or even twisted remains of them. She had no clue where she was. This was wide open, even bigger than the space for the solar array.

The trees were different here. She heard no traffic. She was wherever this thing had deposited her. And probably, so was the kitten. It might not have a mother within miles. So while there was a mild possibility that she was taking it away from its safety, it was far more likely she was the only safety it was going to find.

Giving in, Joule scooped the kitten up. It stopped mewing and she got a good look at it.

Small blue eyes held gratitude and relief. Probably a mistake on its part. She didn't have kitten milk on her. Hell, she didn't have food or water for herself. But the tiny ball of black fuzz seemed a little too long-haired to be the offspring of some standard, feral cat. This was probably the result of somebody's house cat having kittens. *Hopefully nearby.*

If she could find the owner of the kitten, she could find everything—food, water, a phone.

Still she headed toward the ditch, more curious than concerned right now, with the tiny kitten tucked into the crook of her arm. The distance to the edge of the ditch was much farther than she'd first thought, and her muscles protested with every step. She was battered and bruised. And she was grateful she didn't have a mirror. She must look a fright.

But she wanted to see what damage the tornado had done as it had literally carved its way through the earth. As she finally reached the edge of the ditch, she was impressed to see that some sturdy trees still stood within the path.

Of the few that remained, more than one was only a trunk. Its branches had been stripped or ripped off and only gaping splinters of wounds marked where the limbs had once been. Another stood whole, leaves and everything. But what made her mouth drop open was the width of the ditch in front of her.

29

Water.

She needed water.

Joule wasn't thirsty yet, but it was a basic fact of human nature that she would be soon. What she wouldn't give to find a perfectly sealed bottle of water lying amidst the debris, but she'd had no such luck yet. In fact, she wouldn't say she'd had any luck at all.

She and the kitten had created the only sounds she'd heard. There wasn't even wind rustling through the treetops or birds flying through. Everything had gone preternaturally still. The world felt strange, almost too perfect—except for the fact that she was the only one in it.

A rustling sound came quickly from her right side, and she jerked around to assess the threat. Because out here alone, everything was a threat. She might be a mere half mile from her own home, but the unknown was the unknown, and life had taught her not to be a fan.

She and the tiny kitten turned in unison to watch as a huge buck stepped into the wide path. He looked both ways—in a very human, crossing-the-street type gesture—before he moved more fully across the open space.

The expanse of the rut was far enough to be beyond concerning. But, as Joule watched, the deer ventured through it, braver than she—first the buck, and then several does that followed him, and then more came through. After a moment, she was enthralled and began to count them. The kitten sat quietly in her hand and she wanted to believe he was just as enraptured as she was.

Eventually, she saw fifteen of them, but was unsure if that represented a relatively large herd. They'd seen a few deer here and there while working on the array. The fact was, the work itself kept much of the wildlife away. She'd seen a few more deer at the house, but even there, the wildlife tended to much smaller creatures like squirrels and the occasional groundhog or falcon that perched for a moment on Squirrel Log.

Unconsciously, Joule lifted the kitten a little closer to her chest, as though he needed protection from the deer that appeared to be more than a hundred yards away. Or maybe he just needed a better view. Though she held him close, he didn't squirm, but seemed to watch quietly until the deer walked the last bit, their small feet picking their way through the dirt and rubble.

When they almost magically disappeared the moment they hit the tree line on the other side, Joule had a good idea of what the terrain was like.

The tornado had scrubbed the ground and left it soft, churned, and full of rocks and trash. Though she'd been intending to keep going and see what was on the other side, not crossing it might be their safer option.

With the deer now out of sight, the tiny kitten began to squirm. Joule set him down, frowning at him for a moment. There was no telling what he wished other than his own four feet on the ground. Would he try to chase the deer? He couldn't even keep up with her, and she was willing to bet the deer would leave her in the dust.

But she watched as he romped away and disappeared in the grass, much as the deer did. If she hadn't just set him down herself, she'd have no idea there was even a kitten nearby.

Was that it? Was he gone? Had he just decided to let her carry him across the field so he could disappear?

She sighed. Maybe it was stupid, but she was becoming concerned about him. As tiny as he was, he'd be a target for predators—not that she'd seen any. Then again, any decent predator would be wise enough to not be seen.

"Kitten!" she called out, though it seemed really stupid to call him that. She did it again. "Kitten!"

Did he need a real name? Did it matter? Because he was really just a kitten. Maybe his mother was nearby and he was better off without Joule.

She looked around again and didn't see any mother cat, but she didn't see the kitten, either. She sure wasn't going to name him if he squirmed, got down, and simply ran away.

Following in the direction she'd seen him go, Joule searched but still couldn't find him. Her own feet made shuffling noises through the grass, the sound filling the space around her. She wondered how long it had been since she'd been pulled from her friends and the pipe they'd been tied to. She'd been out cold, and when she came to, the tornado was well and over.

Heat flared at the back of her head—not quite pain, but definitely a little off. She possibly had a concussion. But being alone, she had nothing to compare to but the kitten. She paused to let the feeling pass and her mind wander.

In her memory, there had been at least three twisters. The two they'd been warned about—the F2 in Horton and anther F2 in Arab—and then whatever the hell had plowed through here. She had no idea what F-scale rating this one was. She was going to be very disappointed if she'd been plucked away by a 1 or 2.

But none of that gave her any idea of the time and distance between there and here.

She stepped a few more feet, but still didn't see the kitten.

Maybe he was gone. Stopping, she tried to think back and see if she could remember anything helpful. She wished she could remember being hauled away. She had memories of her feet lifting from the ground, but she'd still been holding on to Cage. She had memories of grabbing his hand and being yanked at, but she didn't remember letting go. And she didn't remember flying through a damned tornado. She didn't remember getting dropped out of the sky, or how far up she might have gone before she fell back to earth.

Had she been flung around and dropped, or had she been gently laid in the grass with the trash bag for a pillow? For a moment, Joule wondered if she had died. Was this heaven? It was beautiful. Clear sky, white, fluffy clouds, trees everywhere. The huge rut caused by the tornado made her confident that wasn't the answer.

Was it hell? Because it was empty. She could wander alone, starving to death, dying of thirst, maybe even walking in circles. She told herself she was smarter than to do that. So, maybe it was purgatory—a dear little purgatory containing only herself, a cute kitten, and fifteen deer.

She stood quietly.

The kitten might be gone, but she still had to find water. She couldn't bank on the fact that she was dead and would survive forever without it. How would she find water?

Though she looked around to assess the landscape for anything helpful, she couldn't help but think of her brother. What was Cage doing? Had he managed to stay tied to the pipe? If he and the others had even survived the twister, they'd gotten thrashed around quite a bit.

Joule remembered clearly that she and Izzy had bumped heads and arms more than once. Her foot had gotten stuck and she'd been tossed the other way and her ankle had twisted. If the others had come through, they might not be in good enough shape.

But they were gone—or she was.

She could hear her own breathing. The day was that quiet. And it had gone from being merely strange to becoming eerie. So Joule closed her eyes, pressed her hands against the sides of her pants, and held her breath. If she shut out all the other noise, she might find something useful.

There.

Maybe to her right.

Did she hear it?

30

The noise was close to deafening.

Cage stood in the parking lot, crowded on all sides with moving bodies. Frantic people trying to do the same thing he was. Too many questions and not enough answers.

He'd thought he would be tall enough to see over most heads, but not in this wild, squirming crowd that seemed to have a life of its own. Boomer and Bob had dropped them all here before heading out to fetch another round of survivors. But "here" was even further from what Cage wanted to be doing than the ditch or the back of the truck had been.

The other survivors had disappeared, blending into the writhing crowd, and he was left trying to stick with his friends. Sarah held both his hand on one side and Deveron's on the other, unwilling to let them go. Cage wondered about her bad arm and told her, "Let me stay in the middle."

But Sarah just shook her head and squeezed his fingers tighter. Maybe she was feeling better. Maybe her arm wasn't broken, just bruised. But Deveron seemed to be thinking the same thing as Cage.

"We need to get you to the medical tent." Dev moved as though to nudge her but stopped himself at the last moment. He was on Sarah's right, the side with the injured arm.

But again, Sarah shook her head. "People here are way more injured than me. All I'm going to do is wait in line. I'll be sure to get it looked at when things die down."

But that wouldn't happen for a long time. Cage scanned the crowd again. The line they were in seemed just as long as when they'd joined it. It seemed to be the most popular one. They were constantly being jostled by new joiners as the crowds inflated before their eyes.

It was too big. How would anyone get help?

He had one goal: find Joule.

He needed to find Izzy as well, but hoped he'd find the two of them together. As much as he hated to admit it, he could admit that his only real goal was to find his sister. But everyone insisted that they first report the women to the current missing persons list.

That's what they were waiting in line for. But Cage was doubting that anyone else could find Joule before he did. He pushed up on his toes to see over the crowd again and spotted a woman walking down the line with a clipboard clutched to her chest. She wasn't writing anything on it, but her purpose became clear when she opened her mouth and called out, "This line is for missing people, people you were with when the tornado hit. People who—due to the direct actions of the tornado—lost contact with you!"

She moved a few feet further and repeated the words almost verbatim. But as she moved one more step, Cage turned away, until he heard that she was giving out a new message.

"If you have family members that you were not with at the time of the tornado—people that you can't say for certain are missing, but are maybe just sheltering in a different location—you need to move to the other line. That's the Reconnection line!" She took a deep breath and kept going. She pointed with her free hand as she talked, as though anyone could see her. She was short. But at least she could make her voice carry.

"That line over there is Family Reunion. That's for families with children that were in a different location when the tornado hit. In all lines, priority is given for missing children first and missing adults second."

He watched as she took a deep breath, her caramel-colored ponytail bobbing as she geared up for another yell. "The Reconnection line is there. Yes, you can use Reconnection resources to check for friends who aren't answering their phones—" She pointed again, and Cage thought, *That's dumb, no one's answering their phones.*

As he looked where she pointed, Cage saw what the ranking system was. Family reunification was orange. Missing Persons was red. Reconnection, green.

The woman took another breath, but this time she paused enough to gather everyone's attention, at least as much as she could in this crowd. "Make sure you're in the correct line. If you're trying to reunite with your family, you need to be over there. This line is to report missing persons. If you don't have an actual missing person, you *will* get turned away. You will have to start over in the reunification line!"

It became clear to Cage that this was not their first rodeo.

The local community center was set up for exactly this. They had tents and tables out. People with clipboards or an open laptop or tablet filled two seats at each table, three tables at each tent. A generator sat behind the three tents and each device was plugged in as it was being used. They were organized. They knew what they were doing.

It seemed they'd had this set up for some time, though the crowd felt as if it had doubled in just the time since he and Sarah and Deveron had arrived. The line had moved, shuffling forward while the woman warned them about being in the correct place. He could now hear chugging from the machine, though just barely over the sound of everyone talking at once.

Voices were frantic, mothers listing information about their children, husbands looking for wives. Despite the clear organization, there were no uniforms. Cage suspected that was more an issue of budget in a town this size. The only way to identify if anyone was officially working, was that they carried a clipboard or walked around asking people if they needed help.

As his little trio shuffled forward in the heat again, a short, round man with the ubiquitous clipboard in hand spoke to them. He made quick motions and asked what they were looking for, and in a moment determined that Joule and Izzy did qualify as "missing persons," since the five of them had been in the same location and the two had actually been pulled away by the twister.

It took another fifteen minutes to reach the front of the line. As time passed—far too slowly for his liking—Cage grew more tense. He wanted to believe he would be better off out looking for his sister himself, but he wouldn't.

He didn't have a car. They'd have to get back to the house first for him to find out if he had a car at all. It was plausible that one of the tornadoes had run through the yard again and ripped up the carport and stolen his car. In fact, it could have ripped apart the entire house. Desperado's Hideaway might be no more.

Lord knows, as he'd bounced along in the back of the truck with everyone else, grateful that the bouncing didn't exacerbate his injuries, he'd seen enough homes damaged. One would be perfectly intact and the one next to it blown to pieces, with just a foundation and a chimney left, if that. Or—almost worse— one half of a house would be chewed through. The other half still standing with a gaping wound open to allow the passersby to see everything inside. He'd spotted couches and armchairs, the occasional TV, or book face down on an end table sitting unaffected.

"Isabelle McAlister," Sarah stated, cleanly listing off Izzy's height and guessing at her weight. They'd reached the front of the line while he mused about tornado damage.

"She was wearing jeans and an army green tank top. Gray hoodie."

Cage almost laughed. It's what Izzy could have worn any day, just the same way as if Sarah had been missing, they would have said 'overalls, white t shirt," and so on.

"She was wearing work boots," Deveron added. "She has her hair in a ponytail. At least she did."

That simple phrasing that his friend tacked on brought Cage to a stop.

He listened as they filled out the report for Izzy, and he thought so much of it would just be repeated for Joule. She was wearing the same work boots as Izzy. Same as all of them. But it was his turn and he gave her name adding, "blond hair, shoulder length."

Cage moved his hand, indicating her hair as though they might not understand otherwise. "Curls." He fought to keep his voice under check. Because what he wanted to do was yell, "I don't want to give you information! I want to go *look*. I want someone to find her!"

He explained again how she had disappeared, once again having to tell how her hand had been in his and then she'd been gone.

When he finished everything, he was asked, "Do you have a picture?"

Damn phone. He shook his head, wondering if there was anything he could have done to keep the phone safe. But he turned to Deveron and Sarah.

"Yes!" Sarah said, holding her phone forward to show the picture. "It's the same one I just gave him for our friend Izzy."

In the picture, Sarah stood in the middle of the other two, one arm slung around Izzy, and the other around Joule.

"She's on the left," Cage told the person as Sarah texted the photo to a new number.

When the man had recorded Sarah's number, he made her text Joule's name and case number to him as well, so it would load when the towers were back up. Then he snapped a picture of her phone picture.

Cage was handed a carbon copy in pink of the form he'd filled out for his sister. And that was it. The city had her name, height, weight, hair color, and a picture that they couldn't attach to the documents. The three of them had Sarah's and Dev's phones, which at least still came on, even if there was no internet or towers for them, and they had his number, which was thoroughly pointless. They could show people Joule's picture, but that was it.

He'd waited in line and all they could do was call him to identify fifteen blond young women at the morgue with that. No one was going to actually help them find Joule. The place didn't have the manpower, and he could hear other people crying over lost loved ones.

There would be no search party. Just him and Deveron and maybe Sarah, depending on how her arm felt. The people at the desk motioned for them to move away and let someone else step in.

Pushing their way through the crowd, the trio tried to get out of the way and away from everyone else. He needed some damn space to breathe, he thought.

But as they neared one side, the noise level began to rise at the other end of the lot. Excited sounds came from the edge, and everyone turned as one to see the newcomers.

31

"We got more!" Boomer called out the passenger window as Bob pulled the truck into the middle of the crowd.

His brother was already out, boots on the ground and heading around to the truck bed. As the crowd surged, Bob hopped up on the now-open tailgate and held his hands out. "Back it up."

His voice was calm, but it carried far and clear enough to reach Cage, who once again stretched up onto his toes. *Was Joule in the bed of that truck?*

He couldn't tell from here. He wanted to push forward, to be the first to look at the faces, worn and weary, still huddled in the truck bed. But the crowd was surging and he couldn't get ahead of them. In fact, he could barely keep up.

Bob was still warning everyone back. "There's three kids here."

Not Joule, Cage thought, and he stopped pushing. Bob was right. Kids first.

He felt Sarah squeeze at his fingers, as they waited, though she was likely waiting equally for Joule and Izzy. While Cage wasn't proud of himself, and while he would be happy if they found Izzy, his sole focus was his sister.

Five minutes later, the truck bed had been emptied and one person—pretty banged up by the looks of it—had been carried from the back seat via stretcher. The team carrying her was cutting a path directly to the medical tent.

Again, Cage nudged Sarah. "You need to go to the medical tent and get your arm looked at."

"I do!" she was quick to agree. "But look at them."

She motioned in the direction of the crowded tent with only her head, apparently not willing to let go of either man's hand. "They're very busy right now, and I won't get in."

He wanted to tell her she was wrong, but she wasn't. She had a bruised and maybe broken arm. But it wasn't even at an odd angle, just causing her pain when she grasped something with that hand. On any other day, he would have been driving her to the ER. But he needed a car and a clear road for that. Hell, he needed an ER, and no one had mentioned if the hospital was still standing.

Cage needed to get out of here.

As the crowd pulled back, releasing the stranglehold it had on Boomer and Bob and their large red truck, Cage had an idea.

The truck was empty now. They had space.

Pushing forward himself, he pressed into the opposing rush of the crowd, he fought to catch the truck. It was like running in Jello.

"Bob! Boomer!" he yelled over as many heads as he could, grateful when he managed to get one brother's attention, if not the other.

"Hey!" Boomer lit up as he spotted Cage, recognizing one of their earlier rescues. "How you doing?"

As Cage got close, he realized the plaid shirt was the only way he could tell this was Boomer and not Bob. If they changed clothes, he was going to be screwed. He left Sarah and Deveron to catch up and ran to meet the man who'd helped him before. "Where are you headed next? I was curious if my friends and I could catch a ride?"

The two brothers looked at each other cautiously, obviously not used to being a taxi service in this scenario.

Cage held his breath. The chances the truck was going near their house were slim to none, but he needed to get to their car if they were going to have any real chance of searching for his sister.

Boomer rattled off, "We're headed over toward Horton."

"That's us!" He tried to keep his voice calm, but Cage found it hard not to jump forward, grab the door handle, and shove himself into the backseat without an invitation.

His friends had caught up and Sarah had caught on. She quickly rattled off the address of Desperado's Hideaway. "You don't need to get us there. Honestly, if you can get us even a little bit closer, that would be great. We can hitch the next ride until we get there."

Cage felt his breath catch. Sarah might not be safe hitchhiking, but the three of them together? In the middle of a disaster? They should be okay.

"We're likely going to end up close to there," Bob said, still sitting behind the wheel, leaning over and talking out the open passenger window. He tossed a sharp glare to his brother that Cage couldn't decipher. But he added, "We're here to help. Getting you home and to a car is helping."

Boomer took his brother's decision as gospel and opened the back door, waving the three of them into the backseat before climbing in himself. It was Bob, one hand on the wheel, elbow perched on the back of his seat, who turned around and made himself clear. "We're not trying to drive you home, though. We're running a rescue mission, and it may take several hours to get close to your place, depending on who we find when we stop and what help they need. But having extra hands would be a blessing."

Caged nodded. It had to be faster than walking.

Two hours later, the trio had helped the brothers rescue five people.

The first was a woman by herself, who'd woken up in the ditch with no idea where her car or her toddler twins were. She'd done a search for the car, but her memory was too faulty to make that worthwhile for the group. She climbed into the back after being convinced that the best chance of finding her children was getting to the community center.

A short while after that, they found a family of four wandering the street. After peeking out of the cellar where they'd ridden out the storm, they had discovered their house was reduced to matchsticks. They, too, would be headed to the community center,

When they came upon a third group to rescue, Cage counted a cluster of close to ten people. The brothers set everyone up to do a quick medical triage, and Cage now bandaged cuts and splinted limbs like a pro. Sarah—using only her one arm—acted as his assistant.

But as they'd finally managed to get everybody toward the truck, he realized it was full.

"We're turning around," Bob announced. "Heading back to the community center. If you want to head home, this is closest we're gonna get you."

Cage wanted to offer a curt nod and simply say, "Understood." But that wasn't enough.

Instead, he reached out and shook Boomer's hand, and then reached for Bob. "I can't thank you both enough for pulling us out of the ditch, getting us to the community center in the first place, and now getting us close to home. We have people to find, too."

"Well, you do your part," Bob reminded the three of them

as though they were schoolkids reminded of an assignment. "Keep sending people in to the community center as you find them."

It was a stark reminder that they wouldn't simply find Joule and be done.

Cage nodded, but in another two minutes, Boomer and Bob had done a fifteen-point turn, maneuvering the big truck into the other direction and tailing it back toward the community center.

The three watched as the truck maneuvered slowly around some obstacles and simply rolled over others, but once it was mostly out of sight, it was Sarah who declared, "All right. Home should be over that way. I think we're about two miles away."

As they made the first steps, Cage wondered what they would find when they got there.

32

"Mmmrrrwow."

Joule's head snapped around.

The sound was plaintive, worried.

"Kitten?" she asked into the air and then watched as the grass rustled. She stood still until the tiny black head and bright blue eyes appeared.

Jesus, it looked scared.

It occurred to her then that the kitten had simply needed to use the restroom; it wasn't leaving her. Now, *obviously*, it was afraid to leave her.

"Come here, buddy." She used her softest voice and knelt down. Putting her hands out in front of her, she waited. He was still a good ten feet away and she decided that, if he came to her, that would let her know what the kitten really wanted.

She didn't have to wait long at all. Though he stalked slowly closer, when the tiny creature arrived at her fingertips, instead of sniffing, he literally jumped into her hands. He couldn't weigh more than a pound.

"I'm sorry I left you. I thought you'd found your Mom." She

felt the old tug of wishing the kitten could have found his mother. Joule knew what that felt like.

"You have to not walk away in the future," she admonished. Likely, he'd just had to pee.

She felt more than heard the purr as the tiny creature began to vibrate.

"Well, fuck," she said to the open air, though she tried to say it with a smile, not wanting the kitten to feel bad. "I guess I've got a buddy now."

He snuggled deeper into her hands, as if echoing the sentiment. But it was nice, she thought, having something alive to hold onto.

Turning, she continued on her path, convinced she had heard water. She wasn't normally one for drinking from streams, but the protesters had claimed this water was pristine and they were hell bent on protecting it. Of course, maybe it was full of mining or factory runoff and they were hypocrites. But right now, she didn't think she had much choice. Also, she suddenly had a kitten to look after. *Damn, he needed a name.*

In a moment of whimsy, she wondered if she could get him to sit on her shoulder. Sure enough, after a little shuffling to convince him to try it, he took to the perch like a parrot. She waffled for a moment on whether she should name him Polly or something pirate-y. In a flash of foresight, she realized an adult cat would likely not continue to ride on her shoulder. She immediately followed this thought with the fact that she would not have an adult cat. She was merely a foster.

Joule repeated this internal monologue several times, as though knowing it was a losing battle. But she picked her way forward through the tall grass, glad to have her tiny companion back.

"Alright, Toto, we are on our way." She spoke it out loud again, as though the kitten would understand. "Let's see if we can find some water."

It was ridiculous, as the kitten most likely did not compre-
hend English. But as she looked around, wondering if she
should be embarrassed by it, she realized that if someone was
close enough to hear her voice, that would be a good thing.
Finding another person would be a dream right now, particularly if it was a person who knew where water was.

The cynical side of her was betting that she was fifteen feet
away from one of the amazing local Mexican restaurants and
that she could not only have water, but a coke, chips, fresh
queso, and ....ohhhh. She was probably walking the wrong
direction.

But she'd heard nothing to indicate that there were even
people, let alone a sit-down restaurant, nearby. And she had to
make the smart decision, which was to aim toward the water.

The tiny kitten meowed as she moved along, as if telling her
which direction to go. That part was amusing but, if she stumbled, Toto dug his claws into her shoulders.

"Ouch!" She said it like a scold, but he expressed no
remorse.

Maybe she shouldn't have put him there. When she tried to
pull him down, he dug in tighter, seeming to enjoy the view.

Joule had not had a cat before, and she was coming to
realize they communicated through meows and claw use. She
left him on her shoulder. The razor sharp talons were quite
effective.

In a short time, she reached the edge of the trees. Though
she was confident no one was around, anyone watching her—
any satellite footage or any way they were spotting people—
would lose sight of her when she entered the woods. Turning,
she looked back at the field. She had cut a clear path, but that
would end here at the packed dirt and old, fallen leaves of the
forest floor.

She needed to leave a sign.

Ten or fifteen minutes later, she stepped into the shade of

the trees. As the leaves overhead blocked the sun, she wondered if she could manage to stay aimed in the right direction. Well, in the *same* direction at least, as she didn't know if it was the right one. Lord knew, anyone could get lost in the woods quite easily.

With a sharp intake of breath as she realized she'd missed a major check, she patted herself down, feeling for her phone, or anything else that might be useful. When she'd come to in the field, and her head crinkled when she moved it, she hadn't been thinking clearly.

She wondered again if she might have a concussion.

Joule consoled herself that she was thinking relatively clearly now, so it would at least be mild if she did. Still she checked every pocket on every piece of clothing, hoping to find her phone.

It wasn't there, not in her back pocket or one of the side pockets of her cargo pants. Almost panicking, she turned back, gazing toward the center of the field, where she'd first regained consciousness. But she couldn't quite see where that point was.

Was the phone there? Lying in the impression she'd left when she came to? She hadn't even thought of it, and maybe it had slipped out of her pocket and was sitting in the grass nearby.

Joule stopped herself before running back to check. She didn't even know if she could find the exact spot where she'd landed. Surely, there was a Joule-shaped indent in the tall grass, but could she find it? And, if she did, what were the odds that her phone was waiting there? That it had survived being tossed around by a tornado? That it had either stayed on her person or landed in the field near her *and* was still usable... those were very low odds. In fact, she thought, there was every possibility cell service was entirely out of commission right now.

She decided not to go back.

Though she was once again not confident she was making

the right decision, she was making the one she had to make. So she turned back to the trees and checked the sun, hoping to stay aimed in the right direction. Luckily, it only took a few minutes before the sound of water, filtered through the trees, maybe reflecting off of the trunks and the leaves, grew louder.

It seemed to come from so many directions at once that she stopped, feeling Toto's claws dig in until he re-balanced himself. But when she thought about it, if it truly was a stream, it would be cutting her path, and the sound *should* come from several directions. So she simply tried to make sure she didn't walk parallel to the water and constantly miss it, or take a wrong turn and leave it behind her.

Unable to cut a straight path, Joule disoriented herself a bit, but shortly found a clear, running stream.

"Holy shitballs, kitten!" she said before remembering she named him. "Alright Toto, time to drink!"

This time, when she lifted him from her shoulder, he let go easily, seeming to be as eager for water as she was. As his paws hit the hard-packed dirt, he made a beeline for the edge of the stream. She was grateful she'd found this before she grew too thirsty and she took a moment to watch his little tongue lap into the water.

The little fucker was cute.

But she couldn't just watch him. Leaning over, she put her hands into the stream, but pulled back quickly at the sharp bite of the cold.

Alabama was so hot, so humid—how was it possible this wasn't a hot spring? But it wasn't. Pointedly ignoring where the water might have come from, and hoping that the pretty color and clarity meant that it was safe, she dipped her hands in and scooped up mouthfuls until she'd swallowed far too much. Who knew when she would find water again?

She hadn't found so much as a water bottle or a discarded cup as she'd walked across the field. Though there had been plastic bags, pages from books, and splinters of wood, nothing had been a usable container to carry water. So she drank until she almost felt bloated and ignored what she knew about carcinogens and waterborne parasites.

By the time she'd had her fill, Toto was sitting back and licking his tiny paws.

"Where do we go now?" she asked him. Task one had been achieved, but what was next? "Do we follow the water?"

"Mrrwow."

She laughed into the empty air. If only she understood him. But she didn't care.

"Okay. Upstream or downstream?"

"Mrrwow."

"Agreed! Downstream is more likely to lead to civilization." And since she didn't want to walk through the water and deal with wet feet, following along made the most sense.

She had no idea how long she'd be out here wandering alone.

Scooping the tiny kitten back up, she headed down the path, avoiding muddy patches and thinking that as long as they followed the stream, at least they'd still have drinking water.

Water was more important than food, she knew, although that might be their next goal.

It was hard to keep track of time, but she figured it was a good forty or fifty minutes later before she finally saw through the trees. In the open field stood what had been a farm just hours ago.

The barn was only half standing, looking as if an angry toddler had come along and stepped on a block building. Hay and pieces of board—painted red on one side—trashed the yard.

Cows milled about and, as Joule looked at them, she wondered if their numbers matched the original or if any had been picked up by the twister and spirited away.

An almost-empty, square foundation sat a good distance away. She would have to cross the stream to get to the farm, and the farm was the likeliest chance of finding people, even if the house wasn't still there.

Joule began hunting for stones to step across the water, hoping she could do this without getting her feet wet. Why had she not picked up some of the plastic bags she'd passed?

Even as she chastised herself, she thought she heard a truck.

33

"Yes!" Joule thought, spotting a series of rocks protruding above the surface of the burbling creek. She'd been just about ready to splash into the water and run after the truck she'd heard.

"Wait!" she yelled out as she took her first tentative step and the stone tipped a little. When she had her feet steady, she hollered again. *"Wait!"*

The yelling made her ribs hurt. Using her lungs like that for the first time let her know she was more bruised than she thought.

As she clutched Toto close to her chest, Joule picked her way across the stream. Falling in and having to scoop herself out would be far worse than simply wading through. When she hit the last stone, she jumped for the far bank, sliding in the mud on the upside. She scrambled for a moment trying desperately not to squeeze the kitten, drop the kitten, throw the kitten, or slide back down the bank into the water. She managed to make it to the top with just a little bit of mud on her shoe by grabbing a small tree for anchor before she slipped past.

Jumping up, Joule waved and hollered at the receding truck.

She would have waved both hands, but one of them held a tiny kitten. The tail lights faded into the distance, though she waved and yelled, trying to catch their attention.

"Wait. *Wait!*"

But the truck disappeared, never having seen her.

"Fucking fuck monkeys," she muttered to Toto. With nothing else left to do, she headed onto the farmland, checking out what she could.

The farm was an eye-opener.

She was *not* getting closer to civilization. Following the stream hadn't helped. She was still out in the middle of nowhere. The question was, how far out?

The good news was that there was a road and there had been a truck on the road. If there was a truck now, there would likely be another truck in a while.

Should she stay put, or start walking?

If she had any idea where she was, she might have an idea of which direction to go. Walking seemed the smarter choice. If she found another farm, she might find people. If she found people, she might find a phone.

Even if she didn't find people, she might find an intact building, and she was not above breaking in, eating their food, and using their phone line.

"Come on, Toto." Joule cuddled the small kitten close and wondered how to make a sling for him so he could fall asleep. Luckily, she was wearing her jacket. Alabama, had been hot and muggy, most days, but she'd learned that leaving her jacket at home proved inconvenient against the sudden changes in weather. So she often wore it tied around her waist, just to have it handy if clouds marred the sun or the winds picked up.

She remembered shoving her arms down into the sleeves as the weather had changed back at the site. Had that only been this morning? Or had she been out longer?

Joule decided it had to be the same day. She wasn't hungry

or thirsty enough to be missing too much time. So she peeled her hoodie, realizing she was a bit overwarm anyway, and slipped it around her waist. But she pulled it on backwards, creating an apron. The hood hung in front of her, and she slipped Toto into the pouch it created. Within moments, the tiny creature was asleep, bouncing along with her steps.

She found she was wishing for her own giant to pick her up, put her in a hood, and carry her along to safety. But of course, that would be terrifying. So she kept walking along the road.

She couldn't stay here. This farm wasn't functional. If there was food, it was in the grass, and she hadn't reached the point of eating things she found on the ground yet.

If there was a phone here, it had been ripped from the wall. Any lines connecting it were long gone, too. But if she kept going, she might find another farm, and that farm might be intact.

She had to pick a direction. Though she felt fully alone except for tiny Toto, she knew someone would come through here eventually. Ten minutes later, she sat back on her heels. "What do you think, Toto?"

The tiny kitten didn't answer, not even with a cheap meow.

"Fine, it doesn't matter what you think. We're committed to this direction now."

Though she walked and walked and walked, the old road curved around the edge of the farmland and it felt as if she hadn't gotten anywhere.

She saw more furrows in the earth, and, in many cases, there was just a sense that things were missing. The grass still stood, but the trees were gone, pulled up—roots and all— leaving gaping wounds behind. The lawn toys stood unmarked. The family who lived in the house must have small children. Though the plastic playhouse shutters looked like they might have been messed with, no damage was evident. Behind it, the real house was completely gone.

The sun had moved in the sky and she was feeling the road through the soles of her work boots before she saw another farm, but as she got close she saw that this house, too, had been razed.

"Holy crapnuggets," she muttered to Toto, who was still sleeping in the hood. He opened one eye and rolled over, lying on his back. She'd made him a hammock on a beautiful sunny day.

Lucky little sucker, she thought, but she surveyed the damage again, wondering if any of it could help her.

If there was food, it was long gone, but there might be something useful.

Hell. Logic said she should check it out. It looked like it had been a real home, and therefore it should have a kitchen, and a kitchen should have cups or something. Joule would happily take one from the grass. That way, when she went back to the stream, she could carry water with her. Maybe she would get lucky and find a Twinkie or granola bar.

She looked up and down the road, but no more trucks had come along in the time she'd been watching, and there was no one on this deserted road now. So she headed into the grass, hoping to find something.

The distance was deceptive; the farmhouse much farther away than she'd originally thought. The walking wasn't easy, the ground lumpier than it appeared. Apparently, this was a cow pasture.

And after smelling the first pile of manure, she had to make a point of avoiding the patties. The last thing she wanted to do was finally find a savior and smell like cow shit.

The fence around the home was what she'd come to know as black horse fencing. The posts had slats between, tipped vertical, making a flat front fence. And all of it remained intact and easy to climb over.

As she dropped onto the grass on the other side, she was

grateful to find it was mowed lawn perfectly devoid of cow pies. It was not, however, devoid of nails, broken wood, or glass.

Toto squirmed again, wanting to be let down. When she didn't let him, he climbed down her sleeve, puncturing her as he went.

"Ouch! Ouch. Toto!"

But he reached the end of her arm and jumped for the ground. For a moment, her heart stalled. He was too tiny to leap that far, but it seemed all it cost him was a bit of a thump as he hit. Her kitten wandered off, butt and tail twitching as he went.

Shit, she thought, following him. She'd named him. She knew he was too far from his mother now. It was up to her to keep him from getting cut on any of the dangerous things scattered through the yard. And where was she going to find kitten food?

This time, she watched as he squatted in the grass. Yep. Just a bathroom break.

But he was carefully picking his way through, avoiding the sharp edges and not putting everything into his mouth like a human toddler. He'd be okay.

Joule turned away. *It would be easy enough to find him in the low grass*, she thought as she began searching in earnest for anything helpful.

As the two of them wandered to the other side of the house, she saw shots of red in the grass. They turned out to be bottles of energy drinks. One was even intact.

"Toto. Look at this." She held the heavy bottle up toward him. It wasn't just water, but electrolytes. She'd drunk enough back at the stream that she didn't need this right now, so she opened her pocket and shoved the bottle down in. It barely fit, but in two more minutes she realized the farmhouse was home to a fitness nut.

Energy bars, still in their wrappers, were strewn through

the grass. Frosted Flakes lay individually like snow in between some of them.

Okay, so not everyone who lived here was a fitness freak.

But she put the bars in her pockets. She had a bottle. She had water. And she had food.

Next up, she had to find something for Toto. If only these people had a kitten. Fifteen minutes later, she had two pull-tab cans of tuna and she was reaching over to scoop up something that might be kitten-appropriate when she heard a voice.

"What are you doing?"

Joule looked up. *Oh, hell no.*

34

"**Y**ou have got to be shitting me." Deveron, usually quiet, was the only one to speak this time.

Cage, Sarah, and Deveron, still holding hands, stood at the end of the driveway silently scanning the damage.

"Maybe it's not as bad as it looks," Cage offered, looking at the trash strewn across the lawn—trash that he could identify as Sarah's sweater, the crackers that Joule liked, his books, Dev's video game controller. Why had he said that? It was definitely as bad as it looked, and it looked awful for a building that was still standing. When was he ever the optimist?

The driveway was long and they were still a good way down from the house. This time, the gravel road remained intact. Though some of it clearly had blown this way or that, cotton was strewn and mixed in, as was some identifiable trash and a lot of unidentifiable trash.

As they got closer, Cage saw that his assessment from the end of the driveway had been correct. At least one corner of the house was missing. The edges were rough, as if the house were cake and a child had shoved his hand into it, pulling out a piece to eat.

Sarah turned to Cage, her disbelieving expression conveying everything even before she opened her mouth. "Trust me, it's worse than it looks."

She'd been through this before.

Though his feet ached, and he was sure the others' did too, Cage trudged the length of the gravel drive. This was worse than walking on the pavement. Everything wanted to roll under his feet, and somehow he was confident that he could feel the gravel poking through the soles of his heavy work boots. He was grateful they were laced up tight, preventing his ankles from turning.

Their house looked like a lot of the other houses they'd passed, with a gaping wound and some things inside seemingly untouched. The tornado appeared to have chunked out the bulk of the main room that served as both dining room and living area. Given what he could see was missing, Cage could now identify the curved piece of wood he saw as a leg of the dining room table. He stepped over it.

The next thing he stepped over was a small globe, papier-mache, smooth and shiny. It had sat in the wicker basket on the table along with several others and decorative wicker balls. Once purely ornamental, they were now purely trash.

It was a shame the four of them had taken all the skulls off the walls and dressers and hidden them in drawers or the backs of closets. They might have been able to claim that "decor" had blown away with the damage.

He was coming to terms with the fact that the house was unlivable. He might be able to salvage some of his things, but they couldn't stay here tonight.

If Joule—or Izzy—did manage to come home, who would be here to meet them?

He wondered if he should stay anyway. Was the weather warm enough? Would he be okay? Or were there looters outside of Horton, Alabama?

There were no answers to any of these questions—not that he knew—but he picked up his pace to see what he could. Letting go of Sarah's hand, he left her and Dev to come up behind him. He needed to see the car.

The carport had been twisted and warped, its metal legs lifted out of the ground on one side and the whole top tilted. The surface was now facing him, and somewhere behind it was the car... maybe.

The way the ground naturally rolled with small hills and rises, he couldn't quite see underneath. So he began running. He *needed* that car.

As he got closer and more worried, the stinging of the soles of his feet was no longer a concern. He could now see tires, front and back, still inflated.

Good! The car was still there.

The question was, was it drivable? Had one of the posts of the now ripped and twisted carport been jammed through a window? Had the windows or doors been ripped off? Was there a rock sitting on the engine? It was hard to breathe. Because that car was why he'd come back. Not the house.

Though he'd wondered briefly, back at the community center, if Joule was waiting here for him at the house, he'd shoved the hope away. It came surging back to life now.

"Joule!" he yelled, *"Joule!"*

But only silence answered back.

Deveron and Sarah were smart enough to keep their mouths shut. Probably like him, they were simply listening for an answer. But none came.

Hoping to get any response, he called out for Izzy, too. Once more, he held his breath, wondering if the unfairness of life would have her hollering back, but not his sister. He truly did want to find Izzy, but there was nothing he could do about the pure, soul-deep panic that he felt when he worried about his twin.

When he heard nothing, he turned the last edge and peered around the mangled carport. The car was sitting there, appearing entirely undamaged.

His first thought was that he needed to start it and check that it ran. Which led to a second thought. He needed the keys.

Dashing toward the house, he saw that the cement steps leading to the kitchen door had been tossed aside. The door was missing too. But it appeared the brick siding and the flooring was intact.

He had trouble picking through the rubble that piled at the side of the foundation, but he climbed carefully, eventually getting his hands on the edge and testing it to see if it would bear his weight. When it seemed to pass his quick and dirty test, he hoisted himself up to the floor of the small walkway in between the dining room and the kitchen.

The kitchen appeared intact, thank God. The tiny island had been jostled, but that wasn't surprising, given that it was on wheels. It was a shock that it hadn't moved far, given that it was merely fifteen feet from where the wall was missing.

He walked the short path around it to see that the hooks on the other side were now empty. Was that his fault? Had he forgotten to leave his keys there?

Patting his pockets again, he confirmed that—aside from his wallet and phone and work ID—he didn't have anything else on him. Sarah had driven today. He would have left the keys behind. On the hook.

He was already on his hands and knees, searching, as he heard Deveron in the background saying, "Wait here. I want you to come in, but with your arm, you shouldn't be trying to muscle your way up."

"I can jump down. I just need help climbing up," Sarah protested back.

Still Cage frantically searched the room. Napkins were strewn all over the floor. The paper towels had been pulled from the holder and thrown around as though someone had TP'd the inside of the house.

Cage patted at the floor, wondering where the keys might have gone. Dev's keys should have been here, too. It took only a moment to find his roommate's keys and, as he turned, he saw his friend had boosted himself into the house through the same open doorway.

His brain was firing in odd patterns, and it only just now occurred to him that they could have just walked up the front porch and come in the door like normal people.

He hollered that idea to Deveron, who called back, "Well, there you go, making sense." And he walked past Cage, stepping over their things to unlock the front door and let Sarah in.

Cage wanted to laugh hysterically. He wanted to lose it over the fact that the front door had been double bolted while the back of the house was missing. Much of the screen was missing off the back porch and though the back door was intact, the wall next to it was completely gone. But the front door was fully locked.

He clamped down on the rising hysteria and held out his findings with one hand. "Your keys."

He didn't get up though, and the other hand was still patting at the floor, searching for his own keys. Dev didn't have a car, so the find wasn't all that useful to Cage right now. At last, he moved the island aside and found his own keyring underneath.

"Got it!" he yelled, thinking he would run right out the gaping hole and jump to the ground right in front of the car. But what if he landed on something and twisted his ankle? He couldn't afford that.

So he headed out the front door, letting the screen slam behind him. He couldn't see the car from here, and irrational fear gripped him that it had been lost in the last five minutes, or that he'd hallucinated it in the first place.

But it was still waiting and he took a deep, calming breath, reminding himself that he had to stay fed, healthy, and calm if he was going to find his sister.

Not even closing the door, he shoved the key into the ignition and waited.

35

"You've got to be shitting me," Joule uttered into the air or maybe to Toto.

In front of her, Jerry's brows pulled together. Though he was almost too far away to recognize, he'd heard her.

She instantly regretted saying it. Because the fact was, if Jerry could lead her to people, she would take it. She didn't have to be his friend.

"You!" he responded, the single accusing word indicating that all of her feelings were mutual.

She decided that she wasn't quite ready to say, *Oh, it's good to see you*. Because, while it was good to see another person, Jerry would have been the last of her choices. Instead, she asked what she could honestly ask. "Are you okay? Are you injured? Do you need anything?"

"I'm fine." He put his hands on his hips and adopted his best "angry elementary teacher" expression. "But I see you're stealing from the Johnsons?"

"Yes." Joule offered it back with zero expression, because fuck him. "I'm in the middle of nowhere, after a disaster, with no food or water. And I picked up a sports drink, five nature bars, and two cans of tuna. I'll give the Johnsons the twenty bucks the first time I see them. I suspect they were going to claim their 'ground food' on their list of losses on their insurance."

Though she said the last part with emphasis, she realized that she didn't know if the Johnsons actually had insurance. Still, he could go screw himself. "I'm not taking computer equipment or stealing their TV, Jerry."

"I'll hold you to that."

She rolled her eyes.

Clearly, he was fine enough to be his usual asshole self.

When he stayed silent for a moment, she added, "I'm fine, too. Not very injured, just bruised and banged up. Thank you for asking."

He tossed her a sarcastic look but stayed silent.

This was not working. She had one goal, and working against Jerry was working against that. She took a deep breath and tried not to look like she was taking it. "I'm sorry."

It felt like twisting a knife in her own gut to admit that she was sorry. She wasn't sorry she'd been rude to Jerry, though. She was sorry that she'd hurt her own chances of getting home. She pushed a little further. "Listen, you seem to know where we are. Do you have a working cell phone?"

He shrugged. "No one does. Cell towers are all out."

She'd suspected that was the case. "Is there maybe a land-line in any of these houses?"

As she asked it, she looked around and saw that all the buildings were gone. If there had been a plugged in phone, it and the lines connecting it were all gone as well.

But Jerry didn't mock her. "All out, too."

He waved his hands around as if to indicate the things she'd just accounted for. And at least the conversation was proceeding now as if it were occurring between two normal people. But he still didn't offer any help. She tried again.

"Do you have a car?"

"Nope!" He offered that up almost too cheerfully. "I was in my truck when the Twister hit. Got out, got into the cellar here. Came out afterwards ..." He held his arms out and twisted in a full circle as though offering a fashion show. "You see my truck?"

Not now, but she had seen his truck before. It was a massive monster that made him look like he had some insecurities to make up for. She didn't say that now, because she would have loved to have ridden in that ugly behemoth all the way back to town. Instead, she put the pieces together. Incredulous, she asked, "The wind lifted your truck?"

"Damn straight. And the Johnsons weren't home when I got here. It was coming on fast, so I busted the lock on the cellar."

And here he'd been mad at her about a couple cans of tuna and a bottled drink. But this time she managed to bite her tongue. "Do you know where we are?"

"I told you, the Johnson's farm." He said it again as though she was stupid.

And she opened her mouth to call him a few choice words, instead the hood at her stomach squirmed and let out a "mmmrwow."

"What's that?" Jerry pulled back as though she had some disease and he might catch it from how far away he still was.

"A kitten?" she said, by way of explanation.

"What are you doing with a kitten?"

Oh dear God. It was a damned tornado and it followed her! But Joule calmed herself—forcibly—and answered, "I found him. He was going the same direction as me and we decided to travel together."

"You probably stole it from its mom." The accusation was

not surprising and Joule once again bit down her automatic retort.

"Mom was nowhere around." She was almost angry that she'd had the exact same thought as Jerry. "And he followed me. I wasn't going to leave him."

At least Jerry seemed to concede that little bit.

She tried again. "So where exactly is the Johnson farm? Like, which direction is Horton? Or Arab? Or New Hope? Are we close to anything?"

Jerry shook his head and pointed into the distance. "Arab, Horton, and New Hope are all that direction. We're out in the great beyond."

Well, shitballs, she thought. She was in the great beyond with Jerry, of all people, and he didn't even have his truck. "Would anyone else out here have a truck or something we could borrow?"

She was already emotionally tired of walking, and she was going to be physically exhausted before too long. Fueling a car would be easier than fueling herself. Whatever it was, it'd be faster.

"No cars. The Johnsons have one truck and it wasn't here when I stopped." But he added, "There's another farm a ways over. They might be home. It's worth a shot."

"How far is it?" Joule was becoming wary. She'd come a long way and only found him.

He shrugged. "A couple thousand acres."

She had no idea what kind of distance that was. "Should we walk on the road?"

She'd said *we*, as though she stopped and picked up Toto along the way, and now she was simply picking up Jerry, too.

"No. If we take the road, it'll take ten times as long. We can head straight through here." He pointed to a tree line in the distance that seemed to denote a fence on a property.

Joule nodded along, wondering what they would find when they reached the other side.

As he started to take off, she stopped him. "You might want to grab one of those sports drinks, unless you have water or food on you."

"Good point." He didn't acknowledge his accusation from before as he stepped into the side yard and grabbed several things to put into his own pockets.

Luckily, the walk wasn't as far as it looked. They'd carefully picked their way through the barbed wire fence and trees and crossed another yard. This house, though undamaged, was empty.

Together, they circled the place and banged on doors. Joule was getting so tired of having nothing work. She considered breaking in to find car keys, but since there were no cars or trucks available, that seemed pointless.

"Wait," Jerry told her. "I have an idea."

36

"Yes!" he yelled into the empty car, relief running through Cage almost as surely as gas was running through this combustion engine.

The engine had turned over cleanly and easily. Throwing the car into reverse, he backed out of the space, trying to avoid the mangled limbs of the carport and get the car turned around.

The sound must have brought Sarah running, as she appeared quickly in the open gap. She made a face as if to ask, *What was he doing?*

She waved her arm at him, though Cage didn't understand the signal, as she stood precariously at the edge. Deveron came up behind her, quick enough to make Cage wince, afraid his friend would slam into Sarah and she would stumble forward into the pile of rubble that had gathered below.

But Dev pulled up in time and the two didn't tumble down.

Cage pulled the car just slightly forward before turning off the engine and climbing out. "I just wanted to get it out from under the carport. Wanted to be sure that not only did the engine work, but the tires rolled. It sounds good."

He offered a smile, but Sarah put her one good hand to her heart. He noticed then that she was wearing a sling. He figured Deveron must have fashioned it for her.

Good call, but time was wasting, he thought. He waved them out to join him. "Come on, let's go!"

Sarah shook her head and Cage crossed the short distance between them, coming to stand well below their height, not having realized how far the foundation was raised until the stairs no longer existed.

His impatience must have shown on his face, because Sarah started by shaking her head at them. "One of us needs to stay behind. The house line is dead. If they come back here and we're gone, they might come looking for us. That's bad. There's no cell signal yet to connect ..."

She waved her one good arm into the open space, as if to designate all the dead air around them. There were no cell phones and, if there were no landlines, they would need to find people with radios.

"But we're here. We looked, and she's not—*they* aren't— here," Cage protested. He wasn't going to sit and wait. "That's why we need to go now."

He hitched one thumb over his shoulder, not liking that this was even an argument, let alone the direction it was headed.

"Someone should stay here and wait for them." Sarah's tone said her mind was made up. "What if the phone lines come back up? The line here is intact. What if they call? What if they show up?"

Crap, he thought. It wasn't right to sit here and wait; they needed to get on the move. They couldn't simply hope that Joule and Izzy would find themselves and then make their way back home. Without phone lines, contacting other people could very easily depend on face-to-face interactions.

He had Boomer and Bob watching out for the two women. But the fact was, Boomer and Bob were watching out for so many people, that Joule and Izzy could sit in the back of their truck and get dropped off at the community center, and the men likely wouldn't recognize that they'd found his sister. So no one would alert him and his friends. No one could or would call the house, and he could sit here worried for no reason.

"I'll stay," Sarah volunteered. "You two go out and look. I've got a bum arm anyway."

Though Cage was nodding, Dev pushed in front of her into the open gap. Again, Cage worried that one of them would fall, but at least Dev was smoother on his feet and once again, they stayed upright. "We can't do that. There's three of us. We're a prime number—we can't split up evenly and we shouldn't leave anyone alone. We all need to stay together. At least until we get one more person."

"Okay, who can we get to stay here with me?" Sarah asked, looking between them. But they stared silently at each other, each waiting for someone else to produce a recommendation.

When it was clear none was coming, Cage announced, "Then you'll come with us. We'll leave a note."

It wasn't the same as having someone answer the phone, but it was better than all three of them sitting here with no phone, or leaving Sarah by herself.

But she shook her head. "I'll have the house phone soon."

Cage frowned, but Sarah understood and responded, "The phone company makes restoring the lines a priority."

"Before missing people?" That didn't make any sense, and he could feel his hand squeezing the keys, trying not to show how upset he was that they weren't already in the car and down the driveway. He was more than certain he wasn't hiding it very well.

"Yes." Sarah nodded vigorously. She understood the system here and he didn't. "Once we get the phone lines up, then we can find all the missing people faster. It's an issue of necessity. We can stop wasting effort looking for people who are already found, because we can talk to people who located them. I'm sure the crews are already on it." She paused, but then kept going, as though sensing he needed more convincing. "Hospitals need the communication."

She looked to Dev, imploring him to join her side. She *wanted* to stay. "This is a house. I'll be fine here."

Thank God it was Dev who turned around and blurted out exactly what Cage was thinking. "What the hell, Sarah? The side of the house is missing! You might *not* be okay here when the next storm rolls through."

But Sarah shook her head. "It won't come back the same place."

"What? Is it like lightning now?" Dev asked, sarcasm dripping. "Tornadoes *do* come back to the same place over and over again."

"The sky is clear," she protested, once again putting her good arm up to gesture. "Someone needs to stay behind. I'm the one with the bum arm. I can't help pull people out of their cars and I certainly can't climb up and down ditches to find somebody."

Cage hated her logic. He wanted her safe. Though he would never admit it to himself, the thought of losing anyone else when Izzy and Joule were already gone was nauseating, but she obviously didn't want to go, and he *needed* to.

"I don't like leaving you alone." Dev fell back on the best argument.

"Well, honestly, neither do I," Sarah countered, looking like she would have braced her hands on her hips if she could. "But the fact is, somebody needs to stay. If they can find their way back, this is the first place they'll come. And this is what I'm good for. I promise you, as soon as I can contact someone else, I will get someone else here with me. I don't think I'll be alone for long."

"Can you stay at the other house with Mary Allen and Sue?" Deveron asked.

"It's too far away. If Izzy or Joule comes here, I won't be here."

Cage was staying out of the argument now, because he'd be arguing his own, selfish side. He was running every non-rational scenario for himself but was unwilling to unleash them on his friends. He told himself Sarah would be in the house. They did have a safe room. And she did have a damaged arm. She was likely to make things worse if she came out on the road with them. Still, he felt the need to protest to soothe his conscience. "We're leaving you with no car."

He realized as he said it that he'd phrased it as though he and Dev were already out the door. But he didn't correct it.

"Mary Allen and Sue down the street have a car. We saw it on the way in. It looks like it's still in good shape."

That was true, and he appreciated that Sarah was lobbying hard for the job. Cage look to Dev, who only shrugged. It wasn't a great idea. They all knew it. But it was the best use of what they had.

"Alright," Dev finally conceded. "Be safe." And he hopped out the opening, giving himself enough of a leap to clear the rubble and land on solid ground.

"Not yet!" Sarah's protest was surprising after all her arguing for them to go without her. But she made them spend five more minutes packing water bottles, bandages, and anything that might be used for a roadside splint, food, and more. As he filled grocery bags to chuck into the backseat he thought that, even though they'd been eating at home more, their pantry was still woefully understocked.

But when he and Dev were set up to help anyone they found, he tossed the bags into the back and hoped their first discovery would be Joule and Izzy.

The two climbed back in the car, turned the ignition, and

bumped their way down the gravel drive yet another time. Dev didn't speak, and for that, Cage was grateful. When they hit the end of the drive, they had a decision.

"Which way?" Cage asked, not wanting to be the one responsible. If anything truly terrible happened to his sister, and he had picked the wrong direction, how would he live with that?

Dev pulled out actual information, though. "When we were in the ditch, the ditch ran north-south, and the tornado came up behind us heading north. It grabbed both Izzy and Joule. So if it got them, and if it deposited them somewhere, it was probably somewhere north of here."

God love him, Cage thought. Not only had Dev chosen, but he'd given a solid reason. Cage cranked the wheel to the right and made the turn. Unlike Boomer and Bob's truck, the sedan he shared with his sister was not made for wheeling over the detritus in the road.

They carefully picked their way along, maneuvering around some obstacles and hopping out to push others out of the way. The going was painfully slow, and Cage was grateful Sarah wasn't in the car. She would have tried to have helped, and maybe injured herself further.

"Where should we turn off?" he asked. "Do we drive the side roads and just look around? What are the chances we'll find Izzy or Joule?"

But Deveron just turned the radio on and listened. Within moments, the car was full of names and locations, places for family members to report in. There were descriptions of small children who didn't know or couldn't say their own names. None of the information matched Joule or Izzy.

"Let's try to follow the path," Dev told him, pointing to the greater destruction on one side of the highway.

They turned onto a county road that was in no better shape than the one they'd left. Twenty minutes later, they hadn't gotten very far and they hadn't seen anyone, just a few damaged houses and a few animals wandering loose. But when Cage checked the rearview mirror, he didn't like what he saw.

As he watched, the sky grew dark, and he felt his heart do the same.

37

"Hold on!" Jerry called back and Joule grabbed tight to the edge of the flat metal she was calling a seat. Clamping her other hand carefully around Toto, she tried to cage the kitten to stop him from making any bad choices as the tractor bumped along the road, leaving Joule rattled.

Facing backward as she was, she couldn't see what was coming, but it was still the better option. The little front wheels didn't handle much of anything well, but the huge tires in the back ate up the terrain. They rolled right up and over branches, pieces of wood, and even a small tree.

Jerry seemed to know how to handle the equipment. Joule wouldn't have even tried. It had been his idea to pull the odd vehicle out of the barn. While Joule had been surprised to find that the key was waiting in the ignition, Jerry had expected to find it there.

"Who's going to steal a tractor?" he'd asked, and Joule didn't point out that they were doing exactly that.

But the farming equipment made the road pass far faster

than she ever could have walked. She'd even managed to open one of the cans of tuna and feed little flakes of it to Toto, who ate it with glee.

The kitten was having the time of his life, while she was tied in knots of worry.

Had Cage and Dev and Sarah made it through?

Had they stayed attached to the pipe or had the five friends been thrown five different directions?

She wanted to wonder why she hadn't found Izzy yet, but told herself that as long as she hadn't, she could still count Izzy as alive. While her own survival wasn't unheard of, she knew her tornado ride had beaten the odds.

The way she figured it though, she was far better off than she'd been earlier—despite the fact that it was Jerry she was with. She now had transportation, food, and water. By her calculations, she was good for at least another three days.

And surely, with the tractor tooling down the road, they would run into someone else, or some kind of functioning civilization well before then.

"Hold on!" he called back again.

She reached out quickly, now practiced at holding on and letting herself sway with the bounces. The tractor wasn't made for giving rides, and Jerry's warnings were often the only way she knew that she was going to get jostled and bounced around more.

Toto meowed softly but otherwise didn't seem to mind. And when the road settled back down, she let go.

Eww, Joule thought, looking at her tuna oil covered fingers. Toto wouldn't mind that she'd just touched the tractor with them, and she wasn't covered in grease or dirt or anything... just tuna. So she held them out for the little kitten to lick.

"Hey!" She yanked them back as he began to bite. "No, Toto, you don't eat fingers."

"You okay?"

"Just the kitten." She had to holler it, given the sound of the engine.

"Why are you even carrying him around? It's enough to get ourselves taken care of! He's just a burden."

She raised one eyebrow that he couldn't see, and whispered, "Cretin" to the kitten, who snuggled in deeper to her lap. He was small enough that she could see his little belly full of the tuna she'd fed him. She didn't answer Jerry.

Checking the position of the sun, Joule reasoned that they were now headed south or mostly south. Jerry had swung a left at the first crossroads they'd encountered, seeming to know the area.

He'd first retraced part of her steps that had gotten her to the Johnson farm, but now she didn't think she was completely backtracking. She clearly hadn't made the right choices initially. Still, somehow she'd run into another human being, even if it was Jerry. Though he wasn't her optimum "tornado survival companion," he had found them the tractor. She wouldn't have even thought to look for it.

As much as she disliked the guy, she couldn't say she'd wound up too bad off.

"Hold on!" he called back again, and for a moment, she wondered if maybe she should just hold on all the time.

She gripped the seat edge and Toto one more time before she got tossed side to side. It was an effort not to groan out at the way the hard seat—it wasn't actually a seat—hurt her hips and her spine. And she reminded herself to be glad that she hadn't whacked her head on any of the metal all over the big contraption. And again, she could be grateful that she wasn't walking.

She felt Toto purring in her lap and she couldn't help but kiss her finger and press it to his tiny nose. Carrying around

food and water and figuring out how to get them into him was a
bit of a challenge, but having another live creature—one who
was much better company than Jerry—had definitely kept her
hopes up. Joule was not a cat person ... but maybe she was
becoming one.

She swept her gaze across the landscape behind her,
starting to frown.

They bounced along for another few minutes as she
watched the sky slowly crept up behind them. She made her
way through another "Hold on!" which turned out to be Jerry
slowly Landrovering over a large section of siding from someone's house. Not far beyond that, he rolled over an eight-by-
four fragment of tin roofing. She only saw it as it emerged from
under the back tires. The mystery of "what are we bouncing
over now?" had occupied her for the past handful of miles.

If only she had any idea where she was or how far they'd
traveled.

Jerry seemed to enjoy rough-roading over objects rather
than getting out and simply pushing them out of the way.
When he took another small tree, she pulled her legs up
quickly, as one of the branches reached around and tried to
scratch at her.

Toto, awake now, disliked the rough ride, too, and he
climbed up her chest, his little claws sinking in as he made his
way to her shoulder.

She wondered if she might be smarter to put her jacket on,
now that he wasn't curled in it. At least it would put another
layer between her skin and Toto's toes.

But as the tractor settled down to smoother if slow-as-hell
ride, she glanced back up at the sky and realized that what she
thought she'd seen before was right.

And it was getting worse.

The sky was growing darker, though it was only maybe

early afternoon. There was no reason for the day to get so late, so quick, unless ...

Joule fought against the feeling of dread. Darkening skies always brought that out in her, probably some form of PTSD. *And well earned*, she thought.

She told herself that night hunters wouldn't appear at the edge of the shadows, but she wouldn't have been that surprised if they did. She didn't say anything, though, just turned around and looked in the direction they were going, seeing what Jerry saw.

In front of them was blue sky, pale and bright, with white fluffy clouds chugging along. When she turned and looked back, the darkness had crept even closer. "Jerry. You need to look behind us."

She felt the tractor change motion, maybe he'd downshifted or something. They slowed, though he didn't bring them to a complete stop. Joule could feel the motion through the machine as he shifted in the seat.

"Oh, that's not good. It's behind us, though."

"Not for long. It's moving toward us fast," she told him, able to see a change even from when she'd said his name to when he made his declaration. "Seriously, watch it."

He must have looked forward and back a couple of times, keeping the tractor on the road and giving her another "hold on!" which she bounced her way through again.

"Yeah, that's bad. We need to find a place to stop."

Having Jerry agree with her only made her feel worse. But he faced forward again, picking up speed and seeming to try to get ahead of it, even if the vehicle had a max speed of twenty.

They were simply too slow.

She watched the clouds line up and begin to roll. If it was possible, they were organizing the ions inside her to do the same thing, and Joule fought the urge to barf.

The funnel of clouds first formed sideways, then it bent its twisting, dark gray tail downward until it hit the ground.

"Jerry!" she yelled it at the top of her lungs as the wind picked up and Toto dug tighter into her shoulder. "We just got another one!"

38

"Turn it up. Turn it up!" Cage hollered into the car, waving his hand toward Deveron.

His friend handled the radio controls while Cage kept his eyes on the road. He couldn't afford to look away. Possibly damaging the car, or—worse yet—getting themselves into an accident would only compound their troubles.

The sky had turned steel gray in an instant as he watched in the rearview mirror and Cage wondered if Joule had possibly survived the first tornado, only to get killed by this new one.

The voice came through the radio in clipped but measured tones. "A funnel has touched down north of Horton. This sighting is reported by several local residents, though at this time we have no official confirmation or rating."

As the announcer repeated the wording slightly slower and a little more clearly, Cage flicked his eyes to Deveron, who shook his head in return. That's where they were headed—north—where they had previously hoped Joule and Izzy would have been dropped. Now, he wanted to be wrong.

Was the funnel ahead of them? There were trees on either side of the road now, too tall for them to see more than the dark clouds looming at the edges of their vision. And there was more darkness gathering behind them. Cage's eyes flicked to the rear view again... were funnels forming back there, *too?*

Holy crap, it seemed they were coming from every direction.

And what was with this day? They'd already had three!

He must have said it out loud, because Dev responded, "Apparently, it's common to see them in clusters."

"What?" Cage swerved at the last moment around a darting squirrel. The last thing he needed was animals jumping out and making the already obstructed roadway into even more of a hazard.

As he and Deveron righted themselves from the jerking motion, Dev answered, "I looked it up before moving here. The F scale. About the tornado they had here before we arrived."

Cage had done a little of his own research, too, but got the feeling that he and Joule had decided that the area was relatively tornado-safe. It was the whole reason Helio Systems was building the array here. So, he'd been prepared for dust devils, maybe the small kind of funnel that might twist the young trees, but not more.

As he drove into the darkening skies in front of them, the forests gave way to open land. In the not-too-far distance, he could see the roll of clouds forming as if an unseen baker's hand was curling dough.

Not learning more had been a mistake.

"They can drop right down on a sunny day," Dev was still telling him. "They can roll and turn sideways until they touch the ground. They can get bigger, smaller, lift up, touch down, jump, split, and collide."

Cage wished his friend would stop talking. He didn't need any of this. He didn't need to understand that, as he watched the clouds in front of him, they could become deadly in moments. What he'd already seen today was enough—*and why in hell wasn't it over yet?*

"See? We're watching it right now," Dev was still explaining. He leaned forward, one hand braced on the dash, the other pointing. "I don't know exactly what the pressure systems are— like which ones are which—but you can see where they collide and the clouds fold under and roll. Now it's just a question of whether a funnel tips down and touches the earth."

Cage felt his entire body tense. He'd been worried about the darkness behind them, but what was in front was now moving much faster.

The day suddenly looked like dusk. The clock in the car told him it was merely three in the afternoon. He'd seen storms roll in fast before, but this was different. Normal storms affected an entire area and spread their damage across as much as of the land as they could. Houses and structures stood or failed based on their integrity, not so much on the whim of the storm choosing to leave some places intact or focus all their rage on another. Tornadoes were more like lasers; they could pinpoint targets and completely obliterate them. They could leave another place, ten feet away, completely unharmed.

As the two watched, the funnel did exactly as Deveron had described: the left-hand side of it slowly tipped down to earth until it was perfectly vertical. As it hit the ground, it kicked up a skirt of dust and debris. Though still too far away for them to pick out any individual objects, he could see that it was moving.

And it was hungry.

Cage considered stopping the car and pulling to the side of the road, but somehow, it felt safer to stay in motion.

Reaching out, Dev put a hand on his arm as if to calm him. "We need to find a house and get inside somewhere. We need shelter."

So the tornado could lift his car and steal it, too? Cage thought bitterly. It wasn't the car that he was so protective of, it was his ability to search for his sister. The very thought of Joule being alone, on foot, out here tightened everything inside him, though he knew without question that his friend was right.

"Look around," he instructed. "Find us a place with a good cellar or substructure... something."

Maybe they would get lucky and pass a huge "Tornado shelter" billboard with an arrow pointing to a solid structure.

In the distance, the funnel danced softly, almost rhythmically, twisting right then left. The gray color changed ever so slightly as it moved, and Cage wondered if the color was a function of what it ate. But as he watched, it seemed the weight of the clouds pushed down into the funnel, and it grew wider and wider.

With a last sudden change of direction and a moment in which it simply took a breath and grew, the twister headed straight toward them.

39

"Come inside! We have a shelter!"

Cage recognize the sound of a bullhorn, but not the voice. As one, he and Deveron whipped their heads to the right, noticing the man on the porch as he waved his hands high, holding a bullhorn that completed the picture.

Without making a conscious decision, Cage cranked the wheel. The car spun tires as it tracked too quickly from pavement to gravel. The small sedan fishtailed a little before he managed to get it back on track.

The squat house waited for them at the end of the short drive. Cage could see the nice people who had decided to take pity on the pair driving past and save their lives.

As he got closer, he saw more than just the people waving them up the drive. Hands were in windows, pushing them open. The door flung wide, but to let others in. He and Dev weren't the only ones arriving. There must be an entire team of people inside, enacting whatever twister protocol they had. This was a normal-looking house, and it must have survived the first twisters that came through. They must have thought their day fighting storms was finished and already closed the windows from round one.

The man stepped down off the porch, the wind whipping what little hair he had combed over the top into a wild carica-ture. But his kind face matched his hands as he motioned Cage to bring the car to a stop. Then he waved them slightly one way and then the other, until he had them positioned where he wanted them.

He was leaving their car in the open. As Cage twisted the key out of the ignition and climbed out, he must have had an odd look on his face, because the man yelled, his voice pulled away as the winds picked up. "You don't want to be next to a tree or a structure. More likely something will fall on your car. Though honestly, it's a crapshoot."

He shrugged as if to say, "What can you do?" What he did say was, "Come inside, we have a real shelter."

Though he was older and not in as good shape as the two young men, he waited for the two to catch up and even move past him. He settled a hand at Cage's back, steering him up the steps and through the open front door. He didn't even bother to close it behind them. But in the short time it had taken them to enter the house, the wind had grown more forceful and Cage heard it slap the door shut behind them.

Ice flooded his veins—but not for himself. He had people and a shelter. But what about his sister? Where was she? Was she even alive? What about Izzy? Because, to a certain extent, Cage believed that Joule could survive anything.

Joule had faced night hunters on her own before they even knew what they were. Joule had been smart enough to buy boats before the waters rose. And if Joule had a pop-up tornado shelter in her pocket, he wouldn't say he was surprised.

But Izzy? As smart as she was, he didn't know if she was the kind of survivor that would make it through...

The man ushered the two of them into the center of the

house. In the living room, Cage could see the rug had been rolled back, revealing an open square that led down concrete steps into a space that must have been dug out underneath the low house.

Again the man followed behind them, as though to keep them safe. He was short, portly and balding, but still he protected them. He waited on the top step, carefully maneuvering himself through an odd dance to pull the trapdoor up and over. Closing it tightly, he started on a series of heavily bolted locks. As simple as they were, the construction was beyond solid. The bolts and eyes were thick, and the door made of steel.

Once he had the loops lined up, Cage helped the man slide a pin through a series of curved bars. They would stay in place even if they were flung around with high winds. And Cage thought that was smarter than maybe having a padlock that might require someone to have a key. Because as much as the tornado was locked out, the people were locked in.

When all five bars were in place and the door fully secured, Cage's heart settled just a little, feeling that they were safe and secure.

An F6 could raze the building above them, or blow it up, or steal it away. But this place looked like it would stay.

He turned, almost running into Dev, shocked at what must be twenty people— ranging from elderly to infants—crowded into the space at the bottom of the steps. Behind him, the man still hunched under the door he'd closed flat across the top of the steps gave them a small push. "Go on down. Lower is safer."

As they hit the last step, and he pulled up to his full—if short—height, he explained. "We built this fifteen years ago after a big one took out the house and killed my sister."

Cage understood. So many good things were built as a reaction to harsh loss.

"All the neighbors know to come and weather the storms

here," the man added and, as Cage looked at the crowd, he realized this wasn't just all the "neighbors."

These houses were too far apart for this many people. He
did a quick head count, coming up with more than the twenty
he'd originally guessed.

This man wasn't going to lose anyone else.

Holding out his hand, Cage said, "I'm Cage Mazur and this
is Deveron Swan."

The man nodded at both and simply replied, "William
Butler. All are welcome here."

In the corner, a mother curled up with two small children.
She waved to the newcomers, but quickly turned back to the
picture book she held open, hoping to distract her little ones.
Two others, slightly older, asked if they could join and she
welcomed them onto the blanket she'd laid out.

Several folding chairs sat propped against one plain
cinderblock wall. Feeling the sudden need to do something
other than stare or just stand around, Cage helped a man who
was opening the metal chairs and seating the elderly people on
them. One woman unfolded a soft blanket to pad the chair for
a man who must have been her father.

Cage would have done that for his father, but his mother
and father weren't like these people. And that's why they
weren't still here. He turned to ask William, "How can I help?"
But above him, the roar of the wind stole his voice as they all
looked up.

40

The tractor slowed as it hit the gravel of the driveway, making Joule's heart race.

"Jerry, go faster!"

But he called back, "We're fine."

She didn't believe him. The tractor was slow on a good road, and on the gravel, it was pure crap for speed. She watched the rocks crunch under the large tires and wondered if she could jump off safely and make a run for it.

With Toto, she didn't think so. And even without him, she might twist an ankle—something she couldn't afford with this kind of pressing danger.

She grabbed for the kitten, having thrown her jacket on, and hastily shoved him into one of the pockets, holding him in place. He must have been afraid enough to not squirm. She didn't like the funnel in the distance. Her heart raced every time she looked at it, but ignoring it didn't seem to work any better.

"Jerry, we're faster if we run!" Though as she said it, Joule began to wonder if Jerry could even run.

She had no problem making her decisions based on

keeping herself and Toto safe. But keeping Jerry safe? That was a harder call. Maybe she was a shitty person, but she didn't feel that one in her heart.

Joule reminded herself that he'd found the tractor and at least they were trying to work together.

"Not yet! I want to get closer to the house," he called back, and she turned again to face backward in her seat. Compared to what she'd seen earlier, this funnel was slim, twisting and dancing in the distance.

Maybe Jerry was right. Maybe this stupid, slow behemoth of a tractor could outrun it. She clutched the edge of the seat with one hand, the tiny kitten softly with the other, and her jaw tight enough to make her wonder if she was cracking her teeth. And she waited.

This was one of those moments that she didn't get to decide. Fate did.

Would the tornado pick up speed and rush toward them? Would they be too far from the house to run the remaining distance? And when they got to the house, what then?

She turned again and looked, trying to assess what this place might be like. Did it have a raised foundation or a real tornado shelter?

Jerry, still a good one hundred yards from the house, finally stopped the tractor. He stood up awkwardly, the steering wheel at his waist, the seat behind him, but he grabbed the keys and said "Okay."

Joule jumped onto the ground before he even managed to climb down. She was running for the front door, her hand still clutching Toto. The heavy objects in the pockets of her cargo pants bounced against her legs. Surely they were leaving more marks that she didn't need, but bruises were none of her concern right now.

"Around back!" Jerry yelled to her. "They have a cellar."

Jesus, did he know *everyone* in Alabama?

But Joule veered, swiftly changing direction. The extra distance she'd run let Jerry catch up to her as they headed around the house. Sure enough, dark green cellar doors slanted from the back wall, old-fashioned style. They probably stored root vegetables in there. The farmhouse was a slice of history still functioning in rural Alabama.

But she didn't have time to *oooh* and *ahhh* and marvel at the things she wasn't used to. Joule leaned down to lift one of heavy doors. As she wrapped her fingers around the handle, she noticed the lock.

Still bent over, still ready to tug the door open, she turned back to Jerry. The wind picked up, forcing her to yell. "There's a lock!"

The cellar wasn't worth anything if they couldn't get into it. Her second fleeting thought was that people left the keys in their very expensive and shiny, new tractor, but they padlocked their root vegetables?

But Jerry only nodded, not seeming to think too much of it.

Joule looked up, wondering if they could get into the main part of the house. It had to be safer than being out in the open. Once again, she had no qualms about breaking in. No one seemed to be here. Had rural Alabama simply fled during the storms?

The house looked almost too easy to break into. There were too many windows that looked like real glass. A large bay window had graced the front and even the back door had nine panels across the top. She could break one out and undo the locks ... too easily.

If the twister came through, it would pop this house like a packing bubble and all that glass would go everywhere. The cellar was definitely their best bet. She scanned the area, not sure what she was hoping to find until her gaze fell on several fist-sized rocks and she reached down to grab one.

She was going to have to take her hand off the kitten. What if he ran?

But as she looked up, she realized Jerry, too, was looking for rocks and saw that they had each found one about the right size.

Joule had to pray that Toto stayed put in her pocket as she hauled the rock back and brought it down to bash at the lock. She aimed away from the curved part, hoping to snap it free.

The lock wasn't anything spectacular, maybe just a good high school gym locker kind of combo lock. Beside her, Jerry brought his smaller but pointier rock down onto the lock.

The cellar doors shook with each hit. The old plywood was thick and sturdy but it had seen better days. Though it took more tries than she liked, and the lock never loosened, it eventually disintegrated. The metal fell into several pieces. The tumblers inside would have enticed further examination on any day that a tornado wasn't bearing down on her and the leader of some semi-violent protesters.

Joule fumbled the curved bar with heavy fingers, pulling it through the eyes bolted to the doors and chucking the damaged pieces aside. Together, she and Jerry lifted the doors and she spotted even more old school construction in the opening.

A tilted, ladder-like frame held slim steps made of two-by-sixes. They looked like they would at least bend if not maybe split with her weight, let alone Jerry's. Taking the first step downward, Joule felt the board flex beneath her boot. Her hand darted into her pocket and felt nothing but fleece.

Where was Toto?

She turned frantically as she tapped at her pockets, hoping she'd simply chosen the wrong one and he was on the other side, or somehow in a cargo pocket on her pants. Her eyes frantically scanned the yard, but ran into the bulk of Jerry, who blocked almost all of her view.

Even as she began to panic, she tapped at her jacket all the way across her chest and up to her shoulders where she found the tiny kitten. He had his claws dug into her shoulder, holding on tightly. She didn't even feel any of it as her sudden-onset panic at losing him quickly faded.

"Toto," she whispered in relief, and he replied with a frantic, "Mrrwow!"

Yes, there was a tornado bearing down on them. She could only get them both into the shelter of the cellar and then hope that the funnel skipped over this house.

Breathing out, she turned again and bolted down the steps with Jerry on her heels.

41

As Cage listened, the whipping sound of the wind outside turned slowly to the rumbling grind of a funnel on the ground nearby.

All the motion inside the shelter slowly came to a stop. He stood in the middle of the space, feet apart, as if he expected the ground to shake beneath him. And honestly, if it did, it wouldn't surprise him.

In the corner, the mother had stopped reading and now gathered her children close into her arms, their faces buried in her jacket. Cage only counted two kids now. The other two must have returned to their own parents, likely out of fear.

Dev looked to him, as if to say, *now what?* And Cage wondered what they'd done.

They were here—kindly offered an inside position in a very sturdy tornado shelter. As he looked around, he told himself that they would be okay. This place was built for exactly this problem. He didn't have any doubts that everyone down here would make it through whatever might pass overhead.

It might sound awful. Hell, it already did. But the walls would hold.

William Butler had already lost one family member. He wasn't going to lose anyone else.

But Cage and Dev had left Sarah behind at the house. She didn't have a room like this, only the rented Hideaway's central bathroom. The windows were newer, not glass but a polymer resin. Did that make them better or worse? He didn't know.

Sarah had only one usable arm. Had she managed to get some windows open and keep the pressure in the house from building up? Again, he didn't know.

How far had he and Deveron driven? Were they far enough away that maybe this thing wasn't even anywhere near her? There were no answers.

As he looked back to Dev, he could tell his roommate was having the same concerns about Sarah. And the problem was, with Sarah, it had been a choice. Joule and Izzy had been literally ripped from their hands. They'd done everything they could to stay safe, and they'd lost. But with Sarah, they'd made a foolhardy decision, thinking that the worst was over. And they'd bet that Sarah would be okay at the house by herself. Now he feared they were going to lose that bet.

She'd insisted the phones would get hooked up quickly, but that wasn't happening now. Could they even make it back to the house to check on her? What would the roads be like after another sweep of the havoc? The noise was making it clear that —even if this storm didn't hit this house or their house—things would be worse when they got out.

He turned again to Dev, but his roommate was already striking up a conversation with their host. "What happens if the house collapses on top of the door?"

Maybe not the best question in a time of crisis, Cage thought. As he watched, faces around the room turned toward Dev and William, some with curiosity, others with fear.

It seemed their position in the center of the space made Deveron's question ring out, alerting everyone.

Williams, at least, stayed calm. "There's a second door over there."

He said it loudly enough to be sure everyone heard that they had other options. That he'd planned ahead. He pointed to the side, and Cage noticed a door outline behind a pile of supplies. Metal shelves lined a wall with food and jugs of water. It didn't matter if they couldn't get out. Butler had them stocked.

The man kept talking calmly. "You can see that I don't even open it, but it exists for the exact event you just mentioned. So if the house falls on the upper door, we have a secondary exit."

It was almost too easy. A simple answer to a concerning question.

If only everything else could work as well and be as easy to pre-plan for.

Butler was opening his mouth again, but the noise outside seemed to chew at his words and swallow them.

Once again, all eyes turned upward, as if they could see through the ceiling above, through the floor of the house, and all the way up through the roof.

If it was still there, Cage thought, but then told himself that he wouldn't have missed the building getting torn apart above them. As thick as the cinderblock was, it wasn't dampening all the noise. Still, Cage didn't know what they could do about Sarah except pray to any gods that might be listening. He wasn't in a position to be picky.

As the noise ground through the walls, louder and louder, even the soft conversations in the corners came to a halt.

The relentless grind of the wind was now occasionally punctuated by sounds of the house getting beaten and pummeled. A crack made everyone jump, and then a heavy thump followed. But the time Cage heard something wrench above, no one was even fazed by the noises except the smallest of children.

He watched as the young mother pulled them closer, her lips moving as she must have been telling them something soothing. He still stood in the middle of the room, feet apart, though the floor hadn't shaken once.

But then it did.

42

Joule hit the bottom of the twitchy cellar steps and whirled around to watch. Jerry stomped down behind her, each piece of wood bending under his greater weight.

She saw the angry flash of sky in the distance as he turned around in an attempt to stand on the steps and still grab at the cellar doors. Joule realize the problem—there was no light down here. As Jerry tugged at the doors, what little she could see faded into the shadows.

She decided to be grateful that there were handles on the undersides of the cellar doors. But how would they keep them closed as the wind picked up? Hanging onto the doors would prove too dangerous, even for Jerry, who outweighed her by who-knew-how-much. What was down here that she could use?

She scrounged through what she could see, even as she checked the corners of her brain for an idea. They had tossed the pieces of the padlock aside when they yanked it off. Would the small curve of metal even stay in place? She didn't think so.

As soon as the doors rattled, it would bounce around and fall off without the lock to hold it in a secure spot.

Though she wouldn't have said her eyes had adjusted, she could still see a bit with the light that filtered through the gaps. The spaces wouldn't play well if the twister went over them, which was all the more reason to get these doors secured by some means other than "Jerry holds tight."

Sure enough, there were shelves down here, filled with things that might be turnips, or rutabagas. She recognized a bag of potatoes, but they'd clearly been purchased at the grocery store. Joule would have laughed, but it would have burbled out into a high pitched hysteria, so she held it in.

"Got anything?" Jerry called down from his odd perch on the steps.

"Still looking." She didn't look up as she searched as best she could in the fading light.

Jerry stayed put, with his thick fingers laced through the two door handles, holding it shut. It didn't seem yet the wind was actually trying to steal it from him. And it was entirely possible that the storm would shift direction and they'd never be in danger. But having already been carried away by one tornado today and left with very little memory of what she'd endured, Joule wasn't eager to repeat the experience.

She scrounged further until, "A-ha!"

Under the steps was a wooden box with a hinge lid. When she lifted it, it creaked but she was thrilled to find tools.

"Here!" she called, holding up a short crowbar, and watching as Jerry slid it through the door handles. It didn't seem to be the right size to jam into place, leaving Jerry holding it much as he had held the door handles.

That sucked. She rummaged through more, pawing in the dark through rusted screwdrivers and hacksaws and old door knobs. Eventually, her fingers brushed against fabric and she felt her way through the dark box until she pulled out tie down straps and then several bungee cords.

"Here!" Once again, she held her find up to Jerry, who very neatly anchored the crowbar into place with a figure eight of bungees.

"Good," he said into the dark. Between the day being wiped away by clouds and the doors being secured against the remaining daylight, there was little left to see by.

"Do you have a light?" she asked. Her eyes were now useless. Her hand went to her shoulder to check that Toto was still sitting there, claws still dug in. As her hand patted his soft fur and he squirmed a little under her touch, it calmed her racing heart for just one more moment.

"Hold on," Jerry told her, bringing her back to the task at hand as a light flicked on.

Joule blinked, her head automatically jerking back and her hands coming up to ward off the brightness. She hadn't yet adjusted to the dark, but she wasn't ready for the light. Jerry walked down the last two steps with the way well lit.

Only then did she place what he had. "That's your cell phone!"

"Yeah," he replied as if to say, *what of it?*

He'd had his cell phone this whole time?

He seemed to hear her incredulous thoughts. "The towers are out. I've got no signal."

True, she thought, *but still...* "At least turn off the light and conserve the battery, so that when we do get signal, we can call someone."

He didn't comment one way or the other, but the light quickly disappeared.

Once again, Joule blinked as her eyes adjusted. At least this time she'd seen her way around and knew where she was heading.

Jerry started to ask her something, but the roar from

outside grew as it grabbed at the cellar doors and began to pummel them.

"What did you ask?" she called out, glad she couldn't feel the wind down here, even if she could hear it. She pulled Toto from her shoulder and clutched the tiny kitten in front of her.

"I said—" he yelled. "I hope the cellar doors hold!"

She nodded, then realized he couldn't see her either. So she added, "Me, too."

She wondered if he was having the same thought she was. The crowbar and the bungee cords were excellent and he'd put in the same knot she would have. Her dad had showed her how to build and design, and then she'd added a mechanical engineering degree to it. She knew that the doors themselves were likely to be the problem.

But she thought back to what she'd seen ... When she pulled one open, it had been heavier than it had appeared. The plywood was a little warped, indicating it was thin, but the doors weren't.

As Jerry tried to pull them closed, she'd seen the thickness of them, the flat side underneath. Her engineer's brain had cataloged all of this. The hinges looked relatively heavy and new, though the doors were old. But they were bolted into the wood that framed the opening of the stairs, and that wasn't too sturdy. The system was only as solid as its weakest point, and her money was on that wood giving way first.

She realized now what had bugged her about the doors: they had an underlay of newer, fresh plywood. It was done as though someone had seen fit to reinforce what was already there, rather than simply making new doors from the clean plywood ...as if the builder didn't want the repair noticed.

"Can we sit down?" he called out, and it seemed better than just standing here and waiting for the doors to blow off.

"I think so," she said, then slowly began shuffling along, one hand out to feel for the edge of the shelves she'd seen before. "We should sit in a corner. Away from the cellar doors."

The floor was made of wood, old slats that didn't quite look sturdy, and it brought to mind the Little House on the Prairie books she'd read as a kid. But she found the shelf and followed it along to the wall where she slid down and seated herself. Maybe she was glad she couldn't see well. The place had seemed less-than-clean when the light was on. Definitely a root cellar.

"Over here," she called out, using her voice to direct Jerry to sit next to her. She would have put him on the opposite wall were it not for fear of the tornado grabbing one of them and pulling them out. They had better odds together, and she liked those odds more than she disliked Jerry.

He thumped down next to her, taking a moment to arrange his less-than-lithe form. Clearly, sitting on the floor wasn't something he did often, but she didn't say anything.

As the noise outside got higher and higher, it seemed that each moment, the twister must be right on top of them. But in the next minute, the noise would get louder still, and the cellar doors would rattle even more, proving her previous thoughts incorrect.

She and Jerry fell quiet.

The raging noise outside seemed to calm for a moment, but Joule couldn't tell what a calm day sounded like anymore. Maybe it was just a slightly less terrifying noise, but it made her wonder if the funnel had twisted away from them. Joule felt her hopes rise.

Jerry took the reduced noise as a hint that they should make conversation. She couldn't fault him; maybe he was just soothing rough nerves.

"What did you say the kitten's name was?"

"Toto," she replied easily, thinking she could do this. She could make small talk with Jerry, especially about a cute kitten that had burrowed its way into her pocket again. She put her hand against the soft fur and thought that the studies about cats lowering the likelihood of heart attacks was probably right. By his very existence in her pocket, Toto was calming her.

She could survive this tornado, too. *They* could. And she could live to be mad about Jerry's stupid protests another day.

"Why?" he asked. "Did you miss the rains down in Africa?"

She could hear him chuckle.

"Nooooo." She drew the word out and wondered if he'd simply missed the reference. She prompted, "I found him after a *tornado*."

"So?" Jerry asked. "That doesn't explain his name. You could have named him, 'Hold the Line.'"

Something inside her snapped. She'd had enough of this day, enough of these storms, and honestly, she'd had enough of Jerry long before this conversation had ever started. It was not her best foot forward.

"Listen, Scarecrow. It's actually an easier reference to get than an eighties band!"

But whatever Jerry had replied was overpowered by the sound as the winds kicked up and yanked at the cellar doors harder this time. The roar of the wind and the damage and sheer anger of the storm stole everything as the new funnel once again targeted them.

43

J oule pressed her back against the cold earth wall of the cellar, clutching Toto closely to her chest. Given the wind and the noise, the tiny kitten didn't seem to object at all to being held so tightly.

The harsh sound of the storm seemed to scrub at everything beyond the cellar door. It whipped at the plywood, wracking it against the hinges and trying to steal it away. From beyond the dark, she could hear trees cracking, or maybe that was the house above her. She heard splintering noises, pops, thumps, crashes, and more. In here, it was dark, and still. But beyond the tiny space, the world was being ravaged.

For a moment, Joule panicked that she wasn't tied to anything. But this time, she didn't have to be; she wasn't stuck out in the open. She was safe—or at least as safe as she could be.

Her brain ran wild, thoughts leaping radically from one idea to the next. She considered the possibility that she would die here, that—after everything else—this would be where she met her demise. She considered the possibility that she would survive this tornado but be trapped. And who would look for them here? She wanted to ask Jerry if anyone would come, but the effort it would take to yell such a ridiculous question wasn't worth it.

Her heart pounded in her chest, and she broke out all over in a cold sweat. Rubbing Toto's soft fur, she petted him in long strokes from his ears to the tip of his tail until the tiny kitten actually began purring. *Oh*, she thought again, *to have a giant of her own*. Someone who could make her feel safe enough to purr in the middle of all of this.

Certainly, the tiny kitten needed to be fed again by now, but there was no good way to get to a tuna can. Pulling a metal tab in the dark was a good way to cut her finger. She had no supplies, no light, and this cellar was probably the best place to pick up an infection. So she decided to wait at least until the kitten whined.

In the pocket on her pants leg, she still had most of the bottle of red-flavored sports drink. But she realized she might now need to start rationing it. It had been intended to last only several hours while she walked. Either until she found someone or until she got back to a stream where she could scoop up more water. Down here, there was no water and nothing to drink, only a bag of potatoes and some root vegetables. At least she was glad she told Jerry to pick up his own drink out of the yard and that she wasn't rationing the one bottle between the two of them.

But what should Toto drink? Anything other than water or kitten milk probably wasn't appropriate for a kitten his age, but she was equally out of both. At least he wasn't mewing at her. He didn't 'appear hungry and seemed perfectly content to burrow into the front of her jacket and let her pet him.

Her head snapped at a harsh crack above them. Beside her, she felt his movement as Jerry flinched at the same time. He seemed like such a big burly dude that knowing that he cringed at every sound, too, was at least a little comforting.

She didn't know how long she sat there, but the storm seemed interminable. The noise shifted and changed every second, keeping her muscles clenched and never letting her know if the cellar door was going to fly off or crash inward. Never knowing if the roof would cave in on them, because it certainly sounded like it would.

Though the cellar doors flapped and creaked and lifted as though they were going to get sucked away, the hinges held. Every minute that the doors were still there, Joule was grateful. If she'd known any tornado survival prayers, she would have prayed, because it was all that was left.

At last, the noise died down. But still, she held her breath.

Surely it was coming back. Surely, it couldn't be over. Surely another funnel would form and chase her to another ditch, another cellar. Who knew where or when, but she was willing to bet this wasn't the end.

The eerie silence was almost more disturbing than the noise had been. She couldn't place anything, and the disquiet wormed its way into her bones.

Did tornadoes steal the birds and toss them away to distant places? She didn't know.

Was the wildlife gone? Either run off or scrubbed by the beast... She didn't know.

But at last it became clear that sitting here was hurting more than it was helping. If someone was driving by on the road outside, she and Jerry had missed them. It was time to get out and see what the damage was.

She carefully slipped Toto into her pocket again and stood, realizing as she did, that she'd either been there much longer than she thought, or was much more tense than she'd thought. Her knees screamed at her as she tried to unfold them. The pain in her lower back as she stretched upright told her all she needed to know. But she didn't want it to stop her. It was going to hurt anyway.

So she slowly shuffled around, hands out, until she hit the bottom step with her lower shin. She muttered a curse word.

"You hurt?" Jerry asked, followed quickly by, "What are you doing?"

"Checking the doors," she said. She reached up as she climbed the steps slowly. Her hands were out in front of her, crawling upward on all fours. Slowly, she reached up over her head each time she made a move, in hopes that she wouldn't first bonk her head. Joule slowed down as she remembered the short crowbar that held the doors together. It was old and rusted, but the pry edge was still relatively sharp. She moved her hand around above her head again before moving slowly up another step.

This time when she reached up, she felt her fingers slide along the elastic of the bungees, as she felt for the hook at the end. Jerry had wound it tightly and it took a few moments in the dark to get it undone. Behind her he'd stayed quiet. So he'd either stayed put or had skills she didn't know about.

She unwound the bungee cords slowly with her right hand, one by one putting them into her left to hold onto. When she had all of them off and the pry bar was the only thing holding the handles together, she grabbed it and twisted it over her head until she got it oriented the right way and it slid free.

With a deep breath, she grabbed the handle of the cellar door and pushed upward.

It didn't give.

She tried again.

Nothing.

Then she wised up and tried the other handle. But it also didn't budge.

"Jerry?" she asked. "The doors don't move. Do you want to try this?"

He was larger than her. He had to be stronger. At least this made Jerry useful. She heard him moving around behind her and then felt the steps flex under her feet as he stepped on the bottom rung.

"Hold on, let me get down the steps first," she told him, shuffling her way backwards. At the bottom, she brushed past him, not quite gauging how close it was. With her feet on the floorboards, she could feel the equipment in her hand, feel the soft weight of Toto sleeping in her pocket, and she could hear Jerry going up the steps. But she couldn't see anything, just the ghost edges of lines teasing her in the dark.

Before she'd watched the ladder-style stairs sag as he stepped on them. Now she heard them creak in protest under his weight. She wondered what would happen if he broke through them. How would they get out?

She heard the banging sounds of him pushing upward on the doors, again and again, until he declared, "They're blocked. I can't move it."

Joule's shoulders sagged with the news. Her breath huffed out in a half-hearted "shit."

But then Jerry turned to her and said, "This is all your fault."

44

C age stood back, letting William Butler direct a few of the men he knew to unbolt the lid to the shelter. It slid back on creaky hinges, making a slow arc into the open air above them.

Holy shit, Cage thought as he looked up and saw only a blue sky.

It was possible that part of the house was still standing. But he could see that at least a good chunk of it was missing.

"Well, fuck," Butler muttered, issuing the least likely curse Cage had expected of the older man. Now he motioned to the others to stay as he passed them, walking reverently up the stairs and into the space beyond. It was his house and his shelter, after all.

Cage could see Butler's feet, standing on the floor just beyond the door. He gave a little bounce, as if testing the integrity of the floor, before turning in a full circle.

His feet returned to the opening, shiny black shoes making a statement as he walked back down. He carried himself like an actor or politician coming to address the people below. But then he pulled up short, as if coming back into the shelter was simply too much for him.

Leaning over, William Butler placed his hands on his knees, bringing his head into sight to those waiting below for his proclamation. The position looked awkward, but no one cared. They all hung on the silence waiting for any announcement.

"The house is completely gone."

Gasps greeted him from the people in the corner, who hadn't seen what Cage had. He worried about his car, and his first thought was shoving his way up the steps and past the older men, onto the surface of the foundation to see the yard. But in the same heartbeat, it occurred to him that everyone here had a car to check on, if not a home or a family member.

Even as he thought that, Butler began instructing them. "Let's all make a nice, orderly exit. These are your neighbors, so be kind. Before anyone moves, who has family they need to find?"

Butler had clearly thought this through before, but it was the wrong question. All but five of the hands went up.

"All right," he backpedaled a bit. "Who's missing small children?"

Only two hands raised up this time. A couple, it looked like.

"Come on." Butler waved them up as the first ones out, reaching toward them as though he was going to hold their hands and direct them up the stairs. The two other men still standing on the staircase took that upon themselves.

"Who has teenagers to find?" Butler asked. This time four hands went up, and they were escorted up.

"Is anybody willing to wait and go last?" he asked next.

Cage and Deveron weren't in this category either. However, the mother with the two small kids pointed out that they were asleep—sweaty and breathing raggedly, but asleep. She motioned that she was willing to wait right where she was, as did several other older people. So did the woman who was there with her father. They would be happy to go slowly and be last, she told them.

Cage and Deveron awaited Butler's motion for their chance to go, though it was hard to wait patiently in the small line and try not to push their way forward.

When he reached the top, Cage saw that people hadn't scrambled off in different directions. They'd been stopped by what they saw. Some were still standing on the foundation of the house, which was truly all that was left. Some of them looked out or up in awe, turning and taking in the world scrubbed free of so many things that it had had before: houses, trees, fences, outbuildings, and more.

They'd come up first to find family, but now they were struggling to even find focus.

Others were picking through the debris that littered the floor of the once-stately home. One man was walking the edge of the foundation and yelled out, "Here! This is probably the safest place to climb down. Did anyone find steps?"

But no one had.

In a flash of memory, Cage remembered the wooden front deck. As he turned and looked in what he was confident was the right direction, he found there was no deck at all. No sign of it.

Thank God for the cinderblock shelter. And for William Butler, not only letting all of his neighbors in, but standing on his doorstep and calling out for passersby with a bullhorn at the ready. If Cage had ever doubted that preparedness paid off, this would have turned the tide.

"Car looks good," Dev told him, and Cage whipped around, realizing he'd been facing entirely the wrong direction.

While Deveron was right, and the car seemed intact, they were far from ready to resume their search. A huge tree had fallen across the driveway. He wasn't even sure he'd be able to pick a path around it.

So he still had the car, but it didn't look like he could get to a road. As his eyes tracked further beyond the car, Cage realized he couldn't even *see* the road. Or could he?

Trees were down, pieces of homes littered the area, and he realized that he could see bits of tarmac through the debris. The road was still there. But it might be a while before a car could pass it, so it probably didn't even matter if he could drive around Sanders' tree.

He'd never wished for a monster truck more in his whole life. As he surveyed the damage, his heart fell. This looked worse than the last one, though he really had no real frame of reference to gauge by. Maybe it had just hit a little closer. He was sure the radio announcer would tell him everything as soon as he could get the station dialed in.

Maybe it got better once he got beyond this area. Maybe this one had simply taken out more trees and the damage looked worse. He hadn't even seen the funnel this time—not close, not as it went by. He'd seen the other one, but this one he'd only spotted in the distance.

The shelter had made everything so much easier. He hadn't been whipped back and forth, had his head cracked against Deveron's, his arms and legs threatening to form hairline fractures or even full breaks each time the wind grabbed and yanked at him.

As he thought about it now, he and his roommates should have all been checked for mild concussions back when they were at the community center. But as Sarah had rightly complained, the line was too long.

He turned now, looking to Dev and shaking his head. Was he even thinking clearly? And how would he know?

"How do we get to Joule and Izzy now? How do we get back to Sarah?"

45

Joule felt her head snap back at the accusation. Despite the fact that it was still pitch dark, she blinked hard. "This is *my* fault? Me *personally*?"

She sounded incredulous even to her own ears. And she felt that was the right reaction to have. She heard the stairs creaking under Jerry's weight as he moved downward, and she waited for him to poke her in the chest to make his point.

"You people." He ground out the words. "You come in here and you screw everything up."

She was frowning, her head moving forward with a look on her face that suggested he was being a dumbass, despite the fact that he surely couldn't see her. She didn't try to put on her friendly face but released at least some of her sudden tension by letting her expressions loose.

"Did you really just 'you people' me? And *what* did we screw up?" He had to be talking about the Helio Systems solar array.

"You walked in here like you own the place and you stole our jobs!"

"But don't you still have a job?" she asked. Seriously, he did. Radnor had checked after Jerry had made such a big splash in the protests.

"Well, not for long."

"So you *do* still have a job?"

"Not for long," he repeated. "My family's going to starve!"

Interesting. She didn't know he had a family. For a moment, she wondered *who would have him?* Horrible, uncharitable thoughts, she knew, but the man had just blamed her for basically everything.

"Why would you starve? Helio Systems offered you a job."

He didn't reply, but she could hear his angry breathing and wondered if she was far enough away to duck a punch she couldn't see coming. She tried again, this time shifting the topic just a little. "How much are you making now?"

"That's none of your business!"

Fair, she thought, but didn't say.

She was still standing in the dark, still wondering how the hell they were going to get out if even Jerry couldn't budge the cellar doors. But it seemed like convincing the only other person down here that she wasn't responsible for all hell breaking loose was maybe the first task.

"Helio Systems is offering jobs to anyone who's been displaced by the solar array coming in. For anyone losing some of their work from coal. They start at a good rate." She rattled off the opening pay, remembering it from Dr. Murasawa's comments at the town hall. "Can I ask if that's more or less than what you're making now?"

"I don't want to retrain! I work coal!"

His angry response almost surely meant the offer was more than he was currently getting. If it was less, then he had a valid complaint. But he sure wasn't saying that.

"I'm sorry that you don't want to retrain, but it's paid training. Don't you also want to leave your mountains intact for your future generations?"

For that family he was worried about starving?

"Coal is what my family has done for three generations!"

She didn't have a response to someone so entrenched and unwilling to budge. She understood family loyalty. Her family were scientists. Joule felt that research and building were in her blood. Her grandfather had been a Navy CB—construction battalion—a coveted spot. Her great grandfather on the other side had been an engineer in World War II. So she understood the idea of generations following in footsteps. But a four-generation chain didn't seem that long. Was three really a full "family tradition?"

"Well, if your family is in energy," she tried again, "you would still be in energy. You'd still be providing power to the community." She almost added, *It's a noble position*, but she'd really had enough of Jerry. She tried to change the topic once again. "We need to get out of here."

"It's your fault. All these tornadoes. You people brought them here."

"*What?*"

"This is what happens when you mess with God."

Joule shoved her hand into her pocket, stroking Toto for the requisite help to her bite her tongue and not lash out the way she wanted to. "This is a tornado. It's a weather system, a meteorological event, not revenge."

"So, you're one of them atheists, too?"

"No!" she blurted out, quickly and handily. "I just don't believe in a God who takes revenge on his own people! And I don't believe in a God that gets mad at us for trying to do better by the earth He gave us."

"He gave us coal!" Jerry replied.

"Well, he gave us the damn sunlight, too! And we're supposed to be the stewards of the earth, aren't we? Strip mining the mountains hardly seems like the right way to do that."

She wished she'd had something better. But her chest was heaving with anger, and her short temper was keeping her from her best thinking. Joule didn't have a place in her heart for people who thought like Jerry. She fully understood, particularly in agricultural systems, that deities often took the place of meteorological systems. But she wasn't going to take the personal blame for it!

"We have to get out of here. Should we try pushing on the doors together?"

Only silence greeted her in return.

Joule waited a moment, hoping to simmer down and thinking Jerry would come around. When he didn't, she added, "We can die in here together, or we can get out of here together. Should we push on the doors or not?"

"Fine!" He bit the word off, and she wasn't sure about getting close enough to him to help push on the cellar doors. But the only way away from him was out of here.

It took a moment in the dark to maneuver both of them up the steps, with her on a higher step than him because she was shorter. With one foot low and one foot up a step, she tried to brace herself for a good upward shove.

"On three," he said, and she was more than willing to let him feel like a big man by running the count down.

But when they pushed, they only managed to budge the doors a little. All that effort for nothing.

"Feels like something's across it," he said.

Something big, Joule thought, *and heavy*.

She felt around to the sides of the doorway, wondering if the hinges hadn't given way. Had they maybe borne out her theory that they weren't sturdy?

She wondered if she could pry them off. If so, then they

could pull the doors down in. Maybe they could squeeze through whatever was blocking the doors from opening.

"Can you grab me the crowbar?" she asked. "It's down on the floor, to the left of the steps.

Below her on the stairs, she heard and felt him move. Even through the flexing of the old staircase, she could feel his irritation.

But a moment later, he said, "Here. I'm holding it out."

Joule waved her hand slowly and gently through the air until she grabbed it. It took another few moments to locate the hinges and to line the sharp edge of the bent end of the crowbar under the metal.

She leaned in, putting everything she had into pushing. Then she tried pulling down on the bar. The hinges didn't budge.

Now, when she ran her fingers over the pieces she could feel the bolts themselves. They seemed to have unusually large heads for a job like this. She wondered how long they were and why someone had felt such a need to protect their rutabagas?

She had a sinking feeling that they were in more trouble than she'd realized.

46

Cage and Deveron dropped over the edge of the Butler house foundation, leaving the steps at the back for those who needed them.

He clicked the button on his key chain, happy when the car beeped back at him and the lights flashed. He opened the back door and spotted the food bag. He must have been looking for it without realizing it, because he was suddenly ravenous. If the feeling was because he was actually hungry, or because he'd finally seen food, or because he was nervous and needed to fuel it in some way, it didn't seem to matter.

"Here." He'd torn open one of the granola bars and with the other hand held the bag out toward Dev, noticing that his roommate's hand dove into the bag as quickly as his own had.

Reaching into the second bag in the back seat, he pulled out the water bottles that Sarah had sent along. The first granola bar was gone within a second and he grabbed for a pack of chips and basically poured them down his throat. Crackers came next and then the water bottle was polished off. He couldn't comment about Dev doing the same thing because he was stuffing his own face so handily.

When he finally stopped eating, he looked to Dev. "What do we do?"

His roommate only shrugged as he looked around the ravaged landscape. "I think we're stuck."

Cage shook his head. He *couldn't* be stuck. He didn't know how to deal with being stuck. If something attacked him, he figured out how to fight it. In this case, though, nothing was actually attacking him. Nothing hunted him. He was fighting the vagaries of a weather system. And how could he fight something that didn't think, didn't need, didn't hunt?

A fist-sized fluff of cotton drifted past his feet, darting in and out of the tree branches. He wondered if maybe the answer was to be smaller, not bigger.

"Bicycles," he said to Dev.

"Interesting..." He could see his friend thinking it through. "Easier to maneuver, with everything blocking the road—and, if need be, we can lift them and carry them over things."

"Where do we get good mountain bikes?"

"There's a shop on Buffalo Street," a voice said behind them.

Turning, Cage recognized the man only as having been down in the shelter with them. But that was enough. He said hello, introduced himself formally, and it took less than three minutes to strike a deal.

All hands were suddenly on the tree that was blocking Cage's car into the driveway. With everyone pushing at it, the heavy trunk yielded. For a while, they used brute force and slid it back, scraping the gravel with it. Then they wised up and managed to hack at some of the branches and roll it a little farther.

"I think that should do us," the man, Carl, said as he looked back up to the house to wave to Butler. He called up, "Is it okay if we drive around on the grass?"

Butler just laughed back at him. Cage had gotten the

impression that grass down here was not a precious commodity. And, with everything else that was going on in this yard, a few tire tracks on Butler's wet grass wasn't going to make a difference.

"Let's do it," Dev said and he opened the car door for Carl's wife, Brandy, letting her slide into the front passenger seat.

Cage was ready to climb in when he remembered Boomer and Bob's directive. He could still follow it. Looking up, he asked, "Does anyone else need a ride down to the road? We're heading south."

It's not the direction he wanted to go to find Joule, but it was the direction they needed to go next.

Another couple replied quickly that they could use a ride, and Cage wound up with four people crammed across his back seat. But he was grateful to be doing the work the brothers had tasked him with.

The driving was slow and arduous, maybe only a little faster than walking, given that they repeatedly got out to clear the road. Cage was once again glad that there were six of them as they pushed trees, branches, and debris away to make a path. Their numbers definitely made the work faster.

He dropped two of them off roadside about a mile down the road, when they insisted they could walk from there. And then Carl and Brandy made it another mile before getting out. Brandy held the door open, leaned down, and looked in at him. "You're going to go another mile on this road. And you're going to hit a little section of shops, like, just three of them."

She emphasized how small the little strip was and motioned with her perfectly manicured nails. "But the last one is a sports shop. You wouldn't know it from the outside. But if you go in the back, there's bikes."

"How do we get in?"

She looked at him, stood up, looked around, and bent back down to talk to him in the car. "I don't know for sure, but my guess is right now you can walk right through the front of the store."

Seeing the damage on the road in front of him, Cage guessed Brandy might very well be right.

The couple thanked him again. But then she closed the door and she and Carl headed off to figure out what damage their own place had sustained.

It was growing dark by the time Cage and Dev reached the store. With Brandy's directions, it was easy to find and identify. Sure enough, the baseball gloves, bats, and golfing equipment in the front window gave no indication of mountain bikes. But in a stroke of luck, the front windows were, in fact, shattered wide enough for them to easily climb through.

Along the back wall was a small selection of mountain bikes. They picked out two and grabbed tools for adjustment. Then they raided the store. Cage grabbed a basket and added a tire inflation kit, helmets, and lights. He headed to the other side of the store to look at the gloves. Finding a set he liked, he tossed a second pair to Dev.

"Dude," Dev replied, instantly tossing them back. "I'm going to be hard pressed for my half of what we already have."

"I've got it," Cage told him.

Dev raised one eyebrow. "I thought you were making the same as me."

"I am." It was hard to say. Still, Deveron deserved a reasonable explanation. "Joule and I lost our parents just over five years ago. So we're making the same as you, but we have a bit of a stash from the life insurance. My parents would have wanted me to spend it finding Joule."

Dev, always smart, didn't ask how or why his parents had died, but merely nodded and said, "That explains a lot about you and your sister."

This time, when Cage tossed him the gloves, he grabbed them out of the air and added them to his own pile. It was easier to accept gifts in an emergency, and easier knowing that Cage was going to press Dev into service for finding Joule.

A few moments later, they had everything laid out on the countertop except the two bikes. Dev pulled his cell out and took a photo. They left a paper message with both their names and phone numbers, and the address of Desperado's Hideaway, not that they were sure it still existed. They taped the scrawled note down to the countertop and took a picture of that, too.

They couldn't send the photos to anyone yet. Dev's cell bars were still nonexistent, the words "no signal" filling the space at the top of his phone. But at least they had the pictures as backup to prove they intended to pay for the equipment.

Twenty minutes later, they were on the road, the thick bike tires eating up the distance. As predicted, the bikes maneuvered through the small spaces between debris much easier than the car ever had. Cage didn't say anything to Dev, but he understood they were headed back to Desperado's Hideaway first. It was the only real option. But they had no idea what they would find when they got there.

47

I t was full dark by the time they neared the house, and Cage was grateful for getting the headlamps and bolting them to the fronts of the bikes.

They'd attached flashers to the back and had lights on the fronts of their helmets, too. Cage had thought it was better to be seen, even if nobody else was traveling the roads right now.

As the evening grew darker, he'd discovered that the lights were less for others and more for them. The powerful beams were the only thing lighting the road for them.

He'd also grabbed a small radio, which Dev insisted be attached to Cage's bike. That had proved to be another smart installment. They'd listened to announcements, including long lists of names of people who'd turned themselves in at the community center. Others had been located by rescue teams. Some had simply gotten a handheld radio and contacted the station to let people know they were safe. The lists were long, but none had included Sarah Carter, Isabel McAlister, or Joule Mazur.

There were also descriptions of small children. Those were the ones that broke Cage's heart and made him pedal harder when his legs felt like they couldn't go any farther. Despite all the work out in the fields, and his much-improved physique from it, biking was not the same as squatting and catching lizards, and his muscles were not pleased with him.

Cage and Deveron were another mile down the road by the time the announcer began listing off happy reunions. At least, Cage thought, some people had found each other. That meant there was still hope for him.

"Is that it?"

Cage pulled to a stop. Behind him, Dev had his feet planted on either side of the bike, his finger raised. The blue gloves with white reflective tape were another strangely helpful tool in the dark. Cage had just been aiming at protecting their hands, but these, too, turned out to be more necessary than he'd expected.

"Wow!" He'd almost been ready to bike right past it. Riding a human-powered machine made him very cautious about not making any unnecessary motions. "It is."

They'd almost missed the turn for the Hideaway. He frowned for a moment before realizing that he usually recognized this turn at night, directed by the streetlight at the corner.

"Is the light out?... Nevermind," Dev asked, the tone of his voice at the end of the sentence indicating he'd realized his mistake.

Of course it was out. Everything was out.

The only light they had came from the headlamps on their bikes and the ones on their helmets. Thank God they'd been smart enough to pick up every light they could. It must have been a new moon or too much cloud cover, because Alabama was pitch black.

"Nah man," Cage replied. "The entire streetlamp is gone."

If he hadn't remembered that he'd used the light as a landmark, he wouldn't have known the light was missing. The ground was churned up in several places, and now there wasn't any real evidence a lamp post had once stood here.

"Dammmnnnn," Dev drew the word out as he got moving again and passed Cage, making the turn.

The gravel was noticeably harder to bike on than the road had been. Another tree had fallen across their drive, this time a small sapling. Cage considered getting off the bike and moving it out of the path, but Dev waved him away.

"There's no car here to clear the drive for."

They'd left his car at the bike shop. Sara's car was destroyed —whether or not anyone had towed it from a ditch yet remained to be seen. So they biked to the edge of the gravel and hopped off. Lifting the bike made his muscles protest again, but Cage didn't say anything as they picked their way through the branches and then pushed the bikes the rest of the way up to the house.

Halfway there, a light flicked on in a window. The building appeared to be relatively intact, or at least as intact as it had been the last time they were here.

"Hello?" a voice called out. "Hello?"

"Sarah!" they both cried out in unison, their pace picking up.

"Cage! Dev!" The light danced around, moving closer. As it dropped several feet, Cage sucked in a breath for a moment, but realized it was simply Sarah with a flashlight jumping down from the edge of the foundation rather than heading around the steps to the front porch.

As she got closer, he could see her face from the lights on the bikes and the relief that swept through him was over-whelming. She had been their first check for a number of reasons. The main one being that they knew where she was supposed to be. They could easily get a yes/no answer if Sarah was there. And if she needed help, they might be able to find it for her.

Joule and Izzy were still unknown factors.

He felt the hit as Sarah practically attacked him in a hug, her arms wrapped tightly around him. He hugged her back for a moment before pulling away and scolding her. "You're not supposed to use that arm!"

But she was already hugging Dev. "I kind of worked it out. I took several Tylenol. Did some stretches. And it's actually feeling better."

"You cured yourself?'

"Oh god, no. Look." She aimed her flashlight down toward her arm. And he saw it was mottled blue and purple, bruised all to hell and back. "I probably bruised the bone. But I don't think I broke it. So I'm not putting any weight on it, but I can offer my returning journeymen a hug!"

Despite everything, she was still Sarah, still efficient. She'd already turned around and was picking her way through the debris back to the house. "Follow me."

As Cage looked down, directing the helmet light toward her feet, he saw that the yard was worse than it had been before.

"We got rain here this time," she said over her shoulder as though she had read his thoughts. "Which means we got rain *inside* the house."

Oh, he thought, *not good*.

"We have no heat, no power, but check this out." She waved the flashlight beam upward and Cage wondered what he was supposed to be looking at in the dark night. It took a moment to distinguish smoke.

"You have a fire?" Dev asked

"I do!"

They couldn't see it, but they could hear the grin and the pride in her voice. "We can sleep in front of the fireplace tonight. And in the morning, we'll go looking again."

Cage hadn't considered that. His thought had been Sarah

was first—they'd checked her off the list—and then he'd turn around and head right back out to continue the search.

But as he turned and looked behind him, there was nothing to see beyond the small illumination of the headlight from his helmet. There was no way they would find Joule or Izzy tonight, and searching by bicycle in the dark wasn't safe. His body was now protesting as Sarah lithely used her good arm to help push herself up on the edge of the foundation and into the house proper. It was clear she'd been working the whole time they'd been gone.

As Dev followed her, pushing the bike up before him, Cage thought he heard his roommate groan. Yeah, they weren't going anywhere tonight.

His heart crushed inside his chest. He wasn't good with that, but what else could he do? The world was pitch black. His body was protesting from overuse. And he didn't even know which direction to aim.

So he closed his eyes and did the only thing he could. He hoped to any god who might be listening that his sister was safe. Then he turned and followed Sarah and Deveron up into the house.

48

"What are the chances that the Larkins will come back to the farm and find us and let us out of here?" Joule asked into the darkness.

"Well, I mean..." Jerry somewhat hemmed and hawed at what should have been a very simple question. "They will come back. Eventually."

He'd let the words trail off, as if to imply that the Larkins might not let them out. She flashed back to earlier, when she'd asked him why no one was home on any of these farms. He'd told her they locked everything down and left.

But was that really right? The tractor hadn't been locked down.

When she'd mentioned that, Jerry had quickly replied, "No one locks down tractors anyway."

And now he was acting as though they were stuck and the family that owned the home and the farm wasn't going to come back or wasn't going to set them free once they found someone had taken shelter in their cellar but had gotten stuck...

What was here that was more valuable than the tractor they'd ridden up on? She wanted to know, because she sure wasn't seeing it. Then again, she'd never been an Alabama farm girl and hadn't recognized cotton blowing across the road the first time she'd seen it, either. She'd been fascinated by both the softness of the bolls and by the hard sharpness of the shells they left behind.

Here, she couldn't explore, touch, test, or see what happened. She was, unfortunately, stuck in a cellar, and working with Jerry's at least limited and probably biased information.

"So what's our best option?" She tossed it into the middle of the space, thinking that maybe leaving her question open would make him more willing to share information.

"I don't know."

He didn't elaborate, and Joule grew more frustrated. She might still be young, but she knew herself well enough to know that she didn't operate very well at all on "I don't know."

"Well, I'm going to try and get us out of here."

"It's night," he protested. "We should try to get some sleep."

Her erstwhile partner couldn't see her roll her eyes. "Scarecrow, dude, have you looked around? It's always night down here. If we wait until tomorrow to get out, we'll run out of food."

She'd taken only a few sips of her Gatorade. But she'd opened the second can of tuna for Toto when he whined and pawed softly at her jacket. It was the last can. Toto had quickly found the food in the dark and Joule was grateful that it was packed in water. He'd lapped that up. But where was his next meal coming from? There was no tuna left, and no water for him.

"Can you put your cell phone on?" she asked.

She could almost hear his facial expression as he protested. "You told me not to use up the battery with the flashlight."

"Right. So we aren't going to use the flashlight. What you should do now is simply turn the phone on and change the screen brightness to as low as possible. We only need a very little bit of light to be better than what we have right now."

The ghosts of edges around the cellar doors and down the lines of the steps had faded some time ago, making her believe that either night had set in or a storm had. Since she didn't hear anything at all from outside, she was guessing it was well into evening and maybe even later.

"Fine," Jerry huffed, but she listened to his shuffled movement and then threw her hands up to block her eyes as the light filled the room. The phone powered on in a preset pattern at full light.

"Holy crap!" She saw from the corner of her eyes that Toto look startled, where he'd been sleeping on her lap. Reaching down, she put one hand over his little eyes.

The phone beeped and whirred as it ran through its little startup routine. Then, as her eyes started adjusting, she watched as Jerry tapped and frowned at it.

"How do I turn the light down?"

"May I?" She crawled forward, reaching out her hand for the phone. He reluctantly set it on her palm. After touching the screen a few times, she brought up the dialer and turned the brightness almost to zero. "We just need enough to see by. Even the screen light uses up a lot of the battery."

He didn't comment, neither arguing nor conceding.

"Okay." She stood and turned around, finally able to see what she was doing. Toto walked in a circle around her feet, mimicking her movements, as if he were going to help her deconstruct this place. "Let's see how we get out of here."

She scanned the room, looking at the shelves and the walls behind them. On the other side of the room, two walls were dirt. She whipped back to the wood.

"Okay. The wood goes up the ceiling. The dirt walls go to the outside edges of the house down here, but this wall ... the one directly opposite the steps... is wood. Interesting."

The planks were old. Cedar, maybe? They were rough from not being sealed and from years, or maybe decades, of being down in the cool, dry cellar space. Walking over, she touched the wall first, then pushed on it.

Her own shadow got in her way. Though she'd adjusted, and the light was a thousand times brighter than the dark, the illumination the phone provided was still dim. Joule stepped aside, getting better light on it, and then reached out and tested the wall, pushing on it again. She commented as she went, thanking God for an engineering degree.

"From what I saw before we ran down here, it looks like the cellar is in this corner of the house. And the house itself has outside walls, here, and here, and here." She traced the dimensions above her head, making a line with her finger that ended at the thick post in the corner. It anchored that edge of the house above. Definitely old construction. The foundation was raised a little bit, if she remembered correctly. So she added, "The dirt walls down here are the edges of the houses and these two—" she pointed, "—are wood, holding back the dirt from under the house."

Considering that fact, she traced her finger up one of the pieces of wood and then began knocking as she got higher. "Yep. This covers an entry into the crawlspace under the house!"

"Okay?" Jerry asked, as if to say *what good was that?*

"The cellar doors are blocked." She turned, hands on hips. "The walls are dirt and unless we have a method to tunnel out, we're not going to make it. Honestly, I'd be tempted to tunnel out right next to the cellar doors. But that's the place most likely to be blocked."

Because what would fall directly on the cellar doors and not also block the space beside them? They could tunnel out and be just as stuck as they currently were for the effort. Not a good bet. "However, if we head the opposite direction, then we can get under the house. From there, we should be able to get out."

"Won't we just be trapped under the house then?" he asked, still not having moved from his seat on the bottom step.

Joule shook her head. "Crawl spaces have to have entries and exits." At least, they did by modern housing codes, but she didn't mention that. "There should be a doorway to the outside —probably small, but a door!"

"What if it's blocked?"

"It could be, but what if it's not? What if there's another place in the skirt where we can push our way through? And if we can't get out that way, we might be able to find a door up into the house. Some places have one. Lastly, if we really are trapped there, maybe we can bust our way up through the flooring."

This time she could see Jerry's skeptical response.

"We can't get out that way." She pointed to the cellar doors, still shut tight despite their removal of their brace system. "And you don't seem to think the Larkins are coming back to find us."

When he tipped his head this time, she noticed the odd expression.

"What?"

But he only shook his head.

Joule decided it was best to ignore him. He wasn't going to be the brains of this operation. She could hope he would join her and do the work, but apparently she was on her own to get started. She was tall, but not tall enough. So she looked around and, spying the wooden toolbox under the steps, she headed over to drag it back.

Quickly she quit that effort, realizing it was far too full. But that was good. There had been hand saws, the little crowbar, rusty screwdrivers and more. All of which would be good for busting their way out of here.

She looked up where the wood met the reinforced ceiling

above them. How much space was there under the raised foundation of this house? It might be a full crouching area, or merely enough room to army crawl. And the space she had to work in might depend on the size of the I-beams that held up the subfloor. But Joule corrected herself: A house like this probably wasn't constructed with MDF, non-squeak I-beams. And that might make it easier to break out of.

She emptied the toolbox, making it lighter, and began the work of dragging it across to the other wall. She wedged it into a space between two of the shelves, and looked again at the potatoes, root vegetables, and other boxes stored there. If she was feeling it, she might look inside them later.

Testing her weight, she stepped gingerly onto the box. Then, as she decided she trusted it, she reached upward, knocking on the wood again. She was surprised when one of the old one-by-eights fell off into her hand.

The board appeared to have been nailed in place once upon a time, but now she turned it over and saw the nails had been bent back, rounded and hammered down. The piece had been merely set in place, balancing by gravity, to make it look like it was still part of the wall.

This would make it easier to break through, she thought. Now that she had a hole, she could reach behind the other pieces and more easily pry them out.

"Can you help? Bring the phone?" she asked Jerry. She turned around carefully on her uneven perch, startled to see the light was already moving and he was handing it to her.

She lifted the dim screen and aimed it toward the hole, not wanting to put her hand onto a bed of rattlesnakes or rats. But as she looked into the now lit space and saw what was in there...

It wasn't an animal.

Slowly, she turned and looked at Jerry. "You have got to be shitting me."

49

Joule had reached into the opening and grabbed the package before she really thought about what she was doing. Now she stood there, holding a wrapped brick of what she was pretty sure was either cocaine or heroin.

As she turned around to face her trying companion, the look on Jerry's face told her all she needed to know.

"It looks like this isn't much of a surprise to you." She ground the words through her teeth and barely held back from throwing the brick at him.

In her imagination, it smacked him in the chest and exploded into a white cloud of accusation. But even as she envisioned her rage playing out that way, she also envisioned poor little Toto getting high on whatever this was. And then Jerry, too.

Sober Jerry was enough of a bitch to deal with.

She turned around and set the brick back down in its original position, as though that would erase her finding it and touching it. Then she turned back.

"What was that?"

Jerry shrugged.

Though she was tempted to get off the box, as it was slightly less than stable, Joule was currently enjoying being taller than Jerry. So she crossed her arms, cocked one hip out, and asked, "No, really. What is it?"

He shrugged again, but this time added, "I think it's cocaine."

Another thought occurred to her. "Is it cut?" *God forbid it was pure.* If she'd thrown it at him, she might have killed one or all of them.

"I don't fucking know!" he replied.

"You don't know much, do you, Scarecrow?"

This time he blinked at her. "Why do you keep calling me that?"

"Oh dear God." She was down here with her tiny kitten, trapped in a cellar with the leader of the protests and—what? a kilo?—of cocaine.

Her brain was rapidly snapping the pieces together. *Click.* The heavy bolting on the hinges, the reinforced door, and the nice, new padlock over the very old green paint now made more sense. It wasn't obvious enough to look like they had completely fortified the place. But it was enough to let her know now that, yes, they had done a good bit of it.

Click. The second thing that snapped into place was when she'd asked him if the Larkins would come home and let them out. This was why he wasn't willing to just say, of course they will. Because who would leave someone trapped in their cellar and not let them out after a disaster? Drug runners, that's who.

Click.

"The other farm earlier—the one where we got the tractor —them, too?"

Jerry shrugged yet again. She remembered thinking it was a little odd that there was a farmhouse with no farm. There were no fields plowed and no animals mucking about, just open space that seemed to go fallow.

The last thing didn't fit quite so neatly, but it was a question she had to ask. "Are you part of the supply chain, Jerry?"

He shook his head quickly.

He wasn't. Thank God.

Joule huffed out a breath and listened as, beside her, Toto did it, too. That was fucking adorable, and she needed some fucking adorable right now.

Hell, she figured the drug runners probably didn't want Jerry any more than she did. He had a little too much God and not quite enough brains. "Then why were you there?"

"There?" He didn't seem to understand the question.

"Where we met. On the other farm." When he didn't answer right away, she explained more of her thinking. "You'd driven there with your truck. After the first tornadoes hit."

"Why were *you* there?" he asked. Not the most brilliant counter.

And Joule almost smacked herself in the face out of exasperation. He was going to require her answer. "Because I was trying to ride out the tornado in a ditch off Highway 183 when the funnel picked me and my friend up and threw us different directions. I woke up in a field east of that farm. I don't know how much later."

"Whoa!" His mouth and wide eyes were equally open. "You were actually *in* the tornado?"

"Yes. Jerry." She punctuated each word, because he still hadn't answered her question.

"So why were *you* there on the farm, then?" He beat her to the punch, but Joule figured feeding him information might get him to return the favor.

"I started walking. I found a stream, and then I heard a truck on the road. I screamed for help, but they went past and didn't see me. So I checked the farm for people and there you were." She took a breath and steered back to the place she wanted to be. "So the question is, Jerry, you had a truck, and you picked that place to wait out the storm. Why?"

"I wanted to check it out."

"Check what out?"

"I was just curious if the tornado had ... revealed anything."

"So you just drove to that farm to see if there was cocaine around and ... *got stuck*?"

He sounded sullen this time. "Well, I didn't expect another twister to steal my brand new truck, now did I?"

Obviously, he hadn't.

"I didn't see anything there either," she admitted. She sure as hell would have had a different reaction if the first farm had revealed taped up, plastic-wrapped bricks of drugs lying around instead of tuna cans, cereal, and sports drinks.

Jerry just looked at her, waiting for the next question. He wasn't volunteering any information, though she couldn't tell if he was specifically holding back or if he'd just run out.

She needed more. "What were you looking for? Were you going to steal a brick of cocaine and sell it yourself?"

He shrugged yet again.

Oh, good Lord. "Well, Jerry, this cements it. We have to get out of here. Give me your phone."

"I thought we were supposed to preserve the battery."

"We're gonna preserve it the best we can, Scarecrow. But we need it for this."

"Stop calling me that!"

"Then stop acting like it!" She bit off the rest of her rant. "Sooner or later, the Larkins are going to come back and probably kill us both if they find us down here with their cocaine. So I hope you had a lot of battery when this started."

His eyes lit up a little bit. "I had the phone plugged into the dash. I think it was almost at a hundred percent."

She lifted the phone and looked. He was close. *Good.* "We'll do everything we can to keep this running as long as we can. And we pray the Larkins don't come back. We have to find a way out of here. And this phone is our only light that I know of."

If the Larkins found them, Joule was pretty sure she and Jerry would wind up dead. And if the phone battery died, they died, too.

50

"I need something else to stand on," Joule told Jerry.

They both looked around but didn't see anything.

"Maybe they won't know we were down here," he offered up hopefully.

She almost looked back over her shoulder to give him an incredulous glare.

How on earth would the Larkins *not* know that someone had been down there? If she and Jerry either tunneled their way out, broke their way out from the cellar doors somehow—which they didn't seem strong enough to do—or crawled out through the crawlspace under the house, over the top of the cocaine, they were going to leave a gaping hole. The board that had been pushed into place had been pushed from the cellar side. There was no way to leave this place as though they hadn't been here.

She didn't reply, just looked forward.

The crawlspace still seemed like the best bet, but that meant going up and over the cocaine. It meant choosing a direction and a plan and actively trying to get out. The Larkins

A.J. SCUDIERE

would know, likely right away, that someone had been in their stash.

Joule decided faster was better and reached up to grab the wood planking. She pulled and tugged at it, but the old stuff was sturdier than it appeared. The one plank that had come out was the only one that was loose, and she couldn't boost up and crawl through the hole until she'd made the opening wider. She wasn't going to be able to tear it out with her bare hands.

Stepping down from the box, she reached to the floor and scooped up Toto in one hand. With the other, she pulled the sports drink from the pocket on her pants and took a swallow. Then, because she had nothing better and electrolytes for cats had to be about the same as electrolytes for humans, she poured a small bit into the cap and let Toto take a few sips. She screwed the cap back on and scooped the kitten back up, all while Jerry watched.

"It's your turn up on the box," she told him, hoping it didn't break under his heft. "I need you to rip the boards out and make the space wider."

He gingerly climbed onto the box, smart enough to place his feet at the edges and not the middle, where he might go crashing through. He reached up and grabbed the wood tightly. He'd seen her struggling with it and put his weight into the tug.

He managed to get two of the pieces out. Though the hole was noticeably bigger, it was barely wide enough for Joule, and still not wide enough for him. Jerry tried again.

He looked down, checked his foot placement, and put his hands over his head. Grabbing at the bottom of a plank sticking down into the gaping opening, he rocked it back and forth. But it still didn't want to quite give, and he wound up snapping it, leaving harsh shards like evil teeth hanging down into the space.

"I can't get the side ones," he said without turning around.

As he checked out the pieces, Joule walked back to the

space under the steps and rummaged through the tools she'd left. A smallish, square-headed hammer that looked perfectly evil caught her eye.

"Try this." She held it up to him and then stepped back as Jerry swung. He now quickly opened up the space between the shelves.

"All right. Got it." His triumph was hers, too.

"Can I look?" she asked.

He stepped down, but he asked, "Why do you call me Scarecrow?"

He stood in the center of the small space, looking down in the dim light over his flannel shirt, white T-shirt, and old jeans. "I don't think I look like a scarecrow. Is it the clothes?"

"No." Now she felt bad. "It's a Wizard of Oz reference. Just like Toto."

He nodded slowly but didn't comment on her choice for him. "Well, that makes you Dorothy, and you're wearing the wrong shoes."

She almost laughed. At least he got part of it. And he was being kinder to her than she deserved. *If only she had the power to get back home, all along,* she thought.

Turning to the task at hand, she scrambled up onto the box and peered into the hole. She'd already touched one of the bricks of cocaine, leaving her fingerprints all over it. She was stuck down here with no method of erasing the evidence, aside from maybe wasting her drink to wash them off.

She reached in and began shoving bricks aside, her brain still following the track of washing the plastic packages of cocaine in her sports drink. Would it turn the cocaine pink?

When she'd created a wide enough space, she waved her hand back toward Jerry, asking once more for the phone. This time, she put the flashlight on.

"Hey!" he quickly protested.

But she shook her head. "Just for a second. I've got to see what's under here."

She aimed the more powerful beam into the space under the house. Two or three rats scurried away from the light, though there were probably far more. But rats didn't bother her. As long as they weren't completely rabid, they would run away from people.

What she didn't see was any light from the outside. Even if there were gaps in the skirt on the house, they might not show up at night. But it wasn't a good sign. There was no obvious door to the crawlspace or any obvious weak area to break out of.

For a moment, she considered trying the cellar doors again, but she dismissed the thought. They had done everything they could, and the doors wouldn't open. Unless someone had come home—someone they hadn't heard, who also had maybe gone into the house and hadn't heard them—no one had moved whatever was blocking the doors. They wouldn't be getting out that way.

"Boost me in," she said and watched as Jerry laced his fingers together.

While that normally would have been a good lift, his hands weren't too much higher than where she already stood.

"Wait, sorry." She turned around, stepped down, grabbed Toto one more time and stuffed him in her pocket. He wiggled around a little bit, but he didn't try to squirm his way out. She wasn't going to leave him behind but she had to get into the crawlspace.

So she put her foot backward into Jerry's hands, feeling bad about putting her butt in his face, and boosted herself up and through the hole. Her fingers bit into the dirt, but not far enough for purchase. "Sorry! Push me?"

Joule straightened her leg, making it stiff so Jerry could do just that. She was shoved ungracefully into the gap.

Well, she almost coughed, *the dirt down here was dry*. Whatever water systems they'd installed at the farm worked. They funneled the water away from under the house. Reaching up to wipe at her face, she stopped herself just in time. She'd only make it worse.

Joule had just enough space to crawl on her hands and knees, if she kept her head low. So she did exactly that.

She reached out the hole, for the phone. "I need the light. I won't put the flashlight on, though!"

She added the last part to reassure him about her energy usage. As she slowly turned like a mastodon and crawled away, she whispered wryly, "If only we had solar…"

She crawled through the space for another interminable eon. According to the light from the phone it took her a good forty-five minutes, but it felt like forever to check the entire boundary of the foundation.

The place wasn't large, but the foundation was shallower in some places, deeper in others as it followed the dips and curves of the earth. In each spot, Joule stopped and pushed against the wall. She couldn't remember from when they'd plowed their way up to the house, but she was beginning to think the entire skirt was bricked in.

There would be no getting out from the inside. Though there were vents in place, they were too small for her and definitely too small for Jerry to climb through. In another circumstance, she might have tried to push her way through, find someone to help, and come back for Jerry. But she wasn't going to leave him at the mercy of the Larkins.

When she'd circled the whole perimeter, pushing on everything and deciding that it wasn't much hope, she headed back. The phone lit up Jerry's face as he stood in the exact spot she'd left him in. Maybe he'd been standing there the whole time.

"I don't see anything," she reported. "I think the entire base is bricked in. There aren't any gaps, no access doors, and no weak spots that I can find. The only way out would be brute force. I think we have to go up."

"Okay," he readily agreed.

"That means you hand me the tools and we go in together. We'll use the flashlight to find a spot and bust our way up through the sub flooring."

"Okay," he said again. "Which tools?"

She realized then that Jerry was doing something extraordinary given what she'd expected of him: He was letting her be in charge.

"Let's bring them all up."

"Won't that be evidence that we were here?'

"Yes." She was more content now, but still. "We'll also leave a hole in the floor of their house that they'll probably notice."

"Good point." He didn't seem to catch on any more than that, and she let it go.

Once they'd gone through the laborious task of getting all the tools handed up, Joule had braced herself and offered a hand out to Jerry. She'd been careful not to be in a position where she could roll over and squish Toto, who was still sleeping comfortably in her pocket.

Together, she and Jerry started the survey. It was harder for him to maneuver than it was for her, and even she was cramping up. But they had to find the best place, or they'd cost themselves extra work and maybe a failed attempt.

This search took just as long as the first one she'd done. She checked the phone, and sure enough, it was the middle of the night already. Luckily, the Larkins still hadn't come home and the battery on the phone still hadn't died.

"I think this is the best spot," she offered. She'd knocked upward on the floor a few times, noted the construction, and tried to figure out where the overhead walls would be. It would have been much easier if she'd ever been inside the house.

In the spot that she'd chosen, the flooring was already

starting to rot out a little bit, which would make their job much, much easier. She had no idea what she'd hit once they passed the sub floor, though—tile? Carpet? Hard wood?

"Wait," She turned and asked Jerry. "What kind of floors are these?"

"Wood floors," he told her with confidence. Then with less, he added, "I think they got rugs in some of the places. Nice ones with lots of color."

Okay, she thought, but those were details she didn't need. "Wall-to-wall carpeting, or throw rugs?"

"Not to all the corners. You know, just in the middle of the room."

That's better, she thought, but didn't say. Then she made her way back to the tool pile and grabbed what she could, taking the square headed hammer for herself and another ball peen hammer and a wood wedge for Jerry. It was a bitch crawling these things back and forth. But Toto rolled over in her pocket and the warm feel of him, probably asleep, was comforting. She needed that.

Together, she and Jerry started chipping away at the subflooring. It flaked and cracked relatively easily until they'd carved the layer away. Reaching up, Joule pushed against the next layer above it. *Wood flooring*, she thought, just as Jerry had said. But it gave relatively easily against the pressure she applied. *Cheap wood flooring.*

That made her happy and gave her swings of the hammer renewed energy as they cracked at it. They had to make a hole big enough for Jerry because, while she was the least devoted member of his fan club, she wasn't going to leave him here for the Larkins to discover.

When fragments of the ripped-up flooring littered the dirt around them, she tackled the carpet. It should be the last, easiest layer. Joule wondered if she could just push it out of the way.

She tried and though she could push it up into a tent, it was clearly anchored by furniture on several sides. They'd need to cut their way through.

Lord, she was destroying the home of drug runners. Not her finest hour.

"The hacksaw?" she said to Jerry before heading back to the tool pile. Grabbing two of the little saws—one of them with a perfect pointy end—she positioned herself on her butt, directly under the hole. She could only hope this gave her the most forceful position as she pushed the hacksaw up into the carpeting. It gave, rather than cut.

"Let me," Jerry told her, and she felt a moment of gratefulness that he was here as her partner. She watched as he neatly forced the end of the saw through the carpeting above.

If someone was up there, they were watching the craziest cat burglars ever break up into their home. But so far, no one had complained.

Jerry cut a slice into the carpet but it only let in a little more light than what the phone offered up. The dead of night part was woefully accurate right now.

"We need to cut a T," she told him. "It'll make the hole bigger faster."

She grabbed at the carpet, anchoring one side while he again pushed against it with the saw. This time, at least, the cut went quickly. The relief that bloomed through her chest was short lived as the light suddenly changed.

Joule froze.

Through the small front vent she could see headlights coming up the driveway.

51

C age woke to the smell of eggs and toast.

"Whahhh?" The sound was Deveron coming awake—an odd noise that Cage had become familiar with over the past weeks. Cage opened one eye to see his friend roll over cautiously in the bed of pillows and blankets.

They'd slept on the floor in front of the fireplace with Sarah taking care of them. She'd gotten up every few hours to stir the ashes and throw another log onto the fire. Though it wasn't horrifyingly cold in the fall in Alabama, at night it was colder than they wanted to sleep in. Having a chunk of the wall missing didn't help.

Anyone getting sick right now ran a much greater risk, with the hospitals already overloaded and the power out. They probably also ran greater risk of illness or infection, Cage thought, simply because of what they'd been doing: overexerting themselves, handling all kinds of strange materials, and being exposed to every person in the community.

But he was excited about real food and wanted to ask where it came from. He sat up to watch the food reach its spot at the coffee table and the entire center of him sank as he counted plates. Sarah only carried three.

For a moment, everything had been okay. He was on the floor. He was warm. There was the smell of food. He saw his friend. He knew now that the activity he'd heard from the kitchen was Sarah cooking breakfast.

But where was his sister?

The morning soured in his mouth, but he threw off the covers anyway. If he wanted to fix the problem, he had to move. The slightly-too-cool air hit his legs as his heels slapped the floor, and he did his best to push to standing without swaying.

"How did you cook that, Sarah? Do we have power?" But he looked up and the lights were still off, although daylight streamed through the windows.

She shook her head. "We have gas."

He must have frowned at her, or Dev must have, because she talked as she delivered glasses of water to go with the eggs and toast. "I got under the house yesterday. So I first turned on the stove, and then went down and crawled around. I took a bucket of soap solution that I had dyed red and painted the gas line with it. I didn't see anything. So I'm cooking with the range."

Cage nodded but Dev frowned. "Why red soap?"

Cage answered, "If the gas is leaking, it'll create bubbles in a soap solution and you can see where it's leaking from."

He watched as his friend grew a bit wide-eyed at the prospect. Dev was an engineer, so Cage was a little surprised his friend hadn't heard of any of this, but maybe he hadn't grown up with a gas line. Turning back to Sarah, Cage asked, "Do you think it was enough of a check? I mean, surely you couldn't examine the whole line?"

And with only one good arm. But he didn't say that part. Sarah had done it and done was done.

She shook her head. "No, but I did get to most of it—at least the exposed parts, and it doesn't matter if it leaks outside the house. At least not right now. I checked the tank out in the back while it was still light yesterday, and I didn't smell propane while I was under the house."

Sarah did have a good sense of smell, he thought.

"So if it is leaking, it's not leaking enough to blow us up. And we have eggs." She had been pleased when they moved in and she saw the gas range. At the time, Cage hadn't thought much of it one way or the other but now he, too, was pleased at the rural set up with the big propane tank out beyond Squirrel Log.

He sat on the couch next to Dev, while Sarah automatically took the floor. Maybe she understood they would feel the hard wood like old men this morning. Cage tried to ignore the empty space on his other side. Joule would have sat on the floor without compunction. As he and Dev wolfed down the eggs, Sarah commented, "We have gas and water, just not power."

When she was met with silence, she explained further. "You can *shower*."

Cage only then noticed that Sarah herself looked relatively clean for having been in the ditch yesterday and surviving a tornado. He and Deveron were much worse for the wear. "Oh God, yes. We're horrifying."

"I'll get you guys clean sheets for tonight," she told them and motioned with her empty glass as she stood to head back to the kitchen. She was still favoring the one arm and for that he was grateful.

"You two finish eating, get showered and dressed..." She trailed off. But Cage understood. Sarah would stay here and clean up after them so they could get back on the road quickly.

"Can we listen to the radio?" he asked into the space of the room. He didn't want to listen, but he needed to.

Sarah simply fetched it from the kitchen, where she must have been listening to it while she cooked. Placing it in the center of the table, she added, "You might want to hit the community center first. See if they're there. If their names are on the list."

The two men looked to each other and agreed. The list had become everything, and he could only hope Joule's name was on it. He shoveled in the rest of his hot breakfast like it was the first food he'd had in a week.

It was an hour later, after pedaling back to the bicycle shop and making the tough decision to trade out the bikes for the car, that they were finally headed for the community center. Cage wasn't sure if they'd wasted time picking through the empty sports store and snagging the bike rack for the trunk. Or maybe it was brilliant.

Either way, when they arrived at the community center, people were still milling around. Apparently, a crowd had been there all night. The crew was still checking people in. As the two climbed out of the now-battered sedan, he saw a huge red truck pull up and he recognized Boomer and Bob. This time, the load of people they brought in was only five.

Maybe that was a good sign. Maybe it meant that the need for rescue was diminishing. He had faith that Boomer and Bob would find everyone eventually. Heading over to talk to them, the hope on his face must have shown through, puppy-like. Boomer seemed to clearly understand that he was dashing the young man's hopes as he solemnly shook his head.

Did the man really remember Joule and Izzy's picture? Their names?

"No Joule, no Isabelle." The words were a soft, but stark, blow. Yes, Bob and Boomer remembered everyone they were looking for.

Cage only nodded, but the man said, "Be sure to check the list. They still might be there."

That was the hope he and Deveron were still holding on to. He left the conversation without having said a word. But he clung to his hope. They hadn't heard about anything during the night—the radio hadn't gone off, and the storms seemed to have finally abated. Sarah had even charged Dev's cell phone off a battery. The radio announcer hadn't commented about any new storms. If more had happened, they should have heard.

Cage was counting that as a win. He had to.

It took some jostling and then waiting to get to the list, printed and posted on the wall of the community center. A young woman stood by with a badge around her neck and a clipboard in her hand. The clear symbols said she worked here.

She was answering questions, but Cage didn't have questions. He'd known when he saw the ever-expanding list, that his sister's name wasn't going to be on it.

"Izzy's not here either," Dev said, tapping into Cage's thoughts as surely as he was tapping his finger on the list.

They stepped back to get out of the way for the next desperate searchers. Cage knew that the longer they went without finding Joule, the more likely it became that they never would.

52

Joule woke up warm, but when she rolled over, she crinkled and it smelled far too earthy to be home.

She wasn't home.

Not yet, she told herself.

She moved a little more and felt a sharp jab in her side that reminded her she was sleeping on hay bales under a stolen horse blanket. The scent around her bloomed into easy recognition beyond animal to horse, hay, barn, loft.

Slowly, she reached out and felt around her. The hay extended a little beyond her head but was too narrow to hold even her tiny traveling companion. Where was Toto?

Her initial assessment of the space didn't find him. She would have scrambled to search and call out, but she couldn't be noisy. There had been no way to corral him at night, nothing she could safely put him in. Had he wandered off?

Slowly, she sat up, listening to the horses shuffling in their stalls below and waiting. As she moved, she spotted Jerry tucked up against the wall on his own hay bale bed. The blanket over him didn't move, but there was enough light in the barn that she could see his eyes were open.

"Toto?" She mouthed the name to him and was relieved when he pointed toward his feet. It took a moment, but she spotted her kitten attacking the corner of his hay bale. It was absolutely not the time to play, but Toto was romping about, squatting down, wiggling his butt until the wave followed all the way to the end of his tail. He went in for adorable hay bale murder before romping off to tackle something else that caught his eye. Joule didn't know what he'd seen—a grasshopper? Hell, it might be a roach. She didn't want to think about that.

They both watched the kitten for a few moments and again, she realized how much she *needed this*. She needed the injected humor of a kitten at play. She needed the small, soft, warm body curling up next to hers. She put her hand down, dangling her fingers quietly near the floor and watched as Toto romped over, stopped, and dropped into tiny attack mode to get her fingers. He did so with such a gentle bat of his paw that Joule felt her smile form at the soft touch.

She and Toto and Jerry had made it this far.

In the dark of night, they'd run from the Larkin farm. At the first flash of the headlights, she'd busted up through the carpet, leading Jerry through the unfamiliar living room and out the back door. They'd bolted across the yard, protected from view by the bulk of the house.

With only the dimmest light from the sky to navigate by, they'd moved as quickly as they could, but not fast enough. They'd still been close enough to hear every word as the Larkins arrived at the house and discovered things were very wrong.

A woman's voice had screeched with anger and fear. "Somebody was in the crawlspace! They saw it!"

The sound had spurred Joule to keep running. She had no idea if the family had gone down into the cellar, or into the crawl space themselves, or if they'd counted their bricks of cocaine. *Had they seen that their stash was all still there?*

Her heart had pounded the whole time, waiting for a shot to ring out in the dark. While Joule thought she was doing a relatively decent job of being stealthy, Jerry had crashed through the forest like a Sasquatch.

"Running" was too strong a word for what she and Jerry had been doing. The night was pitch black, and though he carried the phone, she'd batted his hand quickly, making him put it out. It was a beacon to their location. When the light went out, she breathed a little easier that she hadn't made it easy for the Larkins to pick them off—but she still didn't breathe *easy*.

Her heart had pounded for possibly two solid hours as they slowly and quietly picked a path away from danger and hopefully toward safety. At least, that's what she hoped. Joule didn't know where they were going. She wasn't even confident they weren't scribing a circle through the woods and heading straight back to the Larkin Farm/Drug Ring.

But after a few hours and who knew how many miles of dark path—maybe only a few? She wouldn't be surprised if they'd covered virtually no ground—they'd found the big red barn.

It looked to Joule like every other one she'd seen when she drove the back roads. But Jerry said he knew this farm, too, and he deemed the Wilbert family almost definitely safe from the plague of drug running that had hit the area some years ago. Joule appreciated now that the barn smelled of manure and hay. That meant there were animals in it. And it meant that the farmland was functioning as a farm—unlike the Larkin place.

Though she'd managed to get some sleep once they'd laid down with the hay and blankets, her tension was back with a vengeance now.

As Toto romped around the loft they'd secreted themselves in, her brain ran wild in a way her cornered body couldn't. She'd wanted to leave another sign for her brother, but she couldn't leave any path for the Larkins to follow. Now, she even regretted the first four she'd left.

If the Larkins found one, they had her initials. They probably wouldn't immediately think of her—she wasn't even sure if she'd ever met them—but it would make it much easier for them to track her down in the future.

She'd not left an arrow at the Larkin farm, thank God, as both her entrance and exit had been under extreme duress. But she'd left one at the first farm she'd been at, before she saw Jerry. She'd left one at the edge of the field and basically tagged herself at each turn.

She probably hadn't covered as much ground as she'd like to believe she had... so it wasn't a stretch to think the Larkins might come across one of her arrows as they searched. Given that they'd seen virtually no one else so far, and that the arrows were an indicator that someone was hoping to be found, it wouldn't be hard to connect that to the people who had been in their basement with their cocaine.

But there was nothing she could do about any of that now. She whispered to Jerry. "That first farm we were at—are they involved with the cocaine running?"

He nodded this time. They'd skirted this conversation before, but now he clarified, "I think. I don't know for sure, not like with the Larkins."

Well, they both knew for sure about the Larkins now.

"But Tommy, he got a new truck last year."

Joule almost laughed. In this area, new trucks were the measure of misplaced wealth.

"But then he got another new one this year. And the farm isn't doing well. Not at all, not enough for that."

"Interesting, for a farm that's not producing," she whispered back. Her own understanding was that the inability to hide the money got a lot of criminals caught.

"Interesting for a family farm around here at all," Jerry replied, and she followed as he explained. "Farms pass a lot of money through—lots of cash, lots of credit, lots of e-transactions. Some very big and some very small."

She must have frowned at him, because he continued to explain.

"They do contracts whenever they can. Large batches of produce to a single distributor or buyer can bring big money in. But then there's large amounts out for farm equipment and supplies. It runs in the hundreds of thousands of dollars sometimes."

"Really?"

Jerry nodded. "But the margins on a farm are slim—very slim most of the time. It's easy to be negative a couple years in a row, even though the farm made close to a million dollars or more."

Had she ever heard that?

"If a farm is profitable, maybe providing something no one else does," Jerry said, seeming to appreciate being the one in the know for once, "you can make bank. But right now, that's organic and heirloom produce. Not many around here going that way. They cling to the old methods that don't work anymore."

Joule didn't comment about him not appreciating the irony of that statement. He just went on...

"But it's gotten harder and harder for family farms to be profitable at all. The commercial farms took over. Lots of these families have been living on a few tens of thousands of dollars a year, even though hundreds of thousands are passing through their fingers."

Joule was starting to see a pattern. "Do you think they're money laundering?"

That seemed to surprise him. He shrugged.

She added, "I don't know all the details of money laundering, but I know the more cash you move and the more transactions you have of a wider variety, the more easily you can hide the extra. A failing farm sounds like a prime operation for somebody who needs their money laundered."

"Interesting," Jerry said.

Joule was growing even more concerned about what they'd stepped into. This might not be just a family distributing cocaine, but a network. Then again, while pot could be run as a solo operation, no one was growing coca plants and running the vats to create the powder around here. The very fact that there were plastic-wrapped bricks in the cellar was enough to indicate a full network.

When she'd first woken up after the first tornado dropped her in a field, Joule thought her sole job was to find people. Instead, she discovered that finding people could be her worst nightmare. She reminded herself that she'd not survived a tornado to get caught and murdered by drug runners. But she was more than aware that absolutely was an option.

It was up to her and Jerry to keep themselves out of the hands of the people whose business they'd already disrupted. With what Jerry had added, she was now very concerned this was a bigger and more entwined network than just the Larkins and the other farm up the street.

"Do you know anyone else who's involved?" she asked, her voice low.

He shook his head, shrugged, and replied, "I have my suspicions. But I don't know anything for certain."

Absorbing that, she nodded. This time she threw the blanket aside and stood. It was time to get going. They no longer needed to find people. They needed to find the right people. One or two of a very limited set of people that either she or Jerry could absolutely trust. Her task had just gotten infinitely harder.

As Jerry stood up, the hay bale crinkled underneath him,

and Toto darted over to attack it. Joule stretched and was trying to think what she needed to gather to leave when she stopped still.

The barn door slowly creaked open beneath them.

53

C age steered the sedan around the fallen trees with much greater ease this morning. The roads weren't miraculously cleared, but it was obvious others had been out and about and had moved the biggest hindrances out of the way. It was also helpful that no other tornadoes had swept through and undone the work that people had put in.

The day was clear and bright. If he only looked up, there was no evidence of the mayhem that had come through yesterday. Now if he could only find his sister...

He and Deveron headed north again, weaving their way through the debris. As he pulled slowly around a particularly large, fluffy tree top that covered three quarters of the road and blocked his vision, Cage hit the brakes. The tires squealed in protest and Dev reached forward to brace himself against the dash.

"What?" his friend asked, as if the word had just slipped from his mouth in surprise.

But it was evident in a moment as they found themselves staring down the grille of a large Jeep coming the other direction. As Cage watched, the Jeep driver waved them off and slowly backed up, though it was Cage on the wrong side of the road. However, he was much further around the curve the tree created and he appreciated the politeness.

As he wove past the now-stopped Jeep, the man rolled down the window and flagged him down. Cage put his own window down, curious for only a moment before it came clear.

With very little introduction, the man launched into, "We're looking for my daughter."

He held up a printed eight-by-eleven picture. But Cage and Deveron both shook their heads. He hadn't seen the woman. But even as he was thinking it, Dev was already pulling out the picture they'd stolen from the frame on Sarah's night stand and held it out across Cage toward the window.

Cage showed the picture to the driver. "We're looking for the woman on the left and the one on the right. Joule Mazur and Izzy—Isabelle—McAlister."

But the man responded as they had, with a sad shake of his head.

"What's your daughter's name?" Cage asked, in case they got so lucky as to find her.

"Julie Jones. Julie Jones McGee."

They all mutually agreed to look for each others' lost loved ones, and Cage wondered now how many more encounters like this they might have.

"Get in the glove box," he ordered Dev. "Write that all down. Add a few identifying characteristics, too. She's blond, blue-eyed, thirty?"

Dutifully Dev transcribed everything onto the back of a long receipt. But with that job done and possibly pointless, they continued north once again. Still not fast, still hindered by the damage, they passed a half-dozen other cars. Each time, they all slowed down and exchanged pictures and info. So far, nobody had seen Joule or Izzy.

They hadn't gotten out of the car at all.

One of the cars had been a state trooper who'd taken a photo of Sarah's photo. At least he had the photo. The cell phones were only good as storage units while there was still no wi-fi signal, but Cage filled out forms just as they had at the community center and added Joule and Izzy to what must have become a very long list.

They passed the point where Sarah's car had gone off road nose-first, in the ditch. Though there were tracks scraping dirt and grass all over where other cars had gone into ditches. But he could tell this one was from their own accident. They'd stopped and looked over the edge and seen the car was still there, nose down and waiting. Nothing had happened—no Samaritan had come by and towed it, but they weren't surprised. This wasn't anyone's priority. They didn't check out the pipe, as no good could come of that.

Then they'd gotten back in the car and driven onward. They stopped for three more cars before Dev got excited and pointed. "Cage, look. That's the tornado path. We can see it now."

They hadn't been able to see it clearly yesterday, because there was simply too much debris in the road and along the sides. Now, with the daylight and the cleanup begun, they could catch glimpses. This time, they had a trail to follow, and they tracked it for five miles, Cage watching the odometer as they went, trying to be more methodical than frantic.

"Turn here!" Dev called out excitedly.

The track of the tornado hopped a road that crossed theirs, and on the other side, it took an obvious turn and veered toward the east. Cage swung a right onto the small road that wasn't quite as cleared as the highway but was still far more drivable than what he'd seen the night before.

They traced the path of damage as best they could. And when the tornado track crossed the large field, Cage pulled the car to the side of the thin shoulder. They couldn't just drive through the field. "What do we do now?"

"Maybe we can loop around and pick it up on the other side of the field," Dev speculated. "It looks like there's a road about a mile up that way."

Here, the ground was flat for a distance, though Cage seriously thought "a mile" was a big overshoot on Dev's part.

They tried driving the perimeter of the field, searching for where the tornado path exited. Probably an hour later, they gave up and turned around. "We've got the track right there, but we've got nothing out here."

They'd never found the other side where the path of destruction exited the field. Had it stopped in the middle? Hopped away? Cage didn't know, and he still didn't have cell access to look anything up.

He motioned to Dev to check his phone, which Dev looked at again and nodded. "It's all good."

They'd plugged it into the car as soon as they got in, which at least maintained the battery until they got out. They had what they needed.

"I say we go back and we track it," Cage sighed. It seemed the only option. "We've got the bikes."

He was glad now that he'd stolen yet one more thing from the bike shop. He had to remember at some point to go back and pay the man for everything. But for now, he was grateful.

"Here, then we need this." Deveron turned around, rummaging through the bags in the back and producing two water bottles. "We should drink these now and eat now, because we don't know how long we'll be on those bikes."

Once again, Sarah had set them up with food and rationed out eight water bottles for them. Because his friend was forward-thinking, they were fed by the time they got back to where the tracks gouged the dirt on the other side of the road.

"We just pull off and park here, I guess." The car wasn't made for off-road driving, and it rocked and bounced as he brought it to a stop in the grass. Cage could only hope the ground was solid enough that, when he got back in and put it in reverse, the tires would grip and get them out.

Dev was already at the trunk, pulling the bikes from the rack and setting them into the grass, where they tipped precariously and threatened to topple. "Water!" he called up to Cage and waited until his friend tossed the bottles over. Cage put an extra in the pocket in his pants.

"More? I think we have enough," Dev said.

But Cage shook his head. "I hope that we don't need more, but that maybe Joule and Izzy do."

His wishful thinking was shining through, and he knew it. There was absolutely no scientific or logical reason to believe that this would lead them to his sister. But as Cage straddled the bike and prepared to follow the tornado tracks, he had a good feeling that he was finally heading the right direction.

Fifty yards later, that feeling turned to stone.

54

Dev jumped back. "No!"

Cage didn't answer his friend. What could he say? Except *Yes, it's exactly what you think it is.*

They'd almost biked right over the body.

Face down, it wasn't easily identifiable. The dark, curly hair had made his stomach clench. Though Cage fought the urge to turn around and throw up, Dev made it reality.

As he listened to the sounds of his friend retching behind him, Cage took another look. *Was it Izzy?*

Dev barfed again behind him, making Cage wonder just what Dev had seen before coming to Alabama. It seemed these days, they'd all seen something—but whatever Dev had been through, it appeared he hadn't had to deal with dead bodies much before. Cage was unfortunately getting far more comfortable with the dead than someone his age should be.

"Give me your phone?" He reached out, but nothing happened.

Turning from the sad sight, he found Dev a few yards away, holding his hand up as if to ward Cage and his needs off. "No, not my phone."

"We don't have another option. We need pictures. And then we need to roll her over and get her face."

As he watched, Dev's body contracted again, his mouth opening as his chest and head whipped over for another round.

Cage looked away. Vomit was worse than a dead body.

He was pretty certain this was a she… or had been. Though none of that mattered until the person was identified. He closed the distance to his friend rather than asking Dev to come closer. "Dude, I really do need your phone."

This time, though Deveron didn't look up at him, he fished the device out of his pocket and handed it backward before returning to his hands-braced-on-knees position of defeat.

Cage walked back and snapped several shots from different angles, his own shadow getting in the way. He told himself the clothes didn't match Izzy, but he also couldn't remember for certain. Without the phone connected to a tower nearby, the metadata on the pictures wouldn't include the GPS location.

"Dev. Where are we?" he called over his shoulder as he took a few more pictures, doing his best to collect evidence.

"We're in a field, man." Dev was still bent over and not even looking, letting Cage do all the foul work.

"I mean, what highway were we on?"

"Ah, I think State Road 34. That's where the car is." He pointed behind him, back the way they came. "Maybe a mile and a half that way."

Cage only nodded, but mentally dialed the estimate back to half a mile. For an engineer, Dev had a solid tendency to over-estimate.

With everything else done, the only thing left was the worst task. He needed to roll her over and see her face. There seemed no easy way to do it, and he wasn't quite willing to reach down and touch the person's clothing. Aside from the ick factor, it simply felt disrespectful to him.

Walking a slow circle around the corpse, he tried to make a

decision. With his toe, he nudged one arm inward. It didn't move quite right, and his stomach pitched again as he figured there was a break somewhere in the long bones, or several somewheres. She looked beaten up.

Using his foot was even more disrespectful than using his hand, but he had no way to wash up, not even hand sanitizer. So, with his shoe, he pushed the arm up flush against the torso and then snapped another picture. He hated using the phone and using the battery. He still worried that this might be Izzy, though he'd basically talked himself out of that by now, because the clothing didn't match.

But the hair did.

None of this was easy. He tried again, and walked to the other side of the body. Clenching his teeth against the churn inside him, Cage pressed hard with his foot, rolling the body up until it reached sideways and flopped itself over.

His insides roiled for several reasons, only one being the way the corpse flopped down to the grass. He didn't recognize the face—and for a moment, that seemed as awful as if he had.

It was some teenager, someone young, definitely.

It only occurred to him now that he'd never questioned that the person was dead. He'd never once wondered if they needed CPR. Maybe that was a skill he had acquired from seeing corpses before. He could recognize that the dead were dead.

Once again, he took a series of pictures. When they went back, they would stop by the community center and deliver this awful information. Then a team could come out and retrieve the body.

Waving his friend along, and holding out the cell phone, Cage said, "I've done everything I can. Let's go."

Though Dev pushed himself upright and schooled his features, he still held out a hand and refused the phone. "You keep it."

Not wanting to argue, even though he'd closed all the apps,

Cage slipped the phone into his own pocket and picked up his discarded bike. He stood up on the pedals, pushing hard over the uneven terrain. It might have been easier without the debris littering the ground, but maybe not. He clearly wasn't an off-road biker, and his muscles were already protesting a second day of this.

With Dev quickly catching up, they skirted the edges of the path. It was rough going. No one had cleared anything in the field, and they had to slow down. He recognized a good bit of weird detritus, like the expected snapped and tossed tree branches, but he also saw pieces of homes that he couldn't identify.

When they'd been on the freeways, he could see the neighborhoods and the spots where the missing houses had stood. His brain automatically assumed that the freshly snapped wood lying in the road belong to the nearby missing structures. But out here, there was nothing to tie the old pipe with the boiler tag to, or the three shingles that had somehow managed to stick together and make it this far from civilization.

As they made their way through, they checked out everything they could. Cage tried to assess the damage to the trees. They picked up a few objects along the way, using the carry bags they'd stolen from the bike shop with everything else. Cage had now bungeed one teddy bear, a set of car keys, and an embroidered dog collar to the back of his bike. In his pocket, he had another cell phone he'd found dead in the grass. But it was blinged out with rhinestones and glimmer to the point that he knew someone would be able to identify it.

Hopefully, it was someone who would say, "Oh, you found my phone. Thank you." He was afraid someone would say, "Yes. That's our daughter's—and we haven't found her yet."

Given the looks of it, he didn't think the phone belonged to the teenager they'd found. The shine and purple glitter didn't match her old, loose jeans and the Grateful Dead T-shirt.

They were still to the left of the tornado track, not having needed to cross the rough ground yet. It was difficult going. Cage had thought for a while that they would simply bike right down the middle of the path the storm had cut, but the tires only sank into the freshly turned dirt. The rocks and debris churned in had forced them to stop every three feet. The grass, as difficult as it was, was still easier to cross.

"What's that?" Dev asked, pulling Cage from his thoughts. He continued to scan the field in front of them, but he didn't see what Dev was looking at. He was grateful that there were two of them and that Dev was clearly catching things that Cage was missing.

"I don't know. Where?"

"Look." Dev pointed to their left. "All this grass is even, and then nothing right there."

They turned their bikes, slowly pedaling through the mess, avoiding what had been dropped from the tornado as they approached the dent in the grass.

It was another dead body.

"Holy shit!" Dev muttered as Cage thought the same.

He didn't like this. This one was face up. And the only saving grace was that he could quickly identify that it was neither Joule nor Izzy.

"No!" The cry sounded like it was ripped from Dev's throat.

As Cage watched, Dev dropped the bike and ran the last few feet.

"No!"

When Cage looked again at the face, though it was gray and laid to the side, eyes closed, this time he recognized it.

55

J oule sat quietly tense, petrified that Toto would meow and give them away.

Distinctly human shuffling noises broke the regular sounds of the animals ... the noises Joule had become used to during her short tenure in the loft.

Somebody was searching the barn. But why?

There was no reason for a search, unless they knew that she and Jerry were up here, or at least suspected it. She waited for the ladder to the loft to creak as someone climbed it. But as she—

"Mrrrwow!" Toto looked up at her, his tiny plaintive cry seeming to echo visibly in the air around her.

Shit.

She tensed every muscle, staying perfectly still except for her gaze, which flicked to the side to look at Jerry. She saw that he, too, had simply frozen, mid-move. The sound didn't seem to faze their searchers though. And Joule suddenly realized her foolishness.

A cat in a barn meant nothing. There was no reason for them to suspect a mewing kitten meant human intruders were nearby. Toto hadn't given them away; his was the only expected sound here. The shuffling below them continued, but now with a murmured conversation she couldn't make out at all.

Relaxing marginally as Toto meowed again, Joule put her finger to her lips and scooped him up. She would have made a hushing noise but was afraid that would have alerted the searchers to humans.

Her heart stopped as she heard the thing she'd been afraid of—the creak of steps on the barn ladder. Someone was rapidly climbing up to the loft. Should she stand and fight? Could she plant her foot in their chest and send them backward off the ladder and probably to their death?

She didn't know who was coming up or who might be searching for them, though their face would clear the top at any moment. Joule would have to decide. And fast.

Then other footsteps broke into the shuffled conversation. Her fingers dug into the hay and she heard it crinkle with her grip. Could they hear it below?

"What are you doing in here?" the voice demanded.

"We wanted to be sure you were okay." The return answer rang insincere, even to Joule, who couldn't see the person's face.

Jerry's eyes widened at the second voice, and Joule could only guess that it was either one of the Larkins or maybe someone worse who was speaking. Whoever it was, her partner in tornado refugee crime seemed to know them.

"No, you're not. You're in my barn for, and I want to know why."

"No, no. No, we just wanted to know how you were doing after the storms." The fawning voice hit the rule of threes—anything said three times in a row was definitely a lie.

"That's bullshit," the voice replied, growing angrier.

Though Joule desperately wanted to lift her head and peer over the edge of the loft to see what was going on, she didn't dare.

"You assholes didn't come knock on my door, where you would have found me. I would have told you I was fine. No. You came straight here and crept into my barn. What are you looking for?"

The silence that filled the space spoke volumes, dragging out until Joule heard it punctuated by the telltale *ch-chunk* of a shotgun being cocked.

Her eyes flew wide, but there wasn't much time to react, not for her and not for the people down below. As the man spoke, she imagined him lifting the butt of the gun against his shoulder and aiming it. "I asked you a question."

Somehow she felt better knowing it was the accusing man who held the gun. Still, she looked to Jerry who shrugged and shook his head rapidly. Joule didn't know if that meant he didn't know what was going on or maybe if he didn't know what the noise was. But that couldn't be the case—the hard *chunk* of a shotgun being racked was an almost universally unmistakable sound.

"I don't want you two here. Now get out of my barn."

Slow shuffling down below let her know that the two who had come in first were finally leaving, albeit reluctantly. She lifted her head slowly, ever so slightly, until she could see the top half of the opening the sliding barn doors left, revealing the world beyond. She could see the edge of the white, wood-sided farmhouse and one black shutter. She could see a corner of the paddock and one brown cow that seemed to have a tense need to push herself into the fencing. And she watched as one woman with caramel hair and a ponytail trailing over her denim jacket walked out the door. Next came a man in overalls, a cap on his head, his shoulders hunched in anger as he exited the barn.

The older man followed behind them, holding the shotgun up and aimed, just as Joule had thought.

She lowered her head. That had been a dumb move. She'd

wanted to see what was going on, but she didn't know any of these people. Seeing the backs of their heads gave her no more information than listening had, and they could have looked up and seen her. But now she heard the barn doors being slid slowly shut as car doors—or more likely truck doors— slammed somewhere in the distance and an engine revved.

Slowly letting her breath out, though she knew it wasn't yet time to be relieved, she felt some of the tension drain from her muscles though she knew she shouldn't relax yet. She figured her body might have surpassed its capacity to stay alert. Even so, she tried not to make a sound as she turned toward Jerry and saw that he, too, had lifted his head just a little. Maybe he could identify the intruders.

As the second barn door slid into place and tapped the first, her lungs fully exhaled, her breath whooshing out. Her grip on Toto lessened just a little, now that they knew the old man was home, and that he didn't like the people who'd come looking for them. By her estimate, it had to be the Larkins, because who else would look for escapees?

She was feeling a little safer with all three of the barn intruders gone—though she and Jerry were the real intruders. But she was also feeling a little more concerned. If no one had been home, it would be easier to get out of the barn. Now they'd have to make alternate plans. She didn't remember seeing another door to the barn, but didn't there have to be one?

Then again, she had noticed that the Larkin's house was older and hadn't really been built to code. Did this barn have to be? She had to follow rules and regulations quite precisely when designing and building; that was half of her job at Helio Systems, creating something and then being sure it fit into regs. But it seemed the further out into the countryside they got, the more things were overlooked or grandfathered in.

Her stomach growled, interrupting her thoughts with the

reminder of the necessity of nature. Toto meowed at her again, also hungry. And while she had a granola bar still waiting—probably smushed—in her pocket, she was out of tuna.

She and Jerry stared at each other for a while. Joule didn't know if he simply had nothing to say or if, like her, he was waiting out the clock to see if anything happened. Joule tucked herself low to the haybale and tried to remember any other ways out of the barn, but it had been dark when they'd come in.

After an interminable wait, which may have been only a few minutes, she swung her legs over the side of the hay bale, feeling the poke of a thousand straws in the back of her jeans and under her butt as she did it. She was opening her mouth to ask if the barn owner was one of the people that Jerry might trust when she heard the sudden squeal of the door again as it flew open. Far too quickly for her to duck and hide. Below her, a horse whinnied at the intrusion.

The man with the gun was back.

56

Cage wasn't ready to deal with what he saw.

"Oh my God." Deveron was still on his knees, his words almost slurring together as, this time, his hands reached out toward the body. He only made it halfway to touching the corpse's clothing before he snatched his fingers back in close to his own body.

Once again, it was clear there was no resuscitation to be done, no attempt at rescue. He wasn't alive. Micah Banner was lying on the ground in front of them.

Had it just been yesterday that Cage and Micah had been collecting plant samples? They'd walked with their hands full of carefully stacked, eleven-by-fourteen cardstock pages, each with a plant sample taped to it and marked with the coordinates and details of where and how it had been found. His mind flashed to Micah's neat handwriting and how he'd asked his friend to scribe the information—because his own awkward scribbles seemed so juvenile in comparison.

They'd taken so many sample deliveries up to the tent where Izzy and Melinda cataloged them. Cage couldn't say that he counted Micah among his close friends—he simply hadn't had the time to build those relationships down here, not with anyone he wasn't living with. But now he felt the sharp cut of the loss of even that possibility.

That was a stupid thing to think about when faced with the body his potential friend had left behind ... in a field.

The group of them had run together as the tornado hit, dropping everything and linking hands, even though they weren't supposed to. They'd made a chain for comfort, but Cage had read it as a gesture that they wouldn't lose anyone. Yet here he and Dev were, trying to process what they'd found. Linking hands hadn't been enough. *They had lost one.*

Cage had initially dismissed the body. He hadn't wanted to look any further than his original assessment. He'd seen it from a short distance, the brown hair meaning it wasn't his sister or Izzy. After that, he'd simply decided that since it wasn't who he was looking for, he needed to look no further. But as they'd gotten closer, it had become clear this wasn't just the body of some random victim.

Dev now walked a circle. They didn't need to flip him over. He was flat on his back, his face angled to one side. And though it wasn't obvious, Cage thought he could detect the kink in his coworker's neck that might have been responsible for his death.

The contents of Cage's stomach slowly congealed and turned hard. He tried not to extrapolate the meaning, but he couldn't help it. The tornado had come through here, and the tornado was leaving dead bodies in its wake. There was no way to avoid the calculation that the odds were now lower that Izzy had survived or—though he didn't even want to admit it to himself—that Joule had.

For a moment, he wallowed in a bleak future. *What would his life be like without his sister?* What would he be if he were the last survivor of the original four Mazurs?

While Deveron walked a circle around Micah's body, Cage stared blankly into the distance. There was nothing he could think of, no alternate future things he would do. There was no better life, even on the small scale, without Joule.

Once, his father had gone missing for a day, trapped in a stalled subway train while he was out of town. Cage had asked his mother later what she would do if his dad died. She had plans. She'd get a cat—her husband was allergic and she'd always wanted a cat. She'd set the house temperature where she wanted it. Plant the pansies his father had vetoed. Small things, and nothing that would make up for the loss, but little things that she would do differently.

Cage had no such fallbacks. Maybe because he hadn't met Joule later in life but had never known a minute without his sister. So there were no things that he would do if he didn't have his sister holding him back, or if he hadn't compromised on certain decisions.

Granted, he might not be here in Alabama now without Joule. He had originally chosen marine biology for his major, but after dealing with the things that might be found in the water, he'd changed to a more diverse bio major. So what would he do? Go scuba diving without her? It didn't change anything. He could just as easily go scuba diving with her. There was no job that he'd wanted that he'd compromised on so they could stay together. He had been offered another position that would pay approximately five thousand more dollars per year. It didn't mean anything.

He simply had to find his sister. And he didn't want to think about what his life might become if he failed.

He already had one family member permanently missing. Though Joule had rattled him once and made it clear that she believed their father was not coming back, she wasn't here to dish harsh truths now. He would have to be the one to rattle himself. And he wasn't up for it.

The alternative was to simply *find his sister*.

"We need pictures," he told Deveron before remembering

that he still had Dev's phone. Pulling it from his pocket, he went about the ugly business of snapping a few shots. For one, he knelt down and got in close to Micah's face. It felt horribly intrusive. Cage told himself that his vision wasn't blurry and he didn't feel that sharp squeeze at the back of his jaw. The picture was necessary for identification.

"Where are we now?" he asked.

"Another two miles, maybe," Dev said looking around and, again, overestimating.

Glancing back the way they'd come, Cage could see the track their bikes had made. If they needed to, they could turn around and exactly retrace their path.

But how long would the banked grass stay that way? *Not long*, he thought.

"We're near the path of the tornado, at least. So there is a relatively permanent landmark for us to follow." Dev pointed to the unmistakable edge of the churned earth about forty feet away. He mentioned the marker as if he understood that Cage was struggling to pinpoint location without the ability to hook up to a satellite and get GPS coordinates.

When they had done everything they could do, they once again climbed back on their bikes and continued on the path they'd chosen. There was now evidence of people as they went past. Some of it was evidence of life, and some seemed to indicate the original bearer might be dead.

They found more than one shoe—and though shoes could come from closets, it was entirely possible they came from feet. There was an entirely untouched-looking lunch pack with now-spoiled meat and cheese slices. Broken glass, and parts of houses, and eventually several parts of cars littered the ground.

There were also tracks through the grass, much like the one he could see trailing him and Dev.

Someone had come through here *after* the tornado. Otherwise, the grass would have been whipped into some other shape by the passing storm, not staying in its uniformly bent position, revealing the track.

In fact, as they moved, they found a point where the grass told them they were crossing the path of whomever had made it before.

"It's a person," Cage said, hopeful that it had been Joule.

"Or a mountain lion," Dev answered quickly, though Cage wondered if they even had those here, and would they disturb the grass this way?

As they crossed the trampled path, Cage turned his head to the left to see a wavy path through the grass. The person—if he was reading it correctly—came up on his left, crossed where they were stopped and headed off to the right, directly toward the path of the tornado.

But something else caught Dev's eye. "There!"

Cage didn't see it.

"The grass is all patted down. Let's go look."

With nothing better to do and the day waning on with still no sign of his sister, Cage was willing to follow Dev's lead.

Sure enough, the grass had been bent in a path leading directly toward this spot and then away from it. In the matted down area, twigs and scraps of wood had been moved—clearly by a human hand—to form a sign.

57

"Come on Dev," Cage called back without looking. He stood up, using his weight against the pedals and bent over at the waist.

He was pretty certain that he was leaning too far forward and likely had not adjusted this mountain bike correctly. His muscles protested with every push. But even so, he continued moving.

"It's far too late in the day to begin a search like this." Dev's voice came from somewhere behind him.

But Cage didn't know how long the search would be and so he just had to keep going. "We have time."

"We can't do this." Dev was speaking for the devil on Cage's shoulder—the one who told him it should wait until tomorrow, that he was hurting himself by pushing so hard.

"It's *Joule*," was all that Cage replied. He had to follow the arrow. The *JM* that had been scratched lightly to the surface was clear, once he'd looked. She'd even added a few extra pieces at the tip of the arrow tail—a sign their father had taught them meant it was *her*, not just an arrow anyone could have laid out.

Though the sign made it clear that it was her, and even told them the direction to aim to follow her, the biggest win was that his sister *had survived*. That alone was enough to keep him going.

"We don't know how far she went," Dev said.

"Exactly. What if she's right over that hill and we turn around? We won't find out if we don't follow the trail."

"We don't even know if this is her."

Cage stopped his bike, turned, and looked back at his friend, who apparently had stopped a little ways back and he hadn't realized. "One, *I* know it's her. And two, she carved the initials *JM* into the tail of the arrow."

Dev was shaking his head, almost as if Cage were being stupid. "No, I know *the arrow* is her, but we don't know about this path we're following. We don't have any tracking skills. We've come a good distance from the sign, and we don't have any idea what we're following at this point. What if this path—" he motioned to the bent grass behind them, "isn't your sister's?"

"It is. We do know."

"How?" Dev looked incredulous. With his feet on either side of the bike, he now put his hands on his hips as if in protest.

"If she changed direction, she would have left us another arrow. And there is a path here."

"We don't know that it's her," Dev repeated his protest a little more forcefully.

"Who else could it be?" Cage argued back, his hands raising as he gestured around. "There's one relatively rough path through the grass that leads here. It came directly from the arrow with her initials on it. It's *her*."

"Right," Dev said. "We could kind of see a path in the grass, but now we're heading in the woods, and we've got nothing."

"So we keep going straight until we find the next arrow!" It all seemed so damn logical to Cage.

But Dev didn't budge. Cage just stared right back at him for a while in a ridiculously stupid grudge match that he was not willing to lose. He had a brief thought that they'd already left Sarah behind and she was okay. He could leave Deveron behind, too, if he had to.

But it wouldn't be a good move. Finally, he said the only thing he could say, "It's my sister. She's alive. And we're following her tracks."

But before he budged, Dev looked at Cage and replied, equally logically, "It's daylight, but not for that much longer. We work until dark and then we come back tomorrow."

"But—"

Dev shook his head. Maybe it was because he didn't have any siblings. Maybe being an only child made him simply not understand. Dev was applying logic as well, but the kind you applied if you were on a rescue team looking for a child whose picture you'd seen but you'd never met. Cage needed the kind of logic that kept you on the trail for your only remaining family member.

Dev kept trying to make his case. "Now we know she's alive. She's not only alive, she's alive enough to get up and move around and think to leave an arrow that you would recognize. She put her initials on it in case those of us looking for her found it. There's every possibility she's already located help and that we're now aimed the wrong direction. We could be getting farther away by following this track."

Cage wanted to argue back. His feeling was that Joule was still somewhere in front of him was very strong. The worst case scenario was that she had walked in a circle, but if he followed her signs, then he would, too. He would eventually catch up to her. But he couldn't crack the fortress that Dev was building.

"Okay," he agreed. "Until nightfall." He didn't clarify that he wasn't agreeing to stop searching at nightfall, but only that he was agreeing to stay with Dev until then.

With renewed hope, he led the two of them into the woods. The ground here was harder going. The tornado hadn't thrown as much junk into their path among the trees, but the ground was strewn with roots and rocks. Just being in the woods held gut-churning memories for him.

Eventually, they hopped off their bikes and simply pushed them along. They ran into a stream where they stopped and looked at each other. Though Cage didn't say it, he thought, *Good job, Joule*. The first thing she'd done was find water.

Together, the two men looked first to the left and then the right. There was no clear direction to go.

"What do we do?" Dev asked now on a heavy sigh, as if to suggest he knew that Cage would have some easy answer. "Do we go straight through?"

Cage had already considered that possibility. If she turned, there should be an arrow. He was checking the appearance of the other side of the creek. The side was slick and muddy, and it should show if someone had climbed up.

"I don't see any evidence that she went through here. So did she go right or left?" Dev's question mirrored his thoughts. But Cage truly had no idea. He and his twin weren't psychically linked as much as they were in tune with each other, though he was confident that he would know if Joule had left this world.

Right now, he could not for the life of him decide if she would have gone left or right. But at just that moment, they heard a noise and both of their heads snapped up.

58

"I know you're up there."

Joule stood frozen by the voice. She couldn't see the man. She had to assume he could maybe see the top of her blonde head. Or maybe she was lucky and her hair color would blend in with the hay.

Could he see them? Or was he just making accusations to get them to come down?

"My horse blanket's missing," he called up.

Joule cringed—they'd left evidence. They could have slept up here without the blankets, because heat rose, but the barn still wasn't what she would call warm. The blanket had made a difference between getting real sleep and not really getting any rest at all.

Next to her, Jerry held up a hand, motioning her to stay put. She clutched Toto to her chest and, once again, the kitten must have discerned the tension in her system, because he curled down into her hands and didn't make any noise or try to escape. She rubbed at his small head as though that would make any difference.

Standing to his full height, Jerry walked out near the edge of the loft and called down as he did. "Hey, Paul. It's me."

When Paul didn't answer, Jerry added, "Jerry McGee."

"What is your dumb ass doing in my loft, boy?" At least now Paul sounded exasperated rather than angry. Less like he was likely to cock the shotgun again and more like he was ready to give Jerry a good verbal lashing about stealing horse blankets.

"Give me a sec, okay?" Jerry asked, slowly grabbing at the two rails of the ladder that extended up past the flooring for support. They were the only thing that made it reasonably easy to get up and down. Then Jerry rotated his large frame around and began the careful process of climbing back down to the ground.

Still, Joule thought, it was a crappy system up here. Not made for people. A good run or a shove and anyone could fall right out of this place. The height was dangerous, too, but she was in no position to suggest Paul follow OSHA guidelines. So she simply held her breath and held her kitten while Jerry made his way down.

It seemed to take forever for Jerry to get to the bottom of the ladder, and he didn't talk while he did it. Joule was wound tight by the time he finally reached the hay-covered floor.

What happened next was not what she expected.

"I found your truck," Paul told him, though the news sounded more accusatory than exciting.

Joule frowned. She must have clutched Toto just a little too tightly, because he began wiggling. She stroked his soft fur again, happy when he settled down.

"That's great news!" Jerry replied, sounding as if he'd missed the tone. The question was, *had he*? Or was he just writing it off? He knew Paul, and Joule didn't. Maybe Paul was just a surly old goat most of the time.

"Let's talk about what I found in your truck."

"Wait a minute!" Joule could easily imagine Jerry holding

his hand up as if to say "Stop!" just as he'd stopped her several times. She wished she could see them, but it was too risky. "Where did you find my truck?"

"I found it because I was up the road a ways. Why was it there and you're here?"

"When this second set of twisters came through, I got shelter and when I came out I saw they stole it."

"Your big truck?"

"Paul, they were huge! Have you been listening to the radio?" Joule almost laughed. What she wouldn't have given to have been listening to the radio.

"It's off the side of the road, ass down in a ditch," Paul replied, though again his tone sounded impatient.

"But it's all in one piece?" Jerry asked, almost as if marveled by the idea that it hadn't been torn limb from limb.

"Yeah, it is. And so is what's inside." Paul's impatience was now something that couldn't be ignored. "It's got three bricks of cocaine in the back seat."

Holy shitastic fuckballs! Joule's head jerked back, even though she wasn't down there in the conversation herself. She almost scrambled backwards from the shock, as though she could backpedal from the accusation. But she stopped herself at the last minute, glad she hadn't made any noise.

Could Jerry explain that?

Joule had not been prepared for that possibility. Silence met Paul's accusation. She was glad that she hadn't blurted anything out or yelped, giving herself away.

Was Jerry running with the Larkins? But that didn't make sense. He could have easily turned around when they fled through the woods. He hadn't seemed really shocked when she found the bricks of coke in the cellar... was that because he was with a counter cartel? Had she not only landed herself in the middle of a drug running operation, but a drug war?

"Are you shitting me?" Jerry finally snarled, and she wondered how real the accusation was.

"There were three bricks of that shit, taped up, and wrapped in plastic."

"What color was the plastic?" Jerry asked, now sounding curious more than anything. "No. Wait!"

Joule had no idea where he was going with this. She pressed her back into the hay bale behind her and waited. But she was ready to bolt and run as soon as she heard anything that let her know she was in real trouble.

Jerry continued. "Let me tell you first what we found at the Larkins."

Crappety Crap! Jerry had just said "we." He'd outed her, seemingly without knowing it. She could only hope that Paul hadn't caught the slip as Jerry continued.

Jerry sounded pretty smart as he told Paul about getting stuck in the cellar during the storm and trapped by what they'd eventually seen was a large tree that had fallen right across the back of the house.

"We found bricks of cocaine in the crawlspace," Jerry told the old man. "Wrapped in plastic. Green plastic, but still clear."

Okay, Joule thought, *that was smart*. Name the color first.

"So, if that's what you found in my car, my guess is the Larkins planted it."

She could almost hear Paul rubbing at his chin as he thought it through. "If I believe your story, then how did the Larkins know it was you in their house?"

"Well, they know I was out there, and they clearly found my truck, just like you did. Maybe they were just planting the coke on me to keep some of the suspicion off of themselves."

Shit, Joule thought, sighing out her displeasure as quietly as she could. It had been a good lead. But Jerry was losing the upper hand.

"You wouldn't lie to me, would you?" Paul asked.

The question struck Joule as dumb, but Jerry answered right away, and sincerely. "No. That's why I'm down here talking to you now. Because I trust you. The reason I'm in your barn is because I fled from the Larkins last night."

Joule almost raised her hand and comically wiped it across her forehead. He had been smart enough to say *I* this time.

But her relief didn't last for long.

"You say you won't lie to me, but you're lying to me now." Paul's tone was low and angry—not the accusing sound from before, but something deeper. "There's two horse blankets missing. And you said *we.*"

Damnit Jerry! He kept putting her in these situations. She clutched Toto closer to her chest and waited.

59

"Come on down, Joule," Jerry called up. "It's okay. I trust Paul."

Well, she thought, still clutching Toto to her chest, *that was it*. It didn't matter if *she* trusted Paul yet or not. Jerry had decided for her. So she stood and walked closer to the edge where she could look down and wave before following Jerry's earlier actions and slowly stepping backwards down the ladder.

As she hit the bottom rung, though, she turned around and learned that Jerry was wrong. No one should be trusting Paul at all.

Paul stood with his feet planted wide, the shotgun pressed into his shoulder and his eye aimed down the sight right at her.

Her—inappropriate—first response was to turn to Jerry, as if to ask, *Did you know about this?* But Jerry's expression was equally incredulous. He hadn't seen this coming.

"Paul, what are you doing!"

It wasn't a question, and Paul didn't answer. Instead, he reached back and pulled a cell phone out of his pocket.

It was remarkably high tech, considering the overalls and

hunting jacket and old ball cap that had seen better days. He looked to be dialing someone.

"I've got them," he said into the line as soon as someone answered. "Come on back."

Shitgibbons. For someone to *come back* had to mean he was talking to the Larkins.

"What are you doing, Paul?" she asked, purposefully using his name. It felt odd rolling off her tongue for the first time in an accusatory tone, but she was not a fan of the shotgun aimed at her.

Her heart was racing, her muscles tensed and ready to go, Toto still clutched to her chest. And she wished to God she had left him up in the loft. He could have been a barn kitten for the rest of his days, happily hunting mice—if he was old enough to catch them and feed himself... she wasn't sure. Her fingers squeezed around his tiny, soft body involuntarily.

She wondered what would happen if she said *Don't hurt my kitten.* Would Paul let Toto go? Or would he shoot him just to make a point? Clearly, Jerry had no idea who Paul really was.

Then the old man moved ever so slightly, turning his torso toward Jerry. "I'm sorry, man. They've got my daughter."

Fuckballs. This wasn't an issue of Paul being an asshole. It was a hostage situation on top of another hostage situation. The phone buzzed, and Paul put it back to his ear. "No! I'm not sending them out. Not until you send my daughter in."

Joule thought she heard something from the other end of the line, but it didn't matter. It was too late and the barn doors were creaking loudly as they slid open.

A woman stumbled in, dropping onto her hands and knees as if pushed. "Sorry, Daddy," she said softly.

Joule wanted to look at her, but she knew it was far more important to keep her eyes on the barn doors. If she could see someone, then she might have an idea what they were up against. But no one showed their face through the slim opening. Instead, they began the process of shoving the heavy door closed.

Did it even mater? She'd never seen the Larkins' faces. In fact, she didn't even know if they were actually the Larkins. She'd just assumed Jerry had no reason to lie about that.

As the woman began to get up off of her hands and knees, the barn door tapped shut. Joule heard the click of a lock and the sound of a chain dragging along metal.

She would have run to the door, because she was pretty certain they were getting bolted in, but the shotgun kept her in place. She turned back to the man wielding it and registered the expression on Paul's face.

He'd begun to move to hug his daughter, but stopped cold, fear painting every muscle. There were four of them in the barn now, Paul still loosely holding the shotgun on Jerry and Joule. But now he stood still, looked around, and seemed confused.

If Joule had heard right, Paul had offered to trade her and Jerry for his daughter. But instead of trading, whoever it was had simply shoved the daughter inside. That couldn't be good.

There were murmured words outside, and Joule wished she could hear, but all she could get was the tone—and the tone wasn't good. Beside her, Jerry stood still, seeming to be equally frozen by the strange and sudden twists of their circumstance. In her hands, Toto remained curled in a tight little ball.

She wasn't fast enough to outrun a blast from the shotgun. But Paul wasn't holding it steadily anymore. His eyes flicked to the side, clearly confused about what had changed. Like her, he seemed to want to know what was happening on the other side of the door.

Joule took that moment to be grateful that she had picked up a kitten and not a puppy. She tipped her hand, quickly tossing Toto to the side and knowing he would land on his tiny feet.

She was maybe four good steps away from Paul, and it still seemed too far. As she began to move, she wondered if it would work. It was supposed to. The martial arts classes she taken as a kid hadn't taught her how to do this, but she'd spent enough time watching the black belts practice disarming assailants. She knew the moves, even if she'd never reached a belt level where they had let her practice them. This one wasn't from muscle memory, it was all brain.

It took forever to cross the short space. Paul's head whipped back and he saw her coming, the barrel of the shotgun lifting and aiming as he did. Only then did she remember a crucial piece. It wasn't just that she had to act the opposite of what was expected—rushing her opponent rather than walking away— she also had to get out of the line of fire.

She dropped low, making it harder to move. It felt like the world was running in slow motion as she maneuvered below the end of the gun and slapped her hands together into a V-shape. Literally under the gun now, and almost barreling into Paul's torso, she shifted and burst upward, pushing at the gun in his hands in a hopefully unexpected way.

In the perfect scenario, this would allow her to grab the gun, yank it away and turn it on him. In her mind, she whacked him upside the head with the butt of the weapon, dropping him cold and giving herself some much needed satisfaction.

But it didn't quite work out that way.

She didn't think she'd ever seen the moves performed with a shotgun instead of a handgun or maybe a knife. Apparently, all the martial artists were convinced they would be in hand fights, and not caught in the middle of drug running rings with shotgun-wielding farmers.

Still, she managed to catch Paul's wrists with her movement, and that burst of power aimed the gun upward. The old man was maybe better at this than she was, because she fully expected the retort of gunfire in response to her attack and he managed to refrain from pulling the trigger in either anger or surprise.

"What in the blazes!" he muttered like the old coot that he was: a farmer who, despite offering a hostage trade to drug runners and being double-crossed and attacked by the stow-away in his barn, still wouldn't quite swear.

Joule had the shotgun barrel in her hands, but Paul's hands were also still clenched tightly on the weapon. She was trying to figure out if she should pull or shove when she felt the hit.

60

"Look!" Cage called out, his excitement ratcheting up another notch.

They'd come across another arrow at the side of the road. After crossing the stream and climbing up the other side, they'd found mud tracks left by someone who'd come through a relatively short while before. Cage was still convinced it was Joule's footsteps he was following.

Another arrow, with another faint JM carved into the back of it, let him know he was right.

"I don't know, man." Dev looked up at the sky.

Somehow, neither of them had noticed before this that the daylight was growing fainter and fainter. Cage didn't care. "I can't turn back."

"You promised."

"I didn't," he said. "I agreed to search until dark. I didn't say I'd quit then. But, look, it's Joule."

This time, Dev didn't try to deny it or offer up a theory that some other local JM was leaving signs. "I don't know. What could we even do? It's already getting dark."

It wasn't yet, but it would be soon.

Cage pulled Dev's cell phone out of his pocket and powered it up. He flicked on the light at the front of his bike and the one on his helmet and motioned to Dev to do the same. They checked each other over while there was still light to repair anything, but the helmets, rear flashers, and high beams were all still working fine.

Better to turn them on a little early than get sideswiped by a car on the side of the road. The last thing they needed was to add their names to the already high toll of injured or missing.

Though they hadn't seen anyone since arriving at the road-side, they'd watched a truck go by while they were still standing in the woods. As they'd followed it, attempting to flag it down, Cage decided that that must be exactly what his sister had done. Either that or she had veered a little off track while going through the woods, but the obvious point where someone had scrambled up the other side of the bank was almost definitely hers, now that they'd found another sign she'd left.

The JM on this one—made of bricks and sticks—was faint, but because he knew where to look, Cage had found it relatively easily. He wasn't going back, no matter what his friend said or did. "There's pavement here. We're not walking through the woods anymore. We'll stay on the road."

Now that it was powered up, the phone readily told him the time. It wasn't quite summer hours, with the long days that carried the sunlight until after eight. But it wasn't winter yet, either. They'd managed to make a good portion of the trip with daylight. Now that they had a road, he could keep going.

Cage was turning to say something but noticed as the screen changed slightly. "Holy shit, Dev!"

"What?"

"Bars!" He started to dial Sarah and realized nothing was in the right place because it wasn't his phone. He handed it over to Dev to call, and even as he did that, the phone began pinging.

He wished he could turn it off. Each sound heralding a little more battery being sucked away. But messages poured in, the next ping starting before the last one had finished. Most came in from Sarah, though there were others from the Helio Systems main line, and a handful of county alerts.

Dev reached over and readily hit the screen, pulling up Sarah's chain almost before Cage could even see what the options were. But he moved in close and the two huddled, straddling their bikes at the side of the road as they got their first taste of civilization in hours.

Cage wasn't even sure if Dev had scrolled all the way back to the top of Sarah's long list of messages. She'd clearly had cell service for a while now.

—*they found Radnor. He went to the hospital but he didn't make it.*

Cage heard Dev let out a weary sigh of sadness as he felt the same thing happening in his own chest, but Dev scrolled to the next one, more messages dinging in even as they tried to read this chain.

—*nothing from Izzy and Joule.*

Then she added —*Leslie, Melinda, Jeremy & Kevin have checked in and are safe. I told them I was good and you were too.*

Then another text came through.

—*heard from Doug. He and his family are good.*

—*no word on Izzy and Joule.*

She listed more names, every third or fourth text punctuated with "No word from Izzy and Joule."

When they got to the last new message, Deveron quickly tapped back. "We found Micah. He didn't make it. We'll report in when we get to the community center."

Once they'd read through the incoming messages, Cage carefully pulled the phone away and took a deep breath. He dialed Joule's number.

Dev watched solemnly as Cage heard a sound of connection and prayed for his sister's voice. Instead he got the digital notification that the line wasn't in service. He hit the button off and told himself it didn't mean anything.

Then there was a pause as the two of them looked at each other. Cage knew there was a decision to be made. There was a cell signal now, and they had one phone between them. If they split up, someone would be left completely alone, without communications.

There wasn't much going on out here. Though they hadn't been on the road long, only the truck they had missed had gone by. Though he had hoped they would see other people, they hadn't yet.

Cage was calculating what he would do if Dev decided to turn back and take the phone with him. But Dev instead seemed to interpret the phone and the link to humanity as more of an indication that it was okay to be out in the dark searching.

"If we're connected, I'm not as worried," he announced.

Cage didn't wait for him to change his mind. He hopped back on the bike and let Dev follow along. However, he once again regretted believing he'd gotten in good enough shape from the work. Everything hurt as he pushed on the pedals, knowing what he was looking for was just ahead. He wasn't going to lose anyone else.

He'd eaten another granola bar while they picked their way through the woods, but it wasn't really enough. He thought about shoveling a huge bowl of pasta into his face. He imagined it drenched in Alfredo sauce, maybe with mushrooms and thin slices of steak. But almost as quickly as he enjoyed the thought, it soured.

It felt bad to be thinking about the physical pleasures of enjoying food and sating his hunger when he still hadn't found his sister. He pedaled harder.

The road wound in between and around farms and their

outbuildings. Though the structures weren't falling down, most of them looked relatively abandoned. Only one had lights on inside and a man outside picking up debris and tossing it into a pile in the corner of his yard.

He waved as the two went by. But they quickly pulled to stop.

Given the size of the lot, it took a while, but the man graciously crossed the long distance to the roadside, where they showed him the picture of Izzy and Joule and Sarah.

"Have you seen either of these two women?" Cage pointed to his sister. "We think she came through here not long ago."

Though he was polite about it, the man dismissed them with a shake of his head. "We grabbed the kids and the dogs as soon as we heard the funnels were forming, and we got the hell out of Dodge. We only just came back maybe an hour ago."

Having told them all he could, or all he was willing to, he turned and headed back toward the house, picking up debris as he went.

Cage and Dev shrugged at each other and hopped back on their bikes. At least the man hadn't been here the whole time. Had he been watching the road and known that Joule *hadn't* passed by, that would have been a blow to Cage's hope.

He told himself there was still a very good chance that she was simply up the road a bit.

Another ping came in, and they stopped yet again to put their heads together and read it. Sarah had sent them a list of about fifteen names still missing from Helio Systems Tech. The last two were Isabel McAlister and Joule Mazur.

Cage didn't quite recognize a few of the others. Dev had to explain, "You know, the older guy? He has black hair with silver in it." But Cage definitely recognized Saskia Kaczmarek, and he knew all the rest at least tangentially.

Dev looked at him with a bone-weary sigh. "Looks like we're on the lookout for more than just Joule and Izzy."

Cage nodded. As if the task of finding the two women wasn't monumental enough, there was this.

As they climbed back onto the bikes, Cage wondered if the phone would interfere the whole way, creating this start-and-stop situation. He pushed on the pedals and pressed farther down the dark road, making their way past farmhouses, barns, paddocks, and open fields.

Another thought rolled through his mind, one he hadn't shared with Dev. They were supposed to be looking for Joule and Izzy. He'd hoped they were together. But from the first arrow they'd found, he'd known Joule was on her own.

He hadn't backtracked down the path to see if he could find the point where she'd landed—to see if maybe she'd had to walk away from the body of one of her good friends. But the arrow had only been signed JM. Not JM / IM. Not J & I.

So the list of lost names was only a bit worse than what he'd already figured out. They wouldn't be done when they found Joule. Izzy was somewhere else. And then so was everyone else on the list.

They stuck to the road, and he thought about staying to one side in case a car came through, but none did. With the farms so far apart, registering the distance they covered was difficult, but being on the road definitely made them much faster.

Then he began to wonder if he'd passed his sister somewhere along the way.

61

The air was knocked out of her as Joule was hit from the side.

Jerry had tackled them, ending the small standoff as she and Paul toppled together in a tangle of limbs and grunts. The shotgun fell to the floor. It hit too softly, landing on the hay-lined floor and not making a thump or clatter to adequately convey her anger at the whole situation.

In their stalls, the horses whuffed and stomped, clearly uneasy with what was going on.

Disoriented from the fall, Joule quickly scrambled up. Though everybody tried to do the same, she managed to get her feet under her and get upright a little faster than the old man and Jerry.

While she scrambled for the shotgun a little quicker than the others, she only managed to get her hand around the barrel as she saw another set of slim fingers grab for the stock.

This was not good. If they both picked up the weapon together, that would leave the barrel aimed at her. Also, having her hand on the barrel of a gun would be doubly bad news if someone pulled the trigger. But again she thought, *Surprise your opponent.*

So instead of yanking at the gun, she shoved it. And, as the woman stumbled backward in surprise, Joule yanked. Hard.

She won. Now in possession of the only weapon, she stepped back and aimed it toward the small crowd. She motioned the daughter to move carefully and slowly over next to her father, but simply ignored Jerry. God help him if he got in her way, though.

Thanks, Dad. She sent the thought out into whatever might be waiting in the beyond. She was grateful that her father had taught her how to shoot and hoped that skill might prevent her from being reunited with her parents too soon.

She remembered the feel of a gun. The weight of it, pushing it up against her shoulder and aiming the barrel toward the two she was trying to corral.

When the Night Hunters had come, her mother and father had argued about whether or not the children should be taught to handle guns. It had finally been decided that, for their own safety, they needed to be prepared to defend themselves. Aiming it at a human had never been the plan. But none of this had been in the plan.

She'd had a fully shit two days, and she wasn't in the mood to be dicked with by anyone.

Backing up slowly to keep her footing, she let her thoughts run wild, because she didn't want to pull the trigger on one of these people, but she was still sorting out who to trust.

Paul shouldn't be the problem. He'd been caught up in this whole thing, the same as she and Jerry. She didn't even know who the woman was, other than "Paul's daughter." It seemed the woman had been held hostage, too. But right now, she was glaring daggers at Joule.

Joule motioned with the gun as if to say, *I know how to use this and I will.*

Another portion of her mind was listening to the animals, now more than uneasy and making concerning noises. Something else was happening outside the barn, but her immediate threat was three pairs of eyes. Only one of which—Jerry's, shockingly—were looking at her as if she knew what she was doing and it was all okay.

Another stray thought tapped at her brain, wondering about the kitten. *Where was Toto?*

She'd tossed him away just a moment ago. Could she afford to turn and look?

"Toto?" she called out as if a kitten would come when called by name—as if this one even knew his name yet.

"Toto!" she called again, frantically, when she got no obvious response. Maybe if she could find the kitten and do one thing, the other things would fall into place. It was illogical thinking, but it was hers.

Though Paul and his daughter glared at her and Paul made small adjustments as though he was going to dive for her, Joule didn't even flinch. She raised an eyebrow at him and motioned with the tip of the gun for him to keep his ass planted. He didn't have the chops to do what she had done. He didn't have the chops to tackle anyone the way Jerry had, either.

"I see him!" Jerry announced happily and, as though there wasn't a standoff going on and there wasn't a loaded shotgun between them. He headed to the corner of the large, open space. At least he wasn't tackling her again. Crouching down, he held out a hand and called softly, "Hey Toto! Come on out, Toto."

It all happened in a matter of seconds. Joule turned her head briefly to see if Toto was coming out. This time, Paul did lunge at her, but he wasn't fast enough.

Joule stepped back quickly, a reaction and not a plan. Again, she jerked at the gun as if to indicate she *would shoot* when it was becoming pretty clear that she wouldn't.

She'd had enough of this. So she motioned to both Paul and his daughter and gruffly demanded, "Sit down!"

As they were moving, a heavy crack sounded through the air and they all jerked in surprise. Paul fell the last foot on his awkward path to the floor, but all heads spun to the side.

Not immediately registering what had made the noise, Joule whipped back to looking at her prisoners. She was grateful she'd already gotten the other two on the ground, or they might have been able to take advantage of the noise and steal the gun away from her.

Beside her, the whinnies and angry huffs let her know that the horses were not calming down. In fact, they were getting worse, as though they could feel the tension in the air. The noise had almost definitely been one of them kicking at the stall or the barn wall. From the sound of it, he'd broken something. But what?

Though Joule couldn't tell, she imagined she could see the wood stalls still shuddering from the impact. But the horses would have to wait.

"What's your name?" she asked the woman.

"Brenda." It was curt and short.

"I don't want to shoot anybody," Joule said, "but don't think that I won't. Now someone needs to explain to me what is going on."

Paul lost all his tension then, his shoulders sagging, his head going into his hands, as if Joule's declaration had stolen the final bit of fight from him. Now, he was not only sad, but ashamed.

"Laura and Levi came through looking for you," Paul told his daughter. "I said I hadn't seen you, but then I told them what I'd found in Jerry's truck, because I was surprised. Apparently, I was being an idiot, because it wasn't about Jerry. It was about them. They played me and I fell for it."

Brenda was nodding, putting her hand out to her father's

arm, as if maybe she'd been there at the time. And sure enough, the next part of Paul's story cleared that up. "I came out to see if y'all were here. Then when I went back to the house to tell Brenda, I found Laura and Levi holding her hostage. I thought they'd left, but they had guns on us both."

He needed a breath, but Joule waited. She had to hear the whole story.

"They told me they'd followed people to my barn and that I needed to come out and get you. They seemed to think I had a better chance of talking you into coming down the ladder. They needed to see your faces. If you were who they wanted, they said I could exchange you for Brenda."

Joule opened her mouth to retort, "Well, that didn't go as planned, did it?" but he already knew that. He was now under threat from his own gun and he'd not exchanged anyone.

Lowering the gun, but still holding it tightly in the one hand—so she could have it at the ready if she needed—Joule put her free hand to her forehead. She needed a break from this damn day. But it wasn't coming.

Jerry still crouched in the corner, Toto not quite warming to the idea of coming out for him. Joule almost laughed at her kitten's stubbornness, but another loud crack shot through the barn and shuffling noises came from outside.

She looked to Paul, as if to ask, *Were the horses trying to get out or the cows trying to get in?* But he only shrugged in response. His concerned and confused expression meant he didn't know, either.

Ultimately, it didn't matter. It didn't matter what he knew or whether she could lower the gun and they could work as a team in case the Larkins came through that door again, because it was only five seconds later that Jerry got a hold of Toto. He lifted the tiny cat with a gentleness that Joule had not suspected.

As he handed the soft ball of fuzz into Joule's waiting hand, the horses began bouncing off the walls.

"Something's wrong," Paul announced as he got to his feet to inspect the animals. Joule didn't protest. She was just as shitty a hostage-taker as Paul had been.

But the older man didn't even make it to the stalls. They all figured out why the animals were going crazy as smoke began to curl under the edges of the door.

62

C age was ready to give up.

He hadn't seen anything, but he hadn't said anything about it, and neither had Dev. They'd been biking for miles—or else, he was starting to think like Dev did, that they'd come much farther than they actually had.

He tried calculating the odds. What did it hurt to be out here? But the answer was, maybe it did. The longer they stayed out tonight, the more likely they were to sleep through good searching hours tomorrow. The daylight had to be better than this. The more they rode, the more his muscles screamed in protest. They'd been complaining harshly for several hours now. And who knew? Maybe tomorrow, some of the roads would be clearer.

Then again, how far had they come? And how far was it back to the car, or even to Desperado's Hideaway?

He wasn't quite sure where they were. Dev had taken his phone back again, which meant he had the only GPS, but it was a battery-eater, and Cage wasn't willing to ask his friend to use it.

"There's a light up ahead," Dev told him.

So there's another house, Cage thought glumly. Most of the houses had seemed empty—either abandoned to rot or the residents had fled the storms. Then again, if it was lit, maybe the people were home.

"Do you think it's worth knocking on doors?" Dev asked.

Cage was still putting effort on the pedals, still feeling the scream in his thighs with every push. His back was angry and protesting, his shoulders making rude comments at every turn of the handlebars. The pain reminded him that he still hadn't properly adjusted his bike.

His return thought was that he wasn't quite sure how to properly adjust a bike in the first place. He wasn't a cyclist. "I think we should. It'll take a lot of time, but Joule's out here."

"She may have stopped at one of the farms back there. We might have already passed her." Dev's words echoed Cage's thoughts from earlier.

It was plausible that people were in most of the homes they passed, but they were simply shutting off the lights for the night. It wasn't like the suburban neighborhoods where people lit up their houses for display. There weren't even lights on the road. Everything they saw was from the moonlight and the headlamps that they bought...except for the light up ahead.

It glowed with the yellow of an old sulfur lamp, twinkling until they biked a little closer and saw that it was actually more orange.

The light grew in size as they got closer and Cage wasn't sure exactly when he realized what he was looking at. He picked up speed and yelled. "Dev! It's on fire!"

63

Joule hadn't seen the smoke earlier, maybe because it had grown dark outside relatively quickly as night settled. The only light filtering in through the cracks in the barn was coming from the moon, or maybe a lamp somewhere in the distance, she guessed.

But while they'd been arguing among themselves, the thick, acrid smoke had begun rolling in like a predator, all but impossible to miss. They were now trapped inside the barn with fire coming for them. She had heard the murmuring voices beyond the doors, but there had been nothing she could do about it. The bigger threat had seemed to be Paul holding the gun on them.

Now she had the gun, but it no longer mattered. She couldn't talk a fire out of killing her or have Jerry take it out with a good side tackle.

The four of them turned, almost as a unit, and looked at the smoke as if to decide what to do about it. It curled under the doors, coming for them. And Jerry asked, "Now what?"

But Paul was already on his feet and moving. No one else budged. Checking the doors was pointless. There was something burning on the other side, and Joule had heard the Larkins doing something to the doors. They all had. She was confident they were chained inside.

They could see flashes of fire through the cracks and under the door now—not just smoke. So even if they managed to get the doors open, they would jump directly from the smoke into the flames.

As she had that thought, she saw fingers of orange reaching under and grabbing for the hay on the floor. A few of them caught, small sparks lighting small fires, the size of a match-head. Joule ran over and quickly stomped on the two she saw, though she was certain that wouldn't stop anything. It might make it take another minute to get a good foothold—but a minute could change everything, she knew. She stomped on another spark and another as Paul called out.

"There's another door over here!" He raced to the other side of the barn to open it, all three of them following along.

But though the old-fashioned metal latch gave under his thumb as he pressed it, and he tugged on the door, it didn't move more than an inch.

"Damnation!" he yelled. Joule noticed again that this was a man who wouldn't fully swear even when fire was threatening to kill him. "I think they've barricaded this one, too."

Joule was already right behind him and stepped in to yank at the handle. She was about to put her face to the crack she'd made, wondering if the Larkins had simply slid a board through the door handle to block it or something like that. If they had, maybe she could reach through and jimmy it out. But she felt the fire already eating at the other side of the door.

She sensed heat at her feet. Smoke curled in through the crack. And she only watched for a moment before she got smart enough to shove the door shut and let go of the handle that was already growing hot.

Behind her the horses screamed in a hellish choir and her heart kicked at the horrifying noise.

Were they surrounded by fire?

She turned back and saw three pairs of eyes looking at her, all wondering the same thing.

Her brain scrambled and her hand once again darted into her pocket, feeling for the kitten and grateful to find he was still there. If they couldn't get out through the doors, they'd have to get out through the walls. She decided to do what she did best: Get bossy.

"We know there's a fire there and here." She pointed to the large double doors and then to the one right behind her. Even as she said it, she quickly stepped away. She wasn't sure how fire would act, not on a barn like this.

The barn construction was plain with exposed studs. Maybe it wouldn't be too much work to get through it. She turned to Paul. "How thick are the walls?"

"It's exactly what you see. Just a barn." He shrugged as if he didn't know what else he might add. "The animals provide the heat. The structure just kind of holds it in."

Right now the fire was providing the heat and the animals were providing terrified and terrifying noises. Sharp cracks indicated hooves kicking at the stalls. Joule didn't like any of it, but she stayed focused.

She nodded. That was good. "We need to find a place where there's not a fire on the other side. Check for heat!"

The four of them dispersed in different directions, moving to opposite walls and placing their hands flat against the wood to check the temperature. They stomped out tiny embers as they saw them, fighting against time to slow the fire. Again and again, Joule saw them either jerk their hands back or shake their heads.

She found a few spots she couldn't be sure about. Most felt warm to her.

"Here!" Jerry called out excitedly, pointing to a spot he still held one palm to, as if to prove it was cool enough.

"That side leads into the paddock," Paul replied quickly, as he headed toward Jerry. But halfway across the space, he turned and changed directions. He darted into the small alcove near the front and hollered out, "Let me grab some tools! Maybe we can get through!"

Joule still loosely held the shotgun in her hand. "You got more shells for this thing?" she asked as she held it up.

Paul patted his pockets before nodding, but came toward them and handed out a crowbar, a pitchfork, and a shovel. Jerry and Brenda were now armed with farming implements. But as the three of them pulled in close behind her, Joule said, "Step back."

Then she walked up as close to the wall as she dared and aimed, right around her own chest height. Closing her eyes, she pulled the trigger.

64

Cage raced his bike down the long, gravel drive, Dev right behind him. The jolts and jars of the uneven ground clacked his teeth together and jarred his spine as he tried to go even faster.

He was no fire expert, but he would say that the barn wasn't fully up in flames yet. It seemed to have several lines of fire around the outside. And from what he could see, he was pretty certain this wasn't a fire that had occurred naturally or even by accident. It seemed clearly designed to kill the animals inside.

His immediate next thought—as he hit a rock and almost went flying over the handlebars before managing to right the bicycle again—was to wonder what else might be inside.

The cracking boom pulled him and Dev up short. They sprayed gravel as they skidded to a stop in a slick move that Cage would have been proud of at any moment other than this.

Someone was shooting.

"What the hell?" Dev asked, but Cage had no answers.

They were close enough to the barn that they were likely faster on foot now. So Cage swung one leg over the bike and jumped free, letting it clatter to the gravel. He was already several feet away before it hit the ground.

He'd covered half the distance to the barn with Dev right behind him as the second boom echoed through the night. He pulled up short, stepping back for a moment, as though the bullets or shot wouldn't have already whizzed by him if they'd come his way.

But he still couldn't *see* anything. Whatever was happening wasn't happening on the side of the barn facing the drive.

He gave the barn a wide berth as the flames licked at the wood. If the fire made it inside the barn, it would probably go up like a tinderbox. Weren't barns full of hay and other wonderfully flammable things?

But as he rounded the corner, he was certain his eyes were deceiving him. One of the walls appeared to bulge for a moment and then it went flat.

It was surely a trick of the moonlight, and he dismissed it as he heard a noise over his shoulder. He looked back to see Dev was close behind him. But as he turned back to look at the barn, he again saw the wall bulge again.

Only this time, the wood cracked.

"Again!" a voice yelled from inside. Followed quickly by, "Step back."

It took only those three words for Cage to recognize his sister's voice.

His chest swelled with both relief and fear.

Cage beelined for the spot where someone was breaking out of the barn. Joule must have someone with her, as she was shouting orders. *Could it be Izzy?*

He and Dev were close to where he'd seen the wall move when the next crack split the air around him. This time, he felt something shift in the air molecules next to him.

Holy shit, he thought, *they were shooting their way out.*

He immediately jumped back. Surely, his sister had this in hand.

Also, if he stepped in front of her shots, and took a bullet or buckshot, that would not be the happy ending that he'd done all of this searching for. His arm shot out across Dev's torso, like a mother trying to hold her child back in the seat next to her as the car slammed to a stop. The move was probably about as useless.

Dev had surely already figured out what was happening, the same as him. The two of them backed up in tandem as the barn wall cracked, splinters of wood flying. He watched as a pitchfork came through first, tines out, ready to skewer anyone on the other side.

It must have been feet kicking at the wall next. The wood swayed and bulged, and eventually gave way right about waist height. Again, a few splinters flew, but this time a bigger chunk of wood also moved. It seemed hinged slightly at the top, but finally, there was a hole. He watched hands and tools come through as those inside worked frantically to make it bigger.

"*Joule!*" he cried out, wanting to help but knowing that getting shot was the wrong response. Her excited response of "*Cage?*" bloomed in his chest. Any last doubt that it was wishful thinking faded away. He had found her!

"We'll help get you out. Don't shoot us. What should we do?"

But he didn't hear her answer.

Instead, he felt the muzzle of a gun against the side of his head. Just as he recognized what he was feeling, he heard the words, "You're not going to help her. You're going to stand real still until I tell you what to do. Or it'll be the last thing that you ever do."

65

J oule pushed everyone else out through the hole before her. The fire was spreading faster than she had anticipated. She would swear she could hear the crack and whoosh as whole hay bales went up in flame.

Fingers of flame raced along the floor, as if the fire was actively searching for her. There wasn't time to make the hole bigger or cleaner. She shoved Paul out first, because he was the oldest. He'd likely be the hardest to get through the hole. She wasn't sure how well he could climb or land on the grass on the other side.

Even as he forced himself through the small space, he turned back to Brenda and yelled, "Open the stalls!"

Jerry was next, as the biggest. The hole had to fit him, and she wasn't going to leave him behind just because the smaller people went first. Brenda had dashed around behind her as Joule helped push Jerry through, and she must have opened all the stalls, because now there was a herd of frantic horses in the main room of the barn with them.

"We have to go quickly!" Brenda told her, and Joule refrained from answering "No shit."

Then, with just her and Brenda left, she put her hand on the other woman's back and pushed. But Brenda pushed her first, yelling over the heat and flames and wild whinnies. "The animals know me!"

As if that meant anything.

It only occurred to Joule then that it might look selfish to go last, to let the others clear the debris out of the way. But it didn't matter now. The fire was close and breathing was difficult. Stepping one foot high, she put her dirty sneaker out through the hole, following awkwardly with her torso and finally hopping ungracefully into the cool night air.

She immediately crashed into Jerry, wondering why he had failed to get out of the way. She looked up to see that Paul and Jerry were just standing there and staring at something.

Joule turned then to see what had them so shocked. Behind her, Brenda crashed through the hole behind her and pushed right into them making them all stumble.

"Get out of the way!" she yelled at them, pushing as she screamed. "The horses!"

Joule almost fell, but Brenda grabbed for her, keeping her upright. Behind them, the side of the barn cracked as the horses butted or kicked their way out. With the opening now big enough, they thundered through the broken wall. Joule could feel thousands of pounds of horse muscle passing inches behind her. The horses managed to not trample the stunned humans standing in their way, but if that was instinct or her own sheer luck, she didn't know. They bolted into the paddock *en masse* and then easily jumped the fences in their fear. In moments, they had disappeared into the night. Gone, but at least safe.

The same couldn't be said for the people.

The two Larkins were there, and it took a moment to absorb the sight. Again, she thought it *had to be* the Larkins—the man in the ballcap, the woman with the ponytail that she'd seen in the barn just a little while ago. These were almost definitely the people who had tried to burn them to death.

They each held a gun—the woman held hers to Cage's head and looked more steady doing it. But that didn't change the fact that the man had pressed the barrel of his semiautomatic to Dev's temple. His hand shook as the horses thundered by, making Joule's muscles clench with fear for her brother and her roommate.

"This was supposed to be easier than this!" the man yelled, clearly on the verge of a temper tantrum.

Joule tried to surreptitiously scan Laura's face, looking for symptoms of drug abuse and wondering if the woman was strung out on her own product. But there weren't any obvious signs.

It was Jerry who stepped forward, though the woman motioned him back by jabbing the gun against Cage's head a little bit harder. "Stay back, Jerry!"

"You don't want to do this," he said calmly.

Her reply was anything but calm. "No, I fucking don't want to!" she yelled back. "I *don't*. But you've put me in a position I can't get out of otherwise. This is *your fault*."

She motioned a little with the gun, jabbing it as she spoke, and Joule watched as Cage slowly moved his head away.

She wondered if he could quickly duck away or jab his hand up and knock the gun out of her hand. It would be a dangerous move in any situation, but nearly impossible to have a good outcome because there was another gun aimed directly at Deveron's head. Even if Cage could win against Laura, Joule would expect the man to twitch.

Unless the two could act in concert ...

Cage and Dev couldn't. They were both facing the same way and wouldn't be able to read signals from each other. So unless Cage could reach out and grab Dev's hand and tap out a plan in Morse code, and then Dev could understand it—which

Joule thought was a long shot. Even then, it was highly unlikely the two of them could make a move in tandem.

But while Cage and Dev couldn't, Cage and Joule could.

They were facing each other. They understood each other's subtle signals. So, while Jerry distracted the Larkins by trying to talk them out of the situation, Joule moved in the slow beginning of a slide toward Dev, hoping no one would notice.

Hell, maybe Jerry would talk these asshats into becoming better people and putting their guns down, but Joule wasn't going to bank on that.

"Why are you doing this?" Jerry demanded.

"Come on, Jer," the woman whined. "You know what it's been like since the big farms came through."

Joule didn't know, but Jerry did. And honestly, even she could take a good guess. The local economy was tanking. Jerry had told her the farms weren't even getting bought out anymore. The big firms just plowed their way in, moved into other sections of the state, or even the country, and then undercut the contracts.

At that moment, it clicked for her: Why Jerry was so mad at Helio Systems. It didn't matter that they were solar or that it would save some of the local environment or that they would pay him more. Helio Systems Tech was another big company coming in and taking the livelihood from the locals. It wasn't that he loved his job so much. Helio was just a corporation bullying their way into his home town and he didn't trust the big corporations... with good reason.

He'd probably spent a good part of his life watching the little farms go under. The lucky farmers had taken the cheap buy-outs. For those who didn't, things didn't just get bad, they got horrid. Without a working farm, the land itself probably wasn't even worth much.

She took another slide over toward Dev. And, as of yet, it seemed no one had noticed her.

That was good, she thought. But as she tried for another step, the man's eyes darted around frantically and Joule froze where she was, hoping he wouldn't notice she was in a slightly different place than she'd been just a few moments ago.

"Laura, these people are not involved. And neither am I," Jerry said, trying his best to talk her down. "We're not going to tell anybody."

"I can't trust you to stay quiet, Jerry. This is the only way I'm keeping the farm. The only way I'm keeping food on my table."

"You're going to *murder* people?" Jerry asked incredulously, finally putting into words what was going down.

Laura offered a small shrug. She looked exhausted. Behind them, the barn roof began to tilt crazily as the fire consumed the walls.

Joule had the flash of a thought that maybe it had actually been safer in the barn—fire and all. Laura's eyes looked damn crazy.

Joule slid another foot closer to Dev. Cage saw what she was doing, and she offered a subtle nod. When he replied with his own, she looked first at the gun at his head. She didn't flinch, though she wanted to. She and Cage had to live forever. She wouldn't watch him die like this. Not for this stupid woman's drug-running business.

Then she flicked her eyes to the gun at Dev's head.

Cage dipped his chin slightly in acknowledgment.

She wiggled the fingers of her left hand, the side away from Laura and Levi, until Cage noticed. Then she held down three fingers as he watched.

Then two.

One.

Then all hell broke loose.

66

Cage waited until he saw Joule take her first running step before he moved.

He wasn't exactly certain what she was going to do, only that she was going to make sure that Dev didn't get shot. Dev might also have been on board with the plan, though Cage didn't know that, either. Their roommate might have caught on to all the signaling and figured out that Cage and Joule were communicating. He certainly could have seen Joule's fingers counting.

The sky had grown black, but flames that were licking their way out of the barn made the area bright enough to see that the twins were signaling each other. She could only hope no one bothered to look.

As Joule launched herself forward, Cage turned quickly, looking at Laura and for a moment. He twisted his head and found himself staring directly down the barrel of the gun.

He hadn't dropped fast enough. *Drop first, then turn*. Shit, it was too late for that. He dropped low, almost as a reaction from the shock of what he'd done, and waited to feel the burn of a bullet searing through his brain. There wasn't time to wait and see if he died first, so he jammed his hands upward, grabbing at her arm and shoving it skyward. It was not the best execution of the move, and not anywhere near as clean and superhero-like as he'd done it in his mind.

The sound and the movement of the gunshot rocked him, almost throwing him off his feet. He felt the reverberation through her arm and the air the second she squeezed the trigger and the bullet flew upward into the sky.

He could swear he heard another blast. Was she just pulling the trigger over and over? But he was already hearing the rough "Oof!" of someone being tackled, and he was pretty certain it wasn't Dev.

Joule must have aimed for the man in the overalls with the gun. He just hoped she was staying clear of the embers that sparked and burst into the night like escapees on a prison break.

The woman with the ponytail toppled as Cage struggled with her, pulling them both to the ground in a tangled heap. He was equally petrified by both the gun she was waving wildly and a piece of burning wood that landed next to them and began sizzling in the damp grass. The woman didn't look strung out or high, but she was certainly in a rough place where she was making crazy decisions. He felt her poor choices as thumps to his torso and kicks to his shins as she attempted to fight back.

He pulled back a hand to clock her, hoping to get her under the chin, but he spotted her hand still holding the gun. If he hit her the wrong way, she might jerk and shoot off another bullet. So he held himself in check.

He wanted to look back over his shoulder and check on the barn, to be sure it wasn't about to collapse in their direction, dusting them all with wood and embers, but there wasn't time. Looking away might mean losing this fight.

He struggled to get into a stable position on his hands and knees. The moment he achieved it, he jammed his elbow into her forearm, hoping to keep her trigger hand pinned to the ground. He could only hope that would keep her from shooting anything more than an ankle.

Then, as he lifted up his head to see where her gun might be aimed, he saw a boot plant itself across her wrist. A hand came into view, and the small semiautomatic was forcefully removed from her grip.

"Noooo!" she howled, as though she were the wronged party.

In his anger, Cage pulled back again to offer a good "shut-up" punch, but again he was thwarted.

"Everybody up! Hands in the air where I can see them!"

Cage shook his head. *Who said that?* Who was trying to take control of this asinine melee? As he rolled off the woman, who was still trying to shake him, he caught sight of Joule.

The man in the overalls was also trying to toss his sister off himself, but Joule appeared to be remembering some of the martial arts they had studied as kids. And she wasn't quite tossed like a rag doll. It was more that she jumped and scrambled out of the way, avoiding kicking legs, flailing arms, and crackling pieces of burning wood.

Cage could only hope that she'd managed to get the gun out of the man's hand as well. Hell, Cage would trust the old farmer or even Jerry with the gun far more than this guy.

"Everyone on your feet, hands in the air!"

He thought he heard the voice again, through the ringing that vibrated his eardrums and his skull.

Cage turned a circle, looking wildly in all directions, but he still wasn't upright. He counted far too many pairs of feet and was still unable to hear clearly after having a gun fire so close to his unprotected ears.

He clapped his hands to his head now, trying to stop the roar. The voice must have been very loud or very close, but he still hadn't seen who was saying it.

He could only hope that, while he and Joule had started the chaos, someone else was ending it. He checked his sister as he scanned the small crowd. Joule looked fine—no blood. And she moved appropriately, indicating nothing was broken or too badly twisted as she stepped further from the barn.

Good. Her silhouette against the firelit sky filled him with relief. He'd never been happier to see her.

Jerry, next to her, also appeared uninjured, and so did the two people that had come bursting out of the barn wall right after them. Cage next watched as the man in the overalls and the thin woman with the ponytail stood up and slowly, angrily, put their hands into the air.

But then he spotted the person ordering them around. It was Dr. Chithra Murasawa with a rifle in her hands and an angry expression on her bruised and battered face. She aimed at the center of the small crowd, ready to swing and shoot at whoever displeased her. And she looked very displeased.

Next to her, Izzy stood with a handgun gripped fiercely. Her feet were braced apart, her arms out, elbows locked, and the gun shaking frightfully in her grip. *Izzy was alive!* He breathed a sigh of relief mixed with fear. Izzy wasn't good with that gun, not a very convincing as an authority figure.

Cage stepped forward, motioning to the gun. "Do you want me to take that?"

He wasn't sure if he asked it or maybe yelled. The buzzing in his ears still hadn't quite quelled. But Izzy nodded and said —or maybe he read her lips—"Oh God, yes! Please."

She handed the gun to him, barrel first, and with a few deft moves, he checked the piece. It was loaded and the safety was off. He stepped quickly into place next to Dr. Murasawa.

She was absolutely the last person he had expected to see here. And why was she so beaten up? He had to ask, "How did you guys get here?"

"I got chased by the storm. Skidded on wet road and went

into a tree," Murasawa said. That explained the damage. She answered him without taking her eyes off the others, far more competent with a gun than Cage would have expected her to be. "When I got up, I found a truck with the keys in it and started driving around looking for people. No one is out here!"

Cage could agree with that. "You found Izzy."

He hadn't quite asked it as a question, as the answer was obvious. "Yeah. She was wandering down the street, looking really dazed."

This made Cage question her decision then to put a gun into Izzy's hands but, to be fair, the situation was a fat mess. He was just grateful that he and Dev had managed to find both Joule and Izzy. And Dr. Murasawa! It was three names off the list, all at once. Had there not been loaded guns aimed at too many strangers, he would have sat on he ground and breathed with relief, or hugged everyone. This was not the reunion he'd hoped for.

If they could just survive this standoff, they would be okay. Though he had no clue where the doctor had found these guns, he realized that, now that the two of them were the ones holding the firearms, they had a better chance.

He turned his head slowly to his sister, leaving his eyes and the barrel of his gun turned toward the crowd. "Joule, do you want to explain what's going on here?"

Just as he thought he was going to get some answers, another voice boomed from behind him. This time, the sound was accompanied by the unmistakable cock of a shotgun.

"What the ever-loving hell is going on here?"

67

J oule wasn't facing the right direction to see much of anything. But she could tell that Dr. Murasawa and Cage were far enough back from the edge of the barn to see whoever had come around the corner. Both had been immediately convinced to follow the newest set of orders.

She watched as they each slowly set their firearm on the ground at their feet, the other hand still in the air, and then just as carefully returned to standing.

When the group had broken out of the barn, they'd come out the side and weren't facing the driveway. In fact, the building shielded most of it from view. The smoke and flames didn't do anything to make the view clearer. Jumping out of the way as pieces popped and flew, bringing flames or at least sizzling heat with them, didn't help.

That was certainly how Dr. Murasawa and Izzy had managed to creep up on them. *And here she was, getting snuck up on again*, Joule thought, as two massive forms appeared around the corner of the blazing barn.

The barn was keeping her warm on one side, but she was fighting to find the middle ground. She wanted to be close enough for the light and heat, but far enough to avoid the embers that cracked and arced into the night and onto the grass. Luckily, the ground was still wet from the previous night and—so far—none of the embers had sparked a new blaze. There was enough to worry about without that.

"What is with the damn guns? And why isn't anyone putting out this fire?"

Joule looked around the small group and realized she was central to most everything that had happened.

As the voice stepped into the light of the blaze, Cage smiled and called out, and though he kept his hands in the air, he wiggled his fingers in a friendly gesture. Then he greeted the newcomers by name and asked the question Joule was dying to know the answer to.

"Boomer! Bob! What are you doing here?"

"There's a damn fire, if y'all hadn't noticed," Boomer or Bob answered quickly and in a surly tone. He still had his gun up, though not quite as carefully aimed, maybe because of Cage's friendly overtures.

They all heard a crack and sidestepped quickly to avoid a small handful of embers that rained into their little group.

The other brother didn't lower his gun. "We can see the sky lit up for miles. Everyone's coming."

For a moment, she let that absorb. The Larkins maybe weren't the brightest of criminals then, if they'd set a fire that would have attracted the entire county. Though Joule and the others would certainly be dead if they had remained inside the barn.

Beside her, the blaze crackled with its own life and she could hear the sound of flames rushing up the inside walls and eating the wood.

She took one more step away from it and absently began to lower her hand toward her pocket. But one of the brothers— they were obviously brothers—twisted his head quickly in her direction. Maybe she wasn't quite the most favored nation that she thought she was.

"I have a kitten in my pocket. I want to be sure he's okay." Then she walked over with her hands still in the air. "Here, you check."

Joule held both her hands high, but motioned with her hip out, waiting while the big man softly slipped his fingers into the pocket of her hoodie. His face melted as he touched the tiny kitten, petting it softly.

"You have a kitten in your pocket?" Cage asked incredulously.

"She does," the man answered with a grin.

It was Jerry who huffed, his own hands still in the air. "Dorothy here named it Toto."

She watched as Cage laughed, and she had to admit, this was the most comfortable she'd ever felt with a gun aimed on her. And she'd had three different people point a gun at her in the last several hours, which was up from zero in her entire previous lifetime.

Alabama was not sitting well.

"Toto's good?" she asked.

"He's a sweetheart," the big man said, as if he could know that from just touching the fur.

She grinned, although her heart was still racing. Though she was still under threat, she at least was confident that Boomer and Bob would go for the Larkins if they had to shoot someone.

"Well, boys," she started, acting a little bolder than she actually felt. "Jerry and I found shelter from one of the other twisters—wait, let me go back further. I got picked up by the first twister. When I came to, I walked through the woods, and I only found several empty houses. Then I found Jerry."

She motioned with her hand, still keeping it high in the air. "Jerry and I got a tractor—" she didn't mention that they'd basically stolen it, "—and went tooling down the road until the next twisters hit. At that point, we aimed for the nearest house, but the cellar was the only thing we could get into."

The brothers nodded at her, and she kept going, telling about getting stuck, then finding the cocaine when they tried to get into the crawlspace—this revelation made everyone except the Larkins gasp—and how the Larkins had returned home just as they'd come up through the floor.

The one brother's eyebrows were raising higher and higher as she kept talking. But she didn't miss that his gaze would occasionally flick over to Jerry, who must have been motioning to confirm the whole story.

"I'm assuming these two are the Larkins." Joule pointed to Laura and Levi.

Beside her, Jerry, Paul, Brenda, Boomer, and Bob all nodded along. "Well, they came into the barn earlier, looking for us. I guess to kill us. And then Paul came in, and then apparently they got Brenda here..." She didn't really understand all the nuances of this part.

"Maybe you should explain," she said, handing the story off to Paul. It took a while to round robin the whole thing. The brothers continued to loosely command the situation with their guns held up and the barn continued to burn brightly into the night.

She would have thought the hay would have wooshed up in a big blaze reaching into the night sky and then died out already. The fire still roaring along showed her how little she knew. "Why isn't the fire department here?"

"They're at least thirty minutes away. No local stations out here," Bob explained. "Just the volunteer unit."

Joule was stunned by that. She'd never lived anywhere that didn't have a local, city-funded fire station just around the corner.

But the story was still unfolding, bringing everyone up to

speed, until Boomer and Bob were caught up. Dr. Murasawa and Izzy both had their mouths hanging open by the time Brenda finally finished the part about them breaking out of the barn and finding Laura and Levi threatening to murder them. Again.

The brothers then turned to Chithra and Izzy, who told about the truck and the gun rack in it. When they finally petered out, Boomer and Bob both appeared to have had enough. Slowly, while everyone had talked, their guns had shifted aim toward the Larkins. The two had stood quietly, not allowed to tell their side of the story. Joule figured they'd have time to explain their story to the sheriff, if there was one around here. She was grateful that everyone understood who was on what side here. Meanwhile, the Larkins wore sour looks on their faces about the whole thing.

At last, the brother in the blue plaid turned toward them with a blank look on his face. "I knew your family had too much money. You were in rough straights after your farming got run under. I know it. But you can't run coke and you can't murder your neighbors!"

His voice was booming by the time he finished, and Laura and Levi were squinting, as though the force of the accusation was literally aiming at them. They didn't deny any of it.

"All right." The other brother stayed calmer and motioned with his gun. "You two, down on the ground. Face down."

The Larkins didn't seem to want to comply, and Joule found herself bending her knees, getting ready for anything. She could run away or rush one of these idiots if she had to.

It was then that Izzy, who seemed to be paying attention to everything, looked up. She glanced left then right, and then left again, and Joule didn't have any idea why until Izzy said, "Why is the sky getting so dark?"

68

J oule looked up. Sure enough, dark clouds were sweeping in, cutting the moonlight out.

The blaze from the barn had made everything so bright that only Izzy had noticed.

"Crap," the blue plaid brother muttered, seemingly to himself. Then, louder, he added, "That's funnel weather."

"Is it *always* like this?" Dr. Murasawa asked, incredulous.

Joule understood. They'd been told the area was relatively tornado-free. They knew storms might happen, but this was epic.

"No, we don't get it, not like this. Not two straight days of funnels touching down," the other brother answered her, as the first added, "We've already had seven in the area."

All ten of them turned their faces skyward, the conflicts on the ground paling in comparison to the one threatening from the sky.

They jolted as a unit when the burning barn cracked loudly next to them, but when nothing else seemed to happen, they all looked up again and watched as the sky seem to roll in on itself.

The orange of the blaze reflected off of the thick clouds above, illuminating clearly the way the clouds began to fold.

"Crap," the brother said again, and the second added quickly, "We need shelter. Now."

The barn wasn't going to be any help, Joule thought, looking first to the nearest structure. It was already ablaze and it wouldn't have been good even if it was untouched and sturdy.

The second brother apparently had different concerns. "If a storm or a funnel catches this barn, there's two options for what can happen."

They all waited as the wind began to kick up again and the roar of the approaching storm started to fight the fire for noisiest night creature. He yelled, "It's either going to put the fire out, or it's going to throw pieces of flaming wood everywhere."

That would be even more ass-tastic than this day had already been, Joule thought, as she remembered what she'd seen yesterday when the big funnel had collapsed houses like a fist on gingerbread and flung the pieces into the air. *What if they had been on fire?*

Looking to her brother, Joule's hands dropped now, one tucking into her pocket and checking for Toto. She found him still curled in a tight little ball. The poor thing had to be hungry and petrified, but there was nothing she could do for him now except save him to be fed later.

"I've got a shelter!" Paul hollered at them as the winds rose even higher. "Come on!"

Joule watched the embers start to move in uniform directions as the wind whipped them first one way then another. They all turned to go, but only Boomer and Bob were smart enough to watch for Laura and Levi.

As the sky rolled in and the wind picked up, the fire burned higher, shooting long yellow tongues of flame up into the sky.

A thick, dark funnel turned and touched the ground near

the edge of the property, the heavy roar of the wind beginning to overtake the roaring of the fire.

Joule and her brother were already following Paul, as most of them were, but she turned to check over her shoulder. She counted on Cage and Izzy on either side of her to keep her upright as her feet flew over ground she wasn't watching.

As Joule looked back at Boomer and Bob and Levi, she saw Laura jump up. The woman had found a gun and was brandishing it wildly.

Her eyes looked feral and scared, or maybe that was just the reflection of the flames in them, Joule couldn't tell for sure. But Laura spun around and, swinging erratically, fired three times.

Next to her, Joule felt her chain of friends jerk and start to fall.

69

Cage tripped. He'd stubbed his toe on something or gotten bumped maybe. He didn't know, but the white-hot poker of pain searing through his leg brought him to his knees. He was still holding Joule's hand as his knees hit the wet grass.

It all must have happened very fast, but it seemed that it took forever for him to recognize the sounds he'd heard as gunshots. Behind him, things were going down but he didn't know quite what only that it was bad. He worried about Boomer and Bob. He wondered why his own leg wasn't quite working.

As Joule leaned over to pull him back to his feet, Cage turned and saw past her. Izzy jolted and fell face-forward, into the grass.

Dr. Murasawa screamed, her hands flying to her face as she watched Izzy crumple. Had she been hit, too? It looked like Izzy had, but he wasn't sure.

His brain was a touch fuzzy now. Time was out of scope and flowing oddly, as he struggled to get everything into its proper mental place. He was trying to run, but every time he took a step on the hurt leg, the pain shifted from feeling as though someone had pierced him with a burning arrow to feeling as if it was shooting up his entire left side.

He stumbled forward again, but this time Joule grabbed his right hand and viciously slung his arm around her shoulder. It felt as if she had tackled him, shoving her own shoulder into his ribs and lifting him as she ran. He'd known she was strong, but he hadn't quite known she could do this.

Another retort fired behind him and he wondered if anyone else had been shot. To his right, Paul turned, raising the shotgun—but he looked as if he was too unsure to fire it. Instead, he yelled, waving them all past him. As the wind and fire tried to steal his words, he cried out, "Brenda! Brenda take them down into the shelter!"

Cage tried to be useful and run, but he also wanted to see what was going on behind him. He twisted around but realized he couldn't actually hear anything. Once again, the gunfire had rung his brain like a bell and he was still listening to the echoes inside his skull.

But he saw Laura, Levi, Boomer, and Bob out on the open grass in an epic struggle. One of the brothers—he couldn't tell which at this point—had Laura by one arm. It seemed he'd pulled her hands behind her, as though he were struggling to handcuff her. Cage had a ridiculous thought: *Did the brothers simply carry handcuffs on them all the time?*

As he watched, the other brother took a hard right to his jaw. Levi had managed to make the move without anyone noticing the windup, and Boomer's—or Bob's—head snapped back as he stumbled. The man seemed too big for quick moves, but he countered by bringing his hand up rapidly against the side of Levi's head.

Cage was surprised to see a single punch have such an effect. It appeared that Levi reverberated from the hit, stumbling away and shaking his head until he simply collapsed.

Cage was still trying to focus on putting his feet on the ground—but one leg screamed each time he stepped—to help Joule run forward, but he was clearly doing a crappy job of it. The scene behind him was fascinating. He saw as the brother raised his hand back up that he had a gun in his fist and he must have clocked Levi with it.

Laura had escaped and turned around, still somehow with a gun in her hand. Had she and Levi brought spare weapons? Had they stolen guns from Boomer or Bob? Cage couldn't keep straight who had what, or even what he should be doing.

"Come on, Cage!" his sister protested in his ear, but his brain was even more fuzzy and he was looking at Laura, who had blood running down the side of her head.

She still had the wherewithal to open her mouth and was screaming something—or at least Cage thought she was. He couldn't hear her voice as, behind her, the funnel touched down and ate all the angry words right out of the air.

She waved her gun, but the other brother turned and aimed for her. Cage wondered if she might shoot into the moving crowd, aiming for the house and whatever shelter Paul and Brenda had.

Dr. Murasawa and Brenda were now dragging Izzy along. His friend had blood seeping all through her clothing. Cage blinked, trying to follow all the moving pieces. He felt it was important that he turn back around but could not recall why.

He swung his head over Joule's shoulder again as Brenda led them all up the back steps into the house. Cage tripped over the edge of the porch, pain shooting up his side once again. The intensity of the pain blurred his vision, and his sister tugging him along only made it worse.

He couldn't think, or maybe even breathe, he didn't know. But still he turned his head back, needing to see what was happening behind him.

The brothers stood, each with a gun facing Laura. Closer to

the house, Paul stood with his shotgun ready. But if the shotgun blast reached that far, he would pepper all of them. Laura held her gun unsteadily, but close enough to one of the brothers' heads that her aim wouldn't matter.

It was Boomer she was aiming for, but Bob who was in the most immediate danger.

He saw it then and remembered why he had to turn and look. When he yelled, the pain of the movement cracked his head and radiated up his side, but he did it anyway. He had to.

"Bob! It's behind you!"

70

J oule followed Brenda, rushing as best she could while she bore most of her brother's weight. But as she took the first step through what appeared to be an ordinary closet door, she saw that it led down into the underground space, and she balked.

It was a purely emotional reaction—a sudden, seizing terror that she knew was irrational.

She flashed back to walking into the cellar with Jerry, to climbing down the rickety wooden steps. She'd been stuck there for hours. Then she'd been trapped under the house by the storm debris with no one coming. Though she'd maintained a constant forward motion and sawed a path through the flooring and out from under the Larkins' home, she'd been petrified. Escaping that situation, only to find a worse one, didn't make this sudden seizing of her muscles any better.

She turned her head, as behind her Boomer and Bob dealt with the Larkins. Beside them, the barn blazed and crackled as flaming sections crashed down. Joule was waiting for it to collapse in a fireball and wondered again why it hadn't yet. Was time simply moving too slowly for her?

Beyond them, the funnel ate up the ground, grinding at the trees and puny fences in its path. It broke sturdy structures like twigs as if to flex its power as it aimed directly toward her.

She'd told Jerry that it was random, that the storm didn't have a desire to hunt them, but right now it sure looked like it did.

"Joule!" Brenda yelled, trying to get her to snap out of it. The other woman reached up and physically removed Cage from her arms.

Now, Joule looked. She moved just two steps down, far enough to see. But her racing heart halted her again.

She looked at her brother, finally assessing what had happened. When she'd reacted, she hadn't seen the damage, hadn't fully understood. Now, blood was running down Cage's leg as he moved to sit on the floor. Joule stayed frozen in place, letting Brenda help. Brenda seemed to know what she was doing, and Joule seemed stuck, observing.

Beyond him, Izzy was already laid on out the floor, her head resting in Dr. Murasawa's lap as her boss gently tapped, then slapped, at Izzy's face in an effort to bring her back to consciousness. Dev was hovering over the two of them, blocking part of Joule's view. But she could see that Izzy was covered in blood.

That might have been the thing that jolted her out of it.

As she began to make her way further down the steps, she looked over her shoulder, out the wide glass windows that framed a cute back porch. The funnel was getting closer. It was getting larger. And this time, it *did* sound like a train, barreling directly toward them.

Turning from her position, she saw Boomer and Bob racing across the yard toward her now, Laura and Levi left behind. The Larkins were laid out on the ground, unmoving. Joule could only imagine they were dead. If they weren't, they might be soon. Boomer and Bob were leaving their bodies to the storm and Joule couldn't say she disagreed with that decision.

The large men moved more easily than they should have, and they hit the steps in near unison, taking them two or three at a time. Almost comically, they seemed to get jammed up at the doorway. But they immediately stepped back and, in the typical Southern fashion that Joule had seen while she was there, each tried to wave the other through first.

"Get the fucking fuck in here!" she yelled at them, still on the third step down.

Blue plaid took initiative and stepped through first, with his brother right on his heels. As she waved them forward, they each grabbed one of her arms and hauled her backwards down the stairs as they went. They gave her no choice but to move, and for that, she was grateful. But she still remained frozen on the bottom step, as if it meant she could escape if she needed to.

It was completely irrational, but she wasn't able to override it.

Paul, who'd been standing on the porch, shepherding each of them in, now had his entire flock safely down the steps. Joule could just see him standing in the upper doorway as he took one last look at the oncoming funnel. His hair whipped in the wind and his clothing plastered against him as he watched the funnel. She imagined she could hear his flannel shirt snapping like a flag around him. Joule understood. The storm itself was mesmerizing.

Boomer was yelling up to the man, but Paul had already caught on. He slammed the door behind him, ducking down even as he slid three deadbolts into place. He raced down the steps, passing Joule in a huff before finally hitting the concrete floor and joining the rest of them.

"Levi and Laura?" he asked the two big men, but they shook their heads.

"Tried to kill y'all," Bob added softly, and that seemed all that needed to be said. The rest of them didn't need more of the grim story, and Laura and Levi faded into the background as they all dealt with the problems the two had caused.

Joule looked around the space from her perch, and though she was close to hyperventilating, she saw that Paul had built a real shelter down here. That told Joule, more than anything, that people *did* expect to get tornadoes here. They expected at least enough bad storms to make it worth building all of this. Constructing a shelter wasn't cheap or easy, she'd learned.

"Have you had a tornado before?" she asked Paul. It seemed her a rather innocuous question. Some part of her knew she was avoiding looking at the scene before her—her brother shot in the leg, Izzy even worse.

But they were being tended to, and she would only be in the way. So she pestered Paul to keep her brain occupied. She was quite confident that he would say *Yes, all the time.*

What he said instead was, "One big one, fifteen years ago. We don't get many."

She must have had a strange look on her face. He told her what she should have understood for herself by now. "Haven't you figured it out? Once is enough to learn."

He wasn't distracting her. He wasn't making it better. She wished she'd only had *once!*

Turning, she climbed down the last step, wondering why she'd wasted the time. Her brain turned on full speed now. Her brother was bleeding, shot, and so was Izzy.

Joule headed toward Cage. Brenda had already pulled a large medical bag from the shelf and was directing Cage while she pulled out supplies and handed others off to Dev.

Paul had stocked this place, filling the metal shelves that were bolted into drywall. The walls were spackled and taped but not painted.

Brenda was using scissors to cut Cage's jeans up to the spot where the blood was coming from. As Joule watched, more bubbled out of the wound. It wasn't spurting, but it wasn't stopping, either. To her untrained eye, it looked like too much. His thigh was dripping with his own blood, and Joule fought the abject terror that accompanied knowing her brother had been shot and maybe mortally wounded.

She glanced across the room and made a quick decision. Though she knew Izzy needed her more, Joule needed Cage more. She wasn't proud of making that call, but it was what it was. She knelt down next to her brother and asked Brenda, "Is there an exit wound?"

"You're looking at it," Brenda told her without missing a beat. "It went in the back, and this is where it came out."

"Oh, thank God." Joule didn't know much about gunshot wounds, but she knew the bullet not being lodged inside him was the better option. Her brother was now in a disturbingly good mood for someone watching his own blood ooze steadily from his own leg.

"He's good," Brenda told her sharply. "I've got this. Go help the girl."

Joule looked up at Cage, thinking she would go if he dismissed her. Instead, as Brenda tended to his wounds, applying pressure and trying to get them to stop bleeding, he pointed to another spot. Joule couldn't see it because it was covered in blood, but she knew what he was pointing at.

Cage grinned and told Brenda, "This leg can take it. *Somebody* already stabbed me here and glued me back together once."

"Shut up!" Joule yelled at him, glad for his good spirits. Then she added her usual, "I said I was sorry."

"Go help Izzy," Cage said softly, his expression now serious. His easy instruction and clear gaze convinced her he would be okay.

Joule crawled across the short distance to Dr. Murasawa,

who had given up on trying to get Izzy to wake up and had slipped out from under her. Izzy was now laid out across the floor, with Dev hovering over her. Dr. Murasawa began ripping her shirt open.

Joule jerked back at the sight. Cage's wound had too much blood, but Izzy? This was everywhere, and Joule could see tissue at the edges of the wound. Blood practically poured out each time Dev moved in the slightest bit. He wasn't "hovering" over her, as Joule had thought, but was actively stanching the bleeding.

"Here," Dr. Murasawa said, reaching into the medical supply bag Brenda had set between them. She handed Joule a fistful of gauze already bloody from her own fingers. "Right here. Apply more pressure."

She said it as though there was more pressure to apply. But Joule wasn't sure she could do more than Murasawa and Dev were already doing. Still, she leaned forward, pushing the gauze against the wound, almost as though she were doing CPR. There was no rhythm but the short prayers running through her head.

"What about her back? Do we need to roll her over?"

"In a moment. This side is worse. We have to stop it first."

Was it a blessing that she'd already seen the worst of it? Joule didn't know. As bad as this was, the other side could be much better and still be horrific. Her thoughts numbed as she tried to focus on doing the job.

"Okay, I'm going to tip her. Joule, you hold where you are. Deveron, get gauze ready to stop what's on her back." Dr. Murasawa was taking firm charge. Joule was relieved; she was an engineer, but that didn't include human machines.

As Joule pressed to the spot, now moving as Dr. Murasawa tipped Izzy, her friend jerked. She made a noise that sounded like she was struggling to breathe.

"I think she may have a collapsed lung," Dr. Murasawa

pronounced. Though she wasn't a medical doctor, she seemed to know a lot.

Joule ignored the thought that knowledge alone might not be enough to save her friend.

"How do we fix it?" Joule asked. She wanted to believe that, if they just had a plan, they could make it work. But even as she asked, above her, a roar and a boom made them all look up.

The funnel had finally reached them.

71

Cage was carried up the steps by Joule on one side and Dr. Chithra Murasawa on the other.

They moved sideways. The east Indian woman was shorter than his sister, and she went first in an effort to keep him level. Joule brought up the rear.

It didn't matter that they tried so hard to protect his leg. The pain was excruciating, no matter what they did. They'd managed to make the bleeding stop and he was bandaged using a massive amount of gauze. His thigh was now effectively twice as big around from all the necessary gauze tied on tightly with shirts, strips of fabric, and pressure. He wiggled his toes periodically to be sure he still could.

When they hit the top step and he could see out the open closet door, Cage was impressed to find the house still standing.

It had sounded so much worse. But then again, he was no expert.

Boomer had walked out into the yard, the stillness circling around him. Clean air brought the sharp bite of ions after a storm, but the normal sounds that he'd taken for granted—

creatures scurrying, bugs buzzing, birds chirping in the trees—were all eerily absent.

The only noise was Boomer, talking into the huge brick of a telephone in his hand.

Bob stood at the edge of the porch, watching everything and bouncing a little. He turned to face them, motioning them forward. "It's safe."

Paul had kept them safe with the shelter. He'd had medical supplies enough for both Cage and Izzy, and even for Dev's scratch to the head that they'd only discovered later. There was food and, after they'd stabilized Cage and bandaged Dev, they'd all managed to eat a little.

Joule had been overjoyed to find cans of tuna, and little Toto had been thrilled to eat one. He'd drunk all the water from the can and then lapped up more and more. Joule had refilled the tiny bottle cap over and over until he'd finally had enough.

Cage was quite certain that his sister now had a kitten. And he wondered if Mary Allen and Glenda, who owned Desperado's Hideaway, would let her keep it. He was almost certain that, if they wouldn't, then the two of them—or the three of them—would be moving somewhere that would. Then again, he wasn't certain if any of them would be staying at the Hideaway anymore. There was a huge hole in the side of the house that might take a while to repair.

As the two women, now very mismatched in height without the stairs correcting for it, moved him across the living room, he inadvertently put weight on the leg.

"Ow!" he yelped, unable to stop the sound and gripping their arms too tightly, just as he grabbed everyone's attention before he shook his head. "Sorry, dumb move."

He breathed out through the pain and tried to distract himself. "Boomer's got a phone?"

"Old Sat-phone," Bob replied, still standing at the edge of the porch. "Always carry it."

"Do you to just run search and rescue?" Joule asked him, still holding Cage up. She would literally support him forever if she had to. He knew that.

Bob answered, "Anytime we got something going on, we do. We started with our dad when we were kids."

Cage had a moment to wonder what kind of man produced sons like Boomer and Bob. But they were doing good work.

"We're doing a lot more of it each year. Lost Dad about five years ago." He sighed and shifted the topic a little. "The truck is jacked up high because we get floods. It's heavy because we get high winds and down trees a lot. So we got a winch on the front of it. We get tornadoes every once in a while. Recently we've gotten a lot."

"Like this?" Cage asked, but Bob shook his head.

"This is new." He paused as though there was nothing more to say about that. Then he added, "Boomer and I checked the weather already. The fronts are done. Everything has moved through the area and dissipated. This should have been the end of it."

The sky was once again a bright and bold blue, absent of any clouds.

Out in the yard, Boomer pulled the phone from his ear and turned around, hollering up to the group. "We need to get out to the road ASAP. We've got an ambulance already on the way for this one." He motioned to Cage.

Cage nodded but wondered how he could make it to the road when he couldn't stand and his bike was surely gone.

"Let me see about the truck," Bob said, hopping the steps down to the ground, much more agile than he appeared he would be. The truck was not quite where they'd left it, but it was upright, and in a few moments, Bob had backed it up to the porch.

It wasn't like Cage to let others carry him, but he had to let them do it this time. He was more trouble than help, and it hurt no matter what. At least getting carried was faster. Boomer and Bob, were an evenly matched set, moving like a well-oiled machine. They laid him across the backseat of the truck and let Joule ride in the front.

The ride was rough, the gravel on the driveway a mess, and he gritted his teeth against each bump and jolt. When they reached the highway, the pavement itself was smoother, but it was littered with debris, and the truck rolled over all of it.

"What about Izzy?" he asked the question that no one had asked yet.

"There's another crew that will come back for her tonight or tomorrow," Boomer told them. "They'll get Levi and Laura, too. If they can find them."

Boomer said Brenda had covered Izzy with a sheet, the most respectful way to leave her in the unfinished shelter as they all headed up the stairs.

The group had been stuck in the shelter for more than five hours, but Izzy hadn't made it past the first twenty minutes, despite their heroic efforts. She'd needed a hospital. She'd needed surgery. She'd needed not to have been fucking shot by a drug runner.

Levi and Laura had disappeared, most likely their bodies had been swept up by the storm. Cage hoped they rotted somewhere.

Anger bubbled through every bone. Izzy had been ripped from the pipe with Joule, but she'd survived that! She'd found Dr. Murasawa. And they'd come to help save whatever was on fire.

But Levi and Laura, with their greed and shitty decisions, had shot him and Izzy and probably even left the bullet graze on Dev's head.

Dev would be okay. And Brenda had assured Cage that he would, too. "I've seen worse. Daddy took a bullet to the thigh, and he's walking around just fine."

Cage figured that while Paul wasn't his role model in general, he could certainly serve as a model for this. He flexed his toes again, glad that they still worked and angry that Izzy was still in the shelter.

When they arrived at the crossroad where Boomer had arranged the meeting, the ambulance was waiting. For the first time, as the EMTs loaded him onto a gurney and shoved him into the back of the ambulance, Cage realized his injury was bad enough that they thought he might not survive.

The speed with which they moved, racing him to the hospital, reinforced their concern. Brenda might not be the best judge about gunshot wounds.

The EMTs had given Joule directions to find him in the hospital but refused to let her ride in the ambulance with him. A short while later, he was wheeled into the ER.

The doctor asked him questions as the crew rushed him down the hallway. "How long ago were you shot? Can you wiggle your toes? ... Show me."

He was rapidly whisked into surgery, which made him even more nervous. Brenda was definitely wrong. He knew they wouldn't move him that fast unless his injury was serious.

As they laid him out on the table, hooking him to IVs and machines, Cage turned to the nearest doctor and grabbed her arm. "What's your name?"

"Dr. Patel," she answered kindly, not giving in to his own wild fear. "What do you need?"

"If I don't make it..." Cage whispered as he felt the anesthetic starting to take hold, "Tell my sister about... the... tickets."

72

J oule sat on the soft but still uncomfortable couch in
the hospital waiting room.

She had believed that she and Sarah and Dev were
smart people until they'd been tasked with finding this
particular surgical waiting room in the maze of the hospital
hallways. It had taken five different people and three different
sets of directions to get them here. Of course, once they'd
checked at the desk to be sure they were at the right place, and
had signed in, they'd been summarily dismissed to wait for the
surgeon to come out. So they slumped in the cold, blue-and-
white room with the old print magazines.

Though they clustered together, they stayed mostly quiet.
Sarah graciously shared her phone, and together, they played
stupid little video games, trying to replace their fear with
leveling up.

The fact that they'd rushed her brother in so quickly made
Joule think that Dr. Murasawa's estimates of his chances for
survival had been cheerfully overblown. That may have been a
good thing at the time, but now Joule's worries ran rampant.

What if they'd not taken the job? She wondered why Izzy had made it so far, only to be shot. *Would Izzy have survived if they hadn't been stuck in the tornado shelter for hours?*

Joule wasn't sure if she would ever know the answers. And she hated that.

Her thoughts also took the obvious but morbid turn. *Would Cage survive?*

In an attempt to shake that thought and the crushing sensation that accompanied it, she stood up abruptly. After that, it seemed the only thing to do to quell her nervous energy was to head to the vending machine as though that was what she meant to do. She returned with snacks and disturbingly poor coffee for everyone. No one even bothered to crinkle the wrappers and open the food, though periodically they each seemed to forget how bad the coffee was and take a sip.

She settled back in, played more games and, at one point, did an ill-advised internet search for how long surgery should take for gunshot wounds. But the results were so varied that it didn't let her know if Cage should have been out hours ago or if she should prepare to sit here for five hours more.

Three other families or groups sat waiting in the room with them, leaving her and Dev and Sarah clustered together on one couch. Each time a physician stepped out of the surgical suite, the entire room either stood up or leaned forward. Three times, someone had come out—and three times, it had not been for her.

At last a doctor arrived, her soft voice saying, "I'm looking for the family of Faraday Mazur."

Joule jerked forward immediately, though it seemed to take Sarah and Dev a little longer to put the name together with the roommate they constantly called "Cage."

"Yes!" She rubbed her hands down the front of her jacket and missed the soft feel of Toto curled in the pocket. She'd left him with Boomer, confident he was in good hands. But now, holding Toto would have made the news more bearable.

The doctor nodded, a short, curt movement, as she was clearly very practiced at not giving away any information from her expression. But her next words were, "The surgery was a success. Your brother should have a full recovery, though he'll be in the hospital for at least several days for observation and physical therapy."

At Joule's expectant expression, she continued. "The bullet went all the way through, but it didn't nick an artery or a bone. Our time was spent making sure that nothing else was damaged and then that everything was properly put back together."

Joule was stunned, trying to absorb what her brain told her was only good news. She couldn't feel it yet, though.

The doctor stared at her, as if something might be wrong. But surely she'd seen this before? People must need a moment all the time. She gently asked, "Is there anything else I can answer for you?"

"That's it? Just the one surgery? Then he's good as new?"

"Well, he will have a scar. A gunshot wound scar. He might think that's cool."

Not right now, Joule thought, though Cage would. He'd enjoy matching the scar where she'd stabbed him. She latched onto that and blurted out, "The fact that he was stabbed in that same leg before didn't interfere?"

"It wasn't quite the same place. The old scar isn't deep. Whoever took care of it handled it perfectly adequately."

Perfectly adequately. Joule thought of her time in the attic, frantically trying to glue her brother's leg back together where she'd stabbed him. But she would take it.

She opened her mouth to say *thank you,* but instead, she blurted one more question. "When can I see him?"

73

S ix months later...

DR. MURASAWA'S voice carried across the gathered crowd. Digitized through the loud speakers, it lost only a little of its usual comfort and softness. The sunny day helped deliver the happy news.

She'd taken over for Radnor, a radically different leader than the loud and booming man. But Cage and Joule both liked working for her.

"As many of you already know," she told the crowd gathered in the field, "the ribbon cutting here is mostly symbolic. A good number of you have already been involved in the process of helping the solar array put power onto the grid. Thank you."

She graciously waved a hand toward her left, where a handful of locals had chosen to stand by and be part of their little ceremony. Only it wasn't little anymore. A large number of people from nearby Horton, Arab, and New Hope had turned up, packing the small, cleared space at the edge of the array field.

Cage was aware that Dr. Murasawa had been adamant that people would not be pressured to stand up at the ceremony. She wasn't pushing any locals into it.

He saw Joule suppress a grin and knew that she felt she'd won. Jerry was standing to the far left, his hands clasped in front of him. It hadn't happened immediately. It had taken all of them learning a good spate of local diplomacy. Though Joule had tried to explain a lot of Jerry's protests that she'd learned during the whole tornado run last fall, it had still been far more complicated than even she'd learned. Understanding what had bothered Jerry and the other locals so much about the incoming solar array had led to a great deal of compromise.

There were now programs in place in conjunction with the community center—a place the locals already trusted, unlike Helio Systems Tech. Dr. Murasawa had carefully carved inroads and taken the employees along with her.

It wasn't easy. As Sarah had pointed out, it had taken Jerry a while to accept that the change was coming and that there was nothing he could do about it. He could fight the ocean or ride the waves. He could join in things like putting in a solar array, and maybe even cleaning up his own carbon footprint, or deal with the results of not doing it—which included the devastating tornadoes that had come through in a forty-eight-hour period last fall.

Newscasters nationwide had called the "flash weather event" shocking and bizarre. Fifteen different funnels, ranging from F1 to F5 had come through in two days. Joule had survived. So had Cage.

Others had not.

Helio Systems Tech had shut down for a while, and the

local protesters had cheered as though they'd run the bad guys out of town. Cage had been pleased that at least Jerry hadn't joined them and he credited Joule for that win. But the team hadn't left. They'd gone back and re-crunched the data.

They calculated the odds that this particular section of Alabama—which had previously been a low-level tornado zone—had suddenly become a hotspot. There was no predicting it, only planning for the probablities.

They'd decided that the strange, funnel-producing weather system had, in fact, been a freak event.

Cage didn't know if they'd be back next year to repair the array or not. They'd redesigned and redesigned and redesigned. Because, as had been pointed out early on by Jerry and the protesters, there was a need to protect the Alabama environment from the chemicals and pollutants inside the panels in case another twister passed through.

But thanks to Dr. Murasawa's ingenuity and the local consultants she'd hired, the system was officially opening today to cheers. Most of the Helio Systems Tech people stood to one side, wearing their khaki pants and bright pink polo shirts. *They all looked like Radnor*, Cage thought, and maybe that was a fitting tribute.

He stood quietly while Dr. Murasawa invited the local mayors of the three nearby towns to join hands and cut the wide ribbon together.

The Helio Systems employees were on hand as a show, but they'd also been asked if they were comfortable giving tours of the new array in case any locals asked. The roommates had speculated that they'd get few takers, and the rest of them would stand around trying to look like they were busy. Instead, they were shocked when people piled up, dividing up the employees and asking rushed questions.

Cage had to hand it Dr. Murasawa. She'd done an amazing

job integrating Helio Systems into the nearby towns by hiring key people in each community who could be strategically vocal social organizers. She educated them and then let them educate and advocate within their communities. She'd hired them early and paid them well.

Three hours after the ribbon cutting, Cage had given three different local families a quick walking tour, answering questions about how the array worked and how the panels would track the sun. He'd explained that it would provide cheap power and listened to his sister help another family calculate their savings. Dr. Murasawa had made them all memorize the new numbers they expected local households to be paying. But she believed in under-promising and over-delivering.

Joule had happily spouted, "By our low-end estimate, it should cut your power bill by 40 percent."

"That's not that much," the man said.

"That's four hundred and eighty dollars a year, sir. On the *low* end. What could you do with that? Or more?"

It was the wife who had nodded along; she seemed to be making plans for the savings. But Joule also told them, "A Helio Systems Team will be staying behind for at least the first year."

She explained how they would phase all the daily operations and repairs into the community.

Joule and Cage were not part of that the team, though. They'd been hired as frontline workers, and this hand-off to the community marked the end of their part of the contract.

After they returned home today, they'd have a few weeks of break before they moved to start the next job. They had a few more weeks rent covered at the new apartment building where they now lived with Dev and Sarah and Toto. The insurance had been slow to fix the missing chunk out of the Desperado's Hideaway dining room.

But Cage had other plans now.

He'd made it through the surgery, so Dr. Patel had never told Joule about the tickets.

As the last stragglers left, he walked up behind his sister and tapped her on her hand to get her attention. "Hey, Joule, I have a surprise."

ABOUT THE AUTHOR

A.J.'s world is strange place where patterns jump out and catch the eye, little is missed, and most of it can be recalled with a deep breath. In this world, the smell of Florida takes three weeks to fully leave the senses and the air in Dallas is so thick that the planes "sink" to the runways rather than actually landing.

For A.J., reality is always a little bit off from the norm and something usually lurks right under the surface. As a storyteller, A.J. loves irony, the unexpected, and a puzzle where all the pieces fit and make sense. Originally a scientist and a teacher, the writer says research is always a key player in the stories. AJ's motto is "It could happen. It wouldn't. But it could."

A.J. has lived in Florida and Los Angeles among a handful of other places. Recent whims have brought the dark writer to Tennessee, where home is a deceptively normal-looking neighborhood just outside Nashville.

For more information:
www.ReadAJS.com
AJ@ReadAJS.com

www.ingramcontent.com/pod-product-compliance
Lightning Source LLC
Chambersburg PA
CBHW020258030726
47499CB00001B/247